THE CAS OF SAN JOHNSON, LL.D. And JAMES BOSWELL, Esq.

CONTAINING

A STUDY OF OCCULT AND SUPERNATURAL PHENOMENA

VOLUME II
THE STONE OF DESTINY

Andrew Neil MacLeod MMXXII

Burning Chair Limited, Trading As Burning Chair Publishing
61 Bridge Street, Kington HR5 3DJ

www.burningchairpublishing.com

By Andrew Neil Macleod
Edited by Simon Finnie and Peter Oxley
Cover by Burning Chair Publishing

First published by Burning Chair Publishing, 2022

ISBN: 978-1-912946-27-3

For my Wife,

Forever Amber.

The Casebook of Johnson and Boswell

Vol. II
The Stone of Destiny

Table of Contents

Author's Note

The Stone of Destiny is a road novel in its purest sense (albeit an 18th century military-road novel) and so by its very nature essentially episodic in form. When Pete and Si at Burning Chair suggested I create "bridging episodes" to drive the MCs from point A to point B, I jumped at the chance. It made total sense. Not only would additional material fill in gaps geographically, but new scenes would furnish the book with an overarching narrative, making for a more coherent whole. Pretty soon the extra material began to take on a life of its own. So much so, that The Stone of Destiny Parts I & II (with the inclusion of a brief interlude) may be enjoyed as a single story in its own right. I recommend all the stories be read in the order they are presented in this book, though. A music fan will tell you an album is much more than a collection of singles, and should be listened to as such, so that the final, dramatic, crashing chord feels earned. I hope you feel the same way about The Stone of Destiny, and have a blast following Johnson and Boswell on their quest. I certainly had fun writing it. It's been a trip!

Andrew Neil MacLeod

THE CASEBOOK
OF SAMUEL JOHNSON, LL.D.
And JAMES BOSWELL, Esq.

THE STONE OF DESTINY - PART I

CONTAINING:

A History of the Rise and Fall of Atlantis
and
A Correct Pronunciation of the Word *Scone*

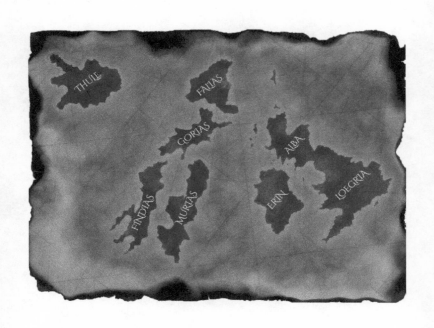

THE BOOK OF ELS

Origins of the Tuatha de Danann

*L*ong, long ago when the world was still young, before the time of the Pharaohs or the Philosopher of Athens, before the fall of Babylon or the sacking of Troy, before the great Mongol horde swept across the plains of Asia, or the ferocious Vikings set their dragon-headed ships for Vinland, before the Phoenicians unfurled their sails of purple silk, or the coming of the Great Ice Age… Before all of this, there stood two mighty pillars at the edge of the world.

Nobody knows who built them, or what purpose they served. Some say to hold heaven and earth apart, thus releasing Atlas from a life of perpetual toil; others say to prevent Fomorian Sea-Giants from devouring the world.

Whatever the reason for their existence, all agreed that the Pillars of Hercules were not raised by mortal hands, but had been put there by the Gods.

Looking west from the Hebridean realm of Eilean Leòdhais, the first settlers could see the twin pillars thrust out of a foaming sea, rising proudly into a sky of stars. The remote island fastness of Hirta lay closer still, its inhabitants dwarfed in the shadow of those mighty pedestals.

Standing forty leagues apart, each marble column would have taken the swiftest ship a full day to circumnavigate.

Few sailors dared venture beyond the Pillars of Hercules. Fewer still returned. Those who did, brought back tales of four mist-enshrouded islands, peopled by a race infinitely superior to man in strength and knowledge. Taller of stature and fairer of face, clad in shimmering garments, with red-golden hair, a bluish tinge to their flawless skin and sea-green eyes, these beings were not from the line of Adam, or even of this Earth.

Local fishermen called this land Rocabarra, and its people they called the *Tuatha de Danann*.

The ancients knew it simply as Atlantis.

Nothing now remains. The Four Kingdoms of Rocabarra were swept under the ocean long ago, and the once mighty Pillars of Hercules lie broken in pieces, scattered across the Abysmal Plain.

But the Tuatha de Danann endured. Scattered to the four corners of the Earth they brought with them their music, poetry, metallurgy, astronomy, medicine, husbandry, and other wondrous arts. For an age of man they walked among us, guiding and influencing us with subtlety and craft.

Not all of them were benevolent. From among the Danann came those they called the Sons of Belial, a corrupted race of immortals who grew to fear the light, seeking out the deepest, darkest places of the earth. From these dark ones came rumours of vampires, werewolves, ghouls and other nameless things to strike terror into the hearts of men.

Some worshipped the Danann as divinities, building shrines and temples in their honour. In later centuries Christians sought to diminish their god-like status. Under their God-fearing influence, the fair folk became the *fairy* folk—little people living under hills and lochs, ready at every turn to play their mischievous tricks on mankind. Tales of their heroic deeds passed from legend into myth, and from thence to folktale, until their once-blinding light had dwindled to a cosy fireside glow.

The Stone of Destiny

Yet the Tuatha de Danann still haunt the twilit groves, troubled waters and weird hills of our dreams, biding their time until the Day of Judgement, a time when the rightful king proclaims himself upon the Stone of Destiny, and the world is made shining and new.

Adamnan the Wanderer, Iona, 566 A.D.

James Court, Edinburgh, December 1773

I remember when it all began like it was yesterday. Johnson and I were sitting alone at a table in the Mitre Tavern of Fleet Street, the rest of our company having long since retired for the evening. There was a warm fire crackling on the hearth, I had a glass of brandy before me, a bellyful of meat, and with my good friend Doctor Johnson by my side, I felt ready to set the world to rights.

It just so happened we were discussing the British monarchy, tracing the divine thread of sang royal all the way back to the High Kings of Ireland. Johnson leaned back on his chair with a self-satisfied air, and hooking his thumbs in his waistcoat pockets said, 'Of course, the fabled Stone on which our monarchs are crowned, which currently resides in Westminster Abbey but was formerly housed at Scone Abbey in Scotland, is almost certainly a fake.'

'Oh?' said I, helping myself to another glass of brandy. 'On what authority do you base such a claim?'

'I have a number of reasons,' said he. 'First of all, Edward Longshanks, who brought the Stone back with him to England by violence, had reached the Scottish border on his way north by mid-March 1296. It would take his army three months to reach Scone. Plenty of time, in other words, for the wily Scots to substitute the true stone for a forgery.

'Secondly, ancient chronicles indicate a black stone of much larger dimensions than the present one here at Westminster, hewn from a solid block of basalt or something similar, with smooth planes, curious hieroglyphs around its circumference, and a slight depression on top where the Kings of Alba perched their royal rumps for over 700 years. The stone at Westminster bears none of these distinguishing features. Indeed, it is a largely unremarkable chunk of masonry.

'Lastly, and most compellingly of all, the Scots never made mention of the stone again, even after their triumphant defeat of the English at Bannockburn, when they were in a position to demand it back, as they did for that other relic of antiquity stolen by King Edward I, the Holy Rood of St. Margaret.'

'Which means...' said I, playing midwife to my friend's thoughts.

'Which means,' said Johnson, 'the stone at Westminster used in the coronation of our current monarch King George III is a spurious relic, and utterly worthless, while the true Stone of Destiny is still out there somewhere, perhaps collecting dust in an attic, or at the bottom of a loch, or serving as an ivy-covered bench in some grand estate.'

'It is a compelling theory, Doctor.'

'But virtually impossible to prove—unless we could lay our hands on the original, of course.'

A wild thought then occurred to me, inspired by that impetuous urge that so often leads men on to folly or to glory. 'I say, wouldn't it be a grand adventure though? The two of us heading off on some quest like the Knights Templar of old, or Don Quixote and Sancho Panza on some knightly errand?'

I was only joking of course, but I caught Johnson nodding quietly to himself.

Little did I know it then, but the seed had already been planted, and from that moment on, our destinies would be linked irrevocably to the Stone of Destiny, for better or for worse.

And yet it wasn't until seven years later that I heard from my friend again, and that in the form of a letter. I was quite taken up with other matters in the interim—a tour of Europe, a happy marriage to my beloved Margaret, a daughter who was the apple of my eye, and a dull but comfortable career at the bar as Advocate of Law. I had resigned myself to a life of cosy domesticity in Edinburgh when the letter arrived. It was laughably brief, almost curt, as if we had only just been talking the previous evening:

My Dearest Boswell,

Having given the matter due consideration, I have decided

to take you up on your proposal. I will be arriving in Edinburgh on the 14th of July, where I would be delighted to meet you at a place of your choosing.

Yours & c.

Johnson

At first I wasn't even sure what "proposal" my friend was referring to. I certainly could not recall making one unless it was in jest. But once the idea had taken hold, it would not let me go. Day and night, my imagination was seized by the image of that mysterious black monolith, accompanied by shameless thoughts of fame and glory. In short, I had become infatuated.

Subsequent letters hammered out the finer details. Doctor Johnson would meet me in Edinburgh, and together with my faithful Bohemian manservant Joseph we would embark on the eastern leg of our tour. Due to the sensitive nature of our inquiry the investigation would be conducted in secret, under the auspices of a sightseeing tour of Scotland's Neolithic ruins. After all, time was not an issue. We anticipated a pleasant jaunt around the coast of Scotland, investigating her mysterious stone circles en route. Meanwhile we could trace the known whereabouts of the Stone of Destiny back to its source, from Scone in the east to the ancient kingdom of Dalriada in the west, in the hope that its origins might provide us with a clue to its final destination.

Little did I know it then, but our investigations would he hampered by a series of perilous undertakings, in which our mettles would be tested to the hilt.

From *The Casebook of Johnson and Boswell*

[The following entries concern events which occurred between the dates of July 26th and October 2nd 1773, specifically our search for the sacred artifact know variously as the "Coronation Stone", the "Stone of Scone", the "Lia Fail", "Jacob's Pillow" or the "Stone of Destiny". In the interests of National Security these documents are marked CLASSIFIED, with precise instructions left with my lawyer to make them public only in the event of my untimely death.

A full account of events immediately prior to those detailed herein—namely the tragedy which befell the town of Edinburgh between the dates of July 14th and July 26th 1773—can be found in The Casebook of Johnson and Boswell Volume I: *The Fall of the House of Thomas Weir* (also marked CLASSIFIED). This earlier document also contains indisputable proof of a conspiracy involving a key member of the British Royal Family and a nefarious organisation known as Ordo Draconis, the infiltration of said organisation by an order of supernatural beings known as the Anunnaki, and the means by which Doctor Johnson came into possession of an otherworldly object known as the "Blue Stone of Enkil". Boswell, 1773]

Chapter 1

'If I hear one more Englishman remark upon my *scones of stone*,' said the proprietress of the famous Brodie's Tearooms in the village of Scone, 'I swear I'll throw the joker out by the seat of his pants.'

'Madam,' replied Doctor Johnson, greatly alarmed, much to Boswell and Joseph's amusement. 'I would never dream of making such a cheap pun. Especially considering it was an Englishman who stole the Stone of Scone in the first place.' He raised a scone to eye-level, much like a jeweller assessing the quality of a precious gem, and popped it in his mouth. 'Besides, it would be patently untrue,' he added, smacking his lips. 'Your scones are light and fluffy, with just the right amount of moisture, making for a most delicious repast.'

'Yes, well...' said Mrs Brodie, her irritation somewhat allayed. She brushed a loose strand of hair from her face and fixed the Doctor with what she considered her most winning smile. 'So what is it you need to know?'

'I merely wish to ascertain the location of the nearest stonemason.'

'A *stonemason*?' said Mrs Brodie. 'That would be Hector Sibbald. He was working on the church spire this morning. If you hurry you might catch him.'

'Excellent woman,' exclaimed Johnson. Then, washing down the last scone with a mouthful of tea, he wiped his lips on a napkin and rose to leave, tossing the napkin onto the table to cover a handful of coins. 'Gentlemen,' he grinned, turning to his two companions and fitting a round, wide-brimmed parson's hat on his head. 'Destiny awaits!'

The medieval village of Scone sat comfortably in a bend of the Tay, hemmed in from the east by a grand sweep of forest. This one-time capital of Scotland was a place of tremendous influence and power, in whose illustrious abbey the High Kings of Scotland from Fergus to John Baliol had been crowned. Apart from the abbey, which stood on the other side of a dense wood, the village boasted a tearoom, a cobbler's, a haberdasher's, a grocery store, a baker, and a hospitable inn where farmers stabled their horses on Sundays.

The Episcopalian Church was located at the north end of the village square directly facing the inn. They found Hector Sibbald halfway up his ladder on the north tower, working on some loose masonry with a trowel and palette. Johnson waved his hat in the air and cried out a greeting to the craftsman, who in his own good time shuffled down the ladder, casting an inquiring look at his visitors as he wiped his hands on his apron. 'How can I help you, sirs?'

'If you would be so kind,' said Johnson, reaching into his pocket for a ragged square of cloth, which he unfolded to reveal a sliver of rock about the size of a pinkie finger. 'Do you recognise this?'

The stonemason held the shard in the palm of his hand to determine the weight, then passed it back to its owner. 'Yes, I've seen something quite like it before. It's unusual, but not rare. Quarried locally, I should think. In fact, you might want to look for an old Culdee chapel in the woods between the village and the abbey. It's only a ten minute walk from here.'

Johnson returned the sample to his pocket, and after thanking Mr Sibbald for his time the three men wandered off in the direction of the Abbey.

It was a particularly fine morning, with cumulus clouds piled on top of one another against a brilliant blue sky, and songbirds flitting cheerfully from tree to tree. As the three men made their way into the wood, Boswell took the opportunity to ask Johnson about his curious keepsake.

'Just a little souvenir I picked up from Westminster Abbey,' said Johnson. 'When the custodian wasn't looking, of course,' he added with a wink.

Boswell stopped in his tracks. 'You don't mean...'

'It's a fragment of the Coronation Stone. The so-called Stone of Destiny.'

'But that's sacrilege... or treason... or... or... something.'

Johnson shook his head and smiled patiently. 'Only if it is the genuine article.'

'And if that should prove to be the case?'

'Then I shall paint myself blue like the ancient Picts, present myself naked before the authorities, and sing Rule Britannia whilst standing on my head.'

*

Scone (sometimes referred to as the Kingdom of Scone, or more poetically still, Scone of the High Shields) was pronounced to rhyme with *moon*, its etymology bearing no relation to the baker's confection made popular in Scotland. Concerning the latter, there was a great deal of debate around the salons and coffee houses at that time as to whether it was pronounced scone as in *bone,* or scone as in *gone*. Johnson, in his capacity as a lexicographer, argued in favour of the former pronunciation, whereas Boswell, in his capacity as a True Scotsman, argued for the latter. With both men claiming authority on this prickly issue, it had been the cause of some contention, much to the long-suffering Joseph's vexation.

They were still bickering when Boswell stubbed his toe on something half-buried on the edge of a small clearing. 'Doctor,' he said, rubbing his foot. 'I believe I have found our ruins.'

The foundations were roughly rectangular in shape, some twenty paces in length and ten in breadth, with blocks fallen over to the side and hidden under a dense mass of undergrowth. Johnson knelt down on one knee, pushing aside a covering of grass to examine one of the blocks. 'It has the same chalky, porous quality as calcareous sandstone,' he observed, producing a magnifying glass and leaning in for a closer look. 'Chiefly quartz, I should think, with light and dark flecks of mica, and some fragments of a reddish-grey clay slate or schist.' After a thorough examination Johnson passed the magnifying glass to Boswell. 'What do you think?'

Boswell made a show of interest, but it was a perfectly ordinary stone so far as he could tell.

'Look again at the sample I chiselled from the Coronation Stone at Westminster,' urged Johnson, tossing the shard of rock to Boswell for comparison.

Boswell was dumbfounded. 'It's identical! But that means...'

'...that the Westminster stone was quarried around here, strongly suggesting that a switch was made, presumably by the Abbot himself, while the genuine article was secreted away, leaving Longshanks with a rather unremarkable block of local masonry.'

'So old Farmer George was crowned on a worthless lump of Perthshire rock,' scoffed Boswell. 'It would seem we Scots had the last laugh after all. Do you think anyone else was aware of the substitution?'

Johnson shrugged his shoulders. 'King Edward himself must have had an inkling, perhaps realising too late he had been hoodwinked. We know he returned to Scone the following year to tear the place apart brick by brick. He also tortured several monks to death, if contemporary reports are to be believed. But in the end it didn't really matter if he had the real stone or not. Look at it this way. If your fellow Scots retained the original, they would want it kept hidden from Longshanks' rapacious eye. And if the stone held at Westminster was a fake, the English would not wish for the shame of it to be made public. Whatever it was Edward Longshanks dragged back with him to Westminster, it's worth as a piece of propaganda was everything. After all, *the stone that the builder refuses...*'

Boswell completed the well-known aphorism: '...becomes the head-cornerstone!'

'On such deceptions, my dear Boswell, empires are built.'

'You never fail to amaze me, Doctor Johnson. If it hadn't been for the Witchcraft Act of 1735, they would have burned you at the stake already. All we need to do now is establish where the former Abbot hid the original.'

Johnson wiped his hands together and climbed back to his feet. 'Easier said than done, I'm afraid.'

Finding little of interest in rocks (sacred or otherwise) Joseph trimmed a willow branch with his pocketknife, cutting away superfluous leaves and twigs to improvise a fishing-rod, then set off in the direction of the river, leaving Johnson and Boswell to make their own way to the Abbey.

The novice monk who answered the door led the two men into a courtyard where the friars kept a well-ordered rose garden, pointing them in the direction of an elderly gentleman in a wide-brimmed straw hat who was busily clipping roses and dropping them into a basket.

'Good day to you, Father,' said Johnson, removing his hat. 'We were just passing through and hoped you might be able to shed some light on the Abbey's illustrious history.'

'You are most welcome, Doctor Johnson,' said the Abbot, straightening as he recognised his visitors. He reached out a hand to clasp Johnson's with surprising firmness and vigour, displaying a dazzling set of teeth when he smiled. 'Please come in.'

The visitors were led through a low corridor running alongside the chapel, terminating in a small room plainly furnished for receiving guests, with a desk, a few chairs, and a simple wooden crucifix attached to the wall. The Abbot invited his guests to be seated and rang the bell for tea, then, as if unsure what else to do with himself, began clipping roses and arranging them in a vase. 'I assume the purpose of your visit is to see the skull of St Fergus?' he asked.

'Erm… no, not exactly,' said Johnson.

'Oh…' The minister appeared vaguely crestfallen.

'We only wish to ask a few questions concerning the Stone of Scone, and perhaps take a look around.'

The Abbot started as he pricked his finger on a rose-thorn. 'Ah! Jacob's Pillow, the fabled relic on which the Patriarch of the Israelites himself rested his head.'

'Or so the story goes.'

'Ever since we lost it in 1296, tourism has taken something of a hit,' sighed the Abbot. 'The only visitors we receive nowadays are the occasional passers-by en route to Perth, or pilgrims come to gaze upon the skull of St Fergus, which we keep in a silver casket by the altar.' The Abbot perked up as he remembered something. 'Do you know, you are the second person to ask about the Stone this month?'

Johnson made a show of seeming unconcerned. 'Oh?'

'Not two weeks ago we received a visit from a scholarly fellow. Obsessed with the idea that the Coronation Stone at Westminster is a fake.'

Johnson's heart skipped a beat. 'And do you give any credence to the rumour yourself, Father?'

'A compelling theory, is it not? That the true Stone of Destiny is still out there somewhere? However I think not.'

'I'd be obliged if you could share your reasoning. It is a matter of tremendous importance to me. From a purely academic point of view, of course.'

Pleased with the invitation to divulge his pet theory, the Abbot drew up a chair and smiled indulgently at his guests. 'When Edward I announced to the world that the Stone of Destiny was in his possession, why then did the Scots not produce the genuine article to refute his claims? And why, if the real stone remained in Scotland, was it not brought out of hiding and used in subsequent coronations?'

'Interesting,' said Johnson. 'Have you examined contemporary records to establish the truth of the matter?'

The Abbot shook his head. 'The Abbot at the time was a man named Thomas de Balermo. Something of the mystic I gather, with Culdee leanings. His correspondence on the matter is cryptic—barely legible, as it goes.'

As Johnson and Boswell reflected on the minister's words, the same novice monk who had received them earlier entered with some refreshments, set the tray down on the desk with barely a glance at the visitors, and withdrew in silence.

'You said someone else has been making enquiries?' said Johnson as the Abbot poured the tea.

'Yes. A Professor John Dunbar of the University of Glasgow. He asked to see the registrum as part of a paper he was presenting. I trust you also wish to have a look?'

'If it isn't too much trouble,' said Johnson, fidgeting with impatience.

After they had finished their tea, the Abbot took an oil lamp from the mantelpiece and led his visitors through the small vestry door and down a short flight of stairs. They entered a low-vaulted basement full of boxes stacked with legal documents and letters. In the midst of all this clutter stood a stout wooden table, upon which had been set a leather-bound record book, a mouldy crust of bread and the stub of a candle.

'The Abbey was seriously damaged during the Wars of Independence,' said the Abbot, rummaging through a selection of boxes, 'and again during Knox's Reformation. Fortunately we managed to salvage most of our records, including correspondence from past abbots all the way back to the Middle Ages.'

'I see your predecessors were nothing if not meticulous.'

'I should think so too,' said the Abbot, *humphing* a box onto the table. 'There is not much else to do around here, apart from our devotional activities and a spot of gardening. Ah, here is Balermo's letter book.' The Abbot drew a pile of letters from the box and untied the ribbon holding them together. 'This is what the professor was interested in… Funny, these feel a little lighter than the last time. Let me see now, 1294, 1295… 1297. Hmm, some letters appear to be missing.'

Johnson and Boswell exchanged wary glances. 'Perhaps the professor mislaid them,' suggested Boswell.

The Abbot went through the letters again. 'This is most irregular. The missing documents allude to Longshanks and the removal of the Stone of Destiny from this abbey, those very subjects of interest to our professor.'

'If we bump into him, I'll be sure to ask him about it,' said Johnson. 'Do you happen to know where Dunbar was going to next?'

The Abbot shook his head. 'He was in such a hurry to leave he barely had time to collect his hat.'

Hiding his disappointment as best he could, Johnson thanked the Abbot for his time, and after a few more pleasantries he and Boswell took their leave.

As they crossed the front lawn, they were startled by a hooded figure stepping out from behind a hedge onto the path in front of them. It was the same novice monk who had first received them, bringing them tea in the vestry. He glanced around to make sure no one else was listening, then lowered his hood and spoke in a low, confidential tone. 'I was coming back from the village last week when I saw your professor cutting through the north field.'

'I see,' said Johnson. 'Do you know where he was headed?'

'I would say he was heading in a north-easterly direction, towards Dunsinane.'

'Dunsinane! And did you notice anything strange or unusual about the man?'

'N-no…'

'Please. Whatever you may have to say, no matter how trivial, is of the upmost importance.'

The young monk seemed to deliberate for a moment. 'Well it struck me as odd at the time, because the gentleman was half running, rather as if he were late for an appointment, or...'

'...or being followed?'

'Yes, I would say so.'

'Well, well,' said Johnson, as he and Boswell made their way back down Abbey Hill. 'This has been unexpectedly enlightening. John Dunbar is an old friend of mine from my Oxford days. A true fanatic, if ever there was one. Also a world authority on ancient relics, as it happens. No doubt the old rogue caught wind of our research, thinking to get there first. If something is making him jittery, you can bet we're not the only ones interested in Balermo's stone. I sense the hand of the Culdee in all of this.'

'There's that name again,' said Boswell. 'The Abbot said something about Balermo's name being attached to a Culdee sect, and the stonemason said those ruins belonged to a Culdee chapel. They were some sort of ancient cult, were they not?'

'The Order of the Culdee,' Johnson explained, 'or Ceili-De, meaning *Companions of God*, are anchorites who seek perfection through isolation, prayer, fasting, confession and penance. They were the original Druids, holy men who foretold the coming of *Righ nan Duil*—The King of All Elements—long before the first Christian missionaries set foot on British soil. Their saints are conceived as Gods or Goddesses, yet they see the divine in every tree, rock and flower. In every dung heap too, for that matter. Legend has it the Ceili-De were entrusted to bring the Stone of Destiny from its original home in Ireland to Iona in Scotland. It would make sense that Balermo was from among their ranks.'

'You speak of the Culdee in the present tense, Doctor Johnson. Do they still exist?'

'Did I? Must have been a slip of the tongue. No, the order was dissolved in the seventeenth century. Yet who knows? Perhaps they are still out there somewhere, fulfilling their sacred oaths to protect the Stone of Destiny from falling into the wrong hands.'

As they reached the base of Abbey Hill, Joseph appeared from among the trees with his catch slung over his shoulder. He seemed a curious oddity, emerging from the woods in his high leather boots, tall black hat and soft woollen cloak, appearing like some peasant of yore to his relieved and grateful companions.

Johnson grinned broadly. 'A rival treasure hunter, rumours of an ancient sect, a clue leading us to a historical location, and now Joseph brings us supper from the river. This is shaping up to be a most edifying day after all, Boswell.'

*

The Abbot peered through a diamond-shaped windowpane of the vestry. Once his guests had disappeared from sight, he made his way down the darkened nave of the chapel to the altar. Hands that clutched rosary beads trembled as he dropped to his knees. Lips moved in silent prayer.

A faint movement from the rear of the chapel caused the row of altar candles before him to flicker, almost imperceptibly, as if the Holy Ghost Itself were present. A disembodied voice spoke from the pew behind him, causing the Abbot to start.

You did as you were bid?

The Abbot looked up without turning, his brow coated in perspiration. 'Yes, damn you.'

And they are going to Dunsinane?

The Abbot lowered his head, all defiance gone. 'Yes.'

Gooood. You have done well.

'Promise me you will not harm them.'

The laughter from the shadows was mocking. *You are in no position to make bargains.*

'I beg of you!' the Abbot's voice rang out.

The stranger's voice then took on a kindly aspect, losing none of its mocking quality. *It is not for me to pronounce sentence. If they violate the sepulcher, they will pay the price.*

The old man cradled his head in his hands. 'Forgive me,' he murmured. Then, looking up at the figure of Christ in his agony, he crossed himself fervently and with the same trembling, faltering voice, he prayed for the eternal souls of Samuel Johnson and James Boswell.

Chapter 2

Three hours later, Johnson, Boswell and Joseph were standing on top of Dunsinane Hill, surrounded by a grand sweep of field and forest, with the silvery-white caps of the Cairngorms just visible in the distance. The first stars of the evening were twinkling in the east, while the sun, slowly sinking in the west, shrugged off its last crepuscular rays, bathing their faces in its warm yellow glow.

The grassy hilltop on which they stood was distinguished by concentric rings of raised turf, the ruins of an ancient hillfort, with a few boulders scattered around. A protective ring of hawthorn encircling the base of the hill had shed most of its summer bloom, exposing a thorny wall of briars which had torn at Boswell's hand as he passed through. He sat on an elevation of rock, a thin stream of blood coursing down his arm to feed the rich soil at his feet. Joseph sat beside him, tut-tutting as he bound the wound with a clean handkerchief, while Johnson pottered around, using his stick to test the surrounding earth.

Boswell felt his eyelids grow heavy. It was eventide, the hour of twilight, a time when the cunning folk were wont to cast their spells of enchantment, only to spirit the unwary traveller away to their dim kingdom under the hill.

As Boswell breathed in the drowsy, almond-scented fragrance of hawthorn he found himself transported back to his youth, to a time when the forest surrounding his father's estate was the only world he knew. He recalled with wistful nostalgia the carpet of bluebells down by the burn, and the first girl he ever kissed, and it filled his heart with such a sweetness of longing that he feared it would burst.

Joseph, sitting shoulder to shoulder with his friend and master, was thinking of the forests of his native Bohemia, where he and his brothers had chased the springing deer, and the daisies on the mountainside, where the soft tread of the cowgirls as they led their lowing cattle up to pasture touched his heart with the first pangs of desire.

Both men had almost fallen under the spell of wood and hill, when their reveries were broken by a splintering crash, as if somewhere nearby a Scots pine had been felled. Boswell snapped his eyes open. 'Doctor?' he cried, scanning the hilltop for his friend.

'Down here,' came the muffled reply. Boswell and Joseph hurried towards the source of the sound, teetering to a halt before a coffin-sized hole. Johnson stood dusting himself off at the bottom, his head just inches below ground level. 'Fascinating,' he murmured to himself, examining the broken edges of wood used to cover the hole, which had proven too rotten to withstand his weight. 'Take note, Boswell. This hole is approximately six feet in depth, six feet long and four feet wide.'

Boswell leaned forward with his hands on his knees. 'Do you think this was a hiding place for the Stone of Destiny?' he asked, sharing his friend's excitement.

'The dimensions correspond quite accurately with ancient reports. Though judging from the quality of the earth, this hole has been empty for quite some time.'

Johnson bent down to examine a flat piece of rock. It was no bigger than the palm of his hand and of a different colour from the rest, as if it had been overturned quite recently. He placed the rock on the edge of the hole and held out his hands for Boswell and Joseph to help him up. Once back on level ground, Johnson made a careful examination of his find, noting several hastily made scratches on the underside. He passed it to Boswell for inspection. Boswell squinted his eyes and tilted his head this way and that, before passing the rock back to his friend. 'It looks like the letter "A" followed by two figure fives, but I can make neither head nor tail of it,' he said with a shrug. 'Though judging from the look on your face,' he added, 'I am sure you are about to tell us.'

'Unless I am mistaken, those figures refer to book, chapter and verse from the Holy Bible.'

Boswell's face lit up. 'Then it must be Acts 5 Verse 5. Let me see...' He reached for the New Testament he kept in his breast pocket and thumbed through the pages until he found the relevant passage. *'Ananias hearing these words fell down, and gave up the ghost: and great fear came on all them that heard these things...'* He glanced up at Johnson. 'Ananias was one of the lesser-known disciples, sent to cure Saul of blindness, was he not?'

'He was. Meaning?'

'I don't know... Perhaps the person who left these scratches seeks to open our eyes?'

'Hmm.'

'You have another idea, Doctor?'

'Acts is not the only book of the Bible beginning with the letter A, Boswell. You are forgetting the Book of Amos.'

'Amos! I'm a little rusty on my Old Testament.'

'Then let me remind you. *"But seek not Bethel, nor enter into Gilgal, and pass not to Beersheba: for Gilgal shall surely go into captivity, and Bethel shall come to nought."*'

'Bethel!' cried Boswell. 'The House of God. The sacred place where Jacob used the Stone of Destiny as a pillow and dreamed of angels climbing a stairway to heaven. Perhaps we are on the right track after all, Doctor. Dunbar himself must have left this message—these scratches are only a few days old.'

'Your suggestion is not entirely without merit, Boswell.'

'But why so mysterious?'

'It's an old game we used to play as divinity students at Pembroke, passing around scraps of paper containing obscure

Bible references only we could understand. Dunbar would delight in making the clues as abstruse as possible, so if we were caught in the act, old Mr Jorden would simply scratch his head and toss the incriminating note in the wastebasket.'

'So Dunbar obviously has something of importance to convey, but doesn't want the information getting into the wrong hands.'

'Precisely.'

'But the Bible passage tells us NOT to look in those places,' noted Boswell.

'He's employing reverse logic,' said Johnson. 'In which case this message should indicate precisely where we *ought* to go next.'

'But Bethel, Gilgal and Beersheba are all in Israel!'

'Which is precisely where you are standing now, according to Dunbar.'

'Now you have lost me, Doctor.'

Johnson sat on a boulder and toyed with his stick, absent-mindedly drawing shapes on the ground as he spoke. 'John Dunbar and I were best friends. As boys we were inseparable. He was a gifted, promising young scholar with a bright future ahead of him, and I suppose I was a little in awe of him. In later years, Dunbar became convinced that the Stone of Destiny was in Scotland, throwing himself wholeheartedly into his studies. At first we shared the same theories, but as time went on Dunbar grew more and more obsessive. In his relentless search for the truth he developed some rather odd ideas; ideas which saw him stripped of his tenure at Oxford.'

'What kind of ideas?'

'You have heard, no doubt, of Scotland being described as *God's own country*?'

'Indeed I have,' said Boswell. 'It is a fine sentiment.'

'Well I'm afraid it's a sentiment John Dunbar took only too literally. To his mind, Scotland was the Promised Land of Israel, while Edinburgh, with its seven hills, he believed to be the Holy City of Jerusalem. The ancient kings of Ireland and Scotland, who were crowned upon the Stone of Destiny, Dunbar believed to be descended from the Ten Tribes of Israel—in which case Bethel, the holy place where Jacob rested his head, must be Scone itself—*For it is the king's chapel, and it is the king's court.*'

'A true fanatic! But if Scone represents Bethel, then where is Gilgal?'

'Use your head, Boswell. Gilgal is Hebrew for *circle of stones,* where the Stone of Destiny was brought after Bethel.'

'But Scotland has a thousand stone circles. It would be like looking for a needle in a haystack. Surely we can't be expected to visit them all?'

'No indeed. We should go directly to the nearest.'

Boswell retrieved *Martin's Guide to Neolithic Britain* from his knapsack and unfolded the map attached inside. 'There are three Neolithic circles in the immediate area,' he announced after studying the map for several moments, 'each within walking distance of the other: Druid's Seat, Blackfaulds, and Colen Wood.'

Johnson paced to and fro, deep in thought. 'Legend has it there were twelve standing stones at Gilgal, representing the twelve tribes of Israel.'

'Well that rules out Blackfaulds, which only has nine stones. So does Druid's Seat.' Boswell turned the next page and immediately his shoulders sagged. 'And Colen Wood also has nine stones. But wait... it says here there are gaps in Colen Circle, suggesting that there were once twelve stones there.'

'Good work Boswell,' said Johnson excitedly. 'If that's not the next marker I'll eat my head. Or a haggis, which is tantamount to the same thing.'

'Well let us hope, for your sake, it does not come to that!' laughed Boswell.

*

As it was a clear night, warm and balmy with only the hint of a breeze, the travellers decided to camp for the night where they stood, and set off for Colen Wood in the morning. Boswell collected fallen branches from the trees surrounding the flanks of the hill, while Johnson gathered handfuls of dried grass and used his flint to set them alight, cupping his hands around the glowing embers and gently blowing to ignite them. Once the flames had caught, he placed a latticework of larger twigs and branches on top, deriving a great sense of satisfaction from his labours.

Joseph prepared and cooked the trout he had caught earlier, adding a little salt from a pouch he kept tied around his neck. The three men ate contentedly, their happy faces illuminated in the flickering firelight.

'These hill forts were of great strategic importance to the Scots,' said Johnson, glancing around as he ate. 'They also feature prominently in fairie lore. Some say the cunning folk live inside hills like these. A mortal will venture in and live for a spell in the land of faerie, only to return years later without having aged a day. Or would return aged and wizened, after only being gone an hour.'

'And you believe such nonsense?' asked Boswell.

'Hardly!' scoffed Johnson. 'But I do believe there is something otherworldly about these old hillforts, whose stone circles are said to act as portals to other dimensions.'

After their meal, the three friends settled down to sleep, using their knapsacks as pillows. Johnson was snoring loudly enough to raise the dead, but was rudely awoken just before dawn by an anxious Boswell. The older man raised his head and scowled. 'Well? What is it?'

'Look at the bushes!' Boswell cried, indicating the ominous foliage surrounding the camp.

'What about the deuced bushes?'

'Don't they appear closer than before?'

Johnson blinked into the dark. Strange as it may seem, Boswell was right. Earlier in the evening the base of the hill had been surrounded almost entirely by a thick wall of briars. They were thicker now, taller, and considerably closer.

'Ye Gods! You are right, Boswell,' said Johnson, jumping to his feet.

The three men gaped at the thicket, at a loss to explain how it could have moved so far up the hill in such a short space of time.

'Hurry!' cried Johnson. 'Make a circle.'

They spread out with their backs to the fire, peering into the darkness, trying to discover some mechanism like a wheel or a system of pulleys that might explain what they were seeing. The tangled mass of vegetation crept forward almost imperceptibly, accompanied by a sinister rustling and creaking as of many leaves and branches. They were surrounded.

'There is witchcraft here!' cried Johnson.

A black tendril separated itself from the tangle of briars and snaked towards Johnson's ankles. Boswell spotted it just in time. 'Doctor Johnson—look out!'

The rogue tendril raised its head like a hooded cobra and writhed hypnotically in the moonlight. Johnson snatched a branch from the fire and waved it defensively before him. The sinuous tendril reared back and hissed. Boswell and Joseph followed Johnson's example, picking up burning branches to wave at the encroaching vegetation. The flames only seemed to enrage the thicket more. One tendril came whirling forward and whipped itself around Boswell's arm. As the branch tightened its grip the thorns dug into Boswell's flesh, forcing him to release his flaming brand. He cried out in fear and alarm as he was yanked away from the protective ring of fire. With a hideous rustling sound the thicket parted, and Boswell was dragged kicking and screaming towards a gaping mouth of thorns.

Before Johnson could reach his friend, a creeper shot forward and twisted itself around his neck. Joseph, standing nearby, tried to prise the thing away with his fingers, but the more he pulled the tighter it wound itself, like a python, constricting Johnson's airways until his breath came in wheezing rasps. He tried to speak, his face turning purple with the strain. The manservant put his ear to the Doctor's lips. 'The fire…' Johnson gasped. 'Put… it… out…'

Joseph turned to stamp on the flames, sending sparks flying everywhere.

The creeper around Johnson's neck briefly relaxed its grip, enough for him to catch his breath. 'I think it's working,' he rasped hoarsely. 'Don't stop.'

Joseph continued to work on the glowing embers, but his frantic efforts only succeeded in fanning the flames anew.

'Drop your trousers!' cried Johnson, still gasping for air.

'What?'

'Relieve yourself on the fire!'

'Cannot when people watching,' muttered Joseph.

'This is no time for modesty, Joseph.'

'Do as the man says,' gasped Boswell, who was now almost completely overwhelmed by the monstrous foliage.

'Close eyes then,' said Joseph.

They did as they were told, only to hear the sound of a belt being unbuckled and the hiss of a fire being extinguished.

Whatever strange magic Johnson had initiated, it worked. The branches slackened, and Johnson and Boswell shrugged themselves free of the loosening coils. 'Quickly,' said Johnson. 'Pass the salt.'

Joseph untied the little pouch from around his neck and handed it to Johnson, who sprinkled it liberally in a circle around them. After emptying the pouch he fell to his knees, motioning for Joseph and Boswell to do the same. The three men knelt together in supplication, eyes shut tight against the advancing horror, their lips moving in silent prayer.

When the first blush of dawn appeared over the horizon, warming their faces, it seemed their prayers had been answered. Johnson risked opening an eye. The rustling menace had retreated several feet back down the hill. By the time the sun had made his glorious appearance the shrubbery had withdrawn to its original position.

The three men finished their prayers, then gathered up their belongings and made for a gap in the bushes at the bottom of the hill. Thorns snagged on their clothes and scratched at their faces and hands as they passed, but the branches behaved more or less like normal branches. Eventually the three exhausted men emerged safely on the other side. They stopped to rest in the field beyond, making a careful inspection of their wounds. Boswell's arms would need dressing, but apart from some minor scratches and abrasions the men had escaped relatively unharmed. They turned to look back up at the hill. The briars looked perfectly harmless in the morning light.

Boswell rubbed eyes and looked again. 'Did that really happen?'

'I believe so,' said Johnson. 'Unless we all shared identical nightmares, which is unlikely.'

'I thought we were done for. What gave you the idea to douse the flames?'

'An old housewife's tale, Boswell. I must say, I'm surprised at how little you know of faerie lore. That thicket is hawthorn, which is common to knolls such as these. Hawthorn is said to guard the entrance to the fairie realm. To destroy or damage a hawthorn tree is to risk incurring the wrath of its resident spirit. We set fire to half the wood. Then I remembered that salt, running water or human urine is traditionally used to ward off attacks from vengeful sprites. Thanks to Joseph we were able to employ a devastating combination of all three, which seemed to do the trick.'

'You really think we were attacked by a gang of angry faeries?'

'It wouldn't be the strangest thing that's happened to us this week. One thing's for certain: whoever or whatever it was, it has a flair for the dramatic.'

'How so?'

'I am surprised at you, Boswell. What did they teach at that academy of yours? Are you entirely unfamiliar with the Scottish

Play?'

'You mean Macbeth? Of course!' cried Boswell. 'The prophecy said the King would meet his end *when Birnam Wood comes to Dunsinane Hill.*'

'And here we are standing on Dunsinane, the very spot where Macbeth built his fort. It's almost as if some malignant force plucked the thought wholesale from our brains.'

'But surely if some supernatural entity wanted to harm us, they would send something a little more dangerous than an angry hedge?'

'A hedge that could have very easily snapped a neck or torn off a limb, Boswell. But I think perhaps it was meant as a warning.'

'A warning of what?'

'To find the answer to that, we must first consider MacBeth's fatal flaw.'

Boswell thought for a moment. 'I don't know. Perhaps his overweening ambition?'

'Precisely. And what could be more ambitious than a quest for the Stone of Destiny itself?'

'Then you think we should abandon our search?'

'Over an unruly shrubbery? We'd be the laughing stock of every literary salon in London! No, Boswell. If something means to deter us, we must be on the right track after all.' Then slinging his knapsack over his shoulder, the Doctor raised his stout walking stick and cried, 'Onwards! To Gilgal and to glory!'

Chapter 3

*D*on't look now,' said Boswell, 'but I think we are being followed.'

'I know,' said Johnson. 'He's been on our tail since Wolfhill. A tall man in a monk's cassock, riding a dappled grey mare.'

Boswell shuddered involuntarily. 'Should we try to lose him in the wood?'

'We'll pretend to be unaware of his presence, for now.'

'You want me go kill him?' Joseph muttered.

Johnson raised his eyebrows. 'No, Joseph, that won't be necessary. We will carry on to our next marker, then make for the nearest town or village. I intend to be somewhere busy before dark. Whatever is following us, I think their strength is greater by night.'

The three friends emerged from Druid's Wood and risked a backward glance at the line of trees. There was no further sign of their pursuer.

Colen Circle consisted of nine unremarkable boulders unevenly dispersed in a circle around a fallow field. A flagstone was located in the centre, flush with the ground. Boswell knelt down and pushed aside the grass, noting a series of scratches on the flat, mossy surface of the flagstone.

'Here is another clue!' he cried. 'Two clues, as a matter of fact. M27:22 and G5:27.'

'Good work Boswell,' said Johnson. '"*M*" must mean "Matthew".'

'Not Mark?' said Boswell, 'or even Malachi?'

Johnson shook his head. 'The Book of Malachi has only four chapters, whereas the Book of Mark has sixteen. Not forgetting the Book of Micah, which has seven chapters.'

'Matthew it is then,' said Boswell, leafing through his New Testament. 'The Book of Matthew relates to Christ's meeting with Pontius Pilate. "*Pilate saith unto them, What shall I do then with Jesus which is called Christ?*"' Boswell looked up thoughtfully from his Bible. 'That leaves G5:27, which could be either Genesis or Galatians. I'm sure they both have more than five verses.'

'They do,' said Johnson. 'But Galatians chapter five ends on verse 26. There is no verse 27. So it must be Genesis, which refers to Methuselah. "*And all the years of Methuselah were nine hundred sixty and nine years.*"'

'Methuselah and Pilate,' said Boswell. 'The oldest living man, and the Roman official who washes his hands of Christ's blood, metaphorically speaking. But what could be the connection between the two?'

The two men gazed thoughtfully at the mysterious scratches on the stone for a few moments. 'I have it!' cried Boswell, snapping his fingers. 'Fortingall Yew!'

'Huzzah! I think he's cracked it!' cried Johnson, hopping from one foot to the other and slapping his friend on the back. 'Boswell, you are becoming very good at this. Isn't he, Joseph?'

The manservant looked unimpressed. 'Farting... gale?'

'Fortingall was the birthplace of Pontius Pilate, Governor of Palestine,' Boswell explained. 'And the yew tree in Fortingall kirkyard is the oldest living thing in Europe. Four thousand years old, some say.'

Joseph frowned. 'You say Roman man from Bible born here?'

'It's not inconceivable,' said Boswell. 'We know there was once a Roman outpost here in Perthshire, and certainly the timelines match up.'

'Just because *could* be true,' snorted Joseph, 'not mean *is* true.'

'My dear Joseph,' laughed Johnson, slapping the shrewd Bohemian on the back. 'We'll make a philosopher out of you yet!'

*

'It is most auspicious that the next marker should be in Fortingall,' mused Johnson. 'A town which lies at the very geographical centre of Scotland.'

Their newly acquired carriage rattled through the Birks of Aberfeldy, a steeply sloping gorge of silver birch trees in the rural heart of Perthshire. Across the breathtaking ravine a series of waterfalls plunged five hundred feet to the roaring waters below, the spray forming a rainbow that spanned the glen, like some faerie bridge. Johnson sat with his hands and chin resting on the head of his staff, absorbed in the wild scenery as it rolled past just inches beyond his window.

'Perhaps it is no mere coincidence that the area has links to Iona,' said Boswell, leafing through his *Martin's Guide*. 'The church is built on an early Christian site dedicated to Coeddi, fourth bishop of Iona, and they say Adamnan the Wanderer himself, ninth abbot of Iona, performed miracles here.'

'It seems inevitable that the Stone of Destiny came this way too,' speculated Johnson. 'On its way to Scone.'

Nestled between the protective paws of a couchant Glen Lyon, the village of Fortingall was an unassuming little hamlet with monastic associations, though the roots of the Old Religion ran deep. The yew tree was a potent pagan symbol and—like other natural phenomena, objects of antiquity and places of worship associated with the Druids—a whole slew of Christian traditions had grown jealously around it.

The church was like any other of its type, a fine old building built on the ruins of a Culdee monastery, with crumbling gravestones dating back a thousand years or more. The yew itself presided over a quiet corner, enclosed in a wall of its own.

Johnson and Boswell entered the kirkyard with growing excitement. When they located the yew tree they stood in admiration before it, impressed by its girth and antiquity. Generations of lovers had scored their initials into its bark, enclosing their names in crudely-drawn love hearts. Eventually the bark would thicken around the letters, absorbing them back into the trunk and sealing the memory of those stolen kisses forever.

'Just think,' said Boswell, reaching out to touch the bark. 'This hoary old fellow was already a thousand years old by the time a young Pontius Pilate clambered among its branches.'

The two friends walked around the tree in search of clues.

'Someone has been here quite recently,' remarked Boswell, observing the softer mud around the base of the tree, extracting his boot with a *shucking* sound.

'Two people, I would say,' said Johnson. 'And it seems there was a struggle.'

Boswell spied something glinting in the mud and bent down to retrieve it. 'Look,' he said, passing his find to Johnson.

It was a broken pair of wire-rimmed spectacles. Johnson took out his handkerchief and polished the lenses. 'These must have belonged to Dunbar,' he murmured, squinting as he held them up to the light. 'Poor devil.'

'Let's hope he managed to leave a clue before he lost them,' said Boswell hopefully. 'That way you may still have a chance to return them in person.'

The two friends searched around the tree until they found a small opening in the trunk about six feet from the ground. Boswell stood on tiptoes and inserted an arm. After feeling around for a bit his face lit up. 'I feel something.'

'Take it out,' said Johnson. 'Gently does it.'

Boswell removed an old rag, which he unwrapped to reveal an even older book, battered and faded with age. Trembling with excitement, Johnson insisted they go somewhere at once to examine their find.

The treasure hunters made their way to a local tavern, which was named, inevitably, the Yew Tree Inn. A dinner of roast pork in a cider sauce was hastily ordered, which was passable, if a little oversalted. Once they had eaten their fill, Johnson wiped his fingers on his napkin and placed the book before him on the table. 'Some kind of leather,' he said, making a careful examination of the cover. 'It seems very old, but the binding is exquisite. Observe the gold-leaf hieroglyphs on the spine.' He raised the book to his nose and took a sniff, before flipping it open. 'Vellum pages, but of a strength and durability I have never seen before.'

'Remarkable,' said Boswell.

Johnson turned the first few pages, and both men caught their breaths.

*

Ever since he was a boy, Boswell had loved looking at maps. Hours spent in the musty old library at Auchinleck, poring over his father's treasured atlases, had instilled in him a lifelong passion for travel and adventure. Curled up in a chair, his lips forming the exotic names of those far-flung continents, he would be whisked away to distant lands; in an instant he was Marco Polo crossing the Silk Road, or Hannibal driving his elephants through the Alps, or Christopher Columbus setting his sights for the New World, or Sir Francis Drake circumnavigating the globe in a single expedition.

Before him was a map unlike anything he had ever seen before. Here was the familiar coastline of the British Isles, though the names were different. Erin for Ireland, Alba for Scotland, Cymru for Wales and Loegria for England. Far to the north, the landmass known as Iceland was labelled Thule. But strangest of all were the four unfamiliar continents to the west of Ireland that did not exist on any ordinary map.

'Extraordinary,' said Johnson. 'Falias, Murias, Findias and Gorias. Are you familiar with the names?'

'I'm afraid not, Doctor.'

'Then you do not know your Celtic mythology. This group of four islands constitutes the mythical land of Rocabarra, from whence the High Kings of Ireland originated, the progenitors of the Scottish people.'

Boswell leaned forward for a closer look. The four landmasses, situated somewhere between the British Isles and Iceland (or "Thule"), resembled in form a great sea-serpent with two tails, whose monstrous head reared over the north of Scotland, as if ready to gobble up the Shetland Isles whole.

'To the north lies Falias, city of air,' said Johnson, tapping the roughly diamond-shaped land mass that represented the head. 'They say her people were schooled in the mysteries of science, and knew the secret of flight.' Johnson moved his finger down the map as he spoke. 'To the south, across a glittering causeway of pure crystal lies Gorias, city of fire. These people were rumoured to be great sorcerers, and practiced witchcraft and necromancy.'

'And what of these twin islands here,' said Boswell. 'Shaped like the forked tail of a serpent?'

'On the west, bounteous Findias, city of earth, whose people tilled the land and knew the art of winemaking. To the east, Murias, city of water, whose people were seafarers, fishermen and lovers of the sea. Fascinating. These islands look like genuine landmasses.'

Johnson turned the next page to reveal a dozen parallel lines running vertically from top to bottom, intersected by scores of shorter lines grouped in bundles of one to five. They reminded Boswell of the silver birch trees they had passed on the Birks of Aberfeldy earlier that day.

'It must be some sort of secret code,' said Boswell.

'Indeed it is,' Johnson replied. 'It is written in Ogham, an ancient Druidic form of writing.'

'Can you decipher it?'

Johnson cast a droll look at Boswell. 'I am afraid that

my language studies at Pembroke did not extend to ancient Druidic.'

Boswell was undeterred. 'Then all we need to do is find some scholar who can. There must be a dozen in Scotland alone. In fact, the University of St Andrews is only—'

'What? And give another potential treasure hunter a head start? I think not.'

'Then how?'

'We must find a Neolithic stone that contains traces of both Ogham and Latin script. That way we can make a translation of our own.'

'I think I know of such a stone!' cried Boswell, flipping through his *Martin's Guide* and running his finger down a list of names. 'It can be found a few days' ride from here, in the town of Fordoun.'

'Good work, Boswell.'

'It seems Dunbar has thought of everything.'

'Either that,' said Johnson, 'or the gods are working in our favour.'

'But whose gods, Doctor?'

'Good question, Boswell.'

*

The next morning, Boswell came downstairs to find Johnson still dressed, his cheek resting on the table beside the flickering stub of a candle. Next to the candle was the book found in the hollow of a tree, with the Blue Stone of Enkil, a sacred relic retrieved from the ruin of Weir House and brought all the way from Edinburgh, being used as a paperweight. Johnson had taken to producing the Enkil Stone whenever he needed to meditate. Something about the way it reflected the light helped focus his mind. Normally a dull, opalescent blue, the Enkil Stone seemed to be glowing, as though a faint blue flame had been kindled from within. Boswell noted with concern the dark rims around his friend's eyes. 'Don't tell me you've been up all night again, Doctor?'

Johnson opened one eye and grunted.

'And has the book yielded up any of its secrets?'

Johnson rubbed his eyes, yawned, stretched, then propped himself up on his chair. 'Not really,' he confessed. 'But I did discover something. Just watch.' Johnson pulled the book from under the Enkil Stone and held it over the candle flame.

'Be careful Doctor!' cried Boswell, instinctively reaching out to rescue the priceless object.

'Hold on a bit,' said Johnson. 'Look.' He removed the book from the flame and showed Boswell the pages were unscathed.

'Remarkable,' said Boswell, taking a seat beside his friend.

'These vellum pages though—I have never seen anything quite like it. Monks traditionally used calf's membrane, but this? It is both finer and stronger than calfskin. Werewolves' hide, for all I know, with vampires' blood for ink.'

Boswell could see Johnson was only half-joking. He picked up the book and flipped through its pages. '*Follow in the footsteps of Dalriada's Kings,*' he murmured.

'I beg your pardon?'

'Here,' said Boswell, showing his friend the carefully printed words on the last page. 'It is written in reverse, like a mirror image.'

'Blast my eyes! How did I not see that before! And in English, too.'

'Perhaps because it was not there before. Look! The letters have already begun to fade.'

'Invisible ink!' laughed Johnson. 'A trick so simple even a schoolboy could figure it out. As a boy we used to pass round notes all the time written in lemon juice—only fire would reveal the secret.' Johnson passed the book across the candle flame, revealing the handwritten lines once more. 'I am sure Dunbar has refined the technique, but the principle is the same.'

'It must have been made quite recently Doctor. Do you think

it was added before he hid it?'

'Almost certainly.'

'What does it mean?'

'The early Kings of Dalriada brought the Stone of Destiny over from Ireland, establishing their Kingdom in the area now known as Strathclyde. Dalriada once covered a broad swathe of sea and land, from the Western Isles and coastal regions of Scotland to the northernmost parts of Ireland, with Iona as its spiritual base. In a sense we are walking in the Kings of Dalriada's footsteps, Boswell, but in reverse, from east to west. Dunbar loved anagrams, backwards messages and reverse logic, so I'm sure the significance was not lost on him. We are close, Boswell. So close I can almost smell it.'

Boswell looked at the book with renewed reverence and respect. It was carefully stowed away in Johnson's knapsack along with the Blue Stone of Enkil, and after the two men had enjoyed a breakfast of ham and eggs, they made their way to the stables.

Chapter 4

To make up for lost time they decided not to stop in Aberfeldy as they had previously planned, but press on to the larger town of Dunkeld. From Dunkeld they were directed a further four miles to a coaching house called the Bankfoot Inn in the village of Auchtergaven, where they paid a stableboy threepence to watch over the horses. Taking no chances with his belongings, Johnson opened his knapsack and stored away the pistols, the book, and the rest of the money. Finally he reached under the carriage seat and retrieved the Blue Stone of Enkil.

The inn was packed to the rafters with guests from some sort of rustic wedding reception, judging from the garlands of flowers adorning the entranceway and rose petals trampled into the straw-covered floor. The bride and groom had already retired to the bridal suite upstairs, and the tavern was now dominated by the rowdier elements. The landlord ushered the three newcomers to a quiet corner and proceeded to make a fuss over them, anxious to secure their patronage and goodwill. Johnson looked around. In one corner an argument was breaking out between the two families, which looked like it might spill over to violence at any moment. Elsewhere men were making the most of the free alcohol, some gazing with maudlin intensity into their cups, while others slammed their drinks on the table in time to the fiddler and sang their bawdy tavern songs. Here and there clusters of shifty-eyed locals who looked like they belonged to neither family observed the new arrivals with watchful eyes beneath hooded lids.

Instinctively, Johnson moved the knapsack under the table closer between his legs. Just as he did so he noticed the blue glow from within. It was the Enkil Stone, and it was telling him that the enemy was close at hand. Johnson scanned the faces round the bar. Some eyes looked back with open hostility, or worse, studiously avoided his gaze. He nudged Boswell in the ribs and lowered his voice. 'Boswell. Listen carefully, but don't acknowledge anything. We need to leave. Don't ask why. Tell Joseph to get the horses ready. Then go to use the washroom and take the back exit to the stables. I'll meet you there in ten minutes. Act casually, as if nothing untoward is going on.'

Boswell leaned over and whispered something to Joseph, who immediately left the table. Seconds later Boswell approached the bar to ask directions to the washroom then disappeared through a side door. Johnson sat casually for a few moments, tapping his finger on the table in time to the music. He was about to leave when a great, lumbering bear of a man in a farmer's smock slammed his tankard of ale down on the table, and before Johnson could object, said, 'Mind if I join ye, squire?'

'Be my guest,' said Johnson, struggling to hide his distaste.

'Nice evening for it,' said the man, almost collapsing onto the chair.

'Nice evening for what?' said Johnson.

'A drink!' roared the man, then tossing back his head he drained his tankard in a matter of seconds, letting the frothy ale pour down his chin, before slamming the empty vessel back on the table.

Johnson suppressed a shudder. 'I suppose so,' he said, looking distractedly over the drunkard's shoulder.

'Barman! Another tankard of ale, and one for my friend here.'

'Oh no, that won't be necessary. I have no intention—'

'Eh? The sassenach won't drink? Whassamatter, too good for us, are ye?'

By now the argument in the corner had turned physical, with the leader of one clan pushing the leader of the other, and the latter responding in kind. Any moment, things were going to turn ugly.

The barman slammed two tankards of ale down on the table with a grin.

'If you'll excuse me,' said Johnson, starting to rise, 'I left something outside, and—'

A restraining hand slammed down on Johnson's. 'Ye'll be going nowhere until ye've had a drink wi' me!' Doctor Johnson glanced around. Everyone's attention was taken up with the fight. 'Well I suppose...' he began, then without warning he swung his tankard of ale in a huge arc and brought it down smartly on his challenger's head, hard. The big man blinked thoughtfully at Johnson for a moment, his hair dripping wet with ale. Then, reaching up, he touched the place where he'd been struck, before placing a finger in his mouth as if to enjoy one last taste of ale. He grinned at Johnson, then tipped forwards, his head swinging downwards onto the table. Johnson reached over and felt for a pulse. Unconscious. He looked around to see if he was being watched, then grabbed his knapsack and made a run for it.

Outside, Joseph was waiting with his hands on the reins.

'What kept you?' cried Boswell, pushing the door open for his friend. 'We thought they might have got you in there.'

'Don't worry about me,' said Johnson, climbing in. 'Just enjoying a drink with a friend.'

As they were making ready to leave a gang of toughs emerged from the tavern and made their way directly towards them. Johnson took one look at their vicious faces then rapped on the carriage roof with his stick, a signal for Joseph to start moving.

When the mob saw the carriage pull away, they broke into a run. More emerged from the tavern to join them. Joseph whipped the horses and they hurtled off down Main Street at a fair clip. They were almost clear when the foremost of the pursuers leaped onto the carriage step and succeeded in opening the door on Boswell's side. He held a knife to the terrified man's throat, while with the other hand he pawed at his victim's pockets. 'Where is it?' he screamed, his ugly face pressed close to Boswell's.

Johnson picked up the first thing that came to hand, which happened to be the Enkil Stone. It was glowing blue. 'Is this what you're looking for?' he cried, and brought it down hard on the intruder's head, knocking him backwards into the dirt. Two other thugs, meanwhile, had managed to get onto the back rail and were climbing onto the roof. Johnson could hear them clambering towards the front of the carriage. He leaned out of the window to warn Joseph, who spun round and cracked his whip at them. The two men raised their arms to shield their eyes. At that moment the carriage bounced over a rock, sending them tumbling over the edge.

At last the pursuers ran out of steam. Johnson and Boswell watched their receding figures from the rear window and laughed with relief. Joseph glanced round to make sure they were gone and eased off a little on the reins.

'That was a lucky escape,' said Boswell.

Johnson agreed.

'Who were those ruffians? What did they want?'

'Who knows? Maybe the book; maybe the Enkil Stone; or maybe they just wanted to kill us. One thing's for certain. The Enkil Stone doesn't glow blue like that for just anybody. If the enemy has been tracking us all the way from Edinburgh, those Culdee horsemen are the least of our worries.'

Chapter 5

The carriage rattled along the fifty miles of well-made military road between Dunkeld and Fordoun, a journey of two days, giving Boswell ample time to consult his guidebook and reflect. 'The Ogham stone is pierced by four circular holes to form the shape of a Celtic cross,' he yelled above the clattering of the wheels. 'It was discovered built into the stone foundations of the chapel during recent renovations.' He cast a sidelong glance at Johnson, who appeared to be sleeping, his face hidden under a newspaper. 'It bears the Latin inscription—'

The shadow of kingdom come,' interrupted Johnson without moving from his repose, *'until sylphs in air carry me again to Beth-El.'*

'Beneath these cryptic words,' Boswell went on, 'is a string of Ogham characters organised around a spiral. The Stone is otherwise distinguished by an engraving of a strange creature—part dolphin, part crocodile and part seahorse—which some claim to be an early depiction of the Loch Ness Monster. Ah, here is Fordoun Parish Church now.'

The church stood on a hill overlooking the town of Auchenblae, an attractive prospect surrounded by orchards, meadows of wildflower and numerous sturdy oak trees. Johnson eased his bulk from the carriage, and after stretching his aching limbs for several minutes he and Boswell made their way inside.

Sunlight streamed in through the rose window on

the eastern wall, diffracted through its many coloured panes to spread across the nave like the wings of some vast and splendid butterfly. Doctor Johnson located the Fordoun Stone on a level with the stone floor behind the pulpit, just as the guidebook had described. He made a careful rubbing using the charcoal and paper he had discovered in the vestibule, taking pains to preserve as much detail as possible. Once the impression was completed, he held it up to the light and grunted with satisfaction. '*The shadow of kingdom come, until sylphs in air carry me again to Beth-El.* See Boswell? Here we have the phrase in Roman script, and here the same phrase repeated in Ogham. This should give us all the tools we need to develop a working translation.'

Carefully, almost reverently, Doctor Johnson rolled the charcoal pressing into a leather cylinder Boswell used for his maps, then passed it to Joseph, who stowed it away carefully under the carriage-seat.

Now all they had to do was find a suitable place to rest while Johnson began work on his translation.

HERE ENDS PART I OF THE STONE OF DESTINY

THE CASEBOOK
OF SAMUEL JOHNSON, LL.D.
And JAMES BOSWELL, Esq.

THE MENAGERIE
OF DOCTOR
MONBODDO

CONTAINING:

A treatise on the nature of MAN, a meditation
on the existence of GOD,
And a dire warning to those who would meddle
with NATURE.

Auchenblae, July 30ᵗʰ 1773.

ince my good friend and boon companion Doctor Samuel Johnson arrived in Edinburgh two weeks ago, we ~~have~~ seen things and shared experiences unique in the annals of science, enough to blanch even the staunchest of hearts.

As the events detailed within these pages defy all conventional forms of classification, I have employed the term praeternaturalis (from the Latin praeter naturam, meaning "beyond nature") to define them. Yet however fantastic these experiences may seem, the essential facts remain, and it follows that there must be some rational, though as yet undiscovered explanation.

Consider the phenomena of Will-o'-the-Wisp, known variously as Jack-o'-lantern, friar's lantern or Ignisfatus, those nocturnal "ghost lights" that lure unwary travellers across bog, swamp or moor to their deaths. Here in Scotland we call them corpse candles, believing them to be the souls of the recently departed. However, new research by esteemed American polymath Benjamin Franklin on the subject of flatulence has led to the theory of flammable air, whereby it is postulated that these so-called corpse candles are merely the result of lightning interacting with subterranean pockets of marsh gas caused by rotting vegetation.

Does it not follow, then, that other such wonders of the preternatural we have encountered on our travels, including warlocks, witches, vampyres, demons, apparitions and so forth, have a rational, scientific basis yet to be discovered? It can hardly be doubted.

Of all the terrors and wonders I have experienced, none can compare to the one I am about to relate. Even now, as I write this, I am tempted to believe the horror of Doctor Monboddo's Menagerie the result of a nightmare or opium dream, and yet the fact that my good friend Doctor Johnson can corroborate events, leads me to only one terrifying conclusion: that it was 'all too true'.

It began so inauspiciously, on a clear, brisk morning in late July, when the Doctor and I pulled into the town of Auchenblae to find suitable lodgings for the night. We had dropped in at Fordoun Parish Church on the way to obtain a charcoal rubbing of an important historical document. Then, after a leisurely tour of the church grounds, we anticipated a pleasant tour of the town before an early dinner at the inn.

From *The Casebook of Johnson and Boswell*

Chapter 1

Fordoun Parish church sits upon a grassy prominence overlooking the picturesque town of Auchenblae, which charms the eye with its thatched cottages, sleepy watermill and languidly rolling river. Johnson and Boswell sat on a bench to admire the view, tucking into some apples which had fallen into the kirkyard from an adjoining orchard.

'This should interest you, Doctor,' said Boswell, reading aloud from his guidebook between mouthfuls of apple. 'Fordoun Parish Church was built next to an older church dedicated to Saint Palladius, who was reputedly buried here. In the graveyard can be found the ancient ruins of Saint Palladius' Chapel.'

'Let's stretch our legs a bit,' suggested Johnson, tossing his apple core over the nearest wall and rising to his feet. 'Nothing like some fresh air to work up an appetite.'

The two friends strolled arm-in-arm among the recumbent tombstones, exploring the ruins of the former chapel and examining with interest the faded inscriptions. Finally they came to a quiet corner of the yard where six graves had been freshly excavated, which seemed to Johnson excessive for such a small town. He called for the sexton, a bow-legged septuagenarian who was busy digging a grave at the far end of the cemetery. The old man paled visibly when Johnson asked about the six empty holes lying side by side in the ground. 'That isn't my work, sir. That's the work of grave robbers.'

Appalled, Johnson asked to see the minister at once, and the sexton hobbled off to find him. Moments later the minister himself emerged from his vestry to greet the visitors. He was a wiry, active man with a physicality more suited to a fishing boat than a pulpit, with deep lines engraved on his kindly face, and a shock of white hair to match his unkempt, protruding eyebrows. His blue eyes shone with a curious intelligence, though the weary expression spoke of some hidden pain. Doctor Johnson liked him instantly. 'Good day, sir. It is my understanding that some of the residents of this kirkyard have had their rests rudely disturbed.'

'You mean the graverobbers? Yes I'm afraid it's true,' said the minister with a sigh. 'Four times this month already. The constables keep a constant vigil, but the scoundrels always manage to evade detection.'

Johnson nodded sympathetically, and asked if there was anything he could do to help.

'I am afraid not, at least not while the graverobbers are still at large,' said the minister. 'But you might join us for prayer on Sunday, if you had a mind to.'

Duly promising to attend, Johnson and Boswell bid the worthy man a good day, then made their way down the hill to a reputable inn on Market Square the minister had recommended, a hospitable house much frequented by farmers, especially on market days, and famed for its rustic fare.

'Damn it,' cried Johnson, slamming his hand on the table. 'If I haven't lost my appetite.'

'With all due respect,' said Boswell, 'I don't see what the fuss is about. I mean, surely medical science can only profit through the work done with these cadavers, unorthodox as it may seem?'

'Unorthodox? How about damned sacrilegious!' Johnson cried. 'How would you like it, Boswell, if someone went digging up your grave after you'd been laid to rest?'

'Well I wouldn't mind it that much,' replied Boswell. 'Considering I'd be dead.'

'But that's just it, don't you see? If your remains are removed from hallowed ground, it is your immortal soul that is in peril.'

'Well, now you put it like that…'

The two men sank into a gloomy silence, each lost in his own thoughts. They had heard about this sort of thing in Edinburgh, where cadavers were in high demand, but graverobbers in this quiet little town? It was unthinkable.

As they sat there ruminating, the landlord's daughter, a pretty girl of eighteen called Theresa, appeared to take their orders. Boswell and Johnson asked the lass about the inn's various comings and goings, and were pleased with her good manners and readiness to answer their questions.

'Doctor Johnson!' she said, as if suddenly remembering something. 'Hang on a minute, I have a letter for you.'

Theresa returned moments later and placed a sealed envelope in Doctor Johnson's hands. Johnson broke the seal and read the contents with great interest.

Dear Sirs,
If you are passing through Auchenblae, would you do me the tremendous honour of coming to dinner? I have a great many things of scientific interest to show you.
Your humble servant,
Monboddo

Johnson had to reread the brief note, mumbling the strange name *Monboddo* several times over, then snapped his fingers. 'Of course! *Doctor* Monboddo! I haven't heard from him in quite some time. He's an eminent professor of zoology and anthropology. I've read quite a few of his papers, always with great interest, and attended some of his lectures at the university. His ideas are, well, quite unconventional, and some call him a crank. Seems to think we're related to monkeys, would you believe. Anyway, he went off to some island in the South Pacific six years ago. Papua New Guinea, as I recall.'

'Oh yes, I remember now,' said Boswell. 'It was in all the papers at the time. Wasn't his ship called *The Covenanter*? They sailed her half-way round the world collecting valuable plant and animal specimens, but I can't recall what happened to her.'

'The scientific community waited years for Monboddo to share his discoveries,' said Johnson. 'But he disappeared without a trace, leaving only the vaguest rumours in his wake, each more preposterous than the last.'

'Well at least,' remarked Boswell, 'we will have a chance to put those rumours to rest, if nothing else.'

Chapter 2

Boswell and Johnson dined handsomely on a saddle of mutton and beef collops with stewed celery and Ayrshire potatoes, and were just about to tuck into some plum dumpling when the door burst open and in rushed a thick-set man in a baker's apron, his hair dripping wet and plastered to his forehead.

'Has anyone seen my boy?' he cried, his fevered eyes searching the faces round the bar.

'Not since yesterday,' the innkeeper replied. 'When did you last see him?'

'He was supposed to come home last night,' the baker said, collapsing onto a stool. 'I've been out all day looking for him. His mother's frantic wi' worry.'

The innkeeper poured a large whisky and brought it over. 'Well you just sit tight and dinnae fret. He's sure to show up sooner or later. Probably got a sweetheart in the next village, eh?'

The baker shrugged his broad shoulders and drained his glass before ordering another, then drained that as well, as the rest of the company resumed their conversations.

Five whiskies later the poor baker, still muttering about his son ('a puir strip o' a lad only thirteen year-auld') had to be helped to his feet and dragged across the floor, while the innkeeper shook his head and tutted. 'Don't worry Sandy,' he called after him. 'We'll organise a search party in the morning if the boy hasn't returned.'

As the evening progressed, more and more revellers arrived,

among them a ragged collection of weavers, distillery workers and horse traders from surrounding fields and villages. It was a boisterous crowd, and a few scuffles broke out. So heated did one quarrel become that Doctor Johnson (who had boxed for Oxford in his youth and had fists like hams) was obliged to intervene. When order was restored, he bought a round of drinks for the ringleaders. No hard feelings.

At the height of the revelry, after polishing off half a bottle of good whisky, Boswell launched into a bawdy tavern song about a drunken corporal who surprises a maiden with his 'long funny dingle-dangle way down to his knees'. Just as Boswell was reaching the climax of his ballad, Theresa happened to walk past. Boswell pulled her onto his knee for the final verse. Horrified, the landlord seized his daughter roughly by the arm and dragged her away, causing the whole company a great deal of amusement, much to Boswell's chagrin.

That night Johnson and Boswell shared a twin room. Johnson upbraided his friend for his intemperance. 'It really won't do, Jamie. You have been drunk three times this week already.'

'I appreciate your concerns, Doctor Johnson, but I am quite capable of managing my own affairs.'

Johnson finished folding his breeches over the chair and turned to face his friend in only his silk drawers and nightshirt, which only slightly lessened his air of authority. 'James. I have no reason to doubt your ability, and yet I cannot turn a blind eye to your capers with that young lady downstairs.'

'Sir! I assure you, I was acting only from the noblest and most honourable of intentions—'

'I promised Mrs Boswell I'd keep an eye on you, and a pox on me if I don't.' Johnson wagged an admonishing finger in his friend's face. 'Now don't let me down, Boswell. At least try to behave in a way befitting a husband and a father. For all our sakes.'

At the mention of his wife's name, Boswell felt the hot sting of tears coming to his eyes. He hung his head like a chastised schoolboy. To have disappointed the man whom he looked on as a father shamed him deeply.

'Now let that be an end on it,' said Johnson, climbing into bed. 'Get some sleep, Boswell. This Monboddo has piqued my curiosity, and something tells me we will need our wits about us if we are to find out what happened to *The Covenanter*.'

*

The following morning, Boswell resolved not to touch another drop of alcohol for the foreseeable future, and ordered a large breakfast of porridge, kippers and poached eggs.

It was a fine, bright morning in Auchenblae, and after breakfast Johnson and Boswell made preparations for their journey.

'You follow the road east for about five miles,' said the innkeeper, the previous night's indiscretion seemingly forgotten. 'Take a left at the blasted oak tree. There's a road there that leads directly to the house. But I wouldn't be going there sirs, not if I was you.'

'Oh?' said Johnson, 'And why not?'

'The professor's not been the same since he got back from that place—Papua-what's-it...'

'Papua New Guinea?'

'Yes, that's it, Papua New Guinea. They say he got a little too close to the natives there. Turned half-savage himself. Some say he even got involved in their heathenish ceremonies: black magic, voodoo and the like.'

'What rot, man!' blasted Johnson. 'A world-renowned scientist going native? Did you ever hear such nonsense? Or perhaps you've witnessed these nocturnal rites yourself?'

'Not likely,' returned the innkeeper. 'You wouldn't catch me within a country mile of that place. But you might want to have a chat with old Edwin there. He's the only one who's seen the professor since he went... funny.'

Sitting in the corner, a little apart from a larger group of sailors, an old man had been nursing the same whisky since opening hours.

'Yes, I run errands for the professor,' said the old sailor, once Johnson had poured him a drink and set the bottle down in front of him. 'I take orders up to the castle, but I don't like it,' he added, draining his glass. Johnson poured him another.

'For one thing,' he said, 'there's something not quite right about that forest. Seems to have a life all of its own.'

'But what about Monboddo,' said Johnson. 'How does he seem to you?'

'Well I wouldn't know, would I? Never says a word. And I never see his face. Always wears a big hat with the brim turned down over his eyes, and a cloak pulled up to cover the rest of his face. There's something queer about the way he just stands there.'

This didn't sound like the Monboddo of old at all.

'And what sort of things does he order?' asked Johnson.

'Oats, grain, stuff like that. And then he sometimes gives me a list for the apothecary: chemicals, medical equipment, glass bottles and stuff like that, all crated up with sawdust and loaded onto my cart. But the thing is, he never lets my boys unload the crates at the other end. Springs up onto the cart himself and hauls them away, one under each arm. I tried to lift one of those crates myself once. Nearly did my back in.'

'And what of his ship, *The Covenanter,*' said Johnson. 'Did you hear aught of what happened to her?'

'I've heard a tale or two, but not from the professor.' The old sailor leaned in, beckoning his audience to do likewise. 'Five years ago a Dutch merchanter spied her off the coast of Africa, going full tilt for the Cape. But when they drew up close, the Dutchman saw something that made him swear off the whisky for good.' He paused in his narrative, indicating his need for further lubrication.

'There was the crew, right enough,' said the old tar once his glass had been replenished. 'Running up and down the rigging as regular as clockwork. But it was no human crew that the Dutch captain saw. No, sirs. *The Covenanter* was manned by a team of monkeys. Every man jack of them. Furry little monkeys, with a great, hairy ape at the helm. All dressed up in a captain's uniform he was, from the bicorn hat down to the buckles on his shoes.'

A sailor at a neighbouring table let out a snort of derision.

'That's not what I heard,' said another. 'I heard he murdered his whole crew and replaced them with cannibals. Fed them the remains of his old shipmates in lieu of wages.'

'Nonsense,' said a third. 'His wife died out there from some tropical disease and it sent him off his rocker. Torched the whole ship, himself with it, until nothing was left but the smouldering skeleton of a hull, left to rot on some Godforsaken beach in Africa.'

'*Tog o do shiapalais!*' said Edwin, slamming his drink down on the table. 'Did I not see the man with my own eyes, only last month?'

Boswell and Johnson excused themselves, leaving the absurd old men to their tall tales, while they went upstairs to get dressed for dinner. They looked at one other and laughed when reached the landing at top of the stairs.

'Well,' said Johnson. 'It seems our bookish professor has got quite the reputation around here. If even half of the rumours are true, we should have a very interesting evening ahead of us indeed!'

Chapter 3

The morning sun sparkled from the granite walls and houses of Auchenblae, bathing the resident oaks in a splendid golden radiance. Johnson stepped out in his riding boots and finest clothes under a warm winter coat, breathing in the smell of fresh manure. Beyond the High Street, blue fields of flax rippled in the summer breeze, and further still forests of pine bristled over distant mountains.

Boswell joined Johnson outside the stables, dressed in the same practical fashion as his friend. They hadn't the slightest idea what Monboddo had in store for them, and had prepared for any eventuality. Joseph would not be joining them. With the baker's boy still missing, the kind-hearted Bohemian had volunteered to remain behind and join the search party, while Johnson and Boswell struck out alone for Monboddo House.

They followed the innkeeper's directions through the fields until they came to the lightning-blasted oak tree on the edge of the forest which marked the beginning of the estate.

The forest path, though rough and uneven, was broad enough to accommodate carriage wheels, though with little left to spare. As the chaise trundled deeper into the wood the tangled vegetation began to take on a strange, forbidding aspect. Creepers and climbing vines as thick as boa-constrictors twisted themselves around primeval trees, suffocating everything in their battle for supremacy.

When the carriage came to a turn in the path Boswell spied an artifact half-hidden in the foliage, and stopped the horses to investigate. He pulled the ivy aside and the two men were stunned by what they found. It was an ancient statue of unknown origin, depicting some sort of monkey god, its lips pulled back in a hideous grimace. An angry phallus jutted out from between its squat legs, grotesque in its proportions.

Johnson recoiled in disgust. 'Whatever else has happened to Monboddo,' he muttered, 'I fear he has gone beyond the realms of Christian propriety.'

The two men climbed back onto the carriage and carried on with renewed caution.

As the forest began to recede, a flash of white through the trees signalled that they had arrived at their destination. A two-storey whitewashed building of middling proportions, Monboddo House was too grand to be called a house proper, and yet not quite large enough to be considered a castle, with twin turrets on the north frontage and a crow-stepped gable, features which commonly mark an old baronial residence.

Johnson and Boswell approached the heavy, iron-studded door and rapped three times, and were shocked almost out of their wits when it was opened by a chimpanzee dressed in formal evening wear.

'Mon*boddo?*' said Boswell.

'Course it's not Monboddo!' snapped Johnson. 'Any damned fool can see this is a monkey.'

The chimpanzee stepped aside to allow the bewildered guests to enter. Johnson and Boswell submitted meekly as the chimp took their coats then, ushering the guests into a study, he loped off to find the professor.

Doctor Johnson took stock of his surroundings. The place was in chaotic disarray, with African masks and spears covering every inch of wall-space, and stacks of scientific journals collecting dust among the threadbare tables and chairs.

Boswell paused to examine a butterfly collection pinned and mounted in a glass display cabinet. One specimen in particular captured his attention. Across the back of its wings, an unblinking set of owl's eyes had been rendered in exquisite detail. 'Look at this, Doctor,' said Boswell, indicating the twin discs of black pupils encircled by amber irises, providing a striking contrast to the mottled, feathery brown of an owl's face. A little white dot on each pupil mimicked the reflection of light, which brought the whole to life.

'*Caligo illioneus*,' said Johnson, leaning in for a closer look. 'The Owl Butterfly.'

'Truly,' remarked Boswell. 'God is a peerless artist, to have rendered one of nature's most terrible predators with such devastating accuracy.'

'And a humourist too,' added Johnson. 'To use His most gentle subject as a canvas.'

'God, sir?' cried a voice from behind them. 'Nay, say not Him. Say, rather, the birds of the air themselves have daubed this miracle of nature, albeit unwittingly.'

Both men turned to meet a tall, gaunt and plainly dressed figure with angular limbs and a massive, hawk-like nose. Monboddo's pate was bald, except for a few shocks of wiry grey hair which stuck out at the back. He wrung his thin, pale hands together as he approached, speaking in a voice that commanded even Johnson's attention, despite its thin, slightly reedy quality. 'Every so often,' he explained, 'nature throws up a mutation. Mostly these are aberrations, such as a snake born with two heads, or a vestigial tail on a human child. Sometimes, however, a random mutation may prove advantageous to the species as a whole. Take, for instance, this humble butterfly, whose distant ancestor emerged from her chrysalis with a pattern vaguely resembling a staring set of eyes on her wings. This random occurrence, a mere chance arrangement of pigments, must have given her an advantage over her siblings, whose brightly coloured wing-markings rendered them vulnerable to any passing predator.

'Thus the lucky mutation is passed on, refining itself from generation to generation, until—wonder of wonders!—the species has achieved the apex of perfection. One is reminded of

Michaelangelo, who when asked to divulge how he sculpts such perfect horses, replied, "I simply take a block of marble, and chip away anything which is *not* a horse."

'In the same way, this butterfly's natural predators have chipped away at any imperfections, until the finished product is as if Vermeer himself had taken up his most delicate paintbrush, and brought his whole creation to life!'

'Bravo!' cried Boswell, clapping his hands together in a flurry of approval.

'Monboddo' said Johnson with a polite bow. 'How long has it been?'

'My dear Doctor Johnson,' replied Doctor James Burnett, Lord Monboddo, clasping his guest's hand in his own pale, thin ones. 'Too long.'

Despite the warmth of their welcome, Johnson detected a slightly forced, unhinged aspect in his host's demeanour. He had aged conspicuously since their last meeting, the black circles around his eyes betraying a man who had not slept in days, yet his whole being seemed to crackle with a nervous energy.

'I see you've already met young Benjamin Franklin,' said Monboddo, referring to the chimpanzee waiting attentively at the door.

'It's extraordinary, Monboddo. How on earth did you train him?'

'Train him? Oh it's quite simple really. I feed Benji a brain serum I have been developing, using a compound extracted from a very specialised kind of orchid. It encourages cellular growth, enhances neural connections and accelerates higher thought processes, until the subject is able to attain a degree of coordination quite unheard of in his natural state.'

'Good Lord, Monboddo,' said Johnson. 'If such an orchid existed, the implications for science would be simply staggering.'

'Oh, it exists, Doctor Johnson,' said Monboddo, leading his guests through the kitchen towards a small back door. 'But don't just take my word for it,' he added, fitting a wide-brimmed straw

ANDREW NEIL MACLEOD

hat to his head and selecting an ivory-headed walking stick from the rack by the door. 'Come and see for yourself!'

Monboddo led his guests out onto the south grounds, where an unruly forest pressed close against the walls of the house. They followed a path through the trees, passing under a canopy of branches that leaned towards one another to form a kind of natural archway. This passage eventually opened, unexpectedly, into a landscaped garden, where a vast swathe of the forest had been cleared.

'Welcome,' Monboddo said with a proud sweep of his hand, 'to my menagerie.'

Boswell and Johnson gazed in wonder at the scene before them, their eyes immediately drawn to a cathedral-like palace of crystal, set amidst a landscaped garden of surpassing beauty, replete with rockeries, hedge mazes, fountains, and traditional Oriental-style outhouses. The central dome sparkled like a multi-faceted diamond in the morning sun, with glass pavilions extending to the east and west.

The two men followed Monboddo through the palace entrance and found themselves in a tropical rainforest of extraordinary richness and variety. Palm fronds brushed the glass ceiling high above their heads, where several varieties of exotic birds had made their homes. A flight of butterflies wafted past, alighting on a nearby rhododendron bush. For perhaps the first time in his life, Samuel Johnson was speechless.

'The Zoological Society writes to me every day,' said Monboddo as he led his guests into the western pavilion, 'begging to be allowed access.'

'And you have no intention of opening your gates to the public?' asked Johnson.

Monboddo scoffed at the notion. 'This is my Taj Mahal, Doctor Johnson; my sanctuary, where I honour my late wife Lady Esther's memory. Why should I invite the masses to trample all over that memory with their muddy footprints?'

They passed through rows of fruit-bearing vines and

bushes—plumcot, rawberry, banapple, tangelo, limequat, tayberry, yuzu—these were just some of the exotically-named hybrids whose succulent flesh Monboddo offered up for their delectation.

The eastern pavilion was home to Lady Esther's hybrid flower garden, a symphony of colour and fragrance to tantalise and delight the senses in equal measure. Each bloom had been carefully bred to achieve the apex of aesthetic perfection; every rose, lily, chrysanthemum, hyacinth or orchid vying to outdo its neighbour in a pageantry of vibrancy and brilliance.

Monboddo stopped before a bed of flame-coloured orchids, stooping to pluck one. 'Behold, gentlemen, the *Flame of Irian*,' he said, holding its translucent petals up to the light. 'I owe the remarkable growth of my menagerie, and the cognitive development of my apes, to this simple flower, and the brilliance of my late wife.'

'You mean to say,' said Johnson, 'that all of this, the forest, the chimpanzee, these monstrous blooms, has been achieved by virtue of this modest little flower?'

'Hard to believe, Doctor Johnson, isn't it? But in a nutshell, yes, though the process for synthesising the compound is complex enough.'

A winding path led down from the south exit of the palace to a little humpback bridge spanning a gently flowing stream, where a willow tree dragged its tendrils lazily in the water. A little way up the hill on the other side of the stream stood an Oriental pavilion, with decorative motifs on its walls, a red-tiled roof and curling finials on the gables and eaves. A tall Scots pine partially shaded the pavilion with its broad, umbrella shaped branches.

Monboddo led his guests over the bridge and up the steps to the outhouse. 'I have spared no expense in the building and fitting of my Aqua Vivarium,' he said, opening the double doors to reveal a seamless series of glass tanks installed on either side of a central viewing corridor. Boswell and Johnson entered, and gazed in awe at the strange mixture of bizarre and familiar drifting past—tiger stripes, leopard spots, antelope horns, porcupine spines—there were fish of every shape and hue, including shoals of chameleon fish that changed colour each time they changed direction, and a fish so translucent one could see its spine and tiny beating heart.

'My marine Aqua Vivarium is the first of its kind,' said Monboddo, pulling a lever by the door which caused light to flood the chamber. 'The shutters on the roof and walls control the amount of sunlight that gets in, allowing me to maintain an almost constant temperature.'

'Good heavens, Monboddo. So this is what you've been working on?'

'Ah, Doctor,' replied their host. 'We have barely even scratched the surface.'

Johnson was surprised at the transformation that had come over Monboddo. He came alive when surrounded by his work. All the awkwardness, absent-mindedness and melancholy of his nature seemed to vanish, and all at once he became an engaging and enthusiastic host, almost childlike in his devotion to science.

The miniature farm on top of the hill beyond the Aqua Vivarium was at first glance an ordinary working farm, though the thatched Tudor farmhouse and stables evoked a simpler, more pastoral age. As the three men approached the gate two horses, one large one small, trotted forward to greet them.

'This one I call a zonkey,' said Monboddo, patting the nose of a striped beast with long ears and prominent front-teeth. 'The offspring of a zebra and a donkey. And this,' he added, patting the smaller horse with feathered ankles, 'is a Shetland mixed with a Clydesdale.'

'But how on earth do you induce such irregular bedfellows to couple?'

'There lies the beauty of it, Mr Boswell. My animals are not the end product of *coitus*. They have been created in my laboratory using a simple yet elegant, and thoroughly *hygienic* process. Indeed, one can only hope that in the future mankind may procreate in a similar fashion.'

It was, thought Boswell, a singularly *depressing* thought; though he knew better than to voice his opinion.

As they approached the farmhouse, they were amazed by the sight of a gorilla sitting on the farmhouse porch in a fetching floral dress and straw hat, bottle-feeding something that looked like a cross between a lamb and a goat. So gently did the ape cradle her charge, with such maternal care and devotion, that it was difficult not to be moved by the spectacle.

'My gorillas make excellent workers,' Monboddo explained, 'and look after the animals with more compassion than a human ever could. Good morning, Mrs Digby. How are you this morning?'

The gorilla looked up and raised a big paw in acknowledgement of the professor.

'*Mrs...* Digby?' said Johnson, aghast.

'Of course,' said Monboddo. '*Mister* Digby is in the next field. The two of them run this farm almost singlehandedly. You don't expect my staff to live in sin, do you? We run a civilised ship, Doctor Johnson. Poor Mrs Digby lost her firstborn last year, which makes her an excellent adoptive mother.'

Mad, thought Johnson. *Quite mad.*

In a paddock next to the farmhouse, another gorilla in a farmer's smock and straw hat, presumably Mr Digby, poured the contents of a sack onto the ground. Once all the seed had been emptied the gorilla raised his fingers to his mouth and emitted a piercing whistle.

'Cheasants or phickens. I haven't quite made up my mind yet,' said Monboddo, as a flock of vividly coloured gamebirds rushed forward to peck at the corn around the gorilla's feet.

'Let me guess,' said Boswell. 'A cross between a chicken and a pheasant?'

'Correct, sir. I'm told they taste delicious, but I would never eat my creations. My hybrid fruits and vegetables provide all the nutrition I need.'

Down in a hollow beyond the farm, a herd of extravagantly-horned cattle grazed on the lush, fertile grass. On the other side of the valley there rose a grassy knoll, with a replica of the Parthenon crowning the summit, its Greek-style colonnade supported on six marble columns. The path to the entrance was lined with poplar trees, and as they approached, Boswell couldn't help but wonder what new marvel their eccentric but brilliant host was about to introduce.

Monboddo paused at the door and raised a finger to his lips. 'And now we come to my most prized exhibits,' he whispered.

The doors swung open, and Boswell and Johnson peered into a massive space lit from above by means of a circular skylight. A tiled corridor ran the length of the building, with caged, straw-lined enclosures on either side.

Monboddo removed a leg of ham from a hook by the door and dropped it into the nearest enclosure. Two lithe forms sprang from the shadows. The larger of the two sported a glossy mane with flaming stripes across his back. The female, squatting on powerful haunches, boasted similar stripes, but of a less marked hue. Though smaller of size, she dominated the male, who circled the meat warily.

'Now, Lady, you naughty girl,' said Monboddo. 'Let Sir Rodger have a taste.'

'They are remarkable, Professor,' said Boswell. 'What are they?'

'Lady is a tigon, the offspring of a tiger and lioness, whereas Sir Rodger here is a liger, the offspring of a lion and tigress. Beautiful, are they not?'

'Doctor Monboddo,' said Johnson. 'All of God's creatures are beautiful. But are these *His* work, or merely a parody created in a laboratory?'

For the briefest of moments Monboddo appeared angry, then thought better of it, composing his features into a benevolent smile once more. 'God's work, of course, Doctor. I merely helped with the process, as I do with all my hybrid children.'

Monboddo turned his attention to an adjacent enclosure where a lithe, sinewy feline rested on the branches of an artificial tree, barely visible at first due to the mottled markings which enabled her to blend in seamlessly with her surroundings. Monboddo tossed in some meat and the cheetah-leopard slunk down from her branch.

'The leopard is a master tree-climber,' said Monboddo. 'And hunts by ambush. The cheetah is the fastest land animal on Earth, and hunts by chasing down its prey. My cheetard excels at both.'

Boswell felt the hairs stand up on the nape of his neck, despite the bars separating him from those watchful, predatory eyes.

*

After the guests had feasted their eyes on the strange wonders of Monboddo's menagerie, they made their way back to Monboddo House. The professor was in high spirits, pleased to have someone at last with whom to share the fruits of his labour. He ushered them into the dining room and rang the servant's bell. Moments later Benjamin Franklin appeared cradling a magnum of French champagne. They watched with fascination as the chimp popped the cork and filled their glasses.

'Gentlemen,' Monboddo cried, raising his glass. 'To science!'

Chapter 4

'And now for dinner,' said Monboddo. 'I have prepared only the finest hybrid fruits and vegetables from my garden. I hope you find them to your liking.' Monboddo clapped his hands twice and cried, 'Thak!' and, to Johnson and Boswell's utter amazement, a fully grown orangutan waddled in with the *hors d'ouvres*.

'By God Monboddo,' said Johnson. 'But how on earth... I mean a monkey taking our coats? A monkey serving us dinner? What next, a monkey reading sermons in the Kirk?'

The orangutan slapped a paw over its eyes.

'My dear Doctor Johnson, now you have hurt Thak's feelings,' said Monboddo. 'Monkeys? No, both Benji and Thak are *apes*, Doctor, and much more closely related to man than monkeys. Consider this question, gentlemen. What is it that sets us apart from the great apes?'

'It is the soul that ennobles mankind,' said Boswell.

'Poppycock!' snorted Monboddo. 'It is the opposable thumb and finger which sets us apart, for it enables us to manipulate tools. But I have made significant developments in this area with my brain serum. Thak, show the doctor your hand.'

The orangutan raised an arm and dexterously touched the pad of each finger with the pad of his thumb.

'Do you see, gentlemen? Not only can Thak serve food, he can make beds, carve tools, he can even write.'

'*WRITE?*' cried Johnson, aghast.

'Oh yes, Doctor,' said Monboddo. 'And not only that. I am

very close to a breakthrough that will give my apes'—and here he paused for dramatic effect—'the power of speech!'

'I must warn you, Doctor,' said Johnson. 'This work of yours is perilously close to blasphemy.'

'*Blasphemy*,' Monboddo echoed contemptuously. 'I expected better from you, Doctor Johnson. What is blasphemy to a man of science? Sheer hypocrisy! Take, for instance, the tribespeople of Papua New Guinea, who have never seen a Bible their entire lives. Do you mean to say that those poor, ignorant souls are damned to burn in hellfire for all eternity?'

'If they behave as heathenish rogues,' replied Johnson heatedly, 'with no notion of the principles of Universal Fraternity, then yes!'

'Come, Doctor. What kind of benevolent creator would allow that? Let me pose you a hypothesis. Let us say you were to burn every last book of science in Christendom, then throw alongside them onto the pyre every Bible and religious text known to man. Where would we be in a thousand years? I say that those books of science would be reproduced word for word. But as for our religious texts, why we'd have some new mumbo-jumbo about pink elephants in the sky, or some other nonsense.'

'Ah,' replied Johnson. 'But that is where you are wrong, Professor. We would always have the doctrines of Christ, whose teachings embody all that is good, noble and generous in mankind. Christ, and Christ alone represents the ideal in Man, which is unchanging and eternal. And so you may burn all the Bibles you please, until there are none left to burn, but *He* will always be born again.'

'I applaud your fervour, Doctor Johnson, but I am afraid I cannot share it. Are we not men of science? Why should we allow such superstitions to get in the way of our work?'

'But my question to you is this, Monboddo: Why? I mean talking apes? Hybrid fruits? Ligers and tigons? What is the purpose of it all, beyond mere novelty?'

'Novelty? My entire life's work—*mere novelty?*' Monboddo

rose from his chair, and with a series of jerky movements paced the room, gesticulating wildly as he walked, reminding Boswell of a Mantis trying to escape the confines of a glass jar. 'Consider this, gentlemen. If you are sick—is it prayer that aids you, or a dose of physick? If you, Johnson, were to suffer a cardiac arrest, here, in my house, and I were to tell you I could take the heart of a pig, and transplant it into your breast so you could live— would you refuse?'

'A pig?' snorted Johnson. 'I most certainly would.'

'But why, man?'

'On moral principles. The pig is a filthy animal.'

'Moral principals. Pah! *Man* is a filthy animal, Doctor Johnson. What about you, Mr Boswell? What if your liver should fail?'

'My liver? There's nothing wrong with my liver,' sniffed Boswell.

'Ah, but if it should? What if I told you I could take the liver from a cow, replace your diseased organ with the healthy one, and in so doing restore your ailing body, would *you* refuse on moral principles?'

Monboddo placed both hands on the dining-table and leaned forward for dramatic emphasis. 'Gentlemen, it is the age of enlightenment, and we are its pioneers! Surely we must use what tools are at our disposal. What is the difference between creating these hybrid fruits you see in my greenhouse, and creating a race of hybrid men and animals? Nay, talk to me not of your feeble morality. God is dead, sirs. It is we who are now gods!'

Johnson slammed his hand down on the table, then removing his napkin he rose and said, 'I apologise gentlemen, but I think I've lost my appetite. If you will excuse me.'

Boswell drained his glass and added, 'Yes, me too. It is getting late, Lord Monboddo, and I'm frightfully tired…'

Monboddo gave a sigh. 'I see I have offended you. It was not my intention. I beg your forgiveness. Thak will show you to your rooms.'

*

That night, Boswell had a terrible dream. He was floating down the River Congo on a small canoe. The dark and impenetrable jungle closed in around him, and the sound of tribal drums filled the air. Everywhere eyes watched from the shadows with malicious, inhuman intelligence.

Suddenly he felt his feet getting wet. He looked down and saw that his canoe was filling with water. As he struggled to stay afloat he caught a glimpse of a huge crocodile on the shore, only yards away, rushing towards the water on human hands and feet!

Boswell bolted upright, bathed in sweat and breathing heavily.

*

The following morning, Monboddo was nowhere to be seen. The men were seated, while Thak served a breakfast of soft boiled eggs with toast soldiers and a pot of tea. Johnson cracked the top of an egg with his spoon, observing it was cooked to perfection, the yolk runny and golden in the middle. He thanked the orangutan warmly, inquiring after the health of his family. 'What am I doing?' he cried suddenly. 'Boswell, if I don't get out of this madhouse soon, I fear I shall go mad myself.'

'I know what you mean, Doctor,' Boswell agreed, and went on to describe in detail his dream of the night before.

'That settles it,' said Johnson, adding a pinch of salt to his egg. 'We shall leave immediately after breakfast.'

There was still no sign of Monboddo as the two men retrieved their coats and made their way from the house. They found their carriage parked where they left it. Benjamin Franklin the chimpanzee was perched on a stool, brushing down the horses' manes. The men climbed into the driver's seat and, after pressing a sixpence into the ape's paw, Johnson took the reins and they were off, rattling away at great speed from the queer house of

ANDREW NEIL MACLEOD

Doctor Monboddo.

Chapter 5

By the time they reached the inn, Johnson and Boswell had descended into a gloomy funk, and even Theresa's considerable charms could not help alleviate their spirits.

Something about their experiences at Monboddo's had drained them, both physically and spiritually, and when they discovered that the baker's boy was still missing and the whole town in a state of panic, it sunk them into even further despondency.

That night a thunderstorm raged that showed no sign of abating, leaving them stranded in the town of Auchenblae for the foreseeable future. Boswell wrote letters to his wife and friends in Edinburgh, while Johnson used the opportunity to work on his translations.

On Sunday, Boswell reminded Johnson of his promise to the minister and, after donning their best clothes, the two men made their way to the church on the hill.

Johnson joined in the worship with the best of intentions, but the sermon proved uninspired and flat, and it was all he could do to keep himself from nodding off.

Afterwards, the minister invited Boswell and Johnson to have tea in the manse, a comfortable home with a warm fire crackling in the hearth, and the familiar tick-tock of a grandfather clock in the hall.

'I am afraid,' said the minister as he poured the tea, 'you will find our home a rather gloomy place. We have forgotten how to laugh since we lost Alan, our only son. His mother begged him not to go to sea but, well, boys will be boys.'

Johnson sat up on the edge of his chair. 'What ship did your son sail on, Reverend Stuart?'

'It was *The Covenanter*. A name that fills me with dread to this day.'

'Of course,' said Johnson quietly.

'Yes,' replied the minister. 'He was the ship's surgeon, though in the end he could not heal himself.'

Johnson asked the Reverend Stuart if he was acquainted with Monboddo. At the mention of the name, the minister's jaw tightened and his hands clutched the arms of his chair. 'I would ask you not to mention that name in this house again, sir. It brings only painful memories.'

'I am truly sorry if the subject upsets you, Reverend,' said Johnson. 'But I must know what happened to *The Covenanter* and her crew.'

'Perhaps this may be of use,' said the minister, taking an old journal from his bureau. As he passed the document to Johnson a pile of letters fluttered to the floor. Johnson stooped to pick one up.

'Those are letters which were never sent, or returned to sender, for one reason or another,' said the minister.

'May I?' said Johnson.

'Be my guest, sir.'

Johnson took the spectacles from his pocket and placed them on the end of his nose. He unfolded the letter he held in his hand with great delicacy. It was written in the spidery handwriting typical of doctors, with a quirky slant to the letters which spoke of some haste. Johnson cleared his throat and began to read.

'My Dearest Mary,

'He has done it! Monboddo has finally done it! The expedition we have so long dreamed about is now a reality, and I can scarcely contain my excitement.

'We set sail next month on a ship called *The Covenanter*. She is barque-rigged, built for strength rather than speed, with a broad, flat bow, a square stern, and a deep hold specially reinforced to support our precious cargo of animals.

'It began as a pipe dream. Doctor James Burnett, Lord Monboddo, my dearest friend and mentor, would often talk of how he wanted to open a zoological garden. It was to be a spectacle of such grand ambition, such special magnificence, that people would flock from miles around just to see it.

'Oh Mary, if only you could hear him speak! The scale and scope of his vision are beyond mere words to convey. Sometimes when he talks I fancy I am listening to Noah himself, and in an instant our humble vessel becomes the Ark—charting a course into the unknown—bearing God's elect towards the New World!

'Only the most humane and ethical considerations will be employed in the day to day running of our menagerie. It is to be a place of research, study and scientific inquiry; a beacon of learning, where visitors can experience the animals in their natural habitat, or as close a facsimile as the Scottish climate can afford.

'The professor has already begun preparations, levelling his estate in readiness for our magnificent endeavour.

'Premature you say? Then you don't know Monboddo! Every last detail has been planned meticulously, leaving nothing to chance. He has employed only the finest craftsmen to erect the structures that will eventually house our beasts.

'He trusts my judgement implicitly, and consults me in every particular—I, Alan Stuart, a simple country doctor—and yet my dear friend and mentor has already promoted me to director of our soon-to-be-realised Garden of Wonders. I, who once dared to scoff at his dreams!

'Monboddo will personally finance the expedition to the South Pacific archipelago. He has spent nearly five thousand pounds in procuring the ship and crew, yet remains optimistic that he will recoup his losses on our triumphant return.

'Tonight I met the captain for the first time, a steady, reliable sort named William Boyd. He brought with him a map of the southern hemisphere which he spread out on the table. My heart was fluttering as I studied those mysterious coastlines, so newly discovered that the cartographer's ink was still wet.

'Over a glass of sherry, Boyd confessed his reluctance to share authority with the ship's owner; but Monboddo gives the captain his full assurance that there will be no conflict of interests. The day-to-day handling of the ship and crew will be entirely in the captain's hands, provided it does not interfere with the scientific aspect of the voyage.

'Both men were satisfied with the arrangement, and parted the very best of friends.

'Monboddo's plan is an ambitious one. We set sail from Glasgow, taking *The Covenanter* all the way round Africa. The craft is furnished with steel cages in the hold, and among the crew are several marksmen equipped with nets and tranquiliser darts. Monboddo aims to capture only the rarest and most exotic species for study, and has equipped a laboratory in the hold for this very purpose.

'From the Ivory Coast we sail round the Cape of Good Hope, heading north to Madagascar, where we hope to add some ring-tailed lemurs to our collection.

'Turning eastwards, we will embark on the final stage of our outward journey, crossing five thousand miles of tropical ocean in search of a mythical flower known as the *Flame of Irian*.

'Burnett's wife, Lady Esther, a renowned botanist in her own right, will be joining our expedition. Last August she received a parcel from the Royal Botanical Society containing a single specimen of the genus *Oncidium*. It is no ordinary flower. Rumour had been circulating for quite some time concerning the *Flame of Irian's* remarkable qualities, and using her husband's influence, Lady Esther sought, and finally obtained, a sample.

'After some careful analysis, she made a startling discovery. From what I can gather, Lady Esther successfully isolated a chemical compound contained in the flower's petals with the potential to accelerate cell growth in organic matter. The implications for science and agriculture are considerable. So important does Lady Esther consider this discovery that the zoological basis for the expedition is to her a mere distraction.

'This brilliant and resourceful woman has been involved in our venture from the very beginning. Her field of interest is plant hybridisation, a relatively new science steadily gaining acceptance, due in no small part to her own endeavours. The tropical specimens she hopes to obtain will be crossed with our native flora to create a new species impervious to Scottish weather. Truly, she is my Lord's equal in every respect; the *flora* to his *fauna,* and the *Flame of Irian* will be the crowning of her achievements.

'My darling, just to see them work together fills me with hope that soon you and I shall achieve the same blissful state of union.

'I hope that your father will approve of my noble undertaking. When I return three years hence, I will be asking for his daughter's hand in marriage as a man of means, rather than a poor minister's son from Auchenblae.

'Please do not forget me. Have patience, my sweet. I shall pray for you every day, and write twice as often.

'With eternal Love and Gratitude, Alan Stuart, M.D.'

After he had finished reading, Johnson folded the letter and gently replaced it between the pages of the journal. 'Reverend Stuart,' he said softly. 'How did your son, Alan, die?'

'*Die?*' The minister looked genuinely puzzled for a moment. 'My son is not dead, Doctor. He is still with us, what's left of him, no thanks to that devil you call Monboddo. I said we had *lost* him. And so we have. Come and I'll show you.'

The minister led Johnson and Boswell up a narrow staircase to a room at the far end of the corridor.

The spectre of loss hung heavy over that house. All the servants had fled, explained the minister, leaving only himself and his poor wife to look after their son; spoon-feeding him, bathing him, dressing him, every day they went through the same empty ritual.

A young man was seated at a chair before the window with a view out to sea. His mother was combing his hair when the men entered.

'He used to love this view,' said the minister's wife, but she could not bring herself to speak further, and covering her face with her hands she fled the room.

Doctor Johnson approached the young man and passed a hand before his eyes. They gazed listlessly out to sea, unblinking and vacant.

'A merchant ship found him stranded on a small launch somewhere off the coast of Africa,' said the minister. 'He was like this when they picked him up.'

'And was there any word as to the whereabouts of *The Covenanter* or her crew?'

'The captain was with my son, but he was dead by the time they found him. Goodness only knows what happened to the rest of them—'

As the minister talked, the young man on the chair began to rock back and forth, his lips moving, chanting something over and over again.

'Listen,' said Johnson. 'He's trying to say something.'

'Nothing of importance,' said the father. 'He gets like this sometimes. He'll soon calm down.'

Doctor Johnson moved closer. 'I can hear numbers. It sounds like... Yes it is,' he cried. 'Latitude and longitude. He is repeating co-ordinates.' Johnson pulled up a chair and leaned in closer. 'Zero degress north, forty-three degrees east,' he repeated, taking the catatonic man's hand in his. 'That's the Atlantic, isn't it? Somewhere on the equator, off the east coast of Africa? Somalia, if I'm not mistaken.'

Eyes were raised to meet Johnson's. A flash of recognition. These were the eyes of a thinking, sentient being, albeit a suffering one. Then in an instant a light went out, and Alan

Stuart had gone.

'Somalia is where they found the launch,' said the minister. 'He is only repeating the last intelligible thought he had, like a parrot.'

The two guests descended the staircase with their heads held low. 'I find it hard to reconcile the hopeful romantic of that letter with that poor wretch upstairs,' said Johnson. 'And yet... And yet I saw *something*; a flicker of recognition, perhaps, that gave me hope.'

'Hope has long since fled from this house, Doctor Johnson,' said the minister. 'And yet I thank you for your kind words all the same. They console me.'

'And what of Mary, the fiancée in the letters?' inquired Johnson.

'We haven't had the heart to inform the lass of his return, much less of his mental condition. She is still young enough to meet someone else and have children. I would not have her play nursemaid to a man who cannot even dress himself.'

'Your selflessness is admirable, Mr Stuart. But perhaps that is a decision that Mary must make for herself.'

'No, Doctor. She is a good woman. I know that she would sacrifice everything to look after my son, and that I would not have her do. It would be presumptuous of me to expect it.'

'And yet some burdens are too heavy for us to bear alone,' said Johnson. 'Mr Stuart, may I borrow this journal? It may provide a vital clue to help us understand your son's affliction, and the key to his cure.'

'Be my guest,' said the minister. 'Though I fear you will find nothing of note, save for the ramblings of a madman.'

'Nevertheless,' replied Johnson, 'perhaps I may find something the authorities have overlooked. Truth lies in the smallest of details, Mr Stuart, no matter how inconsequential they may at first appear.'

Chapter 6

*J*ohnson had confined himself to a corner of the inn on Market Square for the remainder of the evening, the journal of Alan Stuart on the table before him. Finally, in the wee small hours of dawn he removed his spectacles and expelled a sigh, pinching the bridge of his nose between his forefinger and thumb.

'Well?' urged Boswell, installed in a chair opposite the doctor with a good bottle of claret before him. 'What did you discover?'

'A tale of such tragedy and horror,' replied Johnson, 'that it makes the blood run cold. And yet had it not been for the singular misfortunes of that ill-fated crew, Monboddo may yet have crowned his endeavours with success.' Johnson flipped through the pages of Alan Stuart's journal and cleared his throat. 'It began auspiciously enough. After a lengthy and rather uneventful sea voyage, the account of which would only be of interest to seamen and pedants, they came to the Ivory Coast, which proved profitable beyond their wildest expectations. Mondobbo was able to capture a great many exotic animals for his collection. Madagascar yielded equal success, culminating in the discovery of the fabled white lemur, the *Angel of the Forest*. Several weeks later on the island of Borneo, after a long and dismal sea voyage, they captured a male and female of the species *Pongo pygmaeus*. These orangutans quickly became favourites of the crew, particularly the male, whom they named Thak. The curious hoots and whistles Thak produced with his mouth and vocal cords Monboddo understood as the rudiments of speech, and planned to present his prodigy before the Zoological Society on his return.

'Their misfortunes began on the island of Bali, when the crew ran into a vicious troop of macaque monkeys in the Sacred Forest of Padangtegal.

'The hunting party came to the Great Temple of Death, shrine to the goddess Shiva, whose resident monkeys are perceived to be sacred. They had captured a pair of macaques in their nets, and were about to turn back when they spied a row of furry heads peering down at them from the temple walls. At first the crew welcomed the presence of these little Mandarins, with their drooping moustaches and curiously human-like paws. But something about their silent, watchful aspect struck the men as peculiar at first, then menacing.

'As the group backed away, more macaques appeared above the parapet. All at once they began streaming towards them from every direction, a troop of angry primates with fat haunches and tapered, rat-like tails, leaping onto their heads and shoulders and tugging at their supplies. The group turned to flee but they were overpowered by those demons. The ship's carpenter, a burly blonde Dutchman called Van der Bijl, covered in a seething mass of monkeys, smashed them against the walls in his panic. Alan Stuart struggled to remove one grey demon which had fastened its teeth to Lady Esther's hand. Finally he managed to prise open its jaws, sending it packing with a hard kick to the ribs.

'They were almost done for when someone had the bright idea of dropping the supply bags, along with the two captive macaques, and making a run for it.

'As soon as they got back to the ship Alan Stuart attended to Lady Esther's hand, using a red-hot iron to cauterise the wound. Van der Bijl got off lightly, suffering only a few minor scratches to his arms and legs, but Lady Esther's hand would require careful attention.

'On 25th September 1767 they dropped anchor at Amamapare on the western coast of Papua New Guinea, to begin their search for the Flame of Irian. First they would have to secure the trust of the natives. Lady Esther approached the Chief, a cheerful, tattooed fellow with sharpened teeth who answered to the name of Bam Bam. She showed him her sketch of the fire orchid. The chief roared with laughter at the very notion of such a ridiculous enterprise, but promised to provide them with guides all the same. The following morning, against Mr Stuart's better judgement, Lady Esther set off in search of her prize. She returned in triumph, but the journey had taken its toll on her health. A bed was immediately prepared for her in the chief's own hut.

'Over the course of the next few days, Lady Esther's condition deteriorated, despite Doctor Stuart's best efforts. A distraught Monboddo ejected the surgeon from the hut in disgust. The chief then called for the witch doctor, whose pounding drum could be heard all night long from the men's berths across the bay. Inevitably, the shaman's spells and incantations did more harm than good. Alas! Poor Lady Esther didn't last the night. Monboddo, in his unfathomable grief, took her body along with the vasculum containing the fire orchid and returned to the ship. The rest of the crew would remain on the island until sailing conditions improved.

'The following night the natives held a secret meeting. Alan Stuart hid himself behind a bush to see what he could find out. It appears that one of the serving girls who had attended on Lady Esther had gone insane, frothing at the mouth, attacking anyone who came near her. Death had followed swiftly.

'From his hiding spot, Stuart could see the witch doctor. He shook his stick angrily at the mountain where Lady Esther had discovered the fire orchid then pointed towards the ship moored in the bay. His meaning was clear. The strangers had brought a fire demon down from the volcano with them, and the sentence was death. Alan sprinted across the bay to alert the rest of the crew. A terrifying pursuit ensued. Two crewmen were torn to pieces in the surf, while the rest managed to board the ship by the skin of their teeth. With heavy hearts they raised anchor and left behind that island of horror.

'But their troubles had only just begun. Within hours the ship's carpenter fell sick and went down into the holding cells of his own volition. From this moment on Alan Stuart's account becomes increasingly erratic. But one fact is irrefutable. During that first night, someone took the keys to the Dutch carpenter's cell and released him. The Dutchman then went insane and dismembered two crewmembers with an axe.'

Here Boswell interrupted Johnson's dreadful tale. 'My God,' he exclaimed. 'What on earth could inspire such madness?'

Doctor Johnson took off his spectacles and sighed. 'Hydrophobia,' he intoned gravely, cleaning the lenses with a handkerchief before replacing them on the end of his nose. 'It would appear that both Lady Esther and the Dutch carpenter were infected with a particularly virulent strain, though it took the big Dutchman longer to succumb. Hydrophobia is spread through blood and saliva, causing madness and death in the sufferer. The infected may not show any signs at first, other than mild, nonspecific symptoms: malaise, fever, chills, headaches and so on. But as the disease progresses we start to see more violent and aggressive behaviour: biting, scratching, foaming at the mouth, and an inexplicable fear of water. Finally the victim starts convulsing and going into seizures. Death is sure to follow. There was an outbreak of hydrophobia in London not so long ago, that quickly spread among the stray dogs of the city. The authorities thought they had a monster on their hands, such was the savagery of the attacks. It was a singular case in which I myself was consulted, which newspapers called at the time *"The Werewolf of Whitechapel"*.'

'Yes I remember it well,' said Boswell. 'And you think Lady Esther, the chief's wife and the ship's carpenter were infected with the same disease that afflicted those dogs?'

'Unquestionably,' said Johnson. 'The rest of the crew finally managed to subdue him with nets and tranquiliser darts. But the damage had already been done, for in the struggle the Dutchman had managed to scratch or bite two of his captors.'

'Where was Monboddo during all of this?'

'Locked in his laboratory with only his wife's corpse to talk to... and those infernal apes of his. By this point Monboddo appears to have lost his mind, if his continued absence and utter indifference to the fate of his crew are anything to go by.

'Up on deck things were going rapidly from bad to worse. *"The spectre of madness holds sway over all,"* writes Stuart, *"and the men stumble from one duty to the next as if in a delirium. Water is low. What little we have must be shared with the animals. The sun beats down mercilessly, and there is a feverish, oppressive atmosphere which taints the very air we breathe. I can hear van der Bijl down in the hold again, raving and crying like a madman. Reason has left him completely, and I fear the end will come soon. It is only his strength keeping him alive now"*

'That night Alan Stuart couldn't sleep, so he took himself up on deck, where a blood-red moon cast its broken reflection on the rolling sea. There was a blustering south-westerly, and he took a strange notion to climb into the launch and pull the tarpaulin over his head. He must have dozed off, for he was awoken by the padding of footsteps moving past his little snug. He raised his head and peeked through a gap in the tarpaulin. There in the moonlight, a squat, deformed figure was skulking around on deck. Furtively it loped towards the poop deck, where the bodies of the two dismembered seamen had been sewn into a sail and left for burial. To Stuart's supreme horror, he saw that demon pick up one of the bodies as if it were a sack of potatoes and disappear down a hatch. Then he must have fallen into a delirious and tormented sleep, for the next thing he knew it was morning.

'Van der Bijl died during the night. His body was tossed overboard with little ceremony. The seamen wounded in the struggle with the Dutchman were now showing symptoms of hydrophobia. With great reluctance Alan Stuart forced them at gunpoint into the carpenter's vacated cell. After locking them in he climbed the steps to a cacophony of shrieks and whoops, the mocking laughter of hyenas, the rattle of apes shaking their bars and howling, and the screams of entreaty from his former shipmates. He closed the trapdoor, and his heart, to their pleas.

'The remainder of the crew found a cask of brandy in the captain's cabin and began drinking to drown out the memory of those screams. They blamed Monboddo for all their misfortunes. Huddled together on the deck, they spoke in conspiratorial whispers. The only two sane and able-bodied crewmen left, Alan Stuart and Captain Boyd, watched in horror as the drunken sailors made their plans to kill Monboddo, before disappearing into the dark underbelly of the ship.'

Johnson turned the last few pages. 'These are the final written words of Alan Stuart, ship's surgeon on *The Covenanter*:

'The men are going down into the hold. We cannot stop them.
I hear a series of dull thumps from down below, and then nothing.
They are silent now. I do not dare go down there. They are silent.
We have locked and bolted all the trapdoors. Whatever attacked
and killed the crew must not get out.

This morning the captain and I shared the last drop of water,
then finally resolved to break down the door to Doctor Monboddo's
laboratory. I pray it is not too late, and that he may still be saved.
God help us all.'

Chapter 7

And so ends the final entry of Alan Stuart, ship's surgeon on the Covenanter,' sighed Johnson as he closed the logbook. 'It makes for grim reading.'

'So a tropical disease finished off the crew,' said Boswell, 'while Alan Stuart and Monboddo were driven insane, each after their own fashion.'

Boswell's words were cut short by a loud crash of furniture, followed by a rapid series of terrified screams coming from upstairs. The two friends shot a startled look at one another, threw back their chairs and bolted up the stairs two steps at a time. They were met at the top by the housekeeper who, concerned that Theresa had not emerged from her room, had used the innkeeper's key to let herself in, only to discover the empty, unmade bed.

The innkeeper was alerted at once. 'I don't understand it,' he cried, standing in the landing in his nightshirt and stockings. 'I lock my daughter's door every night. There's no way she could have escaped.'

'Leave us, please,' said Johnson, placing his hand on the innkeeper's shoulder. 'I will soon get to the bottom of this.'

The innkeeper stood aside, allowing Johnson and Boswell to enter the bedroom. Everything was in perfect order except for the unmade bed and a solitary doll, lying face down on the floor. The girl's Sunday dress had been folded and placed neatly over the back of a chair. On the dressing table was a mirror, a jewellery box containing a few sad trinkets, and a hairbrush with several golden strands of hair caught in its teeth.

'I don't understand it, Doctor,' said Boswell, glancing around the plain bedchamber. 'Apart from the unmade bed the room is undisturbed. There is no sign of a forced entry. If the poor girl has been abducted, then her captor has left no clues for us to follow.'

'Not quite, Boswell,' said Johnson, standing at the window with something held between his thumb and forefinger.

Boswell joined his friend at the window. 'Let me see. What is it? A red hair! What could it mean?'

'I think, Boswell, that I begin to see the whole picture.'

'Well I wish you'd enlighten me, Doctor. Half of Auchenblae has red hair. Even the cleaning lady.'

'Our young damsel was indeed abducted, and her kidnapper entered and exited her chamber by means of this window, which has not been properly latched.'

Boswell peered down to the cobbled street below. 'But it's impossible. For someone to climb up through the window, grab Theresa and climb back down with the girl under his arm? He would need to be prodigiously strong...'

'Prodigiously,' Johnson agreed.

'So what you are saying is, we are looking for a red-haired madman with superhuman strength?'

'Correct on every detail but one, Boswell. This is not a man we are looking for. Observe the coarseness of this strand.'

'If not a man,' cried Boswell, 'then what?'

'The very same creature that has been running errands for Monboddo all along,' said Johnson. 'The same creature who dug up cadavers from the cemetery, and retrieved those corpses for Monboddo's hideous experiments aboard *The Covenanter*.'

Boswell screwed his face up and let out a blast of air through pursed lips, slamming the palm of his hand to his forehead. 'Thak! Of course!'

'Precisely. Now there is not a moment to lose. If that madman Monboddo gets his hands on poor Theresa, there's no telling what he may be capable of. Quickly now. Tell Joseph to ride directly to the barracks and summon the local militia. I'll get the pistols and meet you in the carriage in five minutes.'

'But it will take hours before the soldiers arrive.'

'Which is precisely why we are leaving now, despite the dangers that may be involved. Hurry now!'

Chapter 8

*J*ohnson and Boswell decided to leave the carriage by the side of the road at the blasted oak, taking the path to Monboddo House on foot. The menacing branches seemed to part as they approached, closing in around them as they stepped into the primordial darkness of the forest. The dank, humid vegetation had a watchful aspect as they progressed. Dwarfed by the immensity of their surroundings, Johnson and Boswell clambered over a succession of vines which seemed to have grown in the short space of time since their last visit, while the path was submerged under a proliferation of strange, alien-looking fungi, glowing with an otherworldly phosphorescence.

Amidst the rank, fetid smell of damp earth and rotting bark, a sicklier scent emerged, a most repugnant smell that warned the men of some approaching horror.

'Do you smell that, Doctor Johnson?'

'Hmm.'

'It smells like rotting flesh. You don't think it's—'

'The body of the missing boy? It is possible. Let's go and investigate—I think the odour is coming from just beyond that elevation there.'

The men left the path and clambered up an incline using the roots of trees as handholds and footholds, until they came to a clearing where the smell was almost unbearable. The air was thick with clouds of flies, the atmosphere infected with such a miasma of evil that the very trees around them seemed to recoil in horror. Swallowing back their repugnance, the two men searched among the tall grasses for the source of the putrescence.

'My God,' said Johnson, staring blankly at the ground before his feet. 'Can it be?'

Boswell came rushing over.

'It is! It is!' cried Johnson, answering his own question. 'Look here Boswell... A giant Rafflesia.'

The bloom before them was huge, squatting low upon a nest of tangled roots and vines. 'The Rafflesia is parasitic,' Johnson explained, 'having no stem, leaves or roots of its own. It infects the host vines, sapping them of nutrients.'

Boswell leaned in close to study the bloom's monstrous triangular petals, which were fleshy pink and covered in livid welts like cancerous sores. 'Observe the petals,' said Johnson. 'They mimic the appearance and scent of rotting flesh in order to attract the carrion flies which pollinate it.'

'I should imagine a stink like that will attract more than just carrion flies,' said Boswell.

'Fascinating,' said Johnson. 'The Rafflesia is a tropical plant with a low resistance to frost. Monboddo's wife Lady Esther must have hybridised the original specimen with some local species to create a strain hardy enough to withstand the Scottish climate. It's almost as if she has taken the entire jungle and transplanted it here. If only we had more time!'

The two men were about to leave when a low growl caused the hairs on the napes of their necks to stand on end. They both looked up at the overhanging branches. A watchful, predatory pair of eyes glared back at them from the shadows. Johnson reached for his pistol—too late. The cheetard sprang, pinning him to the ground. The cat's jaws were poised just inches from Johnson's neck, her hot breath prickling his flesh. Bellowing with all his might, Boswell grabbed the creature's tail and tried to pull her off. Enraged, the big cat spun round and pounced on Boswell. Johnson drew his pistol and cursed, unable to get a clear shot.

Unseen by the struggling men, one of the host vines attached to the base of the Rafflesia plant came snaking forward and wrapped itself around the hind leg of the cheetard. This was quickly followed by three more vines, each snatching a limb of the big cat as Boswell squirmed underneath. A fifth vine whipped itself around the cat's head, pulling her back and away from Boswell's carotid artery. The cheetard writhed in fury, drawn helplessly towards the Rafflesia. The flower's central diaphragm billowed open to reveal a gnashing set of teeth. Johnson beheld the snapping, beak-like aperture as it anticipated its prey and recoiled in horror. Steeling himself, he held his pistol to the cat's head as it was dragged past him and pulled the trigger, putting the poor thing out of its misery. With obscene rapidity the cheetard's carcass was dragged into that chomping set of teeth and devoured, accompanied by the sound of snapping bone and the squelching of blood and tissue.

Johnson didn't notice the vine snaking itself around his own ankle until it was too late. The tendril yanked him to the forest floor and dragged him towards that grotesque maw. In a panic Boswell grabbed for Johnson's arms but the thing was too strong. '*The knife*,' hissed Johnson. Then Boswell remembered. Joseph had insisted on providing them with a small hunting knife with a serrated edge, which Boswell kept strapped to the belt around his waist. He used it now, sawing furiously on the stem until with a squeal of almost sentient pain the vine was separated from the root. Boswell pulled Johnson away just as another tendril came groping towards them, and the two men ran as fast as their legs would carry them back onto the path to Monboddo House.

Chapter 9

Johnson and Boswell used the cover of trees to conceal their approach. When they reached the house, they hurried up the steps and pushed the heavy, iron-studded door, which groaned open onto an empty hallway. Bracing themselves for anything, the two men stepped inside, only to be met with silence all around.

Using a series of hand gestures to signal their intentions, the two men decided on a thorough search of the house, starting with a series of dismal rooms on the first and second floors. Cobwebs hung in great garlands from four-poster beds, years of dust covered every available surface, while outside, monstrous, overgrown branches pressed hard against dirty windows; but save for the pitter-patter of tiny claws behind the wainscotting, the place was devoid of life.

Back on ground floor the men were on the point of giving up the search, when Boswell detected a faint draught coming from under a cupboard door in the kitchen. Further investigation revealed a trapdoor, which opened onto a flight of stairs. A gust of wind swept up from the shadows, causing Boswell to shiver involuntarily.

Gripping their lanterns, the two men descended warily into a cavernous basement of immense proportions. The roughness of the walls suggested the vaulted chamber had at some point been excavated beyond its original dimensions. As their eyes became accustomed to the flickering torchlight, more and more of their surroundings were revealed; and with it, irrefutable evidence that James Burnett, Lord Monboddo, had gone completely, hopelessly and irretrievably insane.

Such was the scale of horror, Boswell and Johnson could only take in one abomination at a time. As they stood there gaping, a pack of rats scurried across the floor, each with a human ear stitched to its back, a crude first attempt at fusing the tissue of different species. Everywhere they looked, the men were confronted with further evidence of Monboddo's insanity. Bell-jars containing pickled, sub-human foetuses lined the walls. One had scales all over its little body, webbed fingers, and a frog-like head fused to its shoulders; another was covered in fur, with little hooves instead of feet, and the nubs of horns poking through its fragile skull. In a third jar, a human brain sprouted two crab-like stalks, an eye on the end of each that stared with unblinking, sentient horror. A label on the jar read simply *"Esther"*.

Cages contained aborted attempts at fusing man with ape. No laboratory creations these, but stitched together, as if some demon tailor had gone mad with a needle and thread. One gorilla wore a human face that hadn't quite taken—a grotesque mask of dried and shrivelled parchment. Another looked sorrowfully at the useless human hands stitched to its wrists, shaking its head, unable to fathom the meaninglessness of its suffering.

Some hybrids were so obscene that it was impossible to tell whether they were looking at a beast with human parts, or a human with animal parts.

On an operating table near the middle of the room the body of a boy was spread out—the baker's son?—with his neck opened longways. The flaps of skin had been pinned back to reveal that his vocal cords had been extracted.

Boswell retched. 'Good God,' he gasped, his eyes filling with tears. 'What kind of monster could do such a thing?'

'Good evening gentlemen,' came a rasping voice from behind them. Before they had a chance to react, both men felt something pressed firmly to their mouths, and tasted the sickly-sweet stench of chemicals, before passing out completely.

*

Doctor Johnson awoke to find himself strapped to a chair in that chamber of horrors. He turned his pounding head with difficulty. A huge orangutan was strapped to a chair beside him. In a bell-shaped cage suspended from the ceiling, Boswell squatted with his arms tethered behind his back and a gag in his mouth, rather like some monstrous parrot. In another cage Theresa was similarly bound and gagged, looking back at Johnson with pleading, tear-filled eyes. She was still alive, at least.

Then, just as he thought things could not get any more disturbing, Thak entered the room. With barely a glance at the captives he began fiddling with dials on a machine directly behind Johnson and the captive orangutan. It was a nightmarish contraption of cogs, levers and wheels, with a spinning centrifugal device in the centre, and a complicated system of copper pipes extending into the ceiling. Thak pulled a brass lever, and with a whirr and a clank the machine coughed into life, belching steam into the air around them.

'Where is Monboddo?' demanded Johnson through the churning noise.

The orangutan looked at Johnson and smiled. 'I am Monboddo, Doctor,' he rasped in a voice like sandpaper.

Doctor Johnson stared at the ape with stark, uncomprehending horror.

'Or rather, Monboddo's genius, his thoughts and his memories, now reside within me. Here is the shell that once contained your professor,' Thak pulled aside a sheet to reveal Monboddo, or what was left of him. He was slumped in the corner of a cage, his head lolling uselessly on his chest, the once alert features sagging and unresponsive.

'Oh, he had his uses,' Thak said. 'He gave me the power of speech, after all. With our prototypes, we used the vocal cords of corpses I took from the graveyard. The results were...

disappointing, to say the least, and had to be incinerated.

'In my case,' the grotesque ape continued, indicating the boy on the operating table, 'we took the vocal cords from a live specimen, and as you can see, or rather hear, the results were far more encouraging.'

'What do you plan to do with the girl, you fiend?' cried Johnson.

'Do you know, Monboddo has been developing a fascinating new procedure. Have you heard of the pineal gland, Doctor? It is the *Ajna Chakra* of Hindu philosophy, the throne of all human consciousness. My mentor discovered a harmless way to extract the pineal fluid from one subject and transplant it safely into the pineal gland of another. A single teardrop containing every memory, dream and thought of the human individual. The soul, if you will. Oh, I've watched him practice on corpses any number of times. It's a very straightforward procedure, if you have the right equipment. Do you know, he planned to inject that brainless tavern wench over there with the pineal fluid from his dead wife? The poor, lovesick fool. But I had a much better idea. I overpowered the doctor and "borrowed" his pineal fluid, so that I, Thak, can continue his exalted work alone.'

'I can see that you have acquired much of the doctor's vanity and arrogance,' said Johnson. 'If little else. What the devil do you need me for?'

'Have you met Zora, my bride to be?' Thak said, indicating the female ape strapped to the chair beside Doctor Johnson. 'If I am to have a partner, I must have an intellectual equal. What better wedding gift, than to inject her with the pineal fluid from Doctor Johnson—the greatest mind in all Europe? After my own, naturally.'

'You'll never get away with this, you monster,' cried Johnson.

'Oh but I shall,' replied Thak. 'And with Zora by my side, together we will create a new race of super-apes to populate the Earth!'

'But it's preposterous!' cried Johnson. 'You can't be serious. It all sounds like some fanciful opium dream!'

'Oh I think you will find, Doctor, that I am quite serious.'

Thak produced a monstrous syringe and waddled towards Doctor Johnson, grinning with maniacal glee. From his cage, Boswell rolled his eyes in horror.

'Hold still, Doctor Johnson,' said Thak. 'This won't hurt a bit. For me, anyway, though I'm afraid that after the initial searing agony, you will be left a drooling vegetable like our friend Monboddo here.'

With painstaking deliberation, Thak extended the syringe towards Johnson's ear.

'Blast your eyes, you damned monkey,' said Johnson between gritted teeth. 'Do you worst.'

Thak stopped dead, his eyes flashing with murderous fury. 'Don't...Call...Me...A...MONKEY!' he roared, and dropping the syringe he raised both fists ready to slam them down on Johnson's head.

Suddenly from upstairs they could hear a pounding on the door. The orangutan clamped a paw over Johnson's mouth, and raised a finger to his lips.

Chapter 10

'There's nothing here, Sergeant,' said Corporal Hendricks of the Royal Fusiliers 21st Regiment of Foot. 'Just a load of old junk and stuff.'

'Just as I thought, Hendricks. I told you it was a waste of time.'

When the strange-looking manservant had turned up at the army barracks raving about graverobbers, missing children, mad scientists and murderous apes, the men had just laughed. But commanding officer Captain Blake spared two men, just in case. Corporal Steven Hendricks and Sergeant Francis Alderdice, having nothing better to do that day, volunteered to check in on the location.

Alderdice was just about to call off the search when he felt a tugging at his sleeve. Looking down, he was surprised to see a chimpanzee trying to capture his attention. 'Well bless me! What's that, little fella? You hungry or something?'

'I think he's trying to tell us something, sergeant.'

Monboddo's pet chimpanzee pointed frantically at the door to the cellar, then drew a finger across his neck.

'So he is! What is it you're trying to say, son? The door? There's something down there?'

Benji nodded vigorously.

'I think it leads to a cellar, Sergeant.'

'Right Hendricks. Let's see if anyone's at home.'

Hendricks pounded the door with the butt of his rifle, then took a step back. The door swung open of its own accord. The two men peered warily into the shadows. 'You go first,' said Alderdice.

Hendricks started off down the stairs, one step at a time, with his superior close behind. From the churning noise emanating from down below, they half-expected to find there some diabolical device. But what they witnessed when they reached the bottom of the stairs made Dante's inferno seem like a walk in the park.

Amidst all the scientific paraphernalia, the dead bodies, the mutations and horror-filled jars, Doctor Samuel Johnson, the greatest literary mind of his generation, was strapped to a chair. And he was in trouble.

'Shoot the monkey!' cried Johnson. 'Shoot the damned thing now, I beg you!'

The creature towering over Doctor Johnson was more demon than ape, its red fur matted thick with sweat, its barrel-chest heaving as its lungs worked like a bellows. The beast let out a blood-curdling scream, and with two extraordinary bounds on its great arms it sprang over the body of the boy on the surgical table and launched itself at the soldiers, its face a murderous mask of fury.

'Bloody hell!' cried Hendricks, instinctively squeezing the trigger on his rifle. The bullet caught Thak in the shoulder but failed to stop him. The orangutan sprang onto Alderdice's shoulders, and with one powerful wrench broke the sergeant's neck.

The ferocity of Thak's onslaught was primal; terrifying. The corporal lunged with his bayonet, but Thak tore the weapon from his hands and swung the stock down on the soldier's head. Then, as the ape raised the rifle to deal the death blow, Joseph Ritter, Boswell's loyal manservant, appeared at the top of the stairs. Rapidly assessing the situation, he flew down and caught the upraised rifle from behind. Man and ape wrestled for the weapon, but Thak proved too powerful. Within moments the beast had overpowered the manservant, throwing him effortlessly to the laboratory floor. Thak pressed the barrel of the rifle down on Joseph's neck, choking the life out of him.

Doctor Johnson struggled to free himself from the wrist braces, watching with impotent fury as Joseph's face turned purple.

Then, miraculously, Corporal Hendricks began to stir.

'Get up man, get up!' cried Johnson.

Hendricks slowly staggered to his feet and looked blankly at the inert body of his comrade, whose head had been twisted almost all the way round. Hendricks seemed dazed, unaware of his surroundings. Joseph started to convulse, his legs twitching and jerking. The sight of a man in trouble roused Hendricks to action. He picked up his rifle and plunged the bayonet into Thak's spine.

The orangutan's eyes glassed over, his grip loosened, and he slumped forward onto Joseph, dead.

'Please,' said Johnson, breathing heavily. 'Release the girl. It's over now.'

Auchenblae, August 3rd 1773

Though we had rid the world of a great evil, we were not inclined to celebrate. The body of the poor baker's son we returned to Auchenblae for burial, and his father's grief was a sight I shall never forget. Those animals we were able to save, including the female orangutan, we donated to the Royal Zoological Society (though I am informed the soldiers kept Benjamin Franklin as their mascot). The rest of the beasts had to be put down with as much mercy as we could afford them.

On Johnson's insistence, all of Monboddo's journals and scientific apparatus were incinerated. 'The world is not yet ready,' he explained, 'for such knowledge. And though one day some foolhardy young scientist may continue the evil that Monboddo started, I can only pray that it is not in my lifetime.'

We stood watching in the rain as James Burnett, Lord Monboddo, was carted off to the sanitorium. I could not help but think, as the carriage rattled away into the distance, that this is what we reap when we choose to meddle with nature.

Finally it was time for us to leave. As we boarded our carriage, Theresa came rushing out with tears in her eyes to thank us for saving her life. I must confess it gratified me somewhat to assume the mantle of the hero, though undoubtedly Johnson was the man of the hour. Surely he is one of God's elect!

Just as we were leaving, Johnson leaned down from the carriage and pressed what looked like a book into Theresa's hands. As we pulled away I could see her staring at it in some perplexity.

I later learned from Doctor Johnson that he had presented the girl with a copy of Cocker's Arithmetick, it being a habit of his to keep spare copies in his portmanteau as gifts to enlighten and inform *the young. I am sure Theresa will be well pleased with the gesture, as any sensible young lady should.*

From *The Casebook of Johnson and Boswell*

Epilogue

'I must confess,' said Boswell, as the carriage rattled back down the High Street, 'I am more confused than ever before. What happened to Alan Stuart after his last journal entry? And how on the earth did Monboddo find his way back to civilisation without a crew?'

Johnson took a long sigh and eased himself back onto the comfortable leather seat. It was a mode of transport he particularly enjoyed; the pleasant sway of the carriage coupled with the rolling scenery, allowing him time to meditate and gather his thoughts.

'I'm afraid that only Alan Stuart and Monboddo himself know the answer to that, Boswell, though I suspect at least half the rumours we heard at the inn were actually true. Certainly, using the serum he developed from that remarkable orchid, Monboddo was able to achieve a great many miraculous things. The scarring I observed on his arm indicates he first tested the brain serum on himself, artificially boosting his intelligence with injections, which would explain the wonders he was able to achieve in such a short space of time. Add to that a burning desire to bring his wife back from the dead, and a ruthless streak that would stop at nothing to bring his work to fruition, and you have a recipe for disaster. Truly, he was a brilliant scientist, in his way, but vanity and ambition were his undoing.'

As they trundled past the kirkyard in the rain, Johnson tapped the roof of the carriage with his cane, a signal for Joseph to stop.

'I would like to pay one last visit to our good friend Reverend

Stuart,' Johnson explained. 'We have unfinished business to attend to.'

The two men knocked on the door of the manse, where they were received with great pleasure.

'So Monboddo has finally come undone,' sighed the Reverend Stuart, as he led his guests through to the drawing room. 'I can't say I'm sorry, though I will pray for his soul.'

'He dared to lift the veil that separates life from death,' replied Johnson, 'and suffered the wrath of God as a consequence.'

As the minister poured the tea, the three men quietly pondered the mysteries of eternity.

Five minutes later there was a frantic knocking on the door. Johnson turned to Boswell and winked, as a scarlet-hooded figure entered the room.

To Boswell's surprise, the cloak was removed to reveal a breathless, beautiful young woman. She fixed the minister with an impatient, questioning gaze.

The minister gave a sigh, and rolled his eyes heavenwards. 'He is in his room, Mary dear.'

With a cry of elation the woman ran upstairs, with Johnson and Boswell close behind.

When the young lady entered the room, Mrs Stuart almost dropped the tray she was holding in surprise.

The girl took one look at the solitary, pitiful figure on the chair by the window, and flew to his side.

He did not move, but the hand resting on his knee fluttered like a captive bird. Mary placed her soft white hand on his, and swallowed back the tears.

The invalid looked up. He seemed to recognise the vision before him. As memory came flooding back, a single tear slid down his cheek.

With a gasp of emotion, Mary dropped to her knees and placed her head tenderly on his lap. Tentatively, slowly, Alan Stuart reached out and touched her hair.

Johnson and Boswell left the room.

INTERLUDE

The Book of Els

Fettercairn, August 4th, 1773

*W*e had removed ourselves to a quiet corner of the *Ramsay Arms Hotel on High Street, a well-ordered establishment with good food, a warm fire, and comfortable lodgings upstairs. The landlord and his patrons were well-mannered and kept mostly to themselves, leaving Doctor Johnson and myself free to discuss matters of a confidential nature. In Johnson's hand was the book he had found—or which had found him—in the village of Fortingall, an ancient text hidden in the hollow of a sacred yew tree.*

From *The Casebook of Johnson and Boswell*

'It was easy enough to make a start on a translation once I had deciphered the Pictish Stone at Fordoun,' Johnson explained, flipping through the pages of his book. 'The Druids wrote from top to bottom, typically down the length of a standing stone or a tree, scratching each letter against a vertical line.' Johnson drew his finger through the dust on the table, warming to his subject. 'The twenty letters of the Ogham alphabet are grouped into four families of five letters each. Each letter is simply a cluster of one to five straight lines, scratched down the vertical edge of a stone, or in the case of the Fourdon Stone, around a spiral. The first group, L, B, F, S, N, feature lines scratched to the right of the line. The second group, H, D, C, T, Q, has lines scratched to the left, while the third group, M, G, NG, Z, R, run diagonally across both sides of the line. The vowels are made from clusters of shorter lines cut straight across, like so. It is a simple, some may say a *crude* system of notation, though there is an elegance and economy of expression that is quite satisfying; ideal for the medium of stone or wood, where a straight line is easier to execute.'

Boswell studied the neat little ink-marks that filled the pages of the book with a new-found respect for Johnson's talents. 'So what's it all about, Doctor?' he said, trying hard to restrain his impatience.

'What's what about?'

'The book, sir!' cried Boswell.

'Oh, this,' said Johnson, turning his attentions back to the book on the table. 'It is hardly any wonder the author uses an archaic language. It deals with a subject matter quite heretical for its time, to say the least.' He pushed forward a few scraps of paper he had been working on. 'See for yourself. It is called *The Book of Els* or *"Book of Angels"*, containing the history of the Tuatha de Danann, the destruction of their homeland, their resettlement in Ireland and their ultimate decline. One can find more detailed accounts in several ancient texts, the *Yellow Book of Lecan*, for instance. What is striking about this one, is that the author identifies the mythical land of Rocabarra with Plato's Atlantis, which lends the account an air of veracity. Other signs indicate that—'

'Just a minute, Doctor. Did you say Atlantis? You mean the lost continent Atlantis?'

'Of all the wonders we have encountered, Boswell, this surprises you?'

'I thought that the story of Atlantis was just an allegory, an intellectual thought experiment dreamed up by Plato, with no more truth than the lost continent of Hyperborea.'

'Tales of an advanced civilisation destroyed by flood are common to almost every culture,' said Johnson. 'We have the book of Genesis, of course, but also the deluge of Mesopotamia, the Epic of Gilgamesh, the Greek legend of Deucalion, the same basic story is found in almost six hundred cultures the world over. I believe, however, that there is more to this than just a story. These four islands probably existed, but were lost under the Atlantic long ago.'

'Lost how?'

'Many thousands of years ago a war broke out between the free peoples of Atlantis, giving rise to two distinct factions. On the one hand were the Order of Keledei, a race of warrior priests who lived in accordance with the Holy Spirit, and walked the path of righteousness. On the left-hand path walked the Sons of Belial, a race of evil men and women who forsook the light, only to descend into the depths of iniquity.

'Sickened of a war that showed no sign of abating, the High Priest of the Keledei flew to the land of Thule, and there took up his staff and struck the ground with all his might, sending a great shockwave that ran the length of the world. Such was the power in his stroke that the ground beneath the sea was rent asunder. From this fissure issued a host of terrible serpents, the Fomorian Sea Giants. Like serpents slithering from an egg they came riding on a crest of a wave that engulfed the four continents, and toppled the Pillars of Hercules.'

'And so what became of the Tuatha de Danaan?'

'Scattered to the four corners of the Earth.'

'And is there any mention of the Stone of Destiny?'

'There is, as a matter of fact,' said Johnson. 'It is identified as the mythical *Lia Fail*, one of four magical treasures brought out of sunken Rocabarra by the High Priests of the Keledei. The Stone was installed on the hill at Tara and used to coronate the

High Kings of Ireland. It was then entrusted to a successor, who brought the Stone to Scotland.'

'And yet legend has it the Stone originated in Israel.'

'I think that the story of Jacob's Pillow was dreamed up by skittish monks in an attempt to obscure the Stone of Destiny's purely pagan origins. It wouldn't be the first time.'

'Does the book provide any clues as to our next destination?'

'The clue is the book itself, Boswell. It's author, Adamnan the Wanderer, was Saint Columba's companion and biographer.'

'Then that is a rare find indeed!' Boswell ejaculated.

'Yes,' said Johnson. 'Columba—or *Colm Cille*—The Dove of the Church, the holy man entrusted to carry the Stone of Destiny to Iona, where he established Scotland's first monastery.' Johnson turned the book reverently in his hand. 'This work was presumed missing long ago, along with a great many other priceless texts. They say the library at Iona was the jewel of Christendom, a beacon of learning whose monks worked tirelessly illuminating texts, making translations, preserving originals and painstakingly copying them out. The Stone of Destiny itself was enshrined within the library's hallowed halls, and produced only to coronate a new King. Ah Boswell, if only a fraction of the things I have heard about the lost library of Iona were true! The legendary Fergus Mór, High King of Dalriada and sacker of Rome, brought back from that city enough treasure to fill a thousand libraries, including the amassed wisdom of Greek and Persian civilisations. But King Fergus was only enlarging an already extensive collection, for the library contained the sum of all druidic wisdom. They say the collection was burned to the ground in a Viking raid, but if this book survived, then perhaps...' Johnson trailed off, leaving the thought unfinished, though his eyes kindled like burning embers.

'If we could find such a library,' suggested Boswell, 'it might provide us with information on how to reach the Stone of Destiny... Aye, and a great many other treasures besides.'

'Ah, Boswell. I would give a hundred, nay, a thousand sacred stones for just one glimpse of such a place!'

'Is there a clue to the library's whereabouts in the book?'

'I am counting on it, Boswell. But it is a painstaking process. So far I have only been able to translate the first two pages. The author uses many archaic expressions and obscure, esoteric references. We should find somewhere to lie low for a while, while I work on a complete translation.'

'Well we won't find it here, Doctor. Half the country knows about our little escapade at Monboddo House, and soon the place will be swarming with journalists. Aye and worse than that, once news reaches Edinburgh.'

'You are right, of course, Boswell.'

Boswell spread the map across the table and traced a line with his finger diagonally through Aberdeenshire. 'There is an old military road that runs seventy miles from Fettercairn here to Inverness in the north, where we might find suitable lodgings, and a guide to take us through the Great Glen.'

'Good thinking, Boswell. First thing to do is get rid of our carriage. It is far too distinctive. We will travel light from now on.'

Johnson struck a deal with a local horse trader, a canny Irishman who was more than happy to exchange their horses and carriage for two pairs of stout Highland ponies. Once all the arrangements had been made, the three friends left Fettercairn with as little ceremony as possible, and a little glumly, it must be said, having traded their fine carriage for an altogether less elegant and commodious mode of transport. Luckily, what the shaggy beasts lacked in length of leg they would more than make up for in strength and stamina.

The winding military road ascended by degrees, until at midday the travellers had reached Cairn o' Mount, a high pass with breathtaking views of the surrounding countryside. Boswell used a hand to flatten the fluttering pages of his guidebook, while Johnson perched his rear on a nearby cairn to catch his breath. 'The Old Military Road from Fettercairn has served as a military route since Roman times,' cried Boswell above the buffeting of the wind. 'Its highest point is here at Cairn o' Mount, the place where MacBeth made his last stand and was mortally wounded in battle. He succumbed to his wounds several days later at Scone.'

From their superior vantage point they could see all the way back to Fettercairn, the road appearing and disappearing between thickly-forested hills. Before them lay the gentle slopes of Angus, while the west and east commanded views across the rugged Cairngorms and the distant grey band of the North Sea respectively. The slate grey ocean sparkled silver where the sun touched its cresting waves, and they could just about make out the billowing white sails of various sailing vessels coming to and from the Port of Aberdeen.

As they started down towards the Bridge of Dye on the borders of Angus, they spied a familiar figure lurking behind them in the shadow of the trees.

'We've got company,' whispered Boswell, inclining his head towards Johnson. 'I think it's our horseman from Druid's Wood.'

'Yes,' Johnson returned. 'He must have picked up on our trail again. And look, he has brought a friend along.'

Boswell glanced back over his shoulder and felt a twinge of apprehension. There was something uncanny about the way the two horsemen dogged their heels, never coming closer than a hundred yards, never quite disappearing from sight.

'Do you think they are from the same group that attacked us at Dunkeld?'

'I think not,' said Johnson. 'Open attack is not their style. Our friends here are wearing the monkish attire of anchorites. They belong to a Culdee sect, if I'm not mistaken, holy men who have taken historic vows to protect the Stone of Destiny, whatever the cost. I daresay they could tell us a thing or two about what happened to Professor Dunbar.'

'How do they know we're after the same thing?'

'They must have got wind of our mission somewhere between

Edinburgh and Scone. We have hardly been discreet, after all.'

'Then we are in grave danger,' hissed Boswell. 'They will waylay us on some lonely highway and sacrifice us to one of their dark gods!'

'What an imagination!' laughed Johnson, then suddenly serious he added, 'They wouldn't hesitate to kill us, of course, if it came to that.'

Joseph, who had been scouting ahead, returned with more disturbing news. Four men dressed in similar dark robes were stationed at the crossroads several miles further along the way, and they appeared to be waiting for something. Johnson looked up at the steeply-wooded incline to their left. 'As soon as we turn the next corner,' he whispered, 'we will leave the trail. Perhaps we can lose them in those hills.'

The moment they turned the corner out of sight they dismounted and led their ponies into the trees, scrambling up the hillside until they found a fallen tree to hide behind.

'Do you think they will catch on to our deception?' Boswell whispered.

'Yes,' said Johnson, still struggling to catch his breath. 'When they meet up with the four riders at the crossroads. I think we should keep going until we find a safer route.'

As dusk fell the three men entered the labyrinth of the Cairngorm Mountains, whose lofty peaks and treacherous ravines had claimed the life of more than one unwary wayfarer before them. The travellers staggered blindly through the pouring rain, driving their ponies west through an endless succession of dismal glens and desolate passes, until at last, footsore and weary, they found their way into the district of Badenoch.

THE CASEBOOK
OF SAMUEL JOHNSON, LL.D.
And JAMES BOSWELL, Esq.

THE WOLF OF BADENOCH

CONTAINING:

A study on the phenomena of Lycanthropy, its
causes and cures,
and some insights into the nature of Demonic
Possession.

*B*ill Chalmers was a poacher. *And a bloody good one too,* he thought as he released the grouse from its snare and snapped its neck. He held it up in front of him. It was a fine, plump specimen, and the fact that it was stolen from His Lordship's estate would only improve the flavour.

He lifted his head and inhaled, letting the sweet pine-scented forest air fill his lungs. Maybe Lord Badenoch held a piece of paper saying that he owned the place, but Bill Chalmers knew who the real master was. He knew every knot of every tree, every tangle or root, and could find his way home blindfolded, even with a pack of hounds on his tail.

No time to gloat. Can't be too careful, even in this mist. He stuffed the bird deep in his pocket and went off to check his other trap.

Damn. A fox. Chewed its own bloody leg off. Bill Chalmers shook his head and looked sadly at the severed limb. *Shame.* He felt a certain kinship with the fox. *Stealth.* That's what he was good at. If he was caught, it would be *his* head in a noose.

Somewhere off in the distance a wolf howled. Perhaps it came from up by the old castle, or somewhere on the hill beyond. An eerie sound that hadn't been heard since the days of the Young Pretender. The last wolf was killed in Badenoch some twenty years ago. Roderick MacLean had heaved its carcass up to the village square and stood panting over it, grinning from ear to ear.

Some claimed that old Roderick had killed one of his own hounds—fixed it up to *look* like a wolf—just to claim the reward. Those dogs of his were likely half-wolf anyway. But Bill Chalmers knew a true wolf when he saw one. No dog had that long, pointed snout, those big yellow teeth…

As he picked his way back through the wood, Bill tried to picture the look on his wife's face when he showed her the grouse. He imagined her strong arms as she expertly plucked the bird, and his two little lads, elbows perched on the table, looking up and asking all sorts of daft questions. His heart swelled with a quickening pride. What was it his father used to say? A fish from the river, a staff from the wood and a deer from the mountain—thefts no Gael was ever ashamed of. *And a grouse from His Lordship's estate,* he added to himself with a chuckle.

A rustling of leaves startled Bill Chalmers from his reverie. He turned to peer into the darkness. A glowing pair of eyes stared back at him from the shadows. Shards of amber, like candle flames, bored their way into the back of his skull.

He began to walk. Another rustle—closer this time. He was being stalked. Something was walking in the dark alongside him. He could hear it.

Just a badger out for his supper, he told himself. *Nothing to see here.*

Then he saw it: a hunched grey figure, at least seven feet tall, stealing from tree to tree.

Not a man who frightens easily, Bill Chalmers started to run. Faster now, branches whipping his face.

He would cut through the field. Not normally a wise decision, but something was coming. Something terrible.

When he reached the clearing and saw the field, Bill skidded to a halt.

Every last sheep—torn to shreds. But what could have...?

Another rustle. Directly behind him this time. No more running now.

He thought of the warm glow of home, just across the field.

He thought of the grouse that his family wouldn't eat.

Finally, he wondered vaguely if that fox had managed to survive.

Bill Chalmers felt the hot, fetid breath on the back of his neck, and started to scream.

Cairngorms, August 6ᵗʰ 1773

t the village of F___ we exchanged a very expensive chaise and a fine pair of horses for a selection of stout ponies of the Scots' variety, called garrons. No matter, as these hardy beasts were best suited for our route through the mountains, following an old drovers' trail which was well defined, if a little rough-going. The weather being inclement, the doctor and I diverted ourselves by discussing the relative merits and virtues of our home countries.

From *The Casebook of Johnson and Boswell*

PART 1 - The Waning Moon

Chapter 1

'Fancy,' said Boswell, slowing to allow his friend to catch up, 'that to the eye of an eagle, these ragged, rain-lashed peaks are a petrified storm at sea, and our little group mere flotsam at the mercy of the currents.'

Doctor Johnson, a man of substantial girth, appeared almost comical on his mount, his boots nearly touching the ground on either side. The hem of his big grey coat was spattered with mud and he seemed thoroughly miserable. 'What I wouldn't give,' he grumbled, 'to be sat outside the King's Head in Lichfield, a mug of warm beer in one hand and a pipe in the other, hearing the pleasant clack of leather against willow on the village green.'

'But Doctor Johnson, you don't drink... You don't smoke either, for that matter.'

'I do now.'

'Come now,' said Boswell, laughing. 'Don't you find it a bracing tonic to the senses, the harsh, untamed beauty of our natural surroundings?'

'Give me the gently-rolling hills of Staffordshire any day,' replied Doctor Johnson, whipping off his wide-brimmed parson's hat and wringing it out. 'For it's one thing to hear of boggy moors, miserable weather and impossible mountain passes by the crackle of a warm hearth,' he cried, placing the misshaped article back on his head, 'and quite another to be caught in the middle of it! Nay, sir,' he continued, going on somewhat in Boswell's opinion. 'Give me the warm bosom of my English rose, and keep your cruel, untamed mistress for yourself. She is an uncouth and altogether fickle bitch.'

Boswell, a native Scot, threw his head back and roared with laughter. 'What do you say, Joseph?' he cried to his manservant. 'How do you like our Caledonian landscape?'

Joseph, a tall, taciturn Bohemian with a drooping moustache, cut an outlandish figure in his traditional *kroje* made from homespun linen, bear-skin cloak, high boots and wide-brimmed hat. He had travelled extensively throughout Europe in his youth, gaining a headful of superstitions along the way. 'Not good,' he said, hawking up a gobful of phlegm and spitting it out on the side of the trail. 'Is like Carpathian Mountains. Bad place. Feel many eyes watch us.'

Doctor Johnson smiled at the comparison. 'All we need to complete this dolorous scene,' he observed, 'would be the howling of wolves.' Then glancing furtively around, he added with as much calm as he could muster, 'Tell me Boswell, you don't happen to have any wolves in Badenoch, do you?'

'Do I detect a touch of apprehension in the brave Doctor's voice?' teased Boswell.

'Certainly not!' retorted Johnson, the colour rising to his cheeks. 'One blast of me pistols would soon see 'em off, eh Joseph?'

The dour manservant merely grunted, then leaned forward and patted his saddlebags.

The mountain path descended by degrees until they reached Moss of Gight, a patchwork quilt of dreary greys and browns stretched out like a blanket over the land. The monotony of the scene was broken only by the occasional patch of purple heather, or a pale and skeletal tree stretching its crooked limbs to a rain-engorged sky.

The marshy ground was too soft for their combined weights, and the men had to dismount and lead the ponies by hand. They trudged through the moor as the rain continued to lash down, and even the ponies struggled in the mulch.

'There lies the town of Drumalban,' said Boswell, indicating the faint corona of light appearing on the horizon. 'We'll soon be settled before a roaring peat fire. It may not be your King's Head in Lichfield, Doctor, but at least it'll be warm and dry.'

'Lead on, MacDuff,' said the Doctor with grim resolve. 'I am sure the worthy innkeeper will seem a veritable Duke, and his establishment a palace, after all we have had to endure today.'

'That's the spirit, Doctor Johnson.'

Drumalban consisted of a stately High Street, with a perfectly symmetrical system of rib-like side streets branching off in either direction, in design not unlike the skeleton of a fish. The eastern part of this thoroughfare forked like a tail, with both roads disappearing into a dense forest.

As the newcomers approached the head of the High Street they heard shutters being slammed, or caught glimpses of pinched faces peering from behind lace curtains. Admittedly they made an unlikely trio: Boswell, his ruined wig and embroidered frockcoat saturated with rain, his grumbling, overweight companion, and their foreign manservant, all perched on small ponies, while a fourth pony brought up the rear with their portmanteaus.

The three weary friends found an inn called The Blasted Heath at the eastern fork of the High Street. It was respectable enough for its type: roomy and clean, with a good fire crackling away in the corner.

Three old crofters, their faces grim and unfriendly, looked up from their whiskies and glowered at the newcomers. Ignoring their stares, Johnson made his way directly to the proprietor to enquire after supper and lodgings for the night. The innkeeper, a short man with a red face, nodded brusquely then called through to the back of the house. Moments later a small boy emerged to stoke the fire.

'Thank you,' said Johnson, placing a sixpence in the boy's hand. 'Now bring me a warm basin of water for my gout. There's a good lad.'

'Aye sir,' said the boy, who dashed off to do as he was told.

Johnson dragged a stool towards the fire, flung out his coattails with a theatrical flourish and plumped himself down like a big pigeon, bidding his companion to do likewise. Moments later the landlord appeared with two plates of mutton. Johnson lowered his head and sniffed the meat suspiciously.

'This mutton's rancid, man. I'd sooner eat my manservant's riding-boots.'

The three men in the corner looked up and scowled.

'Well it's like this, sirs,' said the innkeeper, leaning towards his new customers and lowering his voice. 'We've been having some trouble lately. My boy Jamie found a whole flock of sheep with their throats torn out last night.'

'You don't say?' muttered Johnson. 'How interesting.' Then picking up a piece of mutton with his fork, he shoved it in his mouth and chewed philosophically. 'Well it's tolerable, I suppose. Now where's the boy at?'

'Coming sir,' said Jamie, rushing in with the basin.

'Help me off with these boots, there's a good lad.'

Johnson sunk his feet in the basin of warm water with a sigh of relief. 'Now tell me,' he asked the innkeeper, once he had made himself comfortable, 'who owns the land around here?'

'That'd be Sir William Gight, Lord of Badenoch, sir. His family built this town. Lives in the muckle castle through the woods, about six miles north of here.'

Johnson nodded thoughtfully. 'Well, Boswell, how about we pay our respects to His Lordship tomorrow?'

'A capital suggestion,' agreed Boswell, who liked nothing better than to ingratiate himself with local nobility.

'Innkeeper,' said Johnson. 'Please take some of your mutton out to our manservant. Oh, and some good clean sheets. He'll be bedding down in the stables tonight.'

The innkeeper looked sheepishly at the floor. 'I don't think he'll be wanting to do that sir,' he muttered. 'On account of the dead body that's there.'

Johnson dropped his knife and fork and glared irritably at the innkeeper. 'Tell me, man. Is it customary to keep cadavers near the horses?'

'Not usually, sir. But the dead man's wife came round here last night crying blue bloody murder, and we can't bury the body until the Justice of the Peace arrives. That's if he comes at all. Bill Chalmers wasn't exactly popular round here. And what's another dead poacher to the law?'

Johnson finished the last of his mutton and wiped his greasy fingers on his coat. 'Hmm. You begin to interest me. Let's go and see this dead body of yours.'

The innkeeper grabbed a lantern and led Boswell and Johnson out to the stables at the rear of the inn. The body in question lay covered in a sheet on a bale of hay. The innkeeper whipped back the sheet, revealing a face frozen into a rictus of terror, with glassy, horror-filled eyes and lips pulled back in a hideous grimace. The effect was so startling that Boswell took a step back.

Unfazed, Doctor Johnson leaned over to examine the body. 'Hmmm… Every bone appears to be broken, concurrent with a great fall. And where did you say you found this man again?'

'On the edge of the field, sir.'

'And not at the bottom of a precipice or a cliff?'

'No sir.'

'Extraordinary. Look at his neck, Boswell. Do you see these abrasions? I would like you to show me where you found this body.'

'It was my boy found him, sir. Same place he found the dead sheep. On the way to the castle. Perhaps he can show you in the morning.'

Satisfied with the arrangement, Johnson wandered over to a grouse which had been strung from the rafters. 'And this?' he said, tapping the carcass to make it swing like a pendulum.

'We found that among the victim's belongings,' said the innkeeper.

'Well there's no point wasting good meat. Get it in the pot, man. Your braxy mutton's no good for my digestion.'

Gight Forest, August 7th 1773

We set off early the next morning, following the innkeeper's boy for Castle Gight, ancestral home to the Lords of Badenoch. All the necessary arrangements had been made to our satisfaction, with a messenger sent in advance to announce our arrival.

As we passed through a primordial forest of fir, Doctor Johnson also noted many fine examples of birch, alder, elm, rowan, and willow, all vying for attention from the sun, whose piercing rays slipped through the upturned fingers of the branches to dapple the mossy floor with golden luminescence. The grandeur of the wood inspired us to quote poetry to one another, a pursuit we often indulged in when under the influence of beauty.

From *The Casebook of Johnson and Boswell*

Chapter 2

'From Culbirnie to the sea,' said Boswell, 'You may step from tree to tree.'

'It puts me in mind,' remarked Johnson, 'of the old Celtic poem *The Battle of the Trees*. Have you heard it Bozzie? It concerns a war between Gods and Titans.' The Doctor removed his hat and placed it to his breast, raising a declamatory arm as he recited, '*We will enchant the trees and the stones and the sods of the earth, so that they shall become a host under arms against them, and shall rout them in flight with horror and trembling.*'[1]

'*That will never be,*' Boswell returned. '*Who can impress the forest, bid the tree unfix his earth-bound root? Sweet bodements! good—*'[2]

Suddenly young Jamie let out a yell, pointing to some flattened yellow grass on the edge of the forest. The men climbed down from their mounts and walked over.

'This is where you found the body?' said Johnson.

The boy nodded.

'Hmmm. Look at this tree here, Boswell. Do you see this flaking of the bark, as if it has been struck by something?' Johnson turned to the boy. 'Right, lad. Here's sixpence. Off you go now, we can find our own way from here.'

The boy's eyes lit up when he saw the money, and he disappeared back the way he had brought them before you could say sugared plums.

1   anon
2   Macbeth

'Well, Doctor?' asked Boswell.

'To my mind, there are only two possible explanations. Either the man fell from a great height, and his body was moved...'

'...or?'

'He was grabbed by the neck and flung violently against this tree. Do you see the damage here?'

'Yes but to break every bone in a man's body, would take a creature of considerable strength.'

'Considerable,' agreed Johnson.

The men walked over to the edge of the wood, where an adjacent field presented a grisly tableau of wool, blood and exposed bone. The corpses were bristling with flies, the stench of putrefaction so overpowering that Johnson needed a handkerchief to cover his face as he surveyed the devastation.

Joseph approached and crossed himself with a trembling hand. 'I see this before,' he murmured. 'In my village. We say man become wolf when full moon. Kill everything in path.'

Johnson nodded thoughtfully.

'But surely,' said Boswell, suppressing the temptation to laugh, 'you don't believe... I mean you don't believe in *werewolves*, do you?'

'Ah, you mean Lycanthropy,' said Johnson, touching the nearest carcass with the toe of his boot. 'The legend dates back to ancient Greece. King Lycaon of Arcadia slaughtered his youngest son and roasted him as an offering to the gods. But Zeus, offended by this grisly sacrifice, transformed Lycaon into a wolf as punishment, and killed his remaining children with lightning bolts.'

'Such legends may well serve in Ancient Greece,' said Boswell, 'or among superstitious European peasants. But here? In Scotland?'

'Why not?' said Johnson. 'There have been many eye-witness accounts of the phenomenon.'

'But a man turning into a wolf when the moon is full? On what principle are such transformations founded?'

'What principle is there,' replied Johnson, 'why a loadstone attracts iron? Why an egg produces a chicken by heat? Why a tree grows upwards, when the natural tendency of all things is downwards? Sir, it depends on the degree of evidence that you have, and here we find a man, who having been thrown violently against a solid object, has had the misfortune of breaking every bone in his body. And what is more, last night was a full moon.'

'Wherever the truth of the matter lies,' said Boswell. 'I do not like this place, and the sooner we leave it behind the better.'

'I won't disagree with you there,' replied Johnson.

he air was fragrant with pine, damp earth and rotting bark; a sweet, cloying odour that carried with it the faint suggestion of death.

We passed trees contorted with age, their scaly barks shaggy with lichen, and infested with fleshy lobes of fungi that are called Judas' Ear.

A little further north we came to a lofty battlemented archway, festooned with ivy on the perimeter of the estate, just as the innkeeper had described.

Once through the archway we entered a well-ordered garden of beauty and elegance, substituting the Dionysian riot of growth for an Apollonian world of symmetry and form, where nature had been rolled flat, then pruned, snipped and tamed into submission.

The Grand Avenue was flanked by manicured lawns, trimmed hedges and Grecian statues, with decorative urns placed at regular intervals along the way. At the head of the walk stood a splendid castle, consisting of a tall medieval tower flanked by two spacious wings contrived in the classical style, the whole structure tastefully embellished with a complex arrangement of turrets, embrasures and bastions, giving the house a decidedly baroque appeal, pleasing to the eye despite the eccentric mixture of styles employed.

From *The Casebook of Johnson and Boswell*

Chapter 3

his is more like it, Boswell,' said Johnson, fanning himself with his hat. 'Do you think our shaggy little ponies are suitable mounts for such a fine setting?'

'Quite suitable, Mr Johnson, though I should have packed some better clothes, had I known we would be calling on a peer of the realm.'

As they approached, a flock of crows evacuated the tower battlements, cawing noisily as they took to the air. 'The raven himself is hoarse,' murmured Johnson, 'that croaks the fatal entrance of Duncan under my battlements.'[3]

Alerted by the disturbance, a huge pair of hounds burst from a wooden barn and came racing out, their long shadows stretched before them on the lawn. The dogs stopped just inches short of the horses, snarling and baring their teeth, daring the intruders to move an inch. Johnson aimed a kick at one of the dogs and the beast lunged, attaching its teeth to the heel of his boot. As Johnson struggled to release his leg, the iron-studded oak doors to the castle groaned open and a wiry old highlander appeared, dwarfed by the huge entrance. He put his fingers to his mouth and gave a piercing whistle.

'*Oy! Shamus! Fingal! Thig air mo chois!*'

The dogs immediately lowered their hackles and slunk back across the lawn towards their kennels.

'My apologies, Shentelmen,' said the old man, hobbling down the stairs to greet his guests.

'Good day, sir. My name is Johnson, and this is my friend Mr Boswell.'

'I trust you are not wounded, sir?'

'Not at all. These boots were heeled by Hoby's of London. Hardly scratched the surface.'

'I am glad,' said the old man, his eye flitting suspiciously between the three strangely-dressed visitors. 'I am Malcolm, the groundskeeper here. If you would please come this way shentelmen. I'll show ye to your rooms.'

Joseph led the horses into the stables, while Johnson and Boswell followed the groundsman inside. As they entered, Boswell could not escape the impression of being swallowed up like Jonah in the body of a whale; he stole one last glimpse of daylight before it was snuffed out, then turned to find himself in a vast tower lit only by a few flickering candles.

'And have you served here long?' asked Boswell, struggling to catch up with Malcolm, who was already climbing the stairs with the agility of a man half his age.

'Yes, sir. Ever since I was a bairn. And my faither served the Laird's grandfaither. Here we are sirs,' he said, showing them into the guest rooms. 'I'll take your coats.'

The two men cleaned up with fresh water and soap, then made their way downstairs for their interview with His Lordship.

Once they had made themselves comfortable, the guests had a proper look at their surroundings. Oak balconies on each level ran the perimeter of the keep, looking down on the grand banqueting hall, so that to stand in the centre and look up was to feel oneself in the presence of an invisible audience, or at the bottom of a well. The narrow, stained-glass windows had been reinforced with iron bars, and despite the grandeur of the setting there was little in the way of light, creating a gloomy, almost oppressive atmosphere. Doctor Johnson eased himself onto a tall chair by the fire to check his boots for damage, while Boswell took a turn of the hall, examining the medieval tapestries hanging from the walls. Each depicted a hunting scene rendered in sumptuous, living colour—a merry pageantry of richly-dressed noblemen and women hunting boars, bears, swans, otters, deer and other exotic creatures. One image caught Boswell's attention in particular: a team on horseback pursuing a wolf with their hounds. The artist had rendered the wolf so finely that each white tooth glittered in the candlelight. It seemed to be looking back and taunting its pursuers.

A pair of Lochaber axes formed a cross above the mantelpiece, flanked by two crests, one a stone wolf's head in bas-relief, worn almost smooth with age, the other a stag's head with the motto *Byde and Fecht*.

'Do you like my wolf, gentlemen?' said a voice from behind them. The two men started, then stood as a tall, stately gentleman draped in plaid descended the staircase. 'It is the emblem of the man who built this castle, the dreaded *Wolf of Badenoch*. The stag is my own.'

Sir William Gight, 16th Lord of Badenoch made his way towards his guests, a slender hand extended in welcome. Though handsome, his chin was on the weak side, with a contemptuous cast to his lidded eyes and a small, pinkish mouth which marked him as an aristocrat. 'Doctor Johnson, I presume? I'm a regular subscriber of your periodicals, and your *Dictionary* has pride of place in my library.'

'You do me too much honour, Your Lordship,' said Johnson with a bow.

'The honour is all mine, sir,' replied Sir William, moving towards the fire to warm his rear. 'And have you travelled far?'

'All the way from Edinburgh.'

'Really? And may I inquire as to the purpose of your visit?'

'To see if Scotland is as uncouth as I have been led to believe.'

'And have your suspicions been confirmed?'

'On the contrary, sir. Indeed, on more than one occasion I have been forced to eat my words.'

'Oh I think we can do better than that,' said Sir William, ringing the bell for dinner service.

Moments later the door to the downstairs kitchen swung open, and two maids emerged with a roasted lamb shank on a bed of vegetables. Sir William sharpened his knifes and carved with all the precision of a master butcher, while Malcolm poured the claret and served a thyme and redcurrant gravy to sweeten the meat.

'I am glad to see,' remarked Johnson, 'there is still some livestock left in Badenoch.'

Their host appeared momentarily at a loss for words. 'Ah yes, our recent misfortune,' he said, forking a piece of lamb onto Johnson's plate. 'I have put Malcolm out every night since, to watch over the rest of the flock. Possibly a rogue wolf roaming the area.'

'Don't you fear for your servant's safety?' was Johnson's concern.

'What matter?' laughed Sir William. 'He goes well armed.'

'A man of many skills,' noted Johnson.

'I don't know what I'd do without him,' said Sir William, a weary expression suddenly troubling his handsome features. 'He's been a loyal member of this household since before I was born.'

'And do you retain a large household, Sir William?'

'Not really. Just Malcolm, the gardeners, the kitchen staff and a few maids. I can always hire some extra hands from the village if I'm having guests. Which reminds me. I'm having a bit of a do at the end of the month. A few friends over, dancing, cards, that sort of thing. Young folk too, Mr Boswell, so I trust you won't get too bored. You're both welcome to stay until then. In fact, I insist upon it.'

The Laird of Badenoch, despite his easy manner, was not a man to refuse. Besides, the idea of enjoying His Lordship's hospitality for a few weeks, with the whiff of a mystery to solve, was a combination that both Johnson and Boswell found irresistibly appealing.

The three men talked long into the early hours of dawn, and found to their mutual delight they had much in common. Sir William, eager to know what critics thought of Garrick's latest performance, or whether Goldsmith had published anything worth reading recently, or if the Mitre Tavern on Fleet Street still served fresh oysters with porter, listened intently to everything Johnson and Boswell had to say. Finally, as the first rays of daylight broke through the narrow windows, Johnson stifled a yawn and begged leave to retire, citing his advancing years as an excuse.

'One last thing, Sir William,' he said before climbing the stairs. 'Just before we came to Drumalban, a man was killed.'

'Oh? What was his name?'

'Bill Chalmers.'

'*Bill Chalmers…*' said Sir William, running the name through his mind. 'No, can't say I recall anyone of that name.'

'That's strange,' remarked Johnson. 'I was under the impression that he was a former employee of yours.'

'My dear Doctor, so many people have worked for me over the years, I can't be expected to remember *all* their names. How did he die?'

'His neck was broken.'

'How dreadful. I must see if there's something can be done for his wife and sons. In the meantime, I shall ask Malcolm to be extra vigilant.'

'Please see that you do, sir,' said Johnson. 'Goodnight.'

The guest chambers were at the far end of the west wing, in an isolated section of the castle. Before retiring to their separate rooms, Johnson turned to his friend and asked his opinion of their host.

'He seems like a decent sort of chap,' said Boswell. 'What did you make of him?'

'I was quite impressed. Eton educated, you know. Thoroughly

Anglified. Spends most of his time in London, they say. Indeed, I suspect Sir William Gight enjoys dressing up and *playing* the role of the Great Chief, rather than fulfilling his *obligations* as Chief.'

'I rather thought you would approve of the civilising influence.'

'An unfair observation, Bozzie. I feel full of the old *Highland spirit* tonight. And to my understanding, the first duty of a Chief is towards his tenants, though I'm afraid Sir William has been decidedly neglectful in that respect. There was a lot of *unpleasantness* while he was in London, they say. Raised rents, forced evictions, that sort of thing.'

'Do you think he was telling the truth about the murdered poacher?'

'He was lying.'

'Oh really? How so?'

'Did you not observe Badenoch's hands on the arms of his chair when I mentioned the name of Chalmers?'

Boswell had observed no such thing, and presumed the question was a rhetorical one.

'His knuckles turned white when I brought up the subject,' explained Johnson, 'suggesting a certain level of intimacy. Now as Bill Chalmers was "low born" (so to speak), the only conceivable connection is, or rather *was*, as master and servant.'

'Your logic is compelling, Doctor Johnson.'

'But we are overlooking the most obvious piece of evidence, Boswell.'

'We are?'

'His Lordship presumed Bill Chalmers left a wife and sons. Who's to say he didn't have daughters, or perhaps he was a bachelor, or even a widower?'

'How remiss of me not to pick up on it,' said Boswell. 'But you don't think Sir William had anything to do with the murder, do you?'

'I think not, although it will be interesting to stay around for a while. Let us keep our wits about us, and see what we can find out.'

Castle Gight, August 8th 1773.

This afternoon Doctor Johnson and I were treated to a grand tour of the castle grounds by Lord Badenoch himself, who flatters himself that his house is commonly referred to as the "Versailles of the North". It is no idle boast. The original tower, standing at eighty-five feet and heavily fortified, was acquired by Badenoch's ancestors in 1449. Sir William's great, great grandfather added the impressive north façade and planted much of the surrounding forest, while his great grandfather built the two-storied east and west wings, extending for two-hundred yards in either direction. Progress halted in the early part of the 18th century: Sir William's grandfather Alexander Gight, 14th Lord Badenoch, was an unrepentant gambler who squandered the family fortune. Sir William's father Sir Joseph Gight struggled all his life to pay off the debt. Sir William himself has continued to improve the estate, with the addition of a formal walled garden extending along the south frontage of the castle, symmetrical in structure, and bisected by the Grand Avenue. Further additions include walled orchards to the east and west of the building.

The grounds themselves, locked between the ocean and a mountain range, are hemmed in by extensive woodlands, though much of the forest on the mountainside has been cleared to make way for sheep, whose mysterious deaths have lately been of some concern to Lord Badenoch.

It gratified me that Doctor Johnson, who very rarely concedes there is anything in Scotland to match England for grandeur or majesty, declared himself impressed, and said to His Lordship that he 'Worthily deserved an Englishman's applause for the creation of such a charming house amid such desolation and wildness.'

From *The Casebook of Johnson and Boswell*

Chapter 4

We enjoy a warm climate here,' said Sir William. 'Ideal for growing fruit.' He reached into the nearest tree and picked a ripe plum, passing it to Johnson for inspection. 'We have pears and cherries too,' he added, indicating the individual trees planted in neat rows along the length of the orchard. 'And six different varieties of apple.'

From the orchard they made their way to the formal walled garden at the front of the castle.

'I consider this my *piece de resistance*,' said Sir William, pushing open an ivy-covered wooden door and ushering them into a landscaped garden of beauty and elegance. '*Voila!*'

Everywhere, gardeners were at work pruning rose bushes and clipping hedges. Before them was a circular hedge-maze, and beyond it a pond, in the centre of which a fountain with dancing cherubs sprayed water into the summer haze. Benches had been thoughtfully placed around the circumference of the garden, shaded by a variety of beech, oak and lime trees, and a profusion of vines bearing summer fruit clung cheerfully to the walls.

'I must say, Sir William,' declared Johnson. 'You really have outdone yourself. It's a little corner of paradise you have established on the outpost of the world.'

Sir William beamed with pleasure. 'Well, one does one's best. Come, let me show you my greenhouses.'

After their tour of the castle grounds, the guests spent the rest of the afternoon admiring His Lordship's collection of marble busts, family portraits and ceremonial suits of armour. It was all strangely fatiguing for Boswell, though the library revived his interest. He and Johnson spent several hours poring over the extensive collection.

Afterwards, Lord Badenoch led his guests down a spiral staircase, past the kitchens and into the deepest level of the castle.

'I was rather hoping,' he said as they navigated the staircase, 'you would do me the honour of choosing a bottle to have with this evening's game-pie, Doctor Johnson.'

While Johnson and Sir William ransacked the wine cellar, Boswell took a candle and wandered off on his own, stooping his way through an ancient, vaulted passageway. The passage led into an even older chamber, empty apart from a door on the opposite wall. Boswell moved towards it and placed his hand on the rusty handle. It was stiff to turn, but he managed to wrangle it open. Here was another staircase of roughly hewn stone, descending steeply into darkness. A gust of stagnant air wafted up from the depths.

On the third stair from the top, Boswell caught a glimpse of something yellow against black stone. It was on closer inspection a King James Bible, its open pages yellowed with age. Boswell was just bending down to pick it up when a deep voice made him start. 'I wouldn't touch that if I were you. You might invoke the curse.'

Boswell turned around, relieved to find it was Sir William who had spoken. Boswell was intrigued by the notion of a curse.

'A novice monk, sent by the Bishop of Moray,' said Sir William, 'brought with him a letter of excommunication for the Wolf of Badenoch. The poor lad was thrown down these stairs and left to rot. They say he eventually ate his own hands in an attempt to stave off hunger.'

Boswell shivered at the thought. The Scots loved their gruesome details.

'A morbid little story, isn't it?' said Sir William. 'Rather lends itself to the expression *Don't shoot the messenger,* wouldn't you say?'

'Where do the stairs lead, Your Lordship?'

'An old family crypt, according to my grandfather. After that, who knows? An ancestor of mine once sent a piper down to find out how far the catacombs extend. He was never seen again, though several of the staff claim to hear his pipes in the dead of night. We keep that Bible there to prevent the evil spirits from getting out. One of many sentimental indulgences I extend towards my household, I'm afraid. Their Celtic blood is rather susceptible to such superstitions.'

As Lord Badenoch returned through the passageway, Boswell lingered a while, unable to peel his eyes away from the fecund darkness. For a moment he could have sworn that he saw something, a movement of shadow upon shadow. He shook his head, then turned on his heel and hurried away.

Later that evening, after a hearty dinner of game pie and several glasses of claret, Boswell borrowed a candle from the dining room to claim the sanctuary of the library. Under his arm he carried Johnson's own copy of King James' *Daemonology*, a heavy tome indispensable for those *in the trade*, as the Doctor called it; filled with current knowledge on witchcraft, necromancy, possession, demons, werewolves and suchlike, including spells to counteract their malignant influence. Johnson had made his own annotations, tacking on newspaper clippings, underlining key passages and sketching monstrous things in the margins witnessed with his own eyes.

Boswell placed the book on the reading desk and carefully turned the pages. A series of grisly woodcuts depicted bestial half-men engaged in unspeakable acts of savagery. Here was the Werewolf of Ansbach, whom the townsfolk discovered to be the mayor; the Werewolf of Pavia, who terrorised the Italian countryside until the magistrates caught him and cut off his arms and legs; the Werewolf of Chalons, who brought little children home for his wife to cook and died unrepentant and blaspheming; Gilles Barnier, Werewolf of Dole, who after a chance meeting with a stranger in the forest received a magical ointment which imbued him with the power to transform into a wolf; and Greifswald, a town with a serious werewolf problem, until the townsfolk melted down all the silver in their possession to make bullets. All of the cases detailed were from recent history, and carried with them the whiff of authenticity.

Boswell looked up and felt a shiver course through his body. The notion of werewolves seemed almost plausible in that darkened room, with the flickering candlelight casting shadows on the walls, and the night pressing in against the tall French windows.

Chapter 5

*B*oswell spent the next few days writing correspondence, while Johnson set to work on his translations, the Enkil Stone on the bureau before him. The evenings were spent in conversation with Sir William, who proved to be a warm and engaging host. An unspoken agreement that some rooms were more hospitable than others kept Johnson and Boswell confined to the west wing, where a study had been furnished for comfort rather than to impress. It was the least intimidating of the rooms, the ceiling reassuringly low compared to the grand banqueting hall.

Some parts of the castle hadn't been entered in years, and to Boswell's impressionable mind, someone or something wanted it kept that way.

He was only too happy to oblige.

Sir William was a widower, and though it was a subject he was unwilling to discuss, from what his guests could gather he once had a wife and daughter. Presumably, those locked rooms contained memories too painful for him to confront.

According to Joseph, who turned an ear to much of the servants' gossip and reported back to Boswell, Sir William did have an heir of sorts: an adopted niece at a boarding school in Switzerland. But besides the girl, Badenoch was quite alone in the world—an only child, as he was fond of saying, like his father and grandfather before him.

*

Johnson and Boswell took a turn of the garden each morning after breakfast, a habit from which they derived great pleasure. On this occasion the Laird himself joined them, strolling arm in arm with Johnson, who was keen to learn the common and scientific names for each and every shrub, bush or flower along the way.

Sir William explained in great detail his plans for the garden, including the addition of an artificial lake and summer house, bending down to let the rich soil course through his fingers. Boswell walked a few steps behind, only half listening to their host. The garden, ethereal and otherworldly, seemed particularly delightful at dawn, a time when the slimy trail of the snail on the wall seemed a rich vein of silver, and the spider's web on the wheelbarrow a string of pearls fit for a fairy queen.

The castle seemed dim and grey by comparison, and as they rounded a hedge and the battlements came into view Boswell suppressed a shudder. The ancient tower, frowning, monolithic, seemed to dominate the surroundings, the more recent additions a failed attempt to subdue the impression, serving only to accentuate the stark solemnity of the original edifice.

'Your Lordship,' said Johnson, shading his eyes to examine a turreted room projecting from an upper corner of the tower. A ray of sunlight glanced from its narrow window, and even by day the lofty chamber created a sinister impression, as if by deflecting the light it could conceal its dark secrets from prying eyes. 'May I ask, who uses the uppermost parts of the castle?'

'Nobody goes there anymore,' said Badenoch. 'Why do you ask?'

'Only last night, as I was taking the air, I thought I saw a white face peering down on me from that window. It caused in me an inexplicable feeling of dread. Yet when I tried to discover the entrance this morning, I found that where there should be a door, the corridor comes to a premature end.'

Sir William stopped and turned to face his interlocutor. 'Like

I said, nobody uses that part of the castle, and for very good reason, my friend. Many older parts are unsafe, and have been boarded up. May I suggest you be more careful in future, and only keep to those places you know? I wouldn't want any... nasty accidents on my conscience.'

Perhaps Sir William's warning had been meant kindly enough, but Boswell overheard in His Lordship's words a threatening undertone, and went to bed that evening more convinced than ever they were not alone in Castle Gight.

Later in the night he awoke in a pool of sweat, shaking away fragments of a half-remembered dream; fleeting night-terrors he hadn't experienced since childhood.

As always, when too afraid to go back to sleep, Boswell's troubled thoughts dwelt on his father, a man of strict Calvinistic principles who half-terrified his only son.

Boswell had tried hard to escape his father's suffocating influence; quitting the family residence at the first available opportunity, marrying a woman his father disapproved of and moving to London to start a family of his own. But the scars of a traumatic childhood never really went away, and though he loved his only daughter, Boswell couldn't help inflicting on her the same fears he had experienced as a child, terrifying her with stories of black angels and demons dragging bad people down to hell.

In dreams, Boswell saw his daughter's face being eaten away by worms, slowly revealing the grinning skull beneath. Of all the nightmares that hatched unbidden from the dark recesses of his mind, this one disturbed him the most. Had he been such a bad father? A bad husband, yes. All the whores, the venereal diseases, and the tearful late-night confessions to his wife, confessions that filled him with more self-loathing than the act itself.

As Boswell lay awake with only his thoughts for company, he could hear uneven, shuffling footsteps approach from down the corridor. His quarters were in an isolated wing, some distance from the main keep, and there was no reason why anyone should be up and about at this late hour.

The steps came to a halt outside his room. It seemed as though someone or something was listening at the door.

'*Hello?*' Boswell spoke hoarsely, dreading an answer, his own voice seeming so small and vulnerable in all that silence.

After what seemed like an age, the footsteps moved on, shuffling away into the furthest recesses of the castle. It would be a long time before Boswell had any sleep that night.

Each night the bad dreams would return with increasing intensity. In some, he was running from something that stalked him through the crooked corridors of Castle Gight. Grim portraits stared down from the walls as he ran, until he realised that each one, even the women, wore the judgmental face of his father.

In another dream he found himself in the Great Hall, seated across from a huge, bearded man in a wolf-skin cloak, the same man as the portrait in the corridor upstairs, grinning at Boswell in a way that made his blood run cold. As the bearded man raised a goblet to his lips, the cellar door across the hall bulged painfully inwards, then burst open to admit a multitude of rats, writhing and crawling over one another, streaming over the tables and clambering up Boswell's legs. The bearded man threw his head back and roared with laughter, as rats began pouring in from the holes in the walls. Soon the room was filled with a wriggling, seething mass of rodents. As Boswell opened his mouth to scream, one of them, a fat greasy specimen, clawed its way into his mouth... He woke screaming and clutching at his nightshirt, trying to brush off invisible rodents.

Some nights Boswell couldn't be sure if the visitations were dreams or waking horrors. There was a horrid familiarity about the place, a sense of having lived there before, perhaps in a past life. And always noises—the footsteps behind the door, the scuttling and scraping from the floors above, the wheeze of bagpipes that echoed from deep within the bowels of the castle—Boswell attempted to rationalise these disturbances. He told himself it was natural in an old house: the wind in the lum, rats under the floorboards, the settling-in of joints and hinges, like the creaking of an old ship. But still...

Even Johnson, in his room across the corridor, was not immune to the oppressive atmosphere of Castle Gight. A light sleeper, he too thought he could hear the bagpipes by night and the walker in the corridor. Most nights he paced his room from wall to wall, counting his footsteps, repeating illogical phrases and muttering to himself.

St Vitus Dance, the condition which plagued the man, went some way to explain the grimaces, jerking movements and eccentric behaviour to which he was prone. On more than one occasion, while sitting with his friends, Johnson had astonished the company by throwing himself behind the settee, dropping to his knees and feverishly reciting the Lord's Prayer, before returning to his chair as if nothing had happened. If such compulsive behaviour alarmed Boswell it secretly terrified Johnson, and he developed a very real fear of insanity. These symptoms, he confessed, had only been magnified by the castle's malignant atmosphere. His greater mission, his concern for his friends in Edinburgh, the plight of the Crown itself, all seemed to slip away as he succumbed to a deadly torpor, a listlessness only increased by the stultifying influence of his surroundings. In lucid moments he wondered to himself if it was not all part of some diabolical design.

Chapter 6

The morning sun shone brightly through the windows of Castle Gight, filling Boswell and Johnson with the spirit of adventure. They had decided to go off exploring on their own, leaving a brief note explaining their absence. Both men were pleased, finally, to be leaving the oppressive gloom of the castle behind.

They crossed the castle grounds then made their way up a barren foothill of abandoned corn-rigs, once home to a thriving community of crofters. The ascent was bleak and foreboding. When they reached the valley a more melancholy prospect they could not have envisioned. The wind, whistling mournfully through ruined crofthouses, seemed to recall the laughter of children, while thistles nodded sadly on the lea. A plough had been abandoned nearby, covered over with weeds and left to rust. Plovers pecked the dry earth around it, searching among the waste for morsels on what had once been arable land.

On the other side of the glen, what had at first appeared to be the summit was soon shown to conceal a further peak, with a small loch nestled in between, and a rugged series of peaks beyond. Without a second thought, Johnson climbed out of his clothes and plunged into the water.

Boswell sat watching his friend swim out to a small rock in the middle of the loch, amused by his poise. The older man seemed like a dignified sealion, and at the same time vaguely preposterous, like a giant water-baby.

A passing cloud veiled the sun. Every so often a breeze would trouble the surface of the lake, casting furrows across its glassy surface. Feeling restless, Boswell disappeared into a nearby copse of trees, notebook in hand, to sketch some of the local flora and fauna.

Ten minutes later, Johnson arrived at his rock, then turned to begin the return journey, taking broad, stately sweeps with his arms as he cut through the icy element. Despite his bulk he was a strong swimmer, with a stout heart, a big pair of lungs, and his blubber—not so much a hindrance when supported in water— provided plenty of insulation against the cold.

When he was about halfway between the rock and the shoreline, Johnson spied a figure that was not his friend appear from behind one of the trees. As he swam closer, another figure and then another emerged, until six men were gathered on the shore, all watching the swimmer with amused interest. They were strangely dressed, these strangers, not wearing the half-kilt or philibeg which had become fashionable, but the full plaid, an outlawed costume which had not been seen in the Highlands for nigh-on thirty years. Here were men who seemed to have stepped from the pages of some romantic Jacobite melodrama, from their blue bonnets down to the gleam of their newly-sharpened swords.

Johnson's toes found the coarse gravel of the loch-bed and he emerged dripping wet, wearing nothing but an ill-fitting wig on his head and a half-ironical smile on his lips. With impressive dignity, he snatched up his shirt and began to dry. He dressed calmly, without taking his eyes from the strangers. If he felt any fear, he wasn't about to show it.

'And my friend?'

'Don't worry about him,' said the tallest of the men, who appeared to be the leader. 'He's off clattering through my forest like he owns the place.'

'Your forest?' said Johnson, raising an eyebrow. 'I don't believe we have met. My name is Samuel Johnson.'

'An Englishman?' replied his interlocutor, as if he had just discovered a fly in his soup. 'In my loch?'

'I'm afraid,' said Johnson, fitting his battered hat to his head, 'that is something I cannot help.'

'I believe,' replied the Highlander, 'that is something a great many of your countrymen cannot help.' A sally of wit that provoked appreciative guffaws from his companions.

Boswell reappeared moments later whistling a tune, which died in on his lips when he saw the company his friend was keeping.

'Boswell!' cried Johnson cheerfully. 'This is Iain MacBain, master of this mountain, who has so generously invited us to his home to meet his family.'

'Provided,' added MacBain, producing a rag which he tore into strips, 'you permit me to blindfold you, of course.'

'Naturally, sir. Please proceed,' said Johnson, as business-like as could be.

MacBain's clansmen looked on with bemused interest. Here was this big fat man, who had risen from the water like some pink leviathan, now standing in his rumpled city clothes, suffering himself to be blindfolded as if it were an everyday occurrence.

The journey was a tough, disorientating uphill struggle. At several stages the cautious MacBain insisted his men stop to turn his guests around until they were quite dizzy. Johnson staggered gamely onwards, his hands groping out like some drunken uncle playing a game of blind-man's-buff.

At last MacBain ducked their heads through a small opening and allowed the two men to remove their blindfolds. They were in a deep chasm in the mountainside capable of sheltering at least fifty souls. Ghost-like figures skulked in the shadows, both men and women, watching the new arrivals warily. A goat with ribs like a washboard trotted forward and bleated a welcome. Above their heads hung some half a dozen hares, skinned and carefully prepared. Near the entrance a fire had been lit, surrounded by warm furs, with smoke escaping through a crude hole somewhere high above.

From behind the flames stepped an older man with the same broad jaw and deep-set eyes as his son. 'Doctor Johnson and Mr Boswell, I presume? Your reputations precede you, sirs. I am Duncan MacBain, head of this family.'

The visitors shook hands with the old man, surprised to find formal manners in so rude a dwelling.

'Though I fear our humble lodgings are not quite what you are accustomed to, I trust our simple fare will nourish you. Rory! Put some more baudrons on the fire. Pray, be seated, sirs.'

Johnson, perspiring from the journey, eased his bulk onto a nearby log. 'I thank you. And if I may say, it is not mere frippery and furnishings that are the mark of a true gentleman, but strength of character and nobility of bearing, and I perceive that you and your family have both in abundance.'

'Well spoken,' cried Duncan MacBain, producing a pewter flask from the folds of his plaid. 'Will ye drink to it?'

'No thankee,' said Johnson with a polite wave of the hand. 'Never touch the stuff. No offence, sir.'

'None taken,' replied Duncan with a shrug, and passed the flask on to Boswell.

'I must confess to being a trifle nervous,' admitted Johnson, 'being an Englishman among so many noble defenders of the Stuart cause.' He peered into the back of the cave, where a multitude of eyes watched sullenly from the shadows. 'Allow me to offer my condolences,' he added, moping his brow with a handkerchief, 'for the sufferings and deprivations caused to you and your family through the tyranny of the Hanoverians.'[4]

'Aye, we have suffered,' replied MacBain. 'The army garrison has provoked, harassed and burned us out of our homes, until we have been reduced to what you see now: broken men, who must steal and plunder to get that which is rightfully ours.'

'And what kind of man,' ventured Johnson, 'is the Laird of

4   Dr. Johnson had vehement Jacobite sympathies, though in his own account of this journey he suppressed them; King George himself appears to have read it in manuscript.

Badenoch, in your opinion, sir?'

'Ach, nae kind of a man at all, sir!' said MacBain as he spat into the fire. 'A mercenary bastard, who acts the gentle shepherd to his people, yet thrusts the dirk the moment our backs are turned. Only he lacks the courage to wield the blade himself, sending orders from the safety and comfort of his London mansion. But I tell you this: no amount of washing will clean the blood from those hands. Nay, he is not a man at all, sir, but a wolf in sheep's clothing.'

Around the fire could be heard murmurs and grunts of agreement. Johnson and Boswell could feel their quiet rage as a tangible thing, and realised that this dignified old Jacobite was the only thing standing between themselves and an angry mob.

'But as you are his guests,' continued Duncan, 'honour prevents me from speaking further on the subject. You are welcome here, and will be provided with safe passage back— having enjoyed our hospitality first, of course.'

Duncan MacBain drew four hares from the fire, then set about dividing the meat with his dirk. Nothing was wasted. He distributed a piece to each of the clansman around the fire, then to the women, children and old ones lurking in the shadows. Discreetly, Johnson counted six men of fighting age; though as Iain MacBain was no longer to be seen, there may have been more hidden in the vicinity.

They ate with their fingers while they listened to MacBain, who proved a lively conversationalist. Educated at the University of Aberdeen, he had spent subsequent years in Paris before following Charles Edward Stuart into battle against the Hanoverians.

Boswell, eager for an anecdote about his childhood hero, pressed Duncan MacBain to describe his meeting with the man they called Bonnie Prince Charlie.

MacBain chewed thoughtfully for a moment, tilting his head as he gazed into the flames. He struck Boswell at that moment as very much the noble savage, with his grey hair falling around his shoulders, and his dark eyes glinting in the firelight.

'He was not,' began MacBain, 'what ye might call a manly man, being something of a fop, but he could charm the birds down from the trees, and there was something in his eyes to persuade a man to follow him. I rode with him much of the way north from Derby in '45. He was keen to learn the Gaelic so I taught him a few words. A quick learner, as I remember. He passed a night in this very cave, after the massacre. In fact, he was sitting where you are now, Mr Boswell. But by then he was broken, a shell of the man he once was.'

The cave grew silent, until all that could be heard was the crackling of flames.

'But why stay?' asked Boswell. 'Surely a man of your calibre could easily provide for his family in Glasgow or Edinburgh. America, even?'

'*Why stay...*' repeated Duncan MacBain, as if he had never considered the question before. 'Because it is my home, Mr Boswell. And that is reason enough for me.'

It was a decisive answer, Boswell thought.

'It'll be dark soon enough,' MacBain announced at last, throwing the bones of his meal onto the flames. 'And these hills are not exactly safe by night. There's talk of wolves abroad, for one. My sons will make sure you are escorted back safely to your lodgings, provided you wear the blindfolds again. I will just leave you with a word of warning, or some advice, if you prefer. Leave Castle Gight before the moon waxes full. There is a black curse on that place, and its fall has long been foretold.'

Johnson and Boswell nodded gravely at Duncan MacBain's enigmatic words, but considered it imprudent to press him further.

After taking their leave they were blindfolded again and passed over to Iain MacBain and his brothers, who escorted them gently but firmly down the mountainside.

When they were within sight of Castle Gight, Johnson and Boswell's blindfolds were removed, and the clansmen melted back into the forest.

'We will speak nothing of what happened tonight,' said Johnson, as they cut across the lawn to the castle entrance. The crescent moon hung just above the turret-room of the tower, where Johnson half expected to see a face looking back at him.

Boswell nodded. 'I think under the circumstances that would be prudent.' Then after a moment's hesitation he added, 'Do you think we should take heed of MacBain's warning, and leave Castle Gight before the full moon?'

'What, and miss all the excitement? Not on your life,' replied the doctor, with a twinkle in his eye that Boswell knew only too well.

HERE ENDS PART ONE.

Castle Gight, 16th August, 1773

The days pass sluggishly with little in the way of diversion to commend them, so that I often question our motives for remaining so long at Castle Gight. Only when I observe His Lordship—who despite his bluff, hearty manner cuts a rather lonely and pathetic figure—do I resolve to wait it out, and see what truths the full moon will reveal.

From *The Casebook of Johnson and Boswell*

PART 2 - New Moon

Chapter 7

Johnson and Boswell were breakfasting in the study with Sir William, when the crunch of carriage wheels on the gravel path announced the arrival of a post-chaise. The driver opened the door to reveal a pale little creature swathed in blankets with exquisite, doll-like features. Malcolm the groundskeeper bounded out to greet the new arrival, more lively and full of expression than Boswell or Johnson had ever seen the man. Smiling wanly, the girl stretched out a fragile hand and stepped down from the carriage.

Sir William was standing in the middle of the room with his two faithful hounds Seamus and Fingal by his side, as Malcolm announced the visitor. Johnson and Boswell stood to greet the young lady.

'Ah, Cat,' said the Laird, hooking his thumbs in his waistcoat pockets without moving from his post. 'Gentlemen, allow me to introduce my niece Catriona. Catriona, this is Doctor Samuel Johnson and Mr James Boswell.'

Catriona curtseyed and tried to smile. She was an exceptionally pretty girl, perfectly formed at five-foot-four, with fiery ringlets framing an angelic, heart-shaped face.

'Well,' said Sir William. 'You must be hungry after your long journey.'

'N…no, not quite Uncle,' said the girl, smoothing down her plain black dress.

'Tired then?'

'Hmm, a little tired.'

'Well you go on and lie down. We'll get all your news later.'

The girl thanked her uncle, curtseyed again then made her way upstairs, while a devoted Malcolm followed with her luggage.

'Charming girl,' said Sir William, watching her climb the staircase. 'Been at boarding school in Switzerland. I thought we'd have the dance in her honour, let her meet some of our neighbours. A sort of "coming out" ceremony, if you will.' Sir William lowered his voice. 'I thought it might do her some good. Bad nerves, you see. It's why I sent her to Switzerland in the first place. The doctor said it was the best thing for her.'

'A very wise decision, Your Lordship,' said Boswell. 'I hear their spas work wonders in the treatment of nervous conditions.'

'The Swiss have made great progress in the field of phrenology,' said Johnson. 'Whereby certain emotional and intellectual functions can be understood through a study of the protuberances of the skull.'

'Is that so?' said Sir William, grateful for the change of subject.

'Indeed,' Johnson continued. 'It is my belief that we can determine an individual's character and mental capacity by facial characteristics alone.'

'Doesn't that mean,' said Boswell, 'we could identify a criminal before he commits a crime?'

'Theoretically, yes,' said Johnson. 'But it would be unethical to convict a man of a crime he has not yet committed, based entirely on the shape of his skull. Why, you yourself would have been locked up long ago, Boswell. Your physiognomy bears all the hallmarks of the abject and unrepentant sensualist.'

Boswell blushed under the Doctor's cool appraisal.

'Observe, Your Lordship,' continued Johnson, warming to his subject. 'Our friend's tall forehead, the plump, rosy cheeks, the faint trace of broken veins on the nose. Don't they suggest an intelligent—indeed a *higher*—soul, though with a tendency towards dissipation and licentiousness?'

'Undoubtedly,' Sir William agreed.

'Objection, Your Honour,' Boswell protested, taking the jest in good spirits. 'The counsel is leading the witness.'

'Sustained,' said Sir William cheerfully. 'But come, Doctor. You must apply these formidable powers of observation to my own features.'

Now it was Johnson's turn to blush. 'Your Lordship... I wouldn't presume...'

'But I insist, Doctor. Come now. What can you read from my phizog?'

With a sigh of resignation, Johnson squinted his eyes and focused his full attention on Sir William. After a few moments' thought, he leaned back in his chair and rested the tips of his fingers together to form a pyramid. 'The shape of your skull is somewhat narrow, which suggests you are not a violent man, and indeed your entire physiognomy is pleasing and, if I may say, handsome, bearing none of the hallmarks of criminality. The slight pointedness of the ears, however, indicates a man of substantial appetites, though the thinness of your lips suggest you keep a tight rein on them. Finally, the hooded, almond-shaped eyes, the closeness of the eyebrows and aristocratic hook to the nose betray a deceitful personality, as one who hides a great secret, a secret which if exposed, would provide the key to understanding your entire psyche. Perhaps a family secret, of which you are an unwilling custodian?'

'You are clever, Doctor Johnson,' replied Sir William with a nervous laugh. 'Perhaps too clever! But I'm afraid the only secrets I hide are the commonplace sins of a middle-aged bachelor: an overfondness for wine, snuff, and sleeping the afternoon away in my favourite armchair before the fire.'

'As I said, it is a somewhat unreliable science, still in its infancy.'

The conversation turned to other matters, and the three men talked well into the afternoon. Sir William was in high spirits. The presence of a lady in the house, even a sleeping one, seemed to have a beneficial effect on his temperament.

At six o'clock, Catriona reappeared for dinner.

The sleep had done her some good, and she spoke with a flurry of excitement about the ball, amusing the company with breathless accounts of her schooling in Switzerland, her tutors, and the other girls in her dormitory. Catriona had a particular talent for mimicry, and made even Johnson laugh; now with an impression of her lisping roommate, now the stern nuns who schooled her, emulating not only the inflection of their voices, but assuming the hunched back of one or the mincing step of another, and by doing so was in some small way able to dispel the shadow of tyranny cast by those indomitable sisters. Encouraged by the favourable reception, Catriona even took it upon herself to assume the bow-legged swagger and dour Old Testament drone of her beloved Malcolm, though she blushed despite herself at the thought of her disloyalty.

Johnson took the opportunity to test Catriona on her French and Latin, and was quietly impressed with her breadth of understanding. She was altogether captivating when the spirit took her, Boswell decided, but tended to slip into sudden melancholy for no apparent reason, especially when she thought no one was watching.

Castle Gight, 18th August, 1773

In Catriona, I flatter myself that I have found a kindred spirit, a sister in sorrow, whose ethereal nature mirrors my own poetic sensibilities. I, too, am inclined to suffer from a profound melancholia; there are times when I have lain in bed unable to rise, even to receive my wife or daughter, before rising up, Lazarus-like, to seize the day with all the savage glee of a man possessed.

I alone am qualified to understand Catriona's malaise, and with gentle persuasion and kind perseverance I have resolved to win her trust.

Her black moods notwithstanding, Catriona is an altogether delightful creature, and I had better be on guard, old sinner that I am, against falling in love with my patient.

From *The Casebook of Johnson and Boswell*

Chapter 8

In the days that followed, Boswell lived for the hours spent in Catriona's company. On their morning strolls through the garden he enjoyed a peace of mind unknown since the carefree days of his youth.

As for his companion, Boswell did not flatter himself that she saw him as anything other than a friend or a favourite uncle, and was content simply to play the clown for her amusement, considering the faintest of smiles a minor victory.

When he wasn't with Catriona, Boswell insisted on taking luncheon with the kitchen staff, escaping the gloom and stiff formality of the dining rooms above. It was on such an occasion that he received some startling information concerning Sir William's young ward.

Boswell was sitting with Joseph and Malcolm, while Mary MacKenzie the cook—a handsome, sturdy woman of some thirty years—had her back to them, stirring a huge pot of broth. Her scullery maid Helen, a plain, listless girl, was chopping vegetables nearby.

Boswell found himself entranced by the rhythmic sway of Mary MacKenzie's broad hips, and when she turned he could barely stop himself from stealing a glimpse of her breasts pressing against the starched white linen of her pinafore.

He had nobler reasons for sitting with the servants. By listening to their conversation, he could pick up some gossip and useful information about the castle and its history.

'I expect,' said Boswell, trying to approach the subject of

Catriona discreetly, 'the climate of Switzerland has done the young mistress the world of good.'

'I think it would be better if she had never come back at all,' said the cook, without turning from her work.

'Really?' asked Boswell.

'The little changeling, we call her down here. The master found her on the doorstep one morning, exactly one year to the day he lost his wife and his baby to tuberculosis, God rest their souls.' Mary MacKenzie, a staunch Irish Catholic, crossed herself with the wooden spoon still in her hand. 'None of the village women would claim her, so the master brought her up himself. Did his best by her too, so he did.'

'I imagine that he dotes on the child,' said Boswell.

'Well, I wouldn't say that, exactly. Fact is, I think he's a wee bit scared of her, half the time. She's a proper strange one, the little Madam. Pale and wan the one minute, wicked as a wee imp the next.' Mary turned to face Boswell, and said in a low, confidential tone, 'She killed the kitten he gave her.'

'Now Mary,' warned Malcolm. 'That's no' exactly the truth—'

'Gospel, it is. That's what happened. She goes into these spells, *wee dwams* my mother used to call them. She comes running into the drawing room in tears, holding the poor wee thing all limp in her hands, like she wouldn't hurt a fly. His Lordship said it must have been sick, but the poor wee mite's neck was broken.'

'I'm sure she was just playing wi' the thing over-vigorous like,' said Malcolm. 'She's a strong lassie, though ye widnae think so to look at her.'

Mary tutted and shook her head. 'And then she'd go sleepwalking and not remember a thing in the morning, though her nightgown would be stained and splattered wi' mud.'

Malcolm shot Mary a warning glance that she didn't appear to notice. 'But it was the speaking in tongues that really frightened the master, and made him send her away. Her eyes would roll right up into her head so you could only see the whites, and she spoke in a voice that was deeper than Mr Johnson's upstairs, if you'll pardon me sir, in no language that I have ever heard before.'

'That,' said Malcolm, 'was a fever, and perfectly understandable. No, Mr Boswell, she was sick in body, not in mind, despite what hersel' and her clacking tongue wid have ye believe.'

'Well you would say that,' snapped Mary. 'She can do no wrong in your eyes. But I still say she should have stayed away. This castle is not the place for a lass like that. It works its evil spell on her, and there's no telling where it might lead.'

'Do you think she's seen the ghost?' said Helen, who had been listening to the conversation with rapt attention.

Mary MacKenzie threw her head back and laughed. 'And you believe that daft story, lass?'

'I've *heard* him,' Helen confessed, her eyes wide with childlike intensity. 'Every night, tapping on the cellar door with his skeleton fingers. *Tap tap tap*. It's why I never go down to the cellar alone anymore. And those dreadful pipes, ranting every night. It's awful!'

'Tsk, nonsense,' said Mary. 'Get on with your work, Helen MacGregor, and we'll have no more of mad monks nor of ghostly pipes, or you'll be giving poor Mr Boswell nightmares. Why, he's gone as white as a sheet!'

Chapter 9

It was a fine summer morning as Catriona appeared at the stable doors in her riding costume to take her favourite black charger Satin. Joseph had been there since breakfast, where the simple act of brushing out the horses' tangled manes had calmed his nerves. How had he ended up there, he wondered to himself? The castle, with its nocturnal groans and whispers, was no place for him. He much preferred to sleep in the stables where it was warm and dry, and the dead disturbed him not. If it hadn't been for his sense of loyalty, he would be back in his native Bohemia, kissing his wife and bouncing little Gretchen on his knee.

'Hello, Joseph,' said Catriona. 'Is Satin ready? I would ride him today.'

At the sound of her voice the horses grew restless, and began to snort and wicker with anxiety; some of the stallions nearest to Catriona reared up and kicked their forelegs against the paddock doors.

Catriona turned pale and her lips drew thin. The horses grew more and more agitated. Catriona clamped her hands to her ears to drown out the noise, fleeing the stable in tears.

Only Satin, her beautiful black charger, remained calm. Joseph slung a saddle across the stallion's back and led him out after Catriona.

She was leaning against the stable wall with her head in her hands, her slender frame wracked with sobs.

'There, Miss Catriona. Please not to cry over silly horses.

Here is your Satin. See how he love you?'

Tentatively, Catriona reached out a hand and lightly brushed Satin's glossy flank. The feel of his skin, like warm velvet, seemed wholly alive to her. She looked at Joseph and even managed a smile.

'Come, little Miss. Let me help you.' Joseph put his shoulder to the horse and clasped his hands together, while Catriona placed one dainty boot on his outspread palms and hoisted herself onto the saddle.

'There, you see?'

'Yes, thank you, Joseph,' said Catriona, the unpleasantness in the stables all but forgotten. 'Please tell my uncle I have gone to town.'

Joseph raised his hat, and with a light touch of the whip Catriona was off down the avenue.

'When you will be back?' Joseph shouted after her.

'Before dark!' she cried over her shoulder.

As Joseph stood watching Catriona ride into the distance, Doctor Johnson emerged from a side door to the castle and crossed the lawn, hailing the manservant cheerfully. 'How fares thee, good Joseph?'

'Not good,' replied Joseph, looking gloomily up at the castle. 'Not like this place. Is bad feeling. Many restless things walk at night. The horses tell me so.'

'Well you'll be glad to know,' said Johnson, clapping his friend on the back, 'that you and I are going on a little trip of our own today. Are the horses ready?'

Joseph didn't need to be asked twice.

*

Catriona raced her stallion down the broad walk with the wind flying through her hair. She felt free when she rode, a feeling nothing else could give her. When she reached the archway at the perimeter of the castle grounds she slowed Satin to a canter, enjoying the dank smell of the forest and muted *clump* of her horse's hooves on the carpet of pine needles.

By the time she reached Drumalban her hair was in splendid disarray, her cheeks flushed with the exhilaration of the ride. Gone was the sober, measured expression of Lord Badenoch's young ward, and in its place was the face of youth in all its beauty and vitality. Villagers stopped to watch as she trotted past, her proud stallion rearing his head as if conscious of the grace and dignity of his passenger.

When she reached the blacksmiths, she dismounted and led Satin over to the stables, where the owner was busy at his anvil. Grasping a glowing-hot iron between a set of pincers, he dipped it in a barrel of rainwater with a satisfying sizzle and a cloud of steam, then wiped his face on his apron and grunted at his customer. A hairy, barrel-chested man, MacAdam the blacksmith had always slightly intimidated Catriona, but with her new-found confidence she was not about to let it show.

'Good morning, MacAdam,' she said, pulling off her gloves. 'And how is Mrs MacAdam?'

'Good morning, Miss. As well as can be expected, I suppose.'

'I'm glad. Please give her my regards.'

'I will, Miss. And what can I do for you today?'

'I'd like you to reshoe Satin, but please clean his hooves properly first.'

'Right, Miss.'

As they were talking, the clatter of iron made Catriona start. A tall, thin boy with an ugly face and a mop of curly hair lurked in the shadows at the rear of the workshop.

'Dougie,' cried the blacksmith. 'When ye've stopped gawpin' at the young Miss, ye might go out back and get some more coal for the forge, or ye'll feel the back o' my hand.'

The boy grunted an acknowledgement then slouched off to do as he was told. Only then did Catriona recognise the boy as the blacksmith's son and apprentice, the scrawny whelp she would see in the village from time to time. He had taken on a spurt of growth since Catriona had last seen him. His voice had deepened to a surly baritone, and patches of ginger furze sprouted where his chin jutted out.

While MacAdam busied himself with his task, Catriona wandered off to reacquaint herself with the town. She ordered a dozen yards of silk and mechlin lace from the haberdashers, then stopped in at Mrs Forbes' Tearoom. The old lady was delighted to see Miss Catriona again and made a fuss, while the other old ladies *ooh'd and ahh'd* over her clothes as if she were some exotic bird.

Catriona stayed in Drumalban much later than she had intended, and it was growing dark by the time she left. The forest wore a different face at twilight, and Catriona couldn't be sure if she liked it or not. The birds were all silent now. Nocturnal creatures stirred in the shaded undergrowth. She gave Satin a light tap on his flank, urging him into a brisk canter.

As they approached the landmark of the twin oak trees that loomed on either side of the path, horse and rider were startled by a figure stepping out from the shadows. The horse reared up, throwing Catriona, who landed badly, crying out in pain.

She glared at the figure hovering over her. It was Dougie MacAdam the blacksmith's boy. He must have run on ahead to surprise her. The look of anger on Catriona's face was replaced by one of caution, as she took her measure of the boy. 'What are you standing there for?' she said, trying to sound brave. 'Can't you see I'm hurt?'

'Now, Miss,' said MacAdam, holding out his hands in a calming gesture. 'I won't take up much of your time. I only wanted to talk to you, is all.' He caught Satin by the reins and patted his flank. 'He's a beauty all right, isn't he?'

Catriona sat up and eyed the boy warily. 'You frightened me, and I'm hurt. It's getting dark now, and my uncle will be out looking for me. You don't want us *both* getting into trouble, do you?'

The boy took a step towards her. 'That's a pretty dress you're wearing, Miss Catriona.'

Catriona pulled the hem of her dress to cover her knees, angry now. 'How dare you speak to me in such a way.'

The boy's expression darkened. 'You think you're better than me,' he sneered, matching Catriona's anger with his own. 'I only wanted a kiss, is all.' He took another step towards her and tried to sound more reasonable. 'Just one kiss, and I'll be gone.'

'I'll scream if you come any closer.'

'Scream all you want,' said the boy, emboldened by Catriona's fear. 'There's no one around to hear you.'

As he dropped to his knees and lunged, Catriona's fingers found the nearest rock and curled around it. She swung her arm in a wide arc and cracked MacAdam across the side of the head.

The boy looked stunned as blood spurted from his temple. Catriona fixed him with a look both defiant and fearful. He slapped her, hard, across the face. Catriona let out a desperate cry as he seized her, gripping her throat in one hand, the other sliding under her dress and creeping along her thigh.

From out of nowhere came a strong pair of hands to grab Catriona's attacker from behind, yanking him away. The stranger bent the boy's fingers back so hard Catriona heard the snap. MacAdam twisted round. His assailant stood several inches taller, with muscular arms and a murderous look in his eye. He took a step back, his hand touching the sword by his side. Here was a man, thought Catriona with a shiver of excitement, who scorned the use of fists. Once his steel was drawn, she knew it would not be sheathed until it had tasted blood.

'Get out of here,' the stranger said slowly, deliberately, 'or I'll open you from neck to navel.' The measured tone he used masked a terrible anger, leaving the boy in little doubt he meant every word. Clutching broken fingers to his breast, the lout took off down the forest path back to Drumalban.

Catriona gave the stranger a haughty look, no less afraid than before. But there was a kindness and warmth in his grey eyes.

'Are you hurt?' he asked gently.

'Only my ankle,' said Catriona. 'But I would thank my rescuer...'

'Do ye no' remember me, Cat?' said the stranger, feigning hurt feelings. Catriona stared hard at the handsome youth who seemed willing to commit murder only seconds before. 'Iain MacBain!' she cried, then remembering her place she added stiffly, 'I am very grateful to you for your assistance.'

'*I am very grateful to you for your assistance,*' he repeated in a mocking tone. 'Is that a way to greet an old friend? Where is the Cat I used to know? The one with scabby knees and brambles in her hair?'

Catriona grinned. 'Oh, Iain, it is good to see you again!' She rose to embrace him, but as she stood her knee buckled and she slumped against the tree, wincing.

'Let me take a look at that ankle.' With a concerned expression he knelt before Catriona and slid a dainty white foot from its riding boot.

'Does this hurt?' he asked, tracing a rough, calloused finger lightly across her ankle. Catriona winced again.

'It is a bad sprain, but I think it is not broken.' Iain tore a strip from his plaid, then wrapped it gently but firmly around Catriona's ankle. 'There, that should do for now. It's getting dark. We'd best get you home.'

Iain lifted Catriona onto Satin and leaped up behind her, urging the horse forward with the heels of his brogues. Catriona felt safe and protected in his arms, and snuggled a little closer.

'So,' said Iain, closely in her ear. 'You are quite the lady now, I see.'

'I am at that,' said Catriona.

The rhythmic sway of the horse, the rustle of the wind through the trees and the soft breath of this powerful man on the back of her neck made Catriona feel weightless and drowsy.

'And will you be staying from now on?' he said.

'It is my home, Iain. Yes, I will be staying.'

'I am glad.'

'And how is your father?'

'He is well. He sees far, and talks often of Castle Gight.'

'Yet he will not make the peace with my uncle?'

'It is too late for that, Catriona. Their fates have already been sealed.'

Catriona frowned. 'And did your father leave any word for me?'

'Yes,' said Iain. 'He said *she will remember that which has been forgotten.*'

'Still as mysterious as ever then, I see.'

Iain smiled. 'Aye, he is at that.' Then after a moment's thought he said, 'Will ye no' come and see us?'

'You know my answer to that, Iain MacBain. That my uncle would never allow it.'

'Then I see there is much you have forgotten already.'

They stopped talking then, and spent the rest of the journey in silent communion. It was a habit they had acquired long, long ago, when the forest was still very young.

*

Sir William paced the study floor and glanced at his fob-watch for the hundredth time. 'It's gone eight o'clock. Where in God's name is Catriona?'

Malcolm had been gone for hours. Doctor Johnson and Joseph were missing too, and Boswell was becoming increasingly agitated. He stood at the window, peering into the gathering darkness.

A horse as black as shadow appeared on the drive, with two figures perched on top.

'Here she comes, Your Lordship!'

The two men raced out onto the lawn to greet the arrivals, but when Sir William recognised the rider, whose arms were clasped protectively around Catriona, he stopped dead in his tracks.

Iain MacBain dismounted, then reached up and lifted

Catriona gently from the horse.

'If you have harmed so much as a hair on her head, sir...' muttered Sir William, his fists clenching by his side.

'Calm yourself man,' said MacBain. 'Her horse threw her. I found her stranded in the middle of the wood.'

'It's true,' said Catriona, as she hobbled to her uncle's side. 'Mr MacBain rescued me, and we owe him a debt of gratitude.'

'I... thank you,' said Sir William awkwardly, then reached into his pocket and withdrew a silver coin.

At the sight of the money Iain MacBain stiffened. 'Put away your siller,' he muttered, his face draining of colour. A blow to the face would have been a lesser insult.

Sir William fumbled with the coin and dropped it.

'It was good to see you again Miss Catriona,' said MacBain, without taking his eyes from his adversary. 'Please take care of that ankle, and no more riding in the forest at night.' He flashed his eyes meaningfully at Catriona, then strode off into the night.

Sir William glanced at Catriona, his expression hard to read. 'You will stay away from that... boy and his family,' he said through gritted teeth, then stalked back to the castle. Catriona looked broken. She leaned on Boswell's shoulder while he helped her back indoors.

Malcolm returned at midnight, having searched all evening for Catriona. He was overjoyed to hear she had been delivered safely, though his expression darkened when he learned the identity of her deliverer. He went to the kitchen, then raced upstairs with something hot for her to eat.

Johnson and Joseph returned in the early hours of the morning. Boswell went to the kitchen and brought the two men a cold side of ham, half a loaf of bread and a quart of fresh milk. As they refreshed themselves, Boswell told Johnson of Catriona's misadventures, while his friend hung on every word, nodding thoughtfully.

'But where have you been, Doctor? I was beginning to get worried,' said Boswell.

'Oh, nowhere in particular. Just reading up on some local history.'

Boswell knew better than to press his friend. Doctor Johnson, who had a flair for the dramatic, would never reveal a secret before it was ready to be revealed.

Castle Gight, 23rd August, 1773

This morning I took some books in for Catriona to read, and to share some anecdotes concerning my pilgrimage to Europe, where I had the inestimable honour of being received by Monsieurs Rousseau and Voltaire. Catriona was most anxious to learn every little detail concerning her literary heroes, and it gratified me to be able to satisfy her curiosity.

It strikes me that we are just as eager to know what a person of influence has for breakfast, as we are to know their deepest thoughts, for truly it is in the minutiae of life that we come to know a person, and where their greatest ideas find expression.

I still recall Dr Adam Smith's lectures at the University of Glasgow, where he told the audience he was glad to know Milton wore latches on his shoes instead of buckles, and in the same spirit of inquiry, I was pleased to answer even the most trivial of Catriona's questions.

She delighted to learn, for instance, that Voltaire enjoys up to fifty cups of coffee a day, and has his favourite brand shipped in at great expense, or that Rousseau maintains a strict vegetarian diet, and sees meat-eaters as little more than savages.

It amuses me to consider how Rousseau would perceive our dear Doctor Johnson, a man of Herculean appetites, for whom it is not unknown to devour a whole roast chicken with his fingers in one sitting.

Appetite aside, the Doctor's vices are few. A committed Christian, he never smokes, rarely drinks, and regularly gives alms to the poor. But just as I was extolling my friend's many virtues, I was disturbed in my musings by the gentle sound of snoring and looked down to find dear Catriona asleep like a little dormouse, her tiny fist curled *under her cheek, much like my daughter. I tucked the blanket up to her neck and beat a hasty retreat.*

From *The Casebook of Johnson and Boswell*

Chapter 10

*B*oswell was relaxing in the library with a copy of Shakespeare's Sonnets. After the first few lines he nodded off. He awoke some time later to find the mist rolled up to the window, and the pale moon just a smudge of white in the sky.

As he peered into the murk, he saw a white shape flitting into the walled garden. At first he thought he saw a ghost, before recognising the graceful movements and tilted head of Catriona. The peculiar way she glided across the lawn with no outward display of her injury caught Boswell's attention at once. Without alerting the rest of the household he slipped outside and followed from a distance, watching as she made her way down to the wall at the far end of the garden. Having read it was dangerous to wake a sleepwalker, Boswell decided to wait and watch.

Catriona stood beneath the old oak tree at the bottom of the garden, making a series of rapid, frantic gestures with her hands. She was not alone. A hulking black figure lurked in the shadows, and seemed to be conversing with her. Boswell moved a little closer and stepped on a dry branch. Alerted by the disturbance, the intruder scaled the tree with the agility of a monkey, then slid over the garden wall.

With no discernible sign of emotion, Catriona returned back through the garden, passing Boswell with barely a flicker of recognition. When she reached the castle she slipped inside, disappearing up the stairs to her chamber, leaving her little dark footprint on each step.

The whole episode had disturbed Boswell immensely. Lying in his bed, he couldn't quite shake the feeling that he recognised the intruder. It seemed to Boswell that the black shape he had seen in the garden was none other than the fugitive Jacobite Iain MacBain.

Chapter 11

Fort George, Inverness

Some forty miles away from Castle Gight, Second Lieutenant Hector Grant of the 42nd Regiment of Foot was enjoying a game of billiards with his fellow officers in the mess hall, when an adjunct entered the room.

'Lieutenant Grant, Colonel Crawford requests your presence at once.'

Hector immediately felt his heart sink. When the colonel wanted you, it was never good news. Grant's mind ran through his recent transgressions. Though he endeavoured daily to uphold the honour of the regiment, he was far from a model soldier.

He knocked on the door to the colonel's office, and entered. The old man was at his desk signing papers. Colonel Crawford was typical of his rank, with a face as red as a turnip and shaggy grey whiskers commonly known as *muttonchops*, giving him the appearance of a grumpy West-Highland terrier.

'Ah Grant,' said the colonel, not unkindly, which immediately put Hector's mind at ease. 'I received a communication today from Castle Gight. I believe you have some history with the place?'

'Yes, sir. I flatter myself that I am known to His Lordship.'

'And did you not once have a sweetheart there?'

Hector Grant coloured red. 'I... uh... yes sir. For my own

part, at least. Very much so. But I am sure Miss Catriona will not remember me. It was such a long time ago sir.'

'Yes, well, quite,' said the colonel. 'Lord Badenoch is holding a ball at the castle for all the young officers of his regiment. I trust that it will not be a great inconvenience to you? I gather your young lady has recently returned from her boarding school, and will also be in attendance.'

Hector Grant's heart beat so fiercely on receiving this intelligence that he feared his superior would hear.

The colonel gave young Hector a long, measured look as he lit his pipe. 'I rather thought you might enjoy some leave this afternoon. I am sure you would like the chance to catch up with the lass alone, before the ball.'

At that moment, Hector Grant could have embraced the old man. 'Yes sir. Thank you, sir.'

'I think you will find,' said the colonel, leaning back on his chair, 'that I am not entirely inflexible when it comes to matters of the heart. Nevertheless, I expect you back promptly for duty first thing Monday morning.'

Hector stood to attention and gave the colonel his best salute.

'You are dismissed, Grant. Go and enjoy yourself. And my best regards to the His Lordship.'

*

Castle Gight lay on the other side of an extensive mountain range. To save themselves the long trek round, Hector Grant and his valet Private Tom Lennox decided to leave the military road and take their chances on the mountain pass. At its narrowest, this natural corridor of rock was so sheer that the branches of the topmost trees on either side mingled, providing a perfect canopy of green that filtered the light so effectively it could almost have been twilight, though the sun was shining high and bright in the sky.

No fool, young Hector was aware that those mountains

were home to packs of bandits and "broken men": men who would not think twice about robbing him blind or even killing him. Meanwhile reports of wolves in the district of Badenoch had reached as far as Inverness, reports which did not seem so fantastic when passing though this eerie, desolate gorge.

The men were singing to keep their spirits up, when a voice boomed through the glen like some giant from a fairy tale.

Who passes through my forest?

Grant raised his head and looked around. The voice seemed to have come from nowhere, yet everywhere at the same time.

The two men stopped their horses and waited. Grant placed his hand across his holster to feel the reassuring grip of his pistol. After an agony of waiting the glen erupted with a chorus of whoops and jeers. Clansmen came clambering down either side of the narrow pass, leaping from trees and sliding down ropes made from twisted vines. They surrounded the riders, grinning with obvious delight at their discomfiture.

One of the clansmen, a raggedy old man with dirty hands, made a grab for Hector's reins. Grant's horse reared up, nearly throwing the young officer from the saddle. This was more than Grant could endure, his fear quickly replaced with anger. Leaping from his horse, he gave the impudent old goat a good shove. The clansman staggered back a few steps and his cheeks flared, insulted. Hector raised his fists ready to punish the old man for his insolence.

'Woah there,' cried a voice from the back of the mob. 'We will not have brawling in my forest like common ruffians. Put down your fists, sir.' A young giant Hector hadn't noticed before stepped forward and addressed Hector with polite authority, tipping his bonnet. 'Good day to you. Mr Grant, isn't it? What brings you through my forest on this fine day?'

'I do not believe I have had the honour. Sir.'

'I am Iain MacBain, son of Dominic MacBain, son of Roderick MacBain, and I call these mountains my own. I knew your grandfather James Grant of Glenmoriston. The only branch of the clan to have fought alongside the Prince in the '45, as it happens. How he would grieve, to know his grandson wore the insignia of the enemy!'

Hector almost laughed in his opponent's face. Here was this lad, not much older than himself, speaking of a man infinitely higher than him in birth, rank and nobility, as if he were an old army comrade. Hector was too flabbergasted to be insulted. 'I thank you for your kind words, Mr MacBain,' he said. 'And I know of your kin, to whom these mountains belong. But if you would kindly step aside, we have already lost half the day, and our errand will brook no further delay.'

'Ah. Now there's the rub.' The tall highlander spoke with perfect sincerity, but there was a subtly mocking, arch tone behind his words, that made it sound like a schoolyard taunt. 'You see, we do not suffer any strangers to pass through my forest, without first a test of manhood.'

'This is ridiculous!' cried Private Lennox. 'Let us turn back and take the long way round, Lieutenant. Had we done that in the first place, we would not be here jabbering away to no purpose.'

Hector Grant carefully weighed his options, but it was his youthful sense of daring and adventure that now spoke. 'Come then,' he said. 'What is this test of manhood of which you speak. Swordsmanship? Archery? I must give you fair warning, I have plenty of practice in both those arts.'

'No, Mr Grant, though you will find me no sluggard when it comes to the steel. But we mountain-folk have a simpler test if you would win your passage. This will be a test of strength.'

Hector Grant was shown a natural stairway that cut into the side of the ravine. His eyes followed the trail as it wound its way between the trees and disappeared into the mountain. 'Leave your horses here,' said Iain MacBain. 'They will be quite safe, I assure you.'

Hector Grant clambered up over a latticework of roots until his feet found surer ground, following the lead of the man in front by placing his hands and feet exactly where the leader placed his. Private Lennox took up the rear in a similar fashion. After a while the ascent became easier. Grant discovered that the natural rock made as solid a set of stairs as any in Castle Gight.

As they climbed, Hector couldn't help but notice the white, cabbage-like objects placed at regular intervals on either side of the trail. To his astonishment, Hector realised they were human skulls grinning back at him.

'This is the path of skulls: our Golgotha,' said Iain MacBain, noticing his guest's discomfiture. 'The bones of our ancestors we leave to bleach in the sun, so that we may commune with them and hear their voices.' Then, to Hector Grant's look of disapproval he added, 'You will find that we have adopted many of the ways of our heathen ancestors, since we were evicted from our crofts.' Hector thought it prudent to keep his peace, and nodded solemnly. Eventually they came to a clearing of grass where the ground levelled out, a high place from whence they could observe the densely forested land of Badenoch below. Hector peered over the edge and spied Castle Gight. It seemed so small and fragile from that great height, like a doll's house. Hector turned to study the plateau upon which they stood. Behind them a stream of crystal-clear water issued from a high wall of rock, only to be collected in a natural stone basin. Iain MacBain refreshed himself in the basin of water, inviting his guests to do likewise. Hector was pleasantly surprised at the peaty aftertaste and wholesome effect the water had on his spirits. It was delicious.

'Don't drink too much,' cautioned Iain MacBain. 'Especially at this great height. You are liable to think you can fly.'

Hector was filled with an agreeable sense of well-being and swagger. 'Now what is this test of manhood you were talking about?' he said, wiping his mouth with the back of his hand. 'As much as I enjoy your company, I have an appointment with a lady, and do not wish to keep her waiting.'

At this speech an *ooooh* of excitement rose up from the

clansmen, the same note of challenge heard in the schoolyard, when the new boy defies the reigning champion, and the savour of blood is in the air.

Iain MacBain liked this new tone in the young lieutenant's voice. 'The lifting stane,' he said gleefully, and the phrase was taken up by his clansmen: *The lifting stane! The lifting stane!*

In the middle of the clearing, half covered over with grass, there lay a heavy block of rough marble with rounded edges, rather like a curling stone but several times larger, into which a ring of iron had been set. Attached to this ring was a heavy chain about three yards in length, with an iron bar attached to the other end. The men formed a circle around the stone. Hector Grant nearly laughed at the notion of this absurd test of manhood, but when he saw the reverence with which the MacBains regarded the ritual he closed his mouth again.

'You have three attempts to lift the stane. If it leaves the ground, even for an instant, you have passed the test. You will have earned the freedom of this mountain, and the right to come and go as you please. You will also be welcome at the table of my father.'

'And if I fail?'

'If you fail? We will toss the pair of you over the edge of the mountain and take your steeds.'

Hector looked at his opponent to see if he was joking. It was hard to tell.

'Come, Mr Grant, ye need not worry. It is quite simple— look!' MacBain strode up to the stone, planted his kilted legs like big tree trunks and squatted slightly so his thighs would take the strain, then he spat on both hands and gripped the bar. A hush descended. MacBain closed his eyes, and the veins stood out on his neck. The stone rose a good six inches from the ground, wobbled there for about seven seconds, and dropped back down. A cheer went up from the clansmen. Iain MacBain turned to grip Hector's hand. A fine sheen of sweat coated the Highlander's forehead, but he was otherwise unruffled. 'Now you try.'

Hector Grant observed the faces surrounding him. If not entirely hostile, these were not the faces of men who wished him well.

'Come on,' said Private Lennox. 'You need'na play this childish game. Let us leave now and take the long way round. There is still time—'

MacBain raised a hand for silence. 'I'm afraid it is too late for that, Mr Grant. You are committed now.'

Grant stepped calmly forward and spat on the palms of his hands like he had seen Iain MacBain do. Then he grasped the bar and *pulled*. The veins stood out on his neck, the muscles on his arms bulged painfully with the strain, but the stone did not budge. Eventually his body seemed to sag and he relinquished his hold. 'I cannot...' he gasped. 'It is too heavy.'

The clansmen had gone so quiet you could hear a pin drop. The air was buzzing with hostility; Hector Grant could feel their contempt boring into the back of his neck. He tried again. The veins on his neck bulged so much Private Lennox feared they would burst. Hector's face turned purple, and he groaned in sheer rage and pain. The stone wouldn't budge.

'One more try, Mr Grant,' said Iain MacBain.

Hector studied the faces surrounding him, then looked at his own valet, who looked small and afraid next to these hulking brutes. His limbs were burning and he needed time to relax them. He strolled over to the fountain, scooped the clear liquid into his cupped hands and bathed his face and neck. It felt wonderfully cold. He took a long draught, and felt the icy water cool his burning limbs, restoring health and vigour. He thought about his father, and the honour of his regiment. He thought about Catriona. He walked over to the stone and grasped the bar in his hands. Then he closed his eyes.

Hector Grant didn't know how high he lifted the stone, or how long it remained suspended in the air, but the next thing he knew the men all around him were roaring with joy, Private Lennox the loudest of them all. He opened his eyes, and they all rushed forward to pump his hand and congratulate him.

'Thank God,' said Iain MacBain with genuine relief in his eyes. 'For a moment I though I would have to toss ye over the mountain after all, though I will mourn the loss of the horses.'

Again, Hector looked at his rival to see if he was joking. Again, he couldn't tell.

'And now you have the freedom of my father's fiefdom, Mr Grant. Will ye dine with us?'

'I can think of nothing finer, Mr MacBain, and yet I fear I would be a burdensome guest, for my mind would forever be on matters other than my belly, and the dignity of my company.'

'Och, of course! Your young lady!' cried Iain MacBain, slapping his forehead comically with the palm of his hand. 'Far be it from me to stand in the way of your prize, Mr Grant. But may I inquire as to the identity of the jade? There are many pretty wenches in Badenoch, but few with the power to lure a man from the delights of my father's table.'

'Certainly,' said Hector, full of boyish pride. 'Her name is Catriona of Gight.'

At the mention of the name, all talk stopped dead. A distant bird chirped, cheerfully oblivious, and the wind rustled gently though the leaves. Iain MacBain's brow darkened. 'Well I believe that concludes our business, Mr Grant,' he said, extending his hand. 'My offer of protection still stands, and my men will escort you safely to your destination. You will forgive me if I do not accompany you, but I have other business to attend to.'

'I see my candour has offended you,' said Hector sadly. 'It is my biggest flaw. I apologise.'

'It is not you who has caused the offence,' replied the young giant, 'and you will always be welcome here, aye, and afforded our protection. I like ye well enough, Mr Grant. But I must warn you. My protection will not extend to that House of Sorrows. If ye run with wolves, Lieutenant, have a care, lest ye be hunted with them.'

With this ominous warning still ringing in his ears, Hector

Grant thought it prudent to leave. He and a very relieved Private Lennox were escorted back down the steep incline, finding their horses tethered where they had left them, then led safely through the narrow mountain pass and into the district of Badenoch.

Chapter 12

*L*ord Badenoch was waiting in the study with Johnson and Boswell when the young officer arrived. He seemed pleased by the intrusion. 'Ah, young Hector,' he said, beaming broadly. 'You've grown since last time I saw you. Do you know,' he added, turning to his guests, 'the first time I met this young man he was pilfering apples from my orchard? Malcolm dragged him in by the ear, and I was ready to give him a good thrashing, until Cat spoke up for him. The two of them were inseparable that summer, isn't that right? I take it the purpose of your visit is to see your playmate again?'

Hector bowed his head.

'Malcolm, call Catriona, if you please.'

As they waited, Sir William interrogated the young man on various subjects and seemed pleased with his answers. Hector Grant was quite at ease and projected a confident front, but half an hour later when Catriona descended the stairs, the change that came over the boy was dramatic. He stood to attention, almost knocking over a table, hardly knowing where to look. He even half raised his arm to salute, then let it drop lamely by his side again.

Catriona seemed delighted with the young man's obvious discomfort. Still laughing, she approached and took both of his hands. 'Hector! How tall you've grown. And the moustaches suit you very well.'

With this compliment the young man's cheeks seemed to burn even more fiercely, had that been possible.

'Except when you blush,' she added. 'Then you look like the silly little boy Malcolm first dragged in by the ear.'

Hector Grant stood there opening and closing his mouth without making a sound. 'It's delightful to see you again, Miss Catriona,' he finally managed.

Catriona guided the awkward lad out into the garden, while Sir William shook his head and chuckled to himself, watching from the window.

'They make a rather handsome couple,' said Johnson, appearing at his side.

'Hmm? Oh yes, I suppose they do, now you come to mention it.'

Boswell stared glumly at his sherry. First the renegade outlaw, and now this young officer. Any hopes he may have entertained of becoming Catriona's favourite had finally been crushed, and he was ashamed with himself for feeling the rub so keenly.

As a younger man, Boswell had cherished dreams of a military career himself, but his father had laughed at the notion. The memory was a bitter gall to him. What was he now? An unrepentant drunkard and an absentee father, fast approaching middle age.

He compared his situation to that of Voltaire. How had the Great Philosopher managed to overcome rejection? By quiet fortitude and steady resolve, no doubt. Boswell would try harder to emulate the Frenchman's example. Anyway, the young gallant was so damned likable, it was hard to begrudge him his victory.

He fortified himself with another glass of sherry, then made his way to the library. From now on, he told himself, he would live the life of a monk. He would find solace in books, avoiding the temptation of the fairer sex altogether.

*

Catriona strolled with Hector into the walled garden. *How tall she has grown*, thought Hector. *Nearly up to my shoulder. And*

I had almost forgotten how beautiful she is. Everything seemed delightfully new to him, and his heart brimmed over with unexpected joy to be near her. Whenever her hand happened to brush against his, it would send a thrill through his entire frame.

As they sat together in the shade of the oak tree, Hector closed his eyes and leaned forward to breathe in the scent of Catriona's hair. It reminded him of summer meadows and autumn roses; in such moments all the poetry in his soul would rise up within him. But whenever he opened his mouth to speak, only the commonplace, idle thoughts of everyday life came forth. In those moments he could have kicked himself. How he longed to impress her!

'Sooo,' said Catriona, apropos of nothing. 'Have you killed anyone yet?'

'Killed anyone?' said Hector. 'I don't believe I have. No.'

'How can you call yourself a soldier if you haven't killed anyone?'

'I believe I should feel very bad if I killed someone, Catriona.'

'But what if he were trying to kill you?'

'Then I wouldn't hesitate. But I would hate to do it all the same.'

'If you ever killed anyone,' warned Catriona, 'I would never speak to you again.'

Hector was filled with confusion. 'But you just said...'

'Oh Hector,' laughed Catriona, running off into the hedge maze. 'You're such a blockhead!'

Hector gave chase, navigating his way through the neatly-trimmed, cleverly-angled passageways. Hide and seek was a game they had often played there as children. In the centre of the maze stood a white marble statue of Diana the Huntress, and a bench where they had once scratched their names.

After a few false trials, Hector found his way to the centre, but Catriona was nowhere in sight. He was just about to call her name when he felt a light tap on his shoulder. Catriona had stolen up behind him. She stood on tiptoes with her hands clasped behind her back and closed her eyes, a simple gesture of trust. 'You may kiss me now,' she whispered.

Hector kissed her.

*

After taking his leave of Catriona, Hector Grant made his way indoors to request a private audience with His Lordship. Sir William was filling out invitations as Hector nervously approached. The two hounds snoozing by their master's feet glanced up at the hopeful suitor, then settled back down, disinterested, as Hector formally stated his intentions.

'I see,' said Sir William, once the boy had finished. 'So you love her, eh?'

'Yes sir, I do. Very much so.'

'And have you asked her?'

'No, sir, not yet sir.'

'Well aren't you supposed to ask the lady first? Or is it the other way round? Oh hang it all, I was never much use at these things. But answer me this, Grant. What are your prospects?'

'Well sir, the army is sending me to America in three months. But my uncle has a tobacco farm in Virginia, and I had hopes of leasing some land from him. Father says he would give me a good deal.'

'America, eh?' said Sir William, raising his eyebrows. 'You know it's not easy to make a living out there. It is a thankless, hostile place, full of savages who would scalp you as soon as look at you.'

'I'm aware of the risks, sir, but I believe I'm young and resourceful enough to make a damned good stab at it.'

'And what about Cat? Does she love you?'

The question took Hector by surprise. 'I don't know sir. I mean I hope so. At least I think she does. But then sometimes...' Hector left the sentence hanging in mid-air.

'Hmm... And when were you thinking of proposing?'

'I was hoping to ask her at the dance, Your Lordship.'

'I see. Well, Lieutenant, you have my permission, for what it's worth. Just make sure you choose a fortuitous moment. Catriona is an insufferable romantic, you know, and timing is everything in these sorts of endeavours. Perhaps take her for a walk in the moonlight. Women love that sort of thing... Or so I am told.'

'Yes sir. Thank you, sir.'

'Then all that's left for me to do is to wish you good luck.' Sir William dipped his quill and went back to his papers, a sign the interview was over.

Hector made his way to the stables, where Private Lennox was already waiting with the horses. (He, too, had enjoyed a little romantic intrigue, having stolen a kiss from Helen the kitchen maid while the cook was away.) Lennox and Grant rode side by side through that wilderness to the accompaniment of howling wolves, with only thoughts of their sweethearts to keep them warm.

*

Once Sir William had settled all his business affairs, he removed himself to the main hall and slumped down on a tall chair by the fire.

'Will there be anything else, sir?'

'No thank you, Malcolm,' he said, without looking up. 'You may retire.'

'Thank you, sir,' said the manservant, retreating backwards and closing the double door behind him.

Alone again, Sir William poured himself a double whisky from the crystal decanter and returned to his seat. The wind in the lum sounded to his nerve-jangled senses like the low, sonorous drone of a bagpipe. He eyed the bas-relief wolf above the fireplace. It's leering grin seemed to widen in the flickering firelight. Sir William stuck out his tongue in defiance, then immediately felt foolish.

Young Catriona with her sleepwalking, Boswell and Johnson with their nightmares, they were not the only souls susceptible to the malignant atmosphere of Castle Gight. Ever since the loss of his wife and child, Sir William had become increasingly withdrawn. Never the healthiest of men, some said forcing the MacBains from their crofthouses had affected his conscience, leading to the nervous complaints which now plagued him. *If only they knew the truth*, he thought.

Had his wife still been alive, perhaps Sir William could have exercised a little restraint. But without the guiding influence of Lady Badenoch, he was at the mercy of greedier, less scrupulous voices, among them neighbouring landowners. Sheep farming was the way forward, they all told him.

He had landed in debt through a series of bad investments, and the nasty gambling habit hadn't helped. If he were to give the order of eviction, he wouldn't even have to leave London, or take part in any of the unpleasantness. Just sign his name, and his factor Bill Chalmers would take care of the rest. There was no other choice, really. He simply could not sustain so many families on his land with so little return. Still, the guilt he tried blot out with alcohol was always there, gnawing away at him day and night.

Only the long-serving, loyal Malcolm would know the true meaning of his master's suffering.

The previous Lord Badenoch had called it the Curse of Castle Gight, a secret handed down from father to son, a secret Sir William could barely even acknowledge to himself, let alone Catriona. The Curse was the real reason Sir William had fled to London, sending his beloved niece to boarding school.

He drained his glass and winced, then poured himself another. Catriona had been his only solace. His little miracle. That's what he called her when he first found her wrapped in her swaddling clothes. What a handful she had been! Almost feral. As a child she ran wild with the MacBain boy, coming home dirty, her dress in tatters and her beautiful ringlets in disarray, with an equally wild look in her eyes. The old housemaid Martha Stuart would throw her in the bathtub and scrub her until her skin was raw.

He didn't approve of the friendship. Nor, for that matter, did the boy's father. There was little love lost between Sir William Gight and Duncan MacBain, for obvious reasons. But at least they had agreed on one thing: the two children must be kept apart at all costs.

Hector Grant was the answer to all of Sir William's prayers. A fine, upstanding lad from a good family; he had prospects, young Hector, and was a good influence on the lass. There would be no more tree-climbing and running wild. Together they would take walks in the garden, read to one another, play piano, go riding and other, similarly refined pursuits.

Still, if the wildness had finally been beaten out of the girl, she had lost something of her former exuberance too. Gone was the sparkle in her eye, the wild and reckless laughter, and in its place was a sober, reflective young lady.

And then came the trances and the sleepwalking. Sir William wondered if the curse had not begun to work its malignant influence on his niece too, and sent her away. To see her so sad pained him, but it was for her own good. If she and Hector were meant for each other, then an enforced separation might do them some good. They had become more like brother and sister in the latter stages of their friendship. Perhaps a trial separation would kindle warmer, more mature relations.

And now the boy wanted to marry her. *Good,* thought Sir William. *One less person to worry about.* With Catriona married and packed off to America, perhaps the curse might pass her by.

He drained his glass and prayed it would be so.

Chapter 13

$\mathcal{D}$octor Johnson awoke to find a cryptic note slipped under his door. He stooped to pick it up and flattened it out on his desk, squinting at the handwriting. The author had gone to considerable lengths to conceal their identity, using the left hand instead of the right. The shaky letters said simply: *"I BEG you to meet me in the garden tonight at nine o'clock this evening. My IMMORTAL SOUL hangs in the balance. I will wait for you in the labyrinth. PLEASE come alone, and tell NO ONE."*

The author of this ridiculous letter was, of course, easy to deduce for a man of Johnson's abilities, and following a trail of white pebbles left by the mystery author, Johnson was not entirely surprised when he found Catriona sitting by the statue of Diana, in a dark cloak with the hood pulled over her head.

'My dear Catriona,' began Johnson, sitting down beside her. 'What is all this nonsense about your immortal soul?'

Catriona took Johnson's hands in hers. They were kind hands, she thought, plump and surprisingly soft. 'Thank you for coming to meet me, Doctor.' Her lip trembled and, before she could stop herself, she erupted into tears, much to Johnson's astonishment. 'I am sorry, only I am desperately unhappy, and... *oh, Uncle Sam!*'

Johnson raised a hand to touch her shoulder and she buried her face in his chest, giving full vent to her grief. Eventually her howling gave way to intermittent sobbing. Handing her his handkerchief, Johnson spoke in a voice reserved for those he deemed too fragile for his customary harshness. 'There, now.

Better? Tell me what the matter is, before you drown us both.'

'I think Hector wants to marry me.'

'Well! And is that such a disagreeable proposition?'

'Of course not, Doctor. I love him very much. But I am not fit to be his wife. I... I am bewitched.'

Johnson's brow furrowed. 'Hush now, girl. Whatever has led you to such a conclusion?'

Catriona looked up with big, tear-filled eyes. 'Oh I am in agony, Doctor, and I fear for my soul. A diabolical... thing steals into my room at night and... and takes possession of my body! Oh, it is a beastly thing.'

Doctor Johnson was listening to Catriona very carefully. 'And what happens when you are under the influence of this entity?'

'I... I have no recollection. But afterwards I have the most wicked dreams.'

'What kind of dreams?'

'Dark dreams, Doctor. Dreams of loathsome, unspeakable crimes.'

'And how do these dreams make you feel?'

'That is the worst of it! A terrible feeling of exultation accompanies them. Oh, my blood sings with the joy of it! I am damned, Doctor.'

'Child, stop this blubbing at once,' said Johnson, holding her by the elbows and gently shaking her. 'If you wish me to help you, you must place your trust in me absolutely. Will you trust me now, Catriona?'

Still sniffling, Catriona nodded her head with the simple trust of a child.

'Come then, take my hand, and we will find your uncle.'

'No!' said Catriona, pulling back. 'He mustn't know!'

'Ah, but he must, don't you see? No more secrets now, Miss Catriona.'

*

Catriona sat at the head of the table in the grand hall, with Boswell and Lord Badenoch seated on either side. Doctor Johnson stood behind Catriona's chair, his hands placed lightly on her shoulders. On his insistence, the room had been darkened, with a solitary candle lit in the centre of the table.

He leaned forward and spoke soothingly into Catriona's ear. 'Now, child. I want you to relax your body and focus on that candle. Nothing exists except for the burning flame, and my voice. The room has fallen away into darkness, and all that remains is that single, flickering flame, shining in the abyss. And now you feel your eyes becoming heavy; so heavy, you cannot hold them open any longer...'

Catriona did as she was told; her eyes fluttered closed, and soon her breast was rising and falling with calm regularity.

'Now tell me what you see,' said Johnson. 'What can you hear?'

Catriona's brow, normally smooth as an untroubled lake, suddenly furrowed. 'I can hear the beating of wings. They are drawing near,' she gasped. Her head jolted violently to the side and her hands gripped the arms of the chair. 'I see them! A multitude of black, leathery wings. They are beating around my head!' Catriona raised her arms, swatting at invisible adversaries.

'Fear not, child,' said Johnson in a voice of authority. 'Nothing can harm you. You are protected by the circle of light. Fear no darkness!'

Catriona became still, her face like a sleeping child's once more. Then all at once a leering smile spread across her face, and her eyelids shot open. Boswell gasped. These were not the eyes of Sir William's young ward. The expression was one of such taunting contempt, such gloating sensuality, that the whole company started back.

'To whom am I speaking?' demanded Johnson. 'Speak now.'

The creature that had been Catriona snapped its head round to face Johnson and spoke in a voice that was not her own. '*My name is Mariota Athyn.*'

'And what is your purpose with this girl?'

'I am herald of the Wolf. I am the Bitch of Badenoch.'

'Who is this wolf of whom you speak.'

The witch rolled her head and emitted a thick, gurgling laugh. 'You will see, *sassenach*, on the first night of the full moon. You will all *see*!'

Doctor Johnson removed a small crucifix from his pocket and pressed it to Catriona's forehead in one fluid movement. 'In the name of the Father, the Son, and the Holy Spirit,' he intoned. Catriona's head thrashed violently from side to side. With calm authority Johnson uncorked a small vial of holy water and anointed the demon's head. 'I command thee in the name of Jesus to come out.'

Catriona's features betrayed signs of some terrible inner struggle, then with a final gasp her back arched, and she slumped back onto the chair, her features drawn but still once more. Doctor Johnson removed a handkerchief from his pocket and wiped his brow with trembling fingers. 'She is at peace. For the moment, at least.'

'What a dramatic performance,' Boswell muttered.

'I can assure you,' Johnson replied, 'it was all very real for Catriona.'

'But what does it mean, Doctor?'

'Hard to say,' replied Johnson. 'But clearly Catriona is being used as a conduit for some malignant force. We must take precautions to ensure her safety. Your Lordship, kindly take Catriona to her room and lock the door.' Johnson spoke quickly now, and with a tremendous sense of purpose.

'Boswell, gather fresh boughs of rowan from the garden and hang them from the main doors to the castle. Then place a crucifix over the door to Catriona's chamber. Sprinkle this holy water all around, and draw a pentagram on the floor, like this.' He drew a five-pointed star with his finger on the table. 'With the single point towards her room. Do you see? All of this must be done immediately. Meanwhile, I will leave at once. The demon spoke in riddles. That name, however... *Mariota Athyn*. I am sure I have heard it someplace before.'

'It shall be done just as you say, Doctor,' replied an ashen-faced Sir William. 'And we will send word to the guests, informing them that the ball has been cancelled.'

'No,' replied Johnson. 'We must carry on as normal. The pieces have been set motion, and we must play our parts with courage and fortitude. I must go now. There is no time to lose, and much to learn. Look for me before the full moon.'

*

Catriona woke with a sharp intake of breath. For one horrific moment she was back in the dormitory in Switzerland. Gradually the familiar objects of her own bedroom revealed themselves, and she settled back down with a sigh.

She was glad to be away from that place: the austere nuns gliding down impersonal corridors, the smell of ammonia corroding her nostrils, the unendurable sense of hopelessness and isolation it engendered.

The other girls had feared her strange intensity, and after *that* incident, even the Sisters stayed away. Catriona could remember only disjointed fragments, like pictures in a book: her roommate, the bullying expression gone from her face, the unnatural angle of her arm as she lay screaming on the floor; then the nuns rushing in, the look of horror on their faces, the frightened faces of the girls who came in behind. Catriona looked on—detached, fragmented, far-away, unreachable.

No, thought Catriona. *Much better to be back home.* Except that it didn't feel like a home anymore.

She got out of bed and peered through the window into the garden below. The moon above the treetops, just a sliver away from fullness, illuminated a white mist that crept up almost to her window.

A solitary figure, barely recognisable as a man, stood in

the garden looking up at her. He lifted his hand to show her something. Catriona leaned forward. *A cruel-hearted knight raising a bloody tribute for an even crueller queen.* Despite the horror in her heart, Catriona caught a glimpse of her own reflection in the window and realised she was smiling. As she stepped back from the glass, the figure retreated into the mist.

Catriona felt a shudder of anticipation through her body, and then the ache of thwarted desire. Part of her longed to follow him, to run wild and barefoot through the trees, branches ripping and tearing at her nightgown, until she was naked and free, skyclad, like the pagan witches of old.

He would never let her go, she realised. Her adolescent body responded to his summons with an intensity which frightened her. Was it love? She thought not. Lust? Catriona did not yet truly understand this feeling, though she had an inkling.

She thought of Hector, and experienced a sudden rush of affection laced with guilt. Did she love him? Of that she was certain. Could he save her? If it had been Hector that day in the forest instead of Ian MacBain, he would have challenged the blacksmith's boy to a duel. Perhaps he would have been killed defending her honour. He knew nothing of the thrill of vengeance, nothing of the wild freedom of the hunt. Hector Grant represented all that was good and noble to Catriona, whereas Iain MacBain? She left the thought unfinished, and with a shudder climbed back into bed.

Only when sleep was almost upon her did Catriona acknowledge (her growing sense of unease giving way to a bottomless horror) that the gift her infernal lover had brought for her—the trophy he had so proudly held aloft—was the bloody, severed head of Douglas MacAdam the blacksmith's boy.

*

The same moon that peered into Catriona's bedroom arched high above the town of Dunkeld, as two riders approached on their swift-heeled horses.

Johnson's back was aching from all those hours spent poring over church records, and longer still on the saddle. General Wade's roads may have been a wonder of modern technology promising the last word in luxury, but Johnson's posterior begged to differ. He and Joseph had ridden hard for two days on the trail of the Wolf, stopping briefly at Elgin and Forres, before heading south, skirting the western edge of the Cairngorms on Sir William's fastest horses.

The lightning storm drove them on, and fear of whatever lurked in the shadow of those mountains, watching their progress with lupine voracity.

When they reached Dunkeld the whole town was asleep. Johnson rapped repeatedly on the door of the nearest inn with his stick, until finally the bleary-eyed innkeeper deigned to admit them.

After being shown to his room, Johnson collapsed onto the bed fully clothed, asleep before his head hit the pillow.

He had barely closed his eyes when Joseph came to wake him.

Johnson skipped breakfast and donned his coat, stepping briskly into the morning light, rubbing his hands together to encourage circulation. The church records at Forres and Elgin had provided him with several parts of the puzzle, but there was one last piece to fit before he could make sense of it all. He was convinced that Dunkeld held the answers.

The cathedral stood on the northern bank of the Tay, nestled amidst a green and pleasant landscape of wooded hills and rippling fields of corn, its elegant buttresses complemented by the surrounding pines, which stood as straight as spears of asparagus, as unlikely a final resting place for the Wolf of Badenoch as could be imagined. Such a pleasing impression did the whole create that Johnson readily owned it was as fine a cathedral as any that graced the noble landscape of England, for all her pastoral charms.

'It is a rare privilege, Doctor Johnson,' said the minister, receiving Johnson at the vestry door. 'To what do we owe the honour?'

'I am afraid this is not a social visit, Father, but rather a matter of some urgency. I require access to your records for Alexander Stuart, Earl of Buchan.'

The minister's eyes widened. 'The Wolf of Badenoch? A bad man, Doctor Johnson. A very bad man indeed.'

Johnson left Joseph waiting outside with the horses, and followed the minister into the sacristy.

'He destroyed the town of Forres, and burned Elgin Cathedral to the ground,' said the minister, 'destroying irreplaceable legal and family documents. A shocking act of barbarism, and a nasty business all round. But because of his high status he was received back into the fold of the church and interred here, for better or for worse. Now let me see.' The minister pulled down a heavy leather book and placed it on the reading table with a *whump* and a cloud of dust. 'Here is the family tree of Buchan and his ancestors. I'll leave it with you, Doctor. If there's anything else you need, be sure to let me know.'

The minister withdrew, leaving Johnson to his studies. It didn't take long until he found what he was looking for, tracing a finger through generations of Stuarts. 'Well well well,' murmured Johnson, tapping the page with his index finger. 'There you are, Mariota Athyn.'

After scribbling some notes and replacing the volume, Johnson had one last thing to do.

The tomb of Alexander Stuart, Earl of Buchan, commonly referred to as the Wolf of Badenoch, was to be found behind the high altar in the chancel of the Cathedral. As Johnson approached, his footsteps echoed through the vast chamber, disturbing a silence so profound it seemed part of the very bones of the place.

The tomb itself was carved from a single block of stone, with Stuart's faithful retainers in life carved around its circumference.

An effigy of the Wolf lay on top, in full armour, his longsword clutched for all eternity in gauntleted hands. Johnson leaned over to study the figure's peaceful repose, an image far removed from the notorious sacker of towns and ravisher of women. But if he had expected the likeness of Alexander Stuart to yield any of its secrets, he would be sorely disappointed.

Beneath the opened visor, there was no face at all.

Chapter 14

he night before the ball a strange, shroud-like sense of calm descended on Castle Gight. Joseph slept fitfully in the stables beside his beloved horses. Lord Badenoch's faithful hounds snoozed peacefully at their master's feet. Relieved of duties for the night, Malcolm retired to his quarters with the Good Book for company, while the rest of the staff had already returned to the village and their families.

Boswell and Catriona were reading by the fire in the Great Hall, while Johnson and the laird meditated over a game of chess.

'Do you know,' began Johnson, addressing his opponent, 'I gathered some interesting information concerning your ancestors on my travels.'

'Is that so?' said Sir William, after pausing just a beat too long. Boswell and Catriona looked up from their books.

Johnson knocked over a black pawn with his white knight. 'I was particularly fascinated by the legend concerning your monk, and the circumstances surrounding the Wolf's excommunication.'

'Go on,' said Sir William, moving his black queen out of danger.

'Of course, I do not wish to be indelicate, but it was all so long ago it has acquired the flavour of a colourful piece of rascalry, if nothing more.'

'Come on then,' said Boswell. 'Don't keep us in suspense.'

'Yes, do go on,' begged Catriona.

'Alexander Stuart, Earl of Buchan,' said Johnson, 'Attila of the

North, Wolf of Badenoch, was the bastard son of King Robert II, and a ruffian into the bargain. Unable to conceive an heir with his wife Euphemia, he took on a mistress, one *Mariota Athyn*, and fathered a handful of bastards of his own. Oh, excuse me, Miss Catriona.' Johnson glanced at Catriona to gauge her reaction; she was sitting up on her cushion with an air of unaffected innocence.

'It's quite all right,' she said, her eyes bright with curiosity.

'Little is known of Mariota Athyn,' said Johnson. 'Apart from what little church records could reveal, though she was a handsome woman by all accounts. Also something of a sorceress, if certain rumours are to be believed. Certainly, she was able to bewitch the Earl, who cruelly abandoned his wife in her favour. He immediately stole Mariota away to his lair, a fastness on an island in the middle of Loch Lochindorb, taking her for his "infernal bride" in a pagan handfasting ceremony. There are some who say that Satan officiated at that terrible union.' Johnson glanced at his opponent before moving his bishop across the board.

'On hearing of the scandal, the Bishop of Moray took the side of the aggrieved wife and issued an excommunication, sending one of his apprentice monks, whose grisly fate has become part of the legend of Castle Gight.'

Catriona gave an involuntary shudder, and moved closer to Boswell by the fire.

'But our Wolf was not one to take something like an excommunication lying down. And so with the blessings of his new queen, he and his band of *wild, wykked Hielan-men* went on a rampage of matchless ferocity and cruelty. I followed the Wolf's trail of destruction from Forres to Elgin, where the ruins of the Cathedral he razed to the ground still remain. I also saw the Wolf's sarcophagus at Dunkeld, although for some unknown reason, the face on the effigy has been chiselled away. And so, alas, I was unable to detect any familial resemblance.' Johnson brought his rook forward and knocked aside Sir William's knight, exposing the black king. 'Tell me, Lord Badenoch, is there anything of the Wolf in you? Any... skeletons in your closet?'

'I'm not one of his bastards, if that is what you mean,' snapped Sir William, playing defensively now. 'Alexander Stuart, your so-called Wolf of Badenoch, was nothing but a low brigand and a spoiled upstart. My line derives from the Wolf's legitimate first wife Euphemia, Countess of Ross. She was a widow when they wed, with land, titles and children of her own. When the Bishop of Moray annulled Buchan's marriage, all land and titles reverted to my ancestors, and the Wolf's bastards were disinherited. No, Doctor Johnson, it is noble blood that flows in these veins, and not that of some damned cub of Satan.'

'Quite,' mused Johnson. 'But tell me, do you believe the local legend?'

'What legend?' said Sir William, his hands tightening on the edges of the table.

'A long time ago,' began Johnson, 'during a terrible thunderstorm, a man dressed all in black arrived at Castle Gight. The servants, unnerved by the visitor's appearance, demanded to know the purpose of his visit. The stranger replied that he had come to challenge the Wolf to a game of chess. Intrigued by this challenge, Alexander Stuart, by now an old man, admitted the stranger to his hall and closed the doors behind them.

'The thunderstorm raged all night, yet not once did the doors to the Great Hall open. Once the storm had abated there was no sign of the visitor, but all the Wolf's men were discovered outside the castle walls, killed by lightning. Alexander himself was found dead, slumped over the very chair you are sitting on now, Sir William. His body was unmarked, though the nails in his boots had been pulled out. It was the devil himself, they say, who visited Alexander Stuart on that dark and stormy night. Oh, checkmate, by the way.'

Sir William's jaw trembled. His eyes moved from Johnson to the chessboard with the same incredulous expression. His king had been surrounded, with no way of escape.

'Oh bravo, Uncle Sam!' cried Catriona with a flurry of handclaps. 'I do love a good ghost story. Do you have any, Uncle Bozzie?'

'You must excuse my unpardonable lack of imagination,' said Boswell, standing abruptly and making a bow, 'but I am terribly tired all of a sudden.'

*

Boswell lay in his bed, the sleep he so desperately craved just beyond his reach. A cold wind stirred outside, moaning through the lum; its unseen hand caused the branch of a pine tree to tap against the window like fingers on the glass. A strong gust blew the window open, and Boswell recoiled in fright. He leapt out of bed in his nightshirt, shut and latched the window against the swirling sleet, then ran back to the safety of his bedcovers, ashamed of his own fear.

Somewhere outside in the corridor came a faint tapping, as of fingernails drumming on a wooden floor, or water dripping from a faucet. Boswell listened to the sound getting louder until it became a recognisable pattern, like a man striding down the corridor on hobnail boots, the steady *clip-clop* of his step reverberating through the silence. Whoever it was must have been going at a brisk pace, the violence of the tread suggesting an urgency which affected Boswell beyond all reason. Louder and louder the footsteps rang, until Boswell had to put his hands over his ears to drown out the approaching horror. The footsteps came to a sudden halt outside his room. Boswell looked towards the space underneath the door, where a pair of cloven hooves were clearly visible.

With trembling hands, Boswell pulled the sheets over his head and shut his eyes to the horror outside. The ensuing silence was almost unendurable, when suddenly the door burst inwards with a terrifying violence. Boswell felt the presence of something in the room with him. A large shadow drew near, visible through the cotton bedsheet, looming at the foot of his bed.

Boswell awoke with a start. Normally when he emerged from a nightmare, it was accompanied by an overwhelming sense of relief that he was safe in bed, and the monster only a thing of his mind after all. Sometimes the vision continued to haunt him, and he had to get up and move around, lighting candles and opening windows to banish the night-terrors. Other times he lay paralysed with fear, anticipating any moment the cold, clammy hand on his ankle.

Boswell watched in disbelief as the door handle began to turn—first clockwise, then counter-clockwise. He shook his head and rubbed his eyes to make sure he wasn't dreaming any more. The handle began to rattle. '*Who is it?*' he hissed, trying to sound brave, but he could hear the fear in his own voice.

'Boswell. It's me. Open up.'

Boswell heaved a sigh of relief and hopped out of bed to open the door.

Johnson was standing in the darkened corridor in nightshirt and bedcap, a lighted candle in one hand and his walking staff in the other. 'Come with me,' he whispered, 'if you wish to solve the mystery of our nocturnal footpad.'

Boswell felt a weight lifted from his shoulders. 'You mean you heard it too? Oh thank God, I thought I was going mad.'

'Of course I heard it. It's been going on every night, and I don't think it is an otherworldly visitor either, but something a little closer to home.'

Johnson led Boswell to the end of the corridor. They climbed a creaking set of stairs to the next floor, then carried on down another corridor, past portraits of forgotten relatives, and doors that hadn't been opened for generations. Johnson stopped to peer around a corner, motioning for Boswell to do likewise.

Malcolm the groundskeeper stood before a tall grandfather clock which had been propped against the wall at the far end of the corridor. He reached round to the side of the clock where there must have been a hidden catch, and with a loud click the whole wall swung inwards on groaning hinges, revealing a musty room of circular proportions. The moon shone in through Johnson's turret window, suffusing the room in unearthly silver light.

'*Of course...*' whispered Johnson.

'Good Lord,' said Boswell. 'What the deuce—'

'Shh,' said Johnson. 'Let us wait and watch!'

From their hiding place they could see Malcolm place a bowl of something at the entrance to the hidden recess, then take a step back. With a noisy rattle of chains a huge black figure blocked the entrance.

'Stand back, Malcolm,' cried Johnson. He strode forwards, brandishing his staff like a club. What happened next, however, was the last thing anyone expected.

The old man threw himself trembling to the floor and, clasping his hands in a gesture of supplication, he cried in a voice cracked with emotion, 'He's just an idiot! A poor, helpless idiot!'

'*Huuuurrrr,*' the giant agreed.

As Johnson and Boswell approached, a face was revealed in the flickering candlelight.

When James Boswell was a boy, his father had taken him to see a local production of Shakespeare's Tempest, one of those rare occasions that he and his father did anything together. Boswell remembered well the deformed character of Caliban, the sub-human offspring of the evil witch Sycorax. He had been both appalled and entranced as this hulking, deformed man-beast appeared on stage, with straggly hair, disfigured face and ragged fingernails. Yet somehow, this Caliban had the power to inspire sympathy.

Here before them was Shakespeare's Caliban in the flesh, tethered in chains and blinking stupidly at the intruders. Though atrociously ugly, with one bulging white eye, two holes in his face where a nose should have been, and a few wisps of straggly hair to cover the shrivelled grey parchment of his scalp, this was the face of a blinking, uncomprehending simpleton—a face of such wretched pathos that one could only feel pity to look at it.

'Get up, Malcolm,' Johnson commanded. 'And if you value this creature's life, turn him round now, so I can see his shoulder-blade.'

Malcolm did as he was told. The monster shambled round, and Johnson nodded grimly to himself. Caliban's back was pitted and pocked with ugly welts where he had been tortured with some fiendish device—a poker by the looks of it—but whatever strange mark Johnson had feared to find was wholly absent.

'Be at peace, Malcolm. I mean no harm to His Lordship's great uncle. For it is he, is it not?'

Malcolm nodded. 'Aye. But tell naebody. It wid bring shame doon on the hoose.'

'And the nocturnal noises—the footsteps, the tappings, the pipes in the crypt—that was you? Presumably with the intention of losing some inconvenient guests?'

Malcolm hung his head and muttered an affirmation.

Boswell had a hundred questions, but Johnson merely placed a hand on his shoulder. 'I cannot satisfy your curiosity just yet, my friend; at least not until the final act. Suffice to say that I have learned more on my travels than mere ghost stories. Malcolm, do you value your master's life?'

Malcolm nodded obediently.

'And will you trust me now?'

Malcolm nodded again.

'Then do as I say, and be quick, man. Grab all the silverware you can lay your hands on and put it in a sack. Then I want you to bring me the fastest, strongest horse from the stables.'

'But what on earth does it all mean, Doctor?' cried Boswell.

'I cannot say for certain yet, my friend. But if that creature is as harmless as Malcolm swears he is, then we still have a murderer at large. And the moon waxes full.'

HERE ENDS PART TWO

Part 3 - Full Moon

Chapter 15

On the night of the ball, Catriona was delirious with excitement. She ran around the house all day singing, unable to sit at peace. At six o'clock, two hours before the guests were due to arrive, she dashed downstairs to the servant's quarters and begged Mary to come to her room and help fix her hair.

She chattered incessantly as the cook attended on her. 'Hold still, Miss Catriona, or you'll get a pin in your scalp,' she chided.

'Ow!' cried Catriona. 'You're pulling!'

'Heaven help you, Miss Catriona. I do not know how you get your hair in such a mess. There, that ought to do it.'

When finally she came down the stairs, Boswell and Johnson were struck dumb by the vision before them. Catriona wore a simple tartan dress with an emerald brooch at her breast. Her hair had been tied up elegantly, with a few curled strands falling forward, framing her face beautifully.

'Well well,' said Sir William. 'How charming you look. But why all the effort? Not hoping to capture the attention of anyone in particular, are you?'

'Oh, Uncle, don't tease me!' cried Catriona, blushing in a way that secretly reflected the glow of her heart.

'Well,' said Badenoch, getting to his feet. 'I can hear the first of the guests arriving now.'

Castle Gight, District of Badenoch, 2ⁿᵈ September, 1773

he tragedy that occurred on the night of the ball would change our lives irrevocably; we would never be the same again, and though we suffered terrible losses, those who survived the carnage would forever be united by an experience too terrible and awe-inspiring to forget.

Despite the horrors to come, the evening began promisingly. I was gratified to make the acquaintance of several notable personages, anticipating a night of pleasant diversion. Little did we know, as we quaffed our wine and filled our bellies, what terrors awaited us at the stroke of midnight.

Colonel Crawford and his wife were first to arrive, accompanied by six young officers and their orderlies from the garrison. Captain Colin Campbell, the most senior officer present, was the son of the late Colin Campbell of Glenure, known to his enemies as The Red Fox. The Red Fox's murder at the hands of the Stuart Clan had been highly publicised as the Appin Murder, and Colin Campbell the younger bore a grudge against anyone who bore the name of Stuart. Campbell swaggered in first, followed by Officers Dunbar, Oswald, Fraser, Hector Grant and Army Surgeon Francis Graves, all equally dashing in their regimental tartan. The orderlies, a pleasantly rowdy group of lower-ranking soldiers, took the officers' coats, then made their way to a table of their own adjacent to the main group, happy just to be invited.

Next came the Reverend James Morrison, his wife Elspeth and daughters Charity and Constance. Both girls were strikingly handsome, and as virtuous as their names suggested.

A splendid post-chaise announced the arrival of Lord and Lady Sutherland. The Sutherlands were currently at the centre of a huge scandal, one that Lord Sutherland had tried hard to suppress, though his wife was the driving force behind the evictions carried out on her husband Sir Hilary's estate. If the plight of her former tenants, who had been treated with deplorable savagery, had caused Lady Sutherland any sleepless nights she was not showing it tonight, with her gay, tinkling laughter and ready smiles. The Sutherlands arrived with their daughters Maude, Clarissa, Henrietta, and finally Penelope, who at seventeen was the youngest and by far the prettiest of the four.

As each guest was announced they were seated according to their age and rank, with the younger folk at the far end of the table, and His Lordship himself seated at the head. Doctor Johnson and I had the great honour of being placed alongside our host, much to Lady Sutherland's chagrin.

Once all the guests were seated, Sir William made some preliminary remarks by way of welcome, and after proposing his toast everyone began talking at once. I myself derived great pleasure from contributing to the general conversation, and believe I deployed my arsenal of charm and wit with devastating accuracy.

From *The Casebook of Johnson and Boswell*

Chapter 16

'Of course, in those days we didn't have bloody great knifes stuck on the pointy end of our muskets,' said Colonel Crawford, the man who had led his troops to victory at Villinghausen, had lost his wig and hat at Warburg, and nearly lost his head at Minden. 'If your first bullet didn't find its mark, then there was nothing between you and twelve inches of Ferrara steel. Nothing matches the Highland charge for ferocity and valour, and to that I can personally attest. But in the end, those poor devils were no match for the 42nd Foot and their fixed bayonets. Pass the mustard, dear.'

The colonel turned to his wife and smiled. She smiled back. Lady Mary was a formidable businesswoman who could manage the family textile business as ably as her father, but she was at heart the same Yorkshire lass who had caught the colonel's eye all those years ago.

'Of course, we used bayonets before Culloden,' continued the colonel. 'But with limited success.'

'How so, Colonel?' asked Lady Sutherland, listening attentively from her seat directly opposite the aging war hero.

'Allow me to demonstrate,' said the colonel. 'If you please, Lady Sutherland, pick up that side plate with your left hand, and hold it like so, across your chest. Yes, that's it. Now pick up your breadknife, and brandish it menacingly at me. That's right, now show me your fiercest war face. My goodness, Lady Sutherland, I am glad the Jacobites did not have you among their ranks, or the day might have taken a turn for the worse! Now I want you to imagine you are a desperate clansman, charging the ranks of redcoats with your kilted compatriots by your side. The lucky plate you clutch so winningly to your breast is your shield, or *targe*, whereas the breadknife is your claymore. Now watch...'

The colonel picked up the cane from beside his chair and thrust it across the table. The silver tip glanced off Lady Sutherland's plate with an audible *clink*.

'There, d'you see?' said the colonel, addressing the room. 'Lady Sutherland has successfully intercepted my bayonet thrust, with minimum effort. And with my bayonet now embedded in her wooden targe, she is free to cut me down with her broadsword. And so it was at Sheriffmuir, where I watched a hundred loyal men, bayonets and all, torn to ribbons on Jacobite steel. I was only a lad of eight at the time, having followed my brothers up the hill to watch the battle unfold on the field below. I swore there and then I would never allow such carnage to happen again, and several years later, while dancing a *Strip the Willow* in this very hall, the solution presented itself to me.'

The colonel now turned his attentions to Lord Sutherland, seated beside his wife and listening with great interest. 'Sir Hilary, I would like you to pick up your side plate and butterknife, and wield them in the same way as your charming wife.'

Lady Mary rolled her eyes at her husband, the colonel's, theatrics, while the rest of the company looked on with amused interest.

'I trained each of my men to strike at the Highlander advancing to his *right*, despite his natural instincts, which tell a soldier to tackle the man coming straight at him. Now raise your sword arm aloft, if you please, Sir Hilary.'

As Lord Sutherland, who was also seated across from the colonel but slightly to his right, raised his bread knife, the colonel lunged with his cane again, this time jabbing Sir Hilary under his arm.

'*Oww!*' said Sir Hilary.

'There, you see?' cried the colonel, beaming triumphantly.

'It is all a matter of trust, of course. While you are dealing with the man advancing to the right of you, his sword arm exposed, you must trust that your comrade on your left is dispatching the enemy directly in front of you in a similar style, and so on and so forth, all the way down the line.' The colonel sat back in the chair and lit his pipe, urging the others to admire his ingenuity, which they did unreservedly, applauding his simple demonstration with great enthusiasm.

'A fat lot of good that does the poor bloody sod at the end of the line,' said Lady Mary, and the company roared with laughter. A chastened Colonel Crawford turned to his wife and patted her hand affectionately.

'Ah, the dashing blue bonnets,' said the Reverend Morrison, already misty-eyed from his first glass of whisky. 'What a sight it must have been, watching those gallant Jacobites emerge over the brow of the hill, their claymores flashing in the morning sun. It puts me in mind of Ossian: *Then advanced Cormac, graceful in glittering arms. No fairer youth was seen on Erin's grassy hills.*'

The minister's recital was interrupted by a loud and rather rude snort of derision coming from the corner of the table where Dr Johnson was seated.

'Do the words of our Caledonian Homer offend you, sir?' said the minister.

'Pfft,' said Johnson. 'I consider James MacPherson to be a fraud, and his so-called "ancient texts" nothing but doggerel of his own invention.'

'And yet there is quality there not to be denied, Doctor Johnson,' the minister argued, and went on to quote some more verse in his high, quavering voice. 'Now there's imagery for you, Doctor Johnson,' he concluded, after his impromptu performance. 'There's description! Did you ever know any man write like that?'

'Yes, sir, many a man, many a woman, and many a child,' was Johnson's droll reply.

Boswell leaned back on his chair and smiled, enjoying the

pleasant to-and-fro of conversation. His friend Doctor Johnson seemed to delight in being his usual cantankerous and intractable self.

Lady Sutherland leaned across Boswell to address Sir William, justifying the systematic clearances she had set in motion on her husband's estate.

'The changes we have made I consider necessary, inevitable, and benevolent,' she said, so loudly the whole room could hear. 'And I can almost treble profits by replacing my tenants with sheep. Indeed, each Cheviot is worth a whole family of crofters.'

Sir William nodded thoughtfully and took another bite of lamb, but Johnson could not let this boast pass without an opening broadside. 'Lady Sutherland,' he protested, 'what will become of the poor crofters you evict?'

'Oh, they have been provided for, of course. They will be shipped to America and put to good use on the cotton and tobacco fields. Those who wish to remain will be amply provided for on the coast, where they can make a living foraging for shellfish.'

'But surely,' persisted Johnson, 'the only choice they have then is to be sold into slavery, *if* they survive the voyage, or to starve?'

'Nonsense,' said Lady Sutherland. 'Scotch people are of happier constitution, and do not fatten like the larger breed of animals. They will fend for themselves quite admirably, I am sure.'

'I believe there are some among us,' observed Johnson, 'who would object to being compared to animals.'

Lady Sutherland drew herself up with formidable dignity, a cobra ready to strike. 'And what does the great Doctor Johnson have to say about Scots in his Dictionary?' she returned, in a voice that reverberated around the room. 'Perhaps your true opinion may be found in the definition for the word *oats*. How does it go again?... Ah yes: *A grain, which in England is generally given to horses, but in Scotland supports the people.*' With this rejoinder she threw her head back and brayed like a donkey, albeit a well-bred one.

Johnson's ears turned scarlet. A sure sign, Boswell noted, that the great Dictionary writer was about to explode. Johnson could countenance any argument, but to use his own words against him to score a point—words from his own dictionary at that—was asking for trouble.

'The porridge oat is a hale and hearty form of sustenance,' he muttered between gritted teeth. 'But you, Madame, would have them subsist on seaweed.'

In response, Lady Sutherland leaned over to the minister's wife and began a conversation about the weather. Here was a woman who chose her battles carefully, making note of potential enemies to be dealt with at her leisure.

Lord Sutherland, meanwhile, was questioning Hector Grant on his military record. 'So, young man, seen any action lately?'

'Well nothing too exciting, sir. A few minor skirmishes with Scots rebels. But I hope to be going to the Americas soon, to suppress the uprising there.'

'Ah!' cried Sir Hilary, slapping the young officer on the back. 'That's more like it, lad. Teach those damned arrogant Yankees a thing or two, what? I'd be out there in a flash if I was ten years younger. Do you know I once cherished dreams of a military career myself? But politics is my arena, lad, and where my true talents lie.'

'The military's loss,' said Hector with a bow, 'is Parliament's gain.'

The young ladies were gravitating towards the soldiers, hungry for tales of chivalry and heroics. They focused their attentions on Captain Campbell, whom they had decided (Lieutenant Grant aside) was the most dashing, not to mention highest ranking, of the five officers as yet unspoken for.

Eager to achieve the same renown as his father, Campbell the younger had earned his spurs in America, where he and his comrades had had to endure terrible privations including frostbite, poor medical supplies and attacks from natives before finally engaging the French at the head of Lake George. The ladies lapped up every word as the Captain described the terrible scenes of carnage he had endured.

From his place among the older guests, Boswell stole jealous glances towards the other end of the table. The minister's wife was hard of hearing, and Boswell found himself having to repeat everything he said. After a while he gave up, slumping into a gloomy silence.

He was spared any further misery when several musicians from Drumalban arrived to announce the first dance. The tables were duly cleared and set aside, as a fiddler struck up a cheerful Strathspey.

Lord and Lady Sutherland were first onto the floor, while the young officers, nudging and daring one another, mustered the courage to approach the ladies.

Hector Grant turned shyly to Catriona, bowed, and offered her his arm, which Catriona gladly accepted, her face flushed with pleasure.

The dancers gave a spirited performance, and even Boswell joined in for an Eightsome Reel, his wine glass sloshing around as he cut capers on the floor. Johnson was happy just to look on, tapping his foot in time to the music.

As the guests took their places for the next dance, Hector turned to Catriona and whispered something in her ear, and the two youths slipped away.

Doctor Johnson, quietly observing the young couple from his chair, approached Lieutenant Grant's man, Private Lennox, and told him to grab his weapon and follow the pair.

Hector and Catriona walked arm in arm to the garden. When Hector saw his comrade-in-arms running to catch up with them, he whispered something to Catriona and the two lovers fled laughing into the hedge maze.

By the time they reached the centre, Hector's heart was pounding in his chest. The statue of Diana the Huntress glowed spectrally in the pale moonlight, her alabaster curves like living flesh. The two young lovers sat side by side on the bench, Catriona resting her head on Hector's shoulder.

The full moon shone clear and high above them and, as Hector gazed up, he found himself looking for its face. He once read somewhere that the Chinese do not see a man when they look at the moon, but a rabbit. Hector looked hard for the ears, but he could not see any. Perhaps they see the moon upside down in China, he thought to himself, tilting his head.

'Penny for your thoughts?' said Catriona, startling Hector from his reverie.

'I... I was... just thinking how beautiful you look in the moonlight.'

'Liar!' cried Catriona, punching his arm. 'You weren't looking at me at all.' Suddenly her little brow furrowed. 'Hector?'

'Yes, my darling?'

'Do you ever fear that you will go mad?'

The question took Hector by surprise. 'Erm...no, not really.'

'No, of course not,' replied Catriona. 'You are far too dull for that.' Hector ignored the insult. 'Tell me,' she persisted, with a look of absolute earnestness. 'Do you believe in God?'

'Of course I do, Catriona.'

'And what about demonic possession?'

Hector laughed. 'I confess I haven't given it much thought.'

'Don't laugh,' Catriona chided. 'Have you ever felt that you were someone else? I mean, that sometimes you are made to do things beyond your control?'

'I'm sorry I... I'm not entirely sure I understand your meaning.'

This wasn't going how Hector had envisioned it at all. He decided he would try to steer the conversation in a more fruitful direction. 'Catriona, I won't be here for much longer. I am going away.'

'Oh?' said Catriona. 'Where are you going?'

'America.'

Catriona's face fell, but she quickly regained her composure with a shrug of indifference.

'The thing is,' said Hector, 'I don't want to lose you, Catriona, and I was hoping you might consider coming with me.'

Catriona, a contradictory creature, was about to reply forcefully in the negative, when she was stopped short by the glittering diamond Hector produced.

'Catriona,' he said, getting down on his bended knee. 'Cat. Would you do me the honour of being my wife?'

Hector seemed infinitely gallant in his kilted uniform, and Catriona's eyes shone at the sight of the precious stone winking in the moonlight, but this was rapidly succeeded by a look of caution. 'Get up, you buffoon,' she said, pleased with the look of confusion which came over the lad's face. 'Did you not hear a word I said? Would you like to be married to a madwoman? I might try to do away with you in your sleep!'

'I believe that you asked my opinion on the subject of demonic possession Catriona, and nothing more,' replied Hector, all wounded dignity.

'Yes,' she replied nervously. 'I was only pulling your leg. You should have seen your face; it was a picture!'

'But my question, Catriona…'

'I will give you my answer at midnight,' she said cryptically, before pulling away and dashing off through the maze.

Hector punched his leg in frustration. *Perhaps she is mad*, he mused, feeling ashamed for entertaining such thoughts. *I will ask Doctor Johnson for advice. He seems to know everything. Maybe he can help me to understand the female mind. It is a mystery to me.*

Thus resolved, he walked stiffly back to the castle a little mollified.

Alas, Catriona's answer was going to have to wait.

*

At the stroke of midnight, a rumble of thunder brought the

whole company, eager for diversion, laughing to the windows. The accompanying sheet of lightning, five seconds later, revealed a figure standing on the south lawn. Broad of shoulder in his wolf-skin cloak, with jet black hair and strong, sturdy legs planted like twin oak trees, the intruder addressed those inside in a loud, commanding voice.

'I am Iain MacBain son of Duncan MacBain son of Dominic MacBain, and I have come for you, William of Badenoch.' There was an eruption of noise from all around him—a chorus of barks, howls and jeering whoops that sounded barely human.

The guests all shot questioning, puzzled looks at one another.

The young giant waited for the clamour to die down, then continued. 'Some of you are blameless, and need not share in this fate. Surrender yourselves now, and I shall allow you to walk free. The rest of you will die this very night, as foretold.'

With these ominous words, Iain MacBain produced a dirk and sliced the palm of his hand, letting the rich blood course down his arm onto the grass at his feet.

Urged to action by the spilling of blood, Lord Badenoch's faithful hounds Seamus and Fingal came tearing round the corner, teeth bared, to launch themselves at the intruder. Iain MacBain worked quickly. His blade flashed left and right, and both dogs lay dead at his feet in an instant. MacBain wiped the blood from his dirk on his plaid and shot a look of defiance at the guests within. It had all happened in a matter of seconds, without the young giant breaking so much as a sweat.

In a fit of youthful folly, Hector Grant retrieved his musket, smashed the barrel through a windowpane and fired. The shot took Iain MacBain by the shoulder and flung him backwards. In the stunned silence that followed, the Highlander looked up at the shocked onlookers, his face a livid mask of hatred, his eyes an unearthly, glowing yellow.

Then something entirely inexplicable began to happen before the terrified company's eyes.

MacBain seemed to grow in stature, the fabric of his plaid

ripping at the seams. His arms and legs, already muscular, swelled painfully. Black hairs sprouted rapidly along the surface of his skin. His back arched grotesquely, and the bones of his spine appeared livid white, like the knuckles of a huge fist. But it was MacBain's face that suffered the most dreadful transformation. It *lengthened* into a muzzle. They could see his long incisors and canines glinting in the moonlight. The ears of his head seemed to move *upwards* and sharpen into points like devil's horns, as the hair on his head grew at an alarming rate and joined with the bristling fur that already covered his entire body.

The company stood aghast. It was terrifying to watch, yet utterly mesmerising at the same time.

'Wonder what they'd make of *this* at the Speculative Society,' murmured Johnson.

'I should think he'd be expelled for impertinence,' barked the colonel.

'Damned impertinent,' agreed Johnson.

'It ain't natural, that's for sure,' added the colonel.

With a cry of horror, Lady Sutherland fainted and landed in her husband's arms.

The creature formerly known as Iain MacBain stood to its full height, as more of his kind stalked out from the shadows of the trees. They were as tall as bears with rippling muscles and huge, ape-like forearms. Their leader threw back his great, shaggy muzzle and let out an ungodly howl, a blasphemous noise that was not wholly human, nor wholly animal.

'Please try to remain calm,' cried Sir William. 'My windows are reinforced with iron bars.'

This information provided the guests with little in the way of comfort.

The beasts moved forward as a pack in the moonlight, a terrible fairy tale come to life.

Johnson sprang into action. 'This is the moment, gentlemen. Retrieve your weapons. Ladies, stand back. Stand back I say!' he cried, herding them to safety. 'Away from the windows. Over here, yes that's right. Stand by the fireplace.'

The soldiers returned seconds later armed with muskets, which on Johnson's instruction had been loaded with silver bullets, their bayonets dipped in molten silver.

The men divided into pairs around each narrow window slat, unable to keep their eyes from the dreadful spectacle outside.

The beasts charged the walls before the soldiers had a chance to react. When they collided it seemed the very walls of the keep shook. Branch-like arms exploded between the bars with a shattering of glass. Claws with terrible talons like rusty knives grasped blindly for victims.

Colin Campbell, who survived the Seven Year War unscathed, was seized by the neck, his head smashed repeatedly against the window's iron bars until he dropped down, his face mashed to an unrecognisable pulp.

Poor Private Lennox was caught by the elbow. As he struggled to release himself his arm was pulled clean from its socket with a dreadful popping sound.

The men fired. With a howl of pain and fury two werewolves dropped where they stood. The soldiers reloaded.

Sir William ran to the fireplace, and leaping with the agility of a deer he pulled a Lochaber axe from the wall display. He charged into the fray with the axe raised above his head, and slammed it down with all his might on a hairy arm. The ghastly limb was severed with two blows of Sir William's axe, and dropped quivering at his feet.

A moment later, all was silent. Unable to breach the castle's defences, the enemy retreated, melting back into the forest.

Peering through the narrow window, the soldiers could hardly believe their luck. The bodies of two clansmen, semi-naked and relatively hairless, lay dead on the ground. The arm that Sir William had severed seemed to shrink, the fur along its length receding until they were looking at the bloody, severed arm of a man.

Surgeon Frances Graves ran to Private Lennox and unbuckled

his own belt, using it as a tourniquet. Catriona comforted the lad, cradling his head in her lap and wiping the sweat from his brow as the boy shivered and pleaded quietly for his Mama.

An appalled silence followed, punctuated only by groans and whimpers.

Boswell picked up a whisky bottle and began to drink.

'Now see here,' said the colonel, rounding on Lord Badenoch and poking a finger against his chest. 'I demand that you tell us who these brutes are, and why you saw fit to invite them?'

Sir William could only gape in bewilderment at the colonel.

'They are the ancestors of Alexander Stuart, Wolf of Badenoch,' said Doctor Johnson. 'The devil himself granted Stuart the power of lycanthropy, in exchange for his immortal soul. MacBain and his brood appear to have inherited the knack.' Johnson turned to Sir William. 'Tell me, Your Lordship. Is there any other point of access to the castle apart from the keep?'

'The central tower is impregnable. Unless... The east and west wings are unfortified, and not built to withstand a major attack. Those wolves could smash through the windows like... like...'

'Like a pack of werewolves through French windows?' suggested Boswell helpfully.

'Just so,' replied Sir William.

The east and west wings were connected to the main tower by heavy doors on either side of the hall. 'Quickly now,' said Johnson. 'Block the doors. Use anything to hand.'

The soldiers moved fast, dragging furniture and piling heavy oak chests on top of tables to block the entrances. They were not a moment too soon. The sound of smashing glass erupted all around as the werewolves came in through the windows, smashing and rending everything in their path. The fury of their advance was primal; terrifying. Moments later they converged on the doors to the keep.

'Everyone,' cried Johnson. 'Man, woman and child. Hold these doors! They must not get through.'

On Johnson's orders, everybody, even elderly Lady Crawford, ran towards the doors and pressed their weight against the furniture. But in their haste they had dispersed unevenly. Only four bodies—Johnson, Boswell, Lord and Lady Sutherland—manned the door to the east wing.

A breathless moment of silence, then the doors began to rattle and shake violently in their solid oak frames. They held steady. Another moment of silence, and the fierce battering began again.

The door to the east wing worked its way open a few feet, and from the gap emerged the head of a hideous werewolf. The beast lunged forward, clamping its jaws around the neck of the first person it could find, which happened to be Lady Sutherland.

The werewolf's jaws snapped shut like a pair of garden shears on a flower. The severed head landed on the ground with an audible *dunt* and rolled across the floor. The headless body staggered in circles, hands clawing the air, as blood fountained from the ragged stump. The head tumbled into the fire. Sir Hilary ran to retrieve it. He held his wife's severed head in his hands until they were scorched by the heat from her burning hair. He dropped the grisly article with a heart-rending cry of anguish.

It was a scene of utter chaos. Two soldiers ran across the hall to help Johnson and Boswell in their struggle with the door. Johnson, buffeted this way and that, closed his eyes, as the moonlight shone through the window, gracing his head like a halo.

'*Pater noster,*' he intoned in a voice of grave authority. '*Qui es in caelis, sanctificetur nomen tuum...*'

Across the hall, the Reverend Morrison added his high, quavering voice to Johnson's deep and sonorous one. '*Adventist regnum tuum. Fiat voluntas tua, sicut in caelo et in terra...*'

After what seemed like an age, but was only a matter of seconds, the rattling stopped.

With tremendous courage, Johnson opened the door an inch and peered into the darkened corridor beyond. The werewolves were gone, fleeing the sound of the Lord's Prayer, which had been as molten lead poured into their ears.

Each man turned to look at his neighbour, bathed in sweat, their chests heaving with exertion. Boswell crossed himself and took another swig from his bottle.

Private Lennox lay in a pool of blood by the window, where Catriona had been sitting only moments before. A quick check of his pulse told the army surgeon all he needed to know. He looked at Lieutenant Grant and shook his head.

'Where is Catriona?' cried the young officer.

Another flash of lightning revealed a figure standing at the far end of the hall, by the cellar door.

'*Here I am, my love.*'

All the guests turned slowly towards the sound. It was a venomous voice that made Johnson's hair stand on end: a parody of sweetness, laced with malice and cruelty.

The creature that stepped out from the shadows was no longer Sir William's young ward. It was wearing Catriona's clothes. It even had her face and hair. But it was not she. As it lurched across the hall, with its cruel face and curiously twisted body, each person took a step back, instinctively afraid. The thing that had been Catriona raised the Bible it was clutching in its hands then, cackling like a thing possessed, cast it onto the flames.

The few survivors of that terrible night later agreed that, as the book was consumed and turned to ashes, Catriona's body seemed to be on fire, her red hair wreathed in a halo of unearthly flames. Whether it was a trick of the light or the effect of some diabolical spell, she appeared at the same time a dark queen, as terrible as she was beautiful, and an aged crone, twisted and gnarled beyond recognition from centuries of corruption.

Hector ran towards his beloved, but she threw out an arm, sending him spinning across the room. 'By God, Catriona,' he cried in a voice wracked with anguish. 'Stay this madness.'

'Take courage,' said Johnson. 'That thing is not Catriona.'

This was all too much for Sir William to bear. He fell to his knees and, clutching at his chest, took one last look at his beloved niece before collapsing to the floor.

'Look at you all!' gloated Mariota Athyn, the ancient spirit who had taken possession of Catriona's body. She sneered at the pale white faces that regarded her with horror. 'You call yourselves soldiers? Milksops! You are no better than those sheep that you hold so dear, great white-face of the Cheviots. Do you think you are a match for my kindred and me? We will feast on your flesh and leave the bones for the crows!'

But in her moment of triumph, the witch Mariota had underestimated the strength of Sir William's young ward. From a dark recess of her mind, Catriona fought with all her might for possession of her Self. The struggle was etched clearly on her features as her body writhed this way and that in a torment of agony. The creature that called itself Mariota Athyn released a shriek of fury and anguish. Then, just as it seemed the struggle would destroy Catriona, the leering and hideous spirit that deformed her features faded, before dissolving entirely. At the same instant a shadow flitted into the fire. The flames in the hearth flickered brightly, flared up, and died down abruptly.

Catriona was bathed in perspiration, her hair in wild disarray, but wholly herself once more. Her eyes moved from her uncle, who lay insensible on the floor, to the huddled group of frightened guests, and with a cry of terrible realisation, she fainted.

Only Doctor Johnson, watching the whole drama keenly, realised the full import of what had been done. 'The cellar door,' he murmured quietly to himself, then shouting, 'The cellar door! Bar the cellar door!'

*

Iain MacBain tore through the forest in his wolfskin. The blood lust was upon him.

THE STONE OF DESTINY

Some called it a curse, others called it a gift: the brief but intense agony of the transformation, then the sudden surge of power. The supernatural strength. The desire to rend. To tear.

They had had to conceal themselves, of course, through the ages, those that bore the mark of the wolf, a small crescent-shaped birthmark on the shoulder blade.

But now *she* had returned, the witch Mariota Athyn, in the form of this young girl. She was his true-born sister, a changeling placed in the house of the old man to await the day of prophesy.

As he led his pack through the wood, he could *see* her in his mind's eye. She had the book of the light-that-blinds in her hands. She was throwing it onto the flames. *Good.* The prophecy would be fulfilled. The way was open.

The old man, the usurper, thought it was just a dungeon. Nobody had been down there for years. But *he* knew the way through the old Jacobite tunnels, from the forest directly into the lowest levels of the castle. The Bible had afforded protection that even the strongest door could not against his kind. The excommunicated ones. The Brotherhood of The Wolf.

But now the way was clear. The moon was full, and the way was clear. Now there would be a reckoning, and a baptism of blood.

*

The soldiers ran to the door and fumbled with the lock. From deep within the bowels of the castle they were coming.

'Women and children, up the stairs,' cried Johnson.

Hector Grant ran to Catriona, prostrate with grief over the body of her uncle. Lord Badenoch was breathing very faintly, but alive. Hector scooped Catriona into his arms and carried her to safety, then returned to the hall to join in the fight. Doctor Johnson cast around for Boswell and found him slumped against the wall, giggling and muttering to himself.

'By God, sir, you are *drunk.*'

Boswell turned his head slowly to focus on his friend. 'And what if I am?' he muttered. 'Seems to me the only rational thing to do, considering the circumstances.'

'I see your point,' Johnson allowed. 'But this is no time for lethargy, Boswell. Get up, and help me to move Sir William.'

Boswell staggered to his feet. He grabbed Lord Badenoch by the arms while the Doctor took his ankles, and they half-dragged, half-lifted him up the stairs. After they had seen him safely to the upper balcony, Boswell slumped against the wall and slid to the floor, while Johnson made his way back down to join the soldiers.

'Back up the stairs, Doctor Johnson,' said the colonel. 'As a civilian, it is your duty to protect the women. Besides,' he added with a wink, when Johnson tried to protest. 'What a great loss to the world of literature it would be, should anything happen to you at the hands of these fiends. I should never be able to forgive myself.'

Doctor Johnson felt a warm rush of admiration for the old warhorse. He grabbed Sir William's axe, and turning on his heel did as he was told.

The soldiers stood as far back from the cellar door as space would allow and arranged themselves in a line, muskets raised and loaded with silver bullets.

They could hear something reaching the top of the stairs now. The men looked from one to the other, each recognising the fear on the other's face as visible reflections of their own stark terror.

The scene of the battle could be witnessed from the balustrade, but only Johnson had the stomach to watch. The minister huddled behind the women, his courage broken. Sir Hilary's mind had gone completely. He cowered in a corner, babbling incoherently to himself as he peeled off layers of clothes, while his traumatised daughters pleaded with him to stop. Boswell snored away, oblivious to the unfolding horror, while Catriona sat quietly with her uncle's head on her lap, loosening his collar and massaging his chest.

The door didn't last long. It bulged inwards with a hideous creaking of hinges then exploded, admitting the black bristling demon that was Iain MacBain, his pack of ravening werewolves on the stairs behind him. With painstaking deliberation they filed in and surrounded the soldiers, towering over them.

'On my command men,' cried Colonel Crawford, his voice quivering like a taut bowstring. '*Fire!*'

Simultaneously, the soldiers discharged their muskets. Two silver bullets found their mark, piercing the hides of the enemy. A third ricocheted from the chandelier, which came crashing to the floor.

The soldiers were outnumbered. Lady Crawford, unable to restrain herself any longer, ran to the balustrade and cried for her husband. But the colonel did not look up. He stared down the enemy from beneath his bristling brows and prepared for the final assault.

There were no more silver bullets left. As the werewolves advanced, Colonel Crawford roared, 'Come on, lads! We didn't see off the Frenchies to be cowed by these poodles. *Bayonets!*'

The men lunged forward as one with their thrice-dipped steel. Four bayonets struck home. Two missed their mark or were struck aside.

Meanwhile the fallen chandelier had ignited one of the huge tapestries, pouring black fumes into the hall. The colonel made one last, desperate lunge at a werewolf with his bayonet. The beast caught the barrel in its claws and swung it in the air, the colonel still attached to the other end, smashing both rifle and man against the wall. Colonel Crawford, the man who had led his troops to victory at Villinghausen, had lost his wig and hat at Warburg, and nearly lost his head at Minden, slid to the floor and died without a sound.

The werewolves ripped through the unit like foxes let loose in a chicken-coop. The air was filled with screams of terror as the men were torn to shreds. Frances Graves defended himself valiantly, jabbing with his bayonet. Two werewolves picked him up, and between them tore the surgeon clean in two.

The pack leader took a swipe at Hector with a massive forepaw, knocking the young officer to the ground. Hector took one look at his chest and winced. His tunic had been ripped open to reveal four ugly gashes in his flesh. He looked up at the monster that had been Iain MacBain, staring directly into the yellow, preternatural eyes which shone with a predatory intelligence; eyes with no trace of pity, nor shred of human decency left in them. Hector felt a hatred so keen it overpowered any sense of fear or self-preservation. He staggered to his feet, kissed his mother's crucifix which hung from a chain around his neck, and charged the enemy. Then he did something entirely unexpected.

As he drew close, he collapsed to his knees and slid clean under the monster's legs. The werewolf spun round in surprise. Hector had reached the wall by the staircase. With one hand he grabbed a corner of the flaming tapestry and yanked it free, scrambling to the side as it came crashing down. The heavy, flaming mass of cloth landed full-square on the werewolf. As the creature struggled to release itself, roaring in frustration and flailing in its agony, the cloth clung tighter, burning fur, melting flesh and fusing it to the fibre of the burning material.

Without looking back, Hector found his way to the staircase, ran up the stairs and pounded on the door, begging to be let in.

Catriona reached for the latch. Reverend Morrison put his hand on hers and shook his head grimly. 'It's too late,' he said.

Johnson was there in a flash, shoving the minister aside and pulling the door open. Hector fell forward, gasping and sobbing into Catriona's arms, while Johnson slammed and bolted the door fast.

No sound came from the great hall. Johnson peered over the edge of the balustrade. The whole room was ablaze, great flames licking up the walls to singe his eyebrows, but there was no one left alive. The last of the werewolves had been driven back to the crypt.

Joseph, Malcolm, the kitchen staff and several musicians were gathering on the front lawn. Joseph had brought a bed sheet, and ordered each to take an edge and make a circle. Doctor Johnson, looking down from the open window, understood what was expected of them.

'We must jump now,' he cried to the survivors. The ladies all cowered together, refusing to budge.

'Jump or be damned!' cried Johnson.

The Reverend Morrison, his wife and daughters, and the Sutherland girls edged their way towards the windowsill, then one by one they leapt. Hector helped Catriona, trembling with fright, onto the ledge, then holding hands they took the plunge together.

Poor Lady Crawford wished only to join her husband. She wouldn't budge, her fingers clinging stubbornly to the balustrade.

Johnson ran through the rising smoke to Sir William to check for a pulse. He slapped his cheeks, rousing him back to life. Sir William's eyes flickered open, and he murmured softly for Catriona.

'She is safe, Sir William. But we must leave now, quickly, before the fire consumes us all.'

Lord Badenoch shot up and spied his axe propped against the wall. 'I can't leave without *him*,' he cried, then clambering to his feet he grabbed the weapon, and staggered off down the corridor to his fate.

Sir Hilary, squatting naked in the corner, didn't seem to know where he was. Johnson threw a coat over his shoulders, bundled him onto to the windowsill and shoved him out.

The corridor was now thick with smoke. Doctor Johnson sat by Lady Crawford and implored her one last time. 'Madam. It is your duty as a Christian to save yourself. I must insist you come with us. Believe me, it is what the colonel would have wanted.'

'Don't worry young man,' she said drowsily, patting his hand as if he were a favourite grandson. 'Save yourself. I'm going to meet my Henry.' Then smiling one last time, she gave a long sigh, and was gone.

Johnson shook his head sadly, and closed over her eyelids.

He and Boswell were the last to leave. Everyone on the ground was calling up for them to jump.

'You first,' said Boswell.

'No, sir, you first.'

'I must insist, Doctor Johnson.'

Johnson put a friendly arm around Boswell's shoulders, and pushed.

The Doctor stayed on the windowsill a moment longer, taking a deep breath of clean night air, then looked down at the crowd crying for him to jump, their mouths forming silent O's, voices drowned out by the raging of the fire. He closed his eyes and took the plunge. When his vast bulk hit the sheet they almost dropped him, his rear end bouncing just inches from the hard ground.

The company stood on the lawn as Castle Gight blazed, their faces illuminated by the flames. A strange sense of calm prevailed among the survivors, in spite of the terrors they had endured: a feeling of communion, which can only be experienced by those who have been through war together. Catriona slipped her hand in Hector's. She looked up at him and tried to smile. Even the Sutherland daughters were quiet as they rallied round their father.

They didn't see the werewolves until they were almost upon them. One towered over the rest, cruel eyes flashing on either side of a horribly extended muzzle, dreadful fangs, and bristling grey fur covering its hide. *Duncan MacBain*, thought Johnson vaguely. It was all over.

With a groan of despair, Lord Sutherland produced a pistol from the coat around his shoulders. Before anyone had a chance to react, he pressed the barrel to his temple and pulled the trigger, blasting brain-matter all over his traumatised daughters.

The werewolves, two score and ten of them, encircled their prey, a moving forest of tooth and claw.

Johnson turned to Boswell and held out his hand. 'Well Jamie, it was good knowing you.'

Boswell's drunken eyes were moist with tears. 'Knowing you has been the greatest privilege of my life, sir.'

But even as they stood facing death, a huge shape wreathed in flames appeared on the castle battlements.

Lord Badenoch's hideous relative, the curse of Castle Gight, held aloft the body of his liberator, and let out a cry of terrible triumph, as he and Sir William were engulfed in the flames.

Witnessing the fall of Castle Gight, the werewolves raised their great, shaggy heads and produced a symphony of howls, in which all the grief of their condition, the anguish and the terrible glory, could be heard. Boswell and Johnson put their hands to their ears to block out the deafening sound.

Parts of the battlements began to crumble and collapse. With one last cry, the last two scions of Castle Gight fell backwards into the flames, and as they fell, the werewolves turned as one and returned to the forest.

Catriona stirred in Hector's arms, and murmured a single word. *'Father.'*

Hector tightened his grip on his beloved and shook his head. 'No, Catriona.' Catriona looked up at him. He was no longer a boy, but a man in the full power of youth: full of vigour, determination and moral authority. Catriona then lost all her will to flee, and settled back into his arms.

'So the prophecy is fulfilled,' murmured Johnson.

Hector took the blanket the servants had used in the rescue and wrapped Catriona in it. She murmured softly and pressed her head into Hector's chest, and his heart beat strongly enough for the two of them. Catriona looked up at Hector, her soft eyes shining in the firelight, and breathed, 'Yes.'

The Blasted Heath Inn, Drumalban, 3rd September 1773

All that remained for us was to gather the survivors and make our way to Drumalban. Before we turned our backs on the hollowed out, smouldering ruin of Castle Gight forever, we made a vow of silence. Who would have believed us anyway? That there was a fire, and many died was truth enough: a terrible tragedy, and no more.

We must have made quite a sight, arriving at the inn, the burned-out survivors of Castle Gight. A doctor was summoned, and post-chaises were duly ordered to carry the survivors home. Alas, the Sutherland daughters may never recover from their ordeal, having witnessed both their mother's decapitation and their father's self-destruction at close quarters. Yet they are fabulously rich, and I feel that with the right sort of guidance, they will make excellent wives.

As for myself and Doctor Johnson, we made it through the ordeal unscathed, and though I find myself suffering from an inexplicable headache, dry mouth, shaky vision and nausea, I am otherwise none the worse for wear.

From *The Casebook of Johnson and Boswell*

Epilogue

Weary and dejected, Boswell and Johnson sat nursing their brandies before the fire of the Blasted Heath Inn. There was much to discuss.

'It was easy to establish,' said Johnson, 'that Sir William's grandfather Sir Alexander Gight had a brother. Sir William made a point of stating that he, his father and his grandfather before him were the sole heirs of Castle Gight in their turn, and yet one only had to study the portrait of Sir William's great-grandmother Lady Euphemia Gight in the west wing to find the truth of the matter. She is depicted posing with two little boys, who look very charming in their lace and silk suits. Both children appear entirely normal, though I suspect the artist took a certain amount of artistic liberty with the elder. That, or the brother's deformities only became pronounced in later years. The existence of an elder brother was further confirmed by church records at Drumalban, which state that Sir William's paternal grandfather, Sir Alexander Gight, had an elder brother, christened Archibald. As there were no further records, neither marriage nor death certificates alluding to Archibald Gight, I could only conclude that he was still living, though "hidden away" somewhere. And so indeed he was, in a secret room of the castle. With his peculiar deformities came unnaturally long life and vigour. Guardianship of the deformed and simple-minded heir was passed from grandfather to father, and finally to Sir William himself, who was duty bound to keep his relation protected and hidden from the world.'

'Poor Sir William,' said Boswell.

'Yes. And poor old Uncle Archie too.'

'But where do lycanthropes fit into all of this?' asked Boswell. 'And how on earth did you know to load those guns with silver bullets?'

'I didn't,' said Johnson simply. 'At least not at first. It was merely a precaution, though I was mindful of the old dictum *credo quia absurdum*, a motto we would do well to adopt. The name MacBain was assumed by the patriarch of that family to conceal his true identity. His real name is Duncan Stuart, a dangerous name to be known by back in the heady days of the rebellion. Delving a little further into family records, I realised that the MacBains, or the Stuarts, rather, are the direct descendants of Alexander Stuart, Wolf of Badenoch, and believe themselves to have a claim to the chieftainship and ancestral seat of Castle Gight itself.'

'So that ragged band of Highlanders hiding out in the mountain were disinherited by Sir William's ancestors?'

'In a manner of speaking, yes. Once the Wolf of Badenoch died his claim to the land died with him, and the claim of all his bastards. Ownership passed onto his estranged wife's children from a previous marriage, the grandsires of Sir William Gight.'

'I see. And where does Catriona fit in to all of this?'

'I didn't know at first, though I strongly suspected she had a part to play. It was from her own lips we heard that she was a descendent of Mariota Athyn, a notorious witch and seductress, and Catriona is her reincarnation, if you believe that sort of thing. Catriona is also the true-born daughter of Duncan MacBain, sister to Iain MacBain, deposited on Sir William's doorstep to fulfil an ancient prophecy. I suspect that Catriona herself did not know this, and only in her midnight excursions and trance-like states did she become aware of the terrible connection.'

'But it is one thing to conceive of a band of renegade Jacobites hiding out in the mountains,' said Boswell. 'But a pack of ravenous werewolves is something else entirely.'

'The violent death of Bill Chalmers led me to believe the prophecy may have had a supernatural element. My suspicions were confirmed a few nights ago in a most dramatic fashion.'

Boswell was intrigued.

'In Drumalban I heard tell of an old woman, a local healer with the gift of second sight, who lives in a cave somewhere in the forest. I must confess, Boswell, that when one of the villagers pointed out her lair, I was full of apprehension. But I mustered my courage and approached. There was not a door as such, merely a black curtain of leather, and all sorts of bones and strange charms hanging from the surrounding trees. An old crone appeared from behind the curtain to beckon me inside, and I had a strange notion that she was expecting me. The place was filled with smoke, with all sorts of strangely-marked bottles lining the shelves and a huge cauldron bubbling away in the centre; a scene straight from The Scottish Play, in other words.

'From the crone's own lips I learned that the Wolf of Badenoch received the gift, or curse, rather, of lycanthropy from the devil, in exchange for his immortal soul. I also learned of the Brotherhood of the Wolf—a band of renegade Jacobites who share this power. The soothsayer told me that they may be distinguished by a crescent moon-shaped birthmark on their left shoulders. She even taught me the words of an old prophecy: *When old King James returns to dust, Castle Gight shall thrice be cursed*. It wasn't until I watched Catriona throw that King James Bible onto the fire that I recalled the words of the prophecy, and knew we were in trouble for sure.'

'But what about Sir William?' said Boswell. 'Did he know what dread creatures prowl his forest by the light of the full moon?'

'That is a secret that died with him, I'm afraid. Oh, I am sure he was aware of the prophecy. He may even have known that his former tenants not only bore him a grudge, but had a genuine claim to his title and lands. Certainly, the violent death of Bill Chalmers had given him something to think about. After all it was Sir William who gave the order to evict; Chalmers was merely the blunt instrument used to carry it out. But I feel that His Lordship had secrets and troubles of his own, to pay too much attention to some old prophecy.'

Boswell and Johnson were weary. Wearier than they had been in a long time. Johnson retired first, climbing the stairs to his room with the plodding footsteps of an old man, while Boswell finished the last of the brandy. The liquor burned its way down his throat and filled his veins with a soothing warmth.

Before he retired, Boswell entered Johnson's room to check on the old man. His friend lay snoring fully clothed on his bed. Boswell walked over to the desk, where a notebook had been left open. The great man had written something before going to bed. Boswell picked up the notebook. It was a series of revisions the doctor had been making for the third edition of his Dictionary. The book had been left open at the letter "L", and Boswell noticed that the ink was still drying on one entry. It read:

"Lycan'thropy, s. a species of madness."

And that was all.

THE CASEBOOK
OF SAMUEL JOHNSON, LL.D.
And JAMES BOSWELL, Esq.

THE WYRM OF
LOCH NIS

CONTAINING

An Investigation into Reported Sightings of
THE LOCH NESS MONSTER

Inverness, 4ᵗʰ September, 1773

*F*ree at last from the gloomy confines of Castle Gight, relieved of the burden inflicted on our hearts by that doomed and cursed place, we left the town of Drumalban with gladdening hearts and a joyous sense of release.

Forty miles of well-laid military road lie between Drumalban and Inverness, a ride of two days. We stopped for the night at Nairn, a mean, unremarkable little town, and knew we had crossed the Highland line when we heard Gaelic being spoken openly on the road, passing natives walking barefoot, or standing outside their windowless hovels of mud and grass. On observing their wretched conditions, Doctor Johnson observed that the native Scot prefers to suffer a plethora of little hardships than to discover a means of ending them, which was to my mind a fair but harsh indictment.

Before we reached Inverness we stopped by Culloden Moor, where so many followers of Charles Edward Stuart had lost their lives. We chose an elevated spot that offered a view of the battlefield. I could scarcely contain my grief to behold the scene where two-thousand starved and exhausted Jacobites had been cruelly cut down and bayoneted where they fell. The eerie hour of twilight approached by stealth as we looked across that bleak moor, and I fancied I could hear the skirl of bagpipe upon the wind, and the faint rat-tat-tat-tat of a military drum. Suddenly we were startled to observe a fairy host of dancing blue lights setting the horizon alight, casting their spell of enchantment upon us. Had it not been for recent theories of flammable marsh gas I might have been terrified out of my wits, thinking them to be the very souls of the massacred Scots.

We came at last to Inverness, capital of the Highlands and last bastion of civilisation, which serves as a gateway to the Great Glen and the Western Isles beyond.

We signed the guest book of Mrs MacKenzie's dirty and ill-

furnished inn under our Knights of the Cape pseudonyms, Sir Robert Loin and Sir Edmund Rake, a subterfuge which tickled us both with the sheer novelty of it, and retired early with a tolerable supper sent to our rooms. One glance from the window told us that our monkishly-attired friends had picked up on our trail again since losing us on the Cairngorm Pass. Their dark figures lurked in the shadows on the far side of the street. Leaving before dawn was out of the question, and so we resolved to make ourselves as comfortable as possible for the night.

Doctor Johnson attempted to translate a few more pages of his Ogham script, claiming to be on the verge of a major breakthrough. He showed me a page he had already translated. It concerns a legendary encounter between Saint Columba and a certain Loch Ness Monster, a tale with so many antecedents in popular mythology that it is difficult to separate fact from fiction. According to that ancient chronicle, a Fomorian Sea Giant called Girtha the Insatiable, daughter of the dreaded Balor the Invincible, scourge of the Danann, entered the loch in search of food, and grew so fat from devouring the local populace that she became trapped. Only after her banishment to the depths of the loch by St Columbus was the countryside safe once more from her ravages. Following this remarkable demonstration, the Pictish villagers suffered themselves to be baptised in the same Loch by the same hand that had vanquished their monster, hence it might be said that the Wyrm of Loch Nis is indirectly responsible for the birth of Christianity in Scotland.

Whatever the truth of the matter, tomorrow we travel the length of the Great Glen, and a monster hunt might be just the thing to divert attention from our recent misfortunes.

Loch Ness, 6th September 1773

Our passage through the Great Glen has been hindered somewhat due to storms of the previous week. A number of large trees have fallen onto the road, forcing us to journey via the banks of the loch for much of the way. Progress has been slow. By the end of the first evening we had covered only eight miles, though we took some pleasure in the scenic beauty along the way, and made camp that night rather pleased with ourselves.

From *The Casebook of Johnson and Boswell*

Chapter 1

The three men sheltered in a bay of fern and birch, looking out over the great stillness of Loch Ness. On the other side, a little over a mile away, a faint puff of smoke thicker than the surrounding mist signified a solitary farmhouse.

Boswell studied the surface of the water, which seemed in places to be agitated by something just under the surface. The turbulence would die down, only to re-appear at some other part of the loch. These disturbances had a disagreeable effect on Boswell's nerves.

'There are more things in Heaven and Earth, Horatio, than are dreamt of in your philosophy,' said Johnson, taking notice of Boswell's unease. 'And more things than fish lurking in the gloomy depths of that loch.'

They bedded down that night in the bay, their ponies tethered to a birch tree just beyond the circle of firelight. Boswell had difficulty sleeping; when he did his dreams were troubled by visions of strange and monstrous things lurking in the depths of the water—creatures without eyes, their pale bodies bleached from lack of light, with tentacles for arms and gaping beaks for mouths.

When Boswell awoke, the Loch had assumed its peaceful aspect once more. Its untroubled surface reflected his own image with serene indifference, while the opposite side seemed nearer than before. Several homesteads had sprung to life along its banks, with the gentle bleat of a sheep serving to dispel any residual night-fears.

After washing his face in the Loch and taking a long draught of ice-cold water Boswell disappeared behind a line of trees to relieve himself, then went to check on the ponies. He counted only three. He rubbed his eyes and counted again. One of the ponies, the sturdy one used to carry their portmanteaus, was missing. Boswell called out for Johnson. The Doctor hailed his friend cheerfully as he approached the glade where the horses were tethered.

'Voltaire has gone missing.'

'Voltaire?' said Johnson, raising an eyebrow.

Boswell blushed. He had not shared the fact he named the ponies after the great philosophers. 'The stout one that carries the luggage. He's gone!'

'So he has,' said Johnson. 'Perhaps he wandered off looking for apples.'

'I hardly think so,' said Boswell, showing Johnson the ragged end of rope used to tether pony to tree. Both men turned to look at the water as it lapped innocently against the shoreline.

They divided the luggage between the remaining horses and continued along the banks of the loch, leading their ponies on foot for much of the way to relieve them of their burdens.

The next night another pony was taken. Boswell was awoken by a terrified sound. He shot up and looked at the loch, just in time to see a black tentacle slither through the water and disappear. He ran to where the ponies were tethered. Rosseau was gone.

On the third night Descartes was taken. Joseph had been set to watch over what was left of the team, but the unhappy man fell asleep on his vigil, and did not awake until the dawn.

'Doctor Johnson. If we carry on like this all of our ponies will be gone. Let us leave the banks of this God-forsaken Loch, and entrust our lives to the wilderness, for I fear there is something in the water that has developed a taste for horsemeat, and once it has devoured poor Anselm, I believe it will come for us.'

'I daresay you are right, Mr Boswell.'

The men turned off the beaten track, leading the last remaining pony, laden with luggage, across a bleak moor of bracken and heather until finally, foot-sore and weary, they found the old road to Fort Augustus. In places the road was overgrown or had been destroyed completely, and their journey was a long exhausting slog through a relentlessly unforgiving landscape. The rain poured down in sheets and they almost lost poor Anselm at the ford. Only the ingenuity of Joseph and his ropes saved him from being carried off by the swollen river. Finally they came to Fort Augustus, where the governor Mr Trapaud came out to greet them at the gate. The three men were well-fed and given clean beds for the night, and even poor Anselm was given a dry stable with clean straw to sleep on.

Chapter 2

*T*he following morning Mr Trapaud joined his guests for breakfast. They enjoyed a lavish spread which seemed at variance to the simple fare enjoyed by most military institutions.

'My one concession to luxury,' explained Mr Trapaud, lifting a serving dish to reveal a steaming heap of freshwater trout. 'Our chef Mr Brussard came all the way from France. I asked for him personally. It was my one condition for accepting governorship of this remote outpost.'

The fish was accompanied with a well-balanced sauce of capers and lemon, which was delicious if a little fussy for Johnson's robustly English palate, especially so early in the morning.

A keen amateur meteorologist, Mr Trapaud was pleased to find in Johnson a kindred spirit, and presented his esteemed guest with a copy of Ebenezer McFait's *Essays and Observations*, directing his attention to a chapter entitled *Observations on Thunder and Electricity*. 'Just last night I almost fell off the roof,' Mr Trapaud confessed, 'in an attempt to reproduce McFait's experiments with lightning rods.'

'Our very own Prometheus!' cried Johnson. 'What a great loss to science that would have been.'

Johnson and Boswell were served tea and scones in the conservatory, and were just about to consult their host on the pronunciation of the word *scone,* when Joseph burst in with a look of consternation on his face.

'Joseph,' said Johnson, wiping his mouth on a napkin. 'You

look like you've seen a ghost. What on earth is the matter?'

'I do see ghost! You come quick! You see!'

Joseph led the three men out to the stables, where they found not only Anselm, but Voltaire, Rosseau and Descartes, all happily munching from the same sack of oats. Poor Boswell burst into tears of joy. 'But how… who…' was all he could manage. Even Johnson was struck dumb.

'We caught the thief red-handed this morning,' said the young corporal who had found the missing ponies. 'A well-kent horse thief that goes by the name of Tam Smellie. He was walking down the road with these three garrons as bold as brass, and it was no great difficulty to see they were stolen. We threw him in a cell if you wish to see him. It's your right as the aggrieved party to decide on a suitable punishment.'

A crestfallen Johnson whipped off his hat and sat himself down on a bale of hay. 'And I could have sworn…' he muttered, then laughed at himself. 'I am forgetting my own dictum, Boswell; that only when we have exhausted all natural possibilities, do we turn to the supernatural. I should be soundly whipped.'

'Aha!' said Mr Trapaud. 'Then you saw the monster in the loch.'

'Yes!' exclaimed Boswell. 'Or at least we saw its tentacles moving through the water.'

'I think I may be able to satisfy you on that count, gentlemen. Come with me.'

The battlements of Fort Augustus consisted of a square wall surrounding the entire compound, with high, angled bastions on each corner. Mr Trapaud led his two guests onto the north-eastern bastion, which afforded extensive views across the loch.

'My men often claim to see something in the water,' explained Mr Trapaud. 'Which aroused my curiosity.' He produced a telescope from his coat pocket and passed it to Doctor Johnson, who examined the brass instrument with great curiosity, holding the narrow end up to his eye.

'Now look,' said Mr Trapaud, leaning in close and pointing

out towards the bay. 'There! D'ye see those furrows in the water? And that long surge over there?'

'I see it,' said Johnson.

'Irregular winds agitate the surface, but are not coherent enough to create organised currents. However if the wind direction is persistent those long streaks appear, causing people to think they have just witnessed a sea-serpent cutting through the loch.'

'But yesterday was clear,' argued Boswell, 'with only the faintest hint of a breeze.'

'A similar effect may be caused by earthquakes or underwater landslides,' replied Mr Trapaud. 'Loch Ness lies on a fault line, and is perhaps more prone to turbulence than any other body of water. Sometimes these earthquakes are accompanied by a roaring noise, which has been mistaken in the past for the presence of a monster. Indeed, the word "Ness" is an old Celtic word for *roaring one*.'

'It is a busy puddle,' said Johnson, passing the telescope on to Boswell. 'I'll grant you that.'

'Look there!' cried Boswell, lowering the telescope and pointing frantically at the water. 'That black, undulating form by the jetty.'

'Hy-dro-dy-namics,' pronounced Mr Trapaud impressively. 'Dense water appears darker, and as this dark water undulates under the surface it gives the impression of a snake-like creature moving across the loch.'

'But I saw a tentacle yesterday morning,' Boswell argued. 'It was black and slimy and about ten feet long!'

'Still not satisfied?' said Mr Trapaud. 'Then come with me.'

The governor led his guests downstairs to the kitchen, where three monstrous eels were hanging from hooks on the wall. The chef took one down and slammed it onto his chopping board then lopped off its head with a machete.

'The loch is teeming with them at this time of year, and they are often mistaken for monsters,' said Mr Trapaud. 'This one's a six-footer, but we've caught thirteen-footers before, haven't we Mr Brussard?'

'That's right, Mr Trapaud,' said the chef.

'It tastes just like salmon if you prepare it right. Mr Brussard makes the finest eel pie this side of the border, isn't that right, Mr Brussard?'

'If you say so, Mr Trapaud.'

'I do, Mr Brussard. You *will* stay for tea, won't you gentlemen?'

Johnson roared with laughter and slapped his knee with delight. 'I daresay the eel pie will be a d____d sight more palatable than the *humble* pie I have just been served!'

The very next morning, two soldiers were provided to escort the guests as far as Glenelg, where a vessel could be chartered to ferry them across to the Isle of Skye.

'Well, Boswell,' said Johnson as they took their leave of Fort George. 'It seems I have been thoroughly bested, and by a Frenchman too. I must take my hat off to Mr Trapaud, who was able to provide a satisfactory explanation for the so-called Loch Ness Monster. But I promise you this, I will never be caught with my scientific breeches down again.'

The road to the ferry was a well-trodden drovers' route, a journey of several days through a rolling landscape of verdant hills and scenic ruins all the way down to the coast.

The ferry waiting for them when they arrived was little more than a raft, but large enough and sturdy enough to accommodate all four horses, the passengers and their luggage. To encourage skittish cattle the ferryman had covered the raft's bare wooden boards with turf, as otherwise the beasts tended to panic at the sound of their own hooves drumming on the wood.

As the floating island pulled away from the pier, Boswell glanced up and spied four figures on horseback watching their progress from the crest of a nearby hill. He nudged Johnson. 'We appear to have lost our shadows.'

Johnson nodded grimly. 'Either that,' he said, 'or they have us precisely where they want us.'

THE CASEBOOK
OF SAMUEL JOHNSON, LL.D.
And JAMES BOSWELL, Esq.

A VOYAGE TO
THE EDGE OF
THE WORLD

A Hebridean Odyssey in Three Parts:

Including a Meditation on CABBAGES, their
Medicinal Value, and
Historical Anecdotes concerning their
Practical Application and Usage.

A Hebridean Odyssey

Part I - The Corn Threshers

emons,' said Lizzie Hutton, glancing over her shoulder with a fearful expression. 'They are everywhere.' Her mouth quivered; her eyes betrayed a flicker of indecision. Part of her didn't want to believe. Part of her wanted to take her children home, to tuck them into bed and read them a bedtime story—their favourite, Beowulf and Grendel—while the rain beat harmlessly against the window. She wanted to kiss them both goodnight and tell them that monsters weren't real, except maybe in the pages of a storybook. She wanted to tell them that everything would be all right... but that was before she had looked the devil Himself in the eye.

Now she didn't know what to think. Her faith alone gave her the strength to do what was necessary.

'They seem like ordinary people,' she confided. 'But if you look closely, you can see it in their eyes... their faces... something about their faces....' Lizzie trailed off, momentarily confused, then squeezed her children's hands and dragged them onwards.

'Mammy, I'm scared. I don't like the forest.'

'Weesht, girl. We are going somewhere safe. Somewhere the demons can't hurt you.'

'I want to go home,' sobbed the girl.

'It's not safe,' said Lizzie. 'They will be watching for us.'

'Who? Who will be watching for us?'

'It could be anyone,' whispered Lizzie, glancing nervously from side to side.

'Mammy,' said the boy. *'Is Mr Campbell the minister a demon?'*

'Shut up! Shut up!' said the boy's older sister. *'You're scaring me!'*

Lizzie Hutton knelt before her son and daughter and drew them close. *'Listen, children. The evil one can take many forms. Sometimes he comes to you as a friend, or as a kind old lady, or as a man of the cloth, sometimes even as one of your own kin.'* She looked soberly from her daughter to her son. *'Aye, even as a child.'*

'You are lying!' cried the girl. *'There is no such thing as demons!'*

'There is too!' the boy protested. *'I can see them!'*

'You're a liar!' cried the girl. *'You are just saying that because Mam said that!'*

The little girl's voice had reached fever pitch, her breath coming in wheezing rasps. Lizzie Hutton, little more than a child herself, wrapped her arms around her daughter and held her close. *'Shhh, child...'* she soothed. *'They may hear us. Look! We are nearly out of the forest. Do you see the clearing up ahead?'*

Lizzie Hutton took her children by the hand and dragged them up the slope towards the ruin of Brochel Castle.

Perched on a high promontory, the crenelated tower seemed hewn from the stack of living rock on which it stood. Flanked by two crumbling wings, in the moonlight the keep resembled a slouching vulture.

The little girl looked up at the tower and quailed. *'Why are we going there?'*

'To see your father, of course.'

'Daddy!' cried the boy.

'Father is dead!' rasped the girl. *'He's dead! He drowned at sea!'*

'Weesht!' cried Lizzie, clamping her hand over the girl's mouth. *'Don't speak like that! You will frighten Robert.'*

Suddenly the girl bit down on her mother's hand. She released her with a yelp of surprise. The girl ran on through the rain and climbed the steps all the way to the castle.

'Fiona! Come back!' Lizzie grabbed the boy and went after her daughter.

The rain came in sheets through the roofless tower. Whispering shadows seemed to lurk in every corner. On the far wall, an empty window glared out onto a slate-grey sea. Waves crashed against the rocks far below. The little girl was huddled on the ledge, trying to put as much distance between herself and her mother as possible.

'Fiona! Get down from there at once! Your father shall hear of this...'

'Leave me alone! Pa is dead! He drowned when he was fishing and you are a liar!'

Robert slumped against his mother's side, his face beaded with perspiration. 'Mammy, I don't feel so well...'

'Yes, that is how it starts!' cried Lizzie fervently, bending down and grasping her son's shoulders. 'Soon you will see them too! Do you see them now?'

The little boy nodded solemnly.

'Where?' cried Lizzie feverishly. 'Where do you see them?'

The boy raised an arm to point at his sister. She was trembling on the edge of the abyss, hugging her knees and sobbing softly. Lizzie Hutton looked mournfully from her son to her daughter.

'Robert,' she said softly. 'Close your eyes.'

*

In the village of Inverarnish, Alastair McCrimmon closed the barn door for the night, then turned towards the crofthouse. He staggered slightly and leaned against the barn door. He was still shaking off a nasty cold and had taken to medicating himself with whisky. His wife didn't like it; if he drank too much it made him belligerent, angry. Still, if he drank only in moderation...

A candle light was burning steadily in the bedroom where his wife slept. He saw a tall shadow flit past the window. Strange. His wife had been bedridden these past three days, and was barely able to lift her head from the pillow, let alone move around.

It was when he gripped the door handle that he first heard the voices. Just a murmuring at first, like a tickling in his ear. As he opened the door, one voice sounded clearly above all the rest. It was warning him of some danger ... (demons) ... Alastair MacCrimmon reached into his pocket and felt for his knife. He poured himself another whisky, a large one, then wiped his mouth with the back of his hand and looked towards the back of the house where his wife slept.

He called her name. Softly, at first, then more insistently. No sound came from the other side of the partition. Something was wrong. MacCrimmon put his hand on the curtain, pulled it aside...

The shape under the covers was too big to be his wife... (my, what long legs you have!)... those were not his wife's feet poking out from the bottom of the bed, but a pair of cloven hooves... (all the better to chase you with!)... Gripping the knife in one hand, MacCrimmon leaned over, took a corner of the bedsheet, and... (my, what a bad smell you have!)... whipped it away.

The beast that had devoured his wife was not of this world. Its flesh, as white as a maggot's, was covered in coarse black hairs like the bristles of a fly. Its limbs... how many arms did it have? Four? Six?... (my, what big arms you have!)... were impossibly long and spindly and folded in on themselves, mantis-like, in a parody of prayer. And its face... oh god... Though rigid and immobile as a mask, the insectoid features seemed to mock him... (my, what big eyes you have!)... to dare him to raise his hand against it...

(all the better to...)

'Kill it!' said the voice in his head.

MacCrimmon looked at his hand. It still held the knife.

Chapter 1

'Cabbages.'

'I beg your pardon sir?' said Boswell, staring bleary-eyed at the dish placed before him. Boswell had availed himself of the Laird of Raasay's hospitality a little more liberally than his friend, having caroused all night with MacLeod's ten beautiful daughters, dancing with each in turn and generally making a fool of himself. He sat down to breakfast feeling decidedly under the weather.

'I took the liberty of ordering you a plate of cabbages,' said Johnson, peering over the tops of his reading glasses like a stern but kindly schoolmaster. 'It says here that the cabbage is a sovereign remedy for curing intoxication, and that it even has the power of preventing it; indeed we are informed that, by eating a quantity of cabbage before dinner, we may drink as much wine as we please, without experiencing any inconvenience.'

'Is that so?' groaned Boswell.

'Yes, sir, it is,' said Johnson, with a sly wink at their host. 'The property of the cabbage is mentioned by Aristotle and Theophrastus, who are of the opinion that it proceeds from the antipathy which the vine shows for it. If a cabbage be planted near a vine, the latter retires to as great a distance as possible, or perhaps dies. Hence it is concluded that the vine, owing to this aversion, allows itself to be overcome by the cabbage. Be this as it may, the phenomenon is indisputable, and the recipe, which was declared to be effectual by the ancient Egyptians, is now universally adopted in Germany. I myself am on a strict diet of cabbage. It improves the operation of the bowels, and prevents a great many other disorders to which men of a certain age are prone.'

Boswell took one whiff of the gaseous, pungent pile of greens before him, and his stomach lurched.

'Good God, sir,' said John MacLeod, Laird of Raasay, who was seated at the head of the table. 'Ye have gone as green as that kale. Get ye to bed at once, or I will have a dead man on my conscience.'

Boswell rose to his feet, and with a muttered apology dashed upstairs to seek the solace of his chamber-pot.

MacLeod looked archly at his guest and wagged a finger. 'Ye are an incorrigible rogue, Doctor Johnson.'

'You will forgive an old man for having a little sport at his friend's expense,' said Johnson, grinning like a schoolboy. 'And if he survives, I daresay he will think twice before drinking his host out of house and home again.'

'Oh, he is welcome to it. After all, he won't be the first young rogue to overindulge under my roof, and he certainly won't be the last.'

After finishing Boswell's helping of cabbage, Johnson donned his coat and hat and accompanied the laird outside for a turn of the grounds.

Raasay House was a good family mansion set some three hundred yards from the bay, with a fine verdure about it, a considerable number of trees, and beyond it hills and mountains in gradation of wildness. The house itself was well-ordered with a modest estate, which the laird managed efficiently, utilising the smallholding to the best of his abilities.

In many ways John MacLeod was the ideal chief for his age, Johnson reflected; a man in tune with modern ideas while holding fast to tradition, a man of vision, who retained his sense of justice and mercy, and unlike his contemporaries, the Laird of Raasay refused to evict his tenants in favour of sheep (though the subsequent losses nearly bankrupted him). He lived among them, struggled with them; their hardships were his hardships, their joys his joys.

'The island is fifteen miles long and three at its widest,' said the laird as they made their way down the lawn towards the bay. 'We have wildfowl in abundance, and our lochs also have trout. We have beef and mutton, although the livestock often perish by falling from the precipices. Deer we have none, nor hares, nor rabbits, nor foxes to hunt them.'

'And what grows here?'

'The island affords not much ground, either for tillage or for pasture,' confessed MacLeod, linking his arm in Johnson's as they walked, 'and the winter brings a hard frost. But I have managed to overcome these obstacles with some unique innovations.'

They came to an allotment at the bottom of the garden where row after row of squeaky-clean cabbages popped their heads out of the soil. 'My kale,' said the laird. 'I have succeeded in cultivating a hybridised strain perfectly suited to this climate.'

'Ah, the humble cabbage,' said Johnson. 'If only the poets sang its praises more often, instead of twittering on about roses! They are perennial, impervious to frost, and with your allotment so near to the ocean, they have the added benefit of desalinating the soil.'

'To name but a few of their miraculous properties,' said the laird, pleased to find a kindred spirit in his horticulturally-inclined guest.

'Indeed,' said Johnson. 'Cato the Elder, in his *De Agri Cultura*, waxes lyrical over the humble cabbage, to which he attributes his remarkable health and longevity, whereas Pliny the Elder lists as many as eighty-seven medicinal uses, including cures for gout, colic, paralysis, the plague... and hiccups.'

'Not to mention Captain Cook,' MacLeod added enthusiastically, 'who champions the cabbage for its success in treating scurvy, that bane of the seaman's life.'

The two men walked a little further along the coast, delighting in one another's company, until they came to a field where some women were reaping the last of the summer corn, while the men nearby bound up the sheaves. The women were singing a harvest-song in Gaelic in time to the strokes of the sickle, in which all their voices were united. The effect of this music seemed to cheer the workers and lift their hearts.

'We harvest rye instead of the usual wheat or barley,' explained MacLeod. 'I have it shipped in from Germany at my own expense.'

'A capital idea!' said Johnson excitedly. 'Rye thrives on poorer soil where other grains fail.'

At the sound of the stranger's voice the singing stopped, and the men dropped what they were doing to lean on their pitchforks and stare. The laird raised his bonnet and waved, and one by one the workers resumed their activities. 'Pay them no mind,' he said, taking Johnson's arm and leading him around the edge of the field. 'Folk here are shy of newcomers. You must understand that many of them have never left the island, and we have so few visitors that you must present something of a curiosity.'

They came to a long barn where sacks of grain had been stored for the winter ahead. 'Rye seems to thrive in cold, wet conditions such as we find here on Raasay,' said the laird. 'It produces a dense, dark bread not unpleasant to the taste.'

'And these?' said Johnson, indicating an assortment of barrels stacked against the wall.

'Ah, a little hobby of mine. Rye whisky and rye ale. The ale comes from a Bavarian recipe I found in an old library manuscript. The whisky has a more recent provenance. A fellow from Pittsburgh showed me how to do it. The distilled grain is aged two years in uncharred oak barrels. Would you care for a taste?'

'If it's the same vile concoction that indisposed Boswell, then I think I'll pass, sir.'

'Suit yourself,' said the laird with a shrug, unstopping one of the barrels and helping himself to a dram. 'Come,' he said, slamming down his glass with a wince of pleasure. 'I'll show you where the magic happens.'

At the other end of the barn beyond the threshing room, where the women beat the rye with flails to separate the stalks from the grain, there was a towering chimney-like structure of unmortared brick, shaped like a giant beehive or demijohn bottle. 'This is our kiln house,' said the laird, 'where we dry the grain.' Johnson stepped in through the small door and looked up at a single shaft of sunlight piercing the gloom like a sword.

'Eerie, isn't it?' said the laird. 'The villagers won't enter the kiln house after dark or cut through the rye fields on their way home. They believe there is something that lurks among the crops called the carn witch, and they refuse to enter the kiln at night because of the "feart thing" that bides in the hearth pit.'

'Superstitious balderdash,' scoffed Johnson, then started as the laird placed a friendly hand on his shoulder.

'Maybe so,' the laird said. 'But come, I'll show you the rest of my estate.'

A path wound its way from the kiln house to a walled orchard on the edge of a wood, where the laird cultivated several varieties of apple, pear and plum tree. The two men watched a group of women collect the fallen fruit in their baskets, which would later be pressed and poured into glass jars to make preserves.

The north end of the orchard lay on a gentle incline where the trees were thinner on the ground. A "lean-to" greenhouse had been built against the back wall, consisting of a row of glass panels tilted at forty-five-degree angles, sheltering an abundance of tomatoes, lemons, limes, and cucumbers.

'The wall is southward facing,' the laird explained. 'Which means it gets the sun all day. The greenhouse stores the heat and releases it at night, while the glass defends the young shoots from cold and boisterous winds, even frosts and direct sunlight, allowing us to grow produce all year round.'

'Your ingenuity does you credit,' said Johnson, who was not often so easily impressed, and rarely showed it when he was.

The two men doubled back towards Raasay House, this time taking the scenic route through the wooded foothills of *Carn nan Eun*, meaning "Hill of the Bird".

In a clearing of the wood towards the rear of the estate stood the remains of a small church, its roof long since gone, the surrounding gravestones almost entirely covered in grass.

'This is St Moluags, where my ancestors are laid rest,' said the laird. 'I often come here when I have need of solitude.'

'There is no other church on the island?'

'Apart from here you mean? No, sir. The glades and mountains are all we require to feel the closeness of God.'

Johnson was appalled, though too polite to show it. 'But you have a minister, surely?'

'The Reverend Jeremiah Campbell. His church is a fallow field beyond the village. His parishioners stand in awe of him, though I must confess I have no time for the man myself. I find his style a little too... fanatical for my tastes.'

Johnson was about to speak when he spied a skull grinning back at him from a nook in the wall, showing white against the grey stone of the church. He recoiled in horror. The laird laughed and picked up the skull to show Johnson it was as harmless as the cabbages in his allotment. 'The islanders have a rather cavalier attitude towards death, I'm afraid, and sometimes leave the bones of their loved ones to bleach in the sun.'

Johnson, as a man who took such notions of the afterlife seriously, expressed his disapproval in no uncertain terms.

'Come, Doctor Johnson. Our ways are not your ways, and though you may find some of our traditions a touch... *eccentric*, you will find we islanders are just as moral and God-fearing as your average town dweller, if not more so.'

A clattering of stones echoed from within the empty church, followed by a peal of girlish laughter. Johnson turned just in time to see three young girls disappear over the kirkyard wall.

Inside the church Johnson was startled to discover a life-sized figure of straw propped against the gable wall. The mannequin was dressed in shirt and breeches, with three rusty knives plunged into its breast.

'What heathenish nonsense is this!' cried Johnson, aghast.

''Tis naught but a harmless superstition, Doctor. The corn dolly represents the dying god. Once the harvest has been gathered in, the villagers make a figure like you see here from the last sheaf of corn. They believe that the corn-spirit resides within it, and so it must be ritually sacrificed. The dolly will be taken to the village square and burned on Hallow's Eve, and the ashes will be spread over the field.'

'I have heard of such heretical practices in Medieval Europe, but in this day and age?'

'You have been quite fortunate, all things considered,' the laird said thoughtfully. 'Before we received the light of the gospel, the villagers believed that each passing stranger on harvest day was a manifestation of the corn-spirit. They would catch him and bind him in sheaves of corn, before cutting off his head with a scythe. Why else do you think the workers were looking at you so strangely this morning? Had you not been under my protection, I shudder to think what might have happened.'

Johnson, who had turned quite pale, looked at the laird to see if he was joking. 'But... it's monstrous!' he exclaimed.

The laird released a gale of laughter and slapped his guest on the back. 'Don't worry, Doctor. The last stranger we sacrificed was over two hundred years ago. Things have become a little more civilised since then. On Hallow's Eve, when they burn the corn-dolly, I too, as 'king of the harvest', will be ritualistically "sacrificed", which means I must suffer my neck to be placed within a circle of swords. But it's all quite harmless, I assure you. A mere tradition, the origins of which have been lost in time.'

'And in the past may they remain,' said Johnson, crossing himself devoutly.

Chapter 2

After their tour of the grounds, the two men made their way back indoors, only to find the household in a state of upheaval. Servants were running up and down the stairs with cloths and pails of hot water, while sobbing came from behind closed doors. Lady Raasay stood at the bottom of the stairs, wringing her hands with vexation.

'Whatever is the matter?' said John MacLeod, rushing towards his wife and clasping both of her hands.

'It is Maireadh,'[5] she replied, referring to their youngest daughter. 'She has lain in bed all morning, and I fear she is grievously sick. Oh Doctor Johnson, would you please take a look at her?'

'But madam,' protested Johnson, 'I am no doctor of physick.'

'But they say you are the cleverest man in all of England!' begged the lady. 'And we have need of a doctor here on the island.'

With his vanity—and the well-being of a family who had already shown him much kindness—at stake, Johnson allowed himself to be led upstairs.

Maireadh was a pretty girl of ten years, with blonde tresses and big blue eyes, though her eyes had a sunken, hollow quality and the hair, dark with perspiration, clung limply to her forehead.

A plump nursemaid had established herself in the corner, absent-mindedly twining ears of corn between her chubby fingers, humming some melody not dissimilar to the one

pronounced 'mur+aid'

performed by the women in the field.

Johnson approached the sick bed and placed a palm on the girl's brow. 'Madam,' he barked at the nursemaid. 'I must insist you open that window. Fresh air is the best tonic for the sick. And kindly replace these bedsheets.'

Once he had ensured the patient was made as comfortable as possible Johnson removed himself to Boswell's bedchamber. The shades were drawn and the room plunged in darkness, while the clammy odour of sickness clung to the bedsheets. 'Good Lord, sir. You really are ill!' exclaimed Johnson, taking one look at his friend stretched out on the bed.

'I fear the worst, sir,' said Boswell, raising his head with some difficulty. 'If I do not make it, you must promise to do right by my wife and daughter...'

'Nonsense!' retorted Johnson, pulling open the curtains. 'I shall send up some of the laird's best whisky. Nothing like some hair of the dog to set you to rights. At least that's what I've read.'

With Boswell taken care of, Johnson went to find the laird in his drawing room. He was pacing back and forth before the fireplace with a distracted air when Johnson entered, and rushed forward with an anxious expression on his face. 'How fares my daughter?'

'She is suffering from a serious malady, my Lord. If her condition has not improved by the morning, I must insist she be taken to the hospital in Inverness.'

As it happened, no one would be going anywhere soon. A sudden flash of lightning ignited the sullen skies over Glamaig.[6] The ensuing storm was of such ferocity it was decreed that no boats would be sailing for the foreseeable future.

At midday Johnson received news that little Maireadh's condition had worsened. He hurried upstairs to see what he could do. It didn't look good. The child was sitting up straight on her bed with her back to the wall, clutching the bedsheets in her trembling hands and staring fearfully at a spot at the bottom

6   a conical mountain on Skye – see *The Grey Men of Glamaig*

of her bed.

'Oh Doctor Johnson!' cried the girl's mother, rushing forward and seizing both his hands. 'Save her! She is possessed!'

Doctor Johnson approached the bed. 'What is it, child?' he whispered soothingly, taking her fragile hand in his. 'What do you see?'

Without tearing her eyes from her vision, Maireadh cried, 'It is the devil! It is the devil himself! No! No! He approaches! Save me!'

So convincing was her dread of this invisible assailant that Johnson could have sworn he felt a shadow cross the room, and struggled to keep from looking over his shoulder. 'My dear child!' he cried, squeezing her hand reassuringly. 'There is nothing there—I assure you!'

The girl, having worked herself up to a fit of hysteria, froze suddenly, then slumped forward in a dead faint. With great tenderness Doctor Johnson lowered her body back onto the bed and raised her head on the pillows.

'The fever has passed, for now,' he said to the girl's mother. 'Please get some rest. I will take the first watch, and call for you if there is any change.'

Her eyes dark-rimmed from constant worry, a grateful Lady Raasay retired, leaving her daughter in the capable hands of Doctor Johnson, who for the remainder of the afternoon and well into the evening watched over his charge, holding her hand and bathing her fevered brow with cooling cloths.

At precisely nine o'clock, the laird's wife reappeared to relieve Johnson of his duty.

'My dear Doctor Johnson. You must be positively famished,' she cried. 'Please take yourself to supper.'

Johnson pulled himself away and made his way downstairs to the dining room where he found Boswell already at table, and he rejoiced to see his friend much improved.

The laird's nine remaining daughters did their best to entertain the guests. The twins Morag and Janet sang ballads in Gaelic, while Flora, the eldest and prettiest of the laird's daughters, played the spinet. So pleasing was the effect produced by the girls' voices that Johnson begged for a translation, which the laird promised to provide as soon as he had a spare moment. The other girls demonstrated their dancing and recited poetry, each according to their own ability. Johnson sat patiently throughout and applauded each performance, but there was a strained note to the proceedings, and the laird soon excused them all with a goodnight kiss and sent them early to bed.

Chapter 3

Late in the evening a visitor arrived at the gates of Raasay House, and beat the door so hard it could be heard above the sound and fury of the storm.

An old woman in a tartan shawl that covered her head and shoulders was admitted and led upstairs to the sick room. This, Doctor Johnson was informed, was the Widow Beaton, a local healer of some renown.

'Generally I disapprove of folk remedies or medicine not rigorously tested under scientific conditions,' remarked Johnson. But, seeing the twinge of emotion on the laird's face he quickly added, 'and yet there may still be some virtue in the herbs and poultices of these healing women.'

'She delivered all ten of my daughters, and has nursed them through many a weary hour of sickness.'

'Then I should very much like to interview this woman; after she has completed her examination, of course.'

One hour later Mrs Beaton was brought before Doctor Johnson in the parlour. Though very old, it was clear she had once been beautiful, and her features, lined with care as they were, still held traces of her former comeliness. Her teeth, yellowed with age, were good and straight, and her long silver hair shone luxuriantly in the candlelight.

'Thank you for coming, Mrs Beaton,' said Johnson, offering his chair. 'And how is the patient? Have you determined the cause of her infirmity?'

'A curse has been put on this house,' proclaimed the Widow

Beaton without preamble, fixing the laird with an eldritch eye. This pronouncement was accompanied, as if on cue, by a flash of lightning and a rolling boom of thunder overhead.

The laird was beside himself, and threw his hands up in despair. 'Then what is to be done?' he cried, with an expression of almost childlike credulity.

'Fill a bathtub with hot water,' replied the sage old woman. 'Then take three pebbles from the banks of *Loch na Mna*—one black, one white, one green—and place them at the bottom of the tub. Put the lass in the water, and as you bathe her repeat these words: *In the name of Him that can cure or kill, this water shall cure all earthly ill, shall cure the blood and flesh and bone, for ilka ane there is a stone.*'

The old woman produced a phial from a pouch she wore around her neck. 'Once she has been washed, give her a little of this before she goes to bed. It is mandrake root. Not too much mind! It will ease the pain and help her to sleep.'

'My good lady,' said Johnson, greatly alarmed. 'While I am as broad-minded as the next man, I cannot support the existence of witchcraft in this day and age, or that anyone should bear this house ill will.'

'That is for His Lordship to say,' said the old woman cryptically, and turning to her chief, who had the countenance of someone who had seen a ghost, she extended her hand, into which he placed a silver coin and sent her on her way.

*

Across the narrow Sound, the sharp peak of *Glamaig* rose from a dense bank of cloud, which it cleaved in two like the prow of a ship cuts the foaming waves. The ensuing deluge beat furiously against the windows and doors of Raasay House. Johnson lay uneasy on his bed, the absence of daily distractions serving only to amplify his naturally gloomy and introspective nature. He found himself meditating on the inevitability of death, and contemplating the fragility of the human frame, which like a vessel of clay, once broken, can never be mended.

At the height of his morbid cogitations, a flash of lightning drew his attention to the window. A pair of eyes like red-hot coals flashed beneath a set of devil's horns in silhouette. Johnson bolted upright and covered his face with his hands. When he looked again, the vision had passed. He slumped back onto his bed and felt an icy chill course through his veins. Had he fallen prey to the same bewitchment that tormented the mind of young Maireadh? Or was lack of sleep and a diet of pickled cabbage to blame? With these gloomy thoughts at the forefront of his mind, he buried his head in his pillow and fell into a restless and troubled sleep.

He arose at dawn only to receive more ill tidings. The laird, his wife and daughters, and half of the kitchen staff had fallen sick. Johnson moved from room to room, providing what comfort he could. Even Boswell, who had the night before shown signs of recovery, had retired to his room with a fever.

Maireadh's condition had deteriorated rapidly. Her illness had reached an alarming new phase, causing her to complain bitterly of a burning fire in her limbs. It smote Johnson's heart to see her frail little body, already much weakened from illness, racked with convulsions as she tried to smile. Against his better judgement he administered a few grains of Mrs Beaton's powdered mandrake root, which seemed to have the desired effect, sending the patient swiftly to sleep.

Back downstairs, Johnson assembled those few servants still able to stand, and issued instructions on how best to provide care for the sick. On requesting an inventory from the kitchen, Johnson received some alarming news. The laird's poultry yard had been broken into during the night and all its occupants killed or stolen. More bad news was to follow. The cattle on the surrounding hills lay dead or dying, and with the daily delivery of fish postponed due to the storm, there was nothing left in the larder but rye bread, a few jars of pickled cabbage, and some braxy mutton.

'It will have to do,' said Johnson. 'Ration what little we have left. Make a broth with the cabbage and mutton, and serve it with bread. Feed the sick first. Those well enough to stand can do without for the time being.'

As Johnson was leaving the kitchen, a young farmhand from the village appeared in the hall demanding to see the laird. 'The laird is indisposed,' barked Johnson, pushing past the boy on his way upstairs.

'Please,' begged the visitor breathlessly, seizing Johnson by the hand. 'They're all killing one another!'

'What? Who? What the blue blazes are you talking about, boy?'

'Begging your pardon, sir! But the whole village has gone to the devil!'

Chapter 4

*J*ohnson threw on his coat and followed the boy along the rain-lashed cliffs to the village of Inverarish, a mere scattering of cottages on either side of a muddy track, which lay about a mile further along the coast.

They arrived to find the village deserted. The boy showed Johnson the stables where five bodies had been bound in linen and laid out on a bed of straw. Two of them were mere children, not much longer than Johnson's arm.

Apart from the occasional twitch of a curtain, there were no mourners to be found anywhere in the village. Johnson turned to his guide and asked him the whereabouts of the minister. The boy led Johnson to the end of the village, then over a rickety wooden style to the edge of a field where a small crowd was gathering.

On a mound of earth in the middle of the field stood a throne-like wooden chair, and on the chair sat a tall, austere-looking gentleman in a long black gown with a pair of white linen bands at his neck. This, the boy explained, was the Reverend Jeremiah Campbell from Harris, who had come to bring the light of the Gospel to the island. His influence had grown steadily until it nearly eclipsed that of the laird, who very rarely interfered in village politics anymore.

Those villagers who had not succumbed to grief or sickness were making their way to the centre of the field. Johnson followed the crowd, keeping his head lowered so as not to draw attention to himself. He joined the circle of curious onlookers forming around the mound. As he pushed his way to the front, he could see an old woman being thrown to her knees before the minister. Johnson recognised the accused as the Widow Beaton, and to see her so ill-treated cut him to the quick.

From his lofty perch, the grim-faced clergyman read the charges in his thin, reedy voice. 'Jeanette Beaton,' he rasped. 'You stand accused of witchcraft, for which if you are found guilty the sentence is death. How d'ye plead?'

The old woman lowered her head and kept silent.

'That you did willingly conspire with the Evil One who is called Satan,' continued the minister, 'to bring a plague upon this island; that in the form of a black and monstrous seabird you did summon a storm to confound our fishing boats; that you did seduce the mind of Alastair MacCrimmon to evil, bidding him murder his own wife, before cutting his own throat; that you did willingly cause Elizabeth Hutton to drown herself and her own children, an act of depravity for which she will surely be damned for all eternity; that in the form of a hare you did suck the blood of cattle and spread a pestilence upon the land...'

Having heard enough of these wild accusations, Doctor Johnson pushed his way through the crowd and addressed the speaker directly. 'By what authority are you given to try this unfortunate woman?'

The clergyman narrowed his eyes contemptuously at his challenger, then raised his voice for all to hear. 'By the authority of God!'

This pronouncement was met with a roar of approval, and a hail of rotten turnips and cabbages rained down on the accused, splattering Johnson's coat in the process.

'Stop this at once!' cried Johnson, his wrath rising. 'I will have proof of these crimes, or on my oath, every single one of you shall answer for it before the assizes of Edinburgh.'

With a jeer of derision, the crowd released a fresh hail of rotten vegetables. The poor widow, who up until that point had kept her peace, raised her head and cursed each and every one of them in the most colourful language she knew.

'See?' cried the clergyman, purple with rage, leaning forward in his chair and pointing an accusing finger. 'See? The witch uses the devil's own tongue to put a curse upon us!'

It was at this point, just as things were turning from bad to worse for the unfortunate woman, that the Laird of Raasay himself put in an appearance. Mounted on a handsome white steed, he wore the tartan plaid with becoming grace, gathered together at the shoulder with a fine silver brooch. Though his face was as pale as a winter dawn, he appeared every inch the noble Highland Chieftain.

The crowd parted as their chief approached the Seat of Justice. 'Good day to you, Reverend Campbell,' he said courteously. 'For what reason do you abuse my revered guest, and torment this poor, unfortunate widow?'

The minister fixed the laird with a withering glare, a glare that would have daunted a lesser man, and repeated the charges in his dour, impassive voice.

The laird nodded sadly. Crofter Alastair MacCrimmon and his wife were much beloved on the island, while poor Lizzie Hutton had been a lass of only twenty-one tender summers. 'Clearly some distemper of the brain has destroyed the sanity of these poor wretches,' said the laird. 'We all know MacCrimmon liked the drink a bit too much, and Lizzie Hutton... Well, she's never been the same since her husband left. And yet you place the blame on the doorstep of a woman who has never harmed a soul in all her long days, who has cared for our kin as if they were her own, and who, lest we forget, lives some five miles from the scene of these crimes!'

'May a witch not send her familiar spirit to create mischief, in the name of the Evil One?' sneered the minister.

'What proof do you have that the Widow Beaton conspires with Satan?'

'Did she not place a curse upon your own house?' cried the minister, pointing an accusing finger at the laird. 'Why else is it Your Lordship has no male issue, lest it be a curse from the Witch of Fladda!'

Now it was the laird's turn to be wrathful. 'I would watch your tongue, when you speak of my family,' he cautioned.

'A family that even as we speak languish in their sickbeds,' persisted the minister, appealing to the crowd with a sweep of his hand. 'Along with half the village.'

'It is true,' confessed the laird. 'My wife and daughters are confined to their beds, but that alone does not prove the hand of the Evil One.'

'Go home, then, and look to your daughters, or ye may find that it is too late, and the devil has taken them all for his handmaidens!'

The two rivals stood facing one another from their respective heights: the laird mounted on his fine horse, the minister from his lofty throne, and it seemed to all watching that lightning flashed between the dark eyes of the minister and the grey eyes of the laird. Instinctively, the laird's hand touched the sword by his side, and in his wrath he might have drawn it, had not Johnson appeared between them and spoken with the voice of reason. 'Gentlemen, it profits us nothing to squabble. Let me suggest a compromise. Give me twenty-four hours, and if I have not found a means of proving this worthy woman's innocence, then you may do with her what you will.'

The minister assented with a dismissive wave of his hand. 'It is all the same to me,' he snorted, 'whether the witch burns today or burns tomorrow, provided she be detained in the meantime to prevent further mischief.'

'Away, then, with all of you,' cried the laird, 'and tend to your sick. We will have no more talk of witchcraft today.'

The crowd dispersed with the laird's admonishment still ringing in their ears, though they did not neglect to take their prisoner with them.

Having won for the widow a temporary reprieve, Johnson and the laird made their way back to Raasay House, though they had little cause to rejoice. Johnson led the laird's horse by the reins, picking his way carefully along the slippery coastal path. He would need all his faculties if he were to prove the widow's innocence. It would be no easy task. These people were highly superstitious at the best of times, and it would take a miracle before they surrendered their sacrificial lamb; nothing short of a cure for the sickness they were now calling the "Devil's Plague".

The laird, slumped on his horse, was barely recognisable as the man who had stepped out the previous morning. His confrontation with the Reverend Campbell had drained his last reserves of energy, and his whole frame seemed shrunken with care. 'That was a brave thing you did,' he said at last.

'I have bought us some time,' allowed Johnson. 'Little else.'

The laird looked pained and sank further into his saddle. 'You mean you have no plan?'

Johnson smiled thoughtfully. 'I am reminded of an old parable,' he replied, after walking on for some moments in silence. 'A prisoner condemned to be hanged for murder made a bargain with the king: if he could teach the king's favourite horse to fly within a year, then the king would grant him his freedom.'

'But why make such a ridiculous claim,' the laird protested. 'When the task is impossible?'

'Because a lot can happen in a year,' replied Johnson. 'The king may die before the year is out, or his jailer might forget to lock the prisoner's cell one night, or while training the horse to fly, the accused might seize an opportunity to make his escape over the yard wall. Finally, if all else fails, he has a year to teach the deuced horse to fly.'

The laird laughed long and hard, which terminated in a painful coughing fit. 'An amusing analogy, to be sure,' he conceded at last. 'But we have one night to perform a miracle, not one year.'

'*Dum vita est, spes est*,'[7] was Johnson's good-humoured reply. 'But leave it with me. Perhaps the answer may be closer to hand

7   where there's life there's hope

than you think.'

When they arrived back at the house, Johnson insisted the laird retire to his chamber to rest, while he checked in on the rest of the household. The situation was grave. Maireadh was delirious, moaning softly in her sleep. Her mother, pale and drawn from care, slept restlessly by her side. A corn dolly no larger than the palm of Johnson's hand sat on the windowsill. Johnson opened the window and tossed it out with a grimace of distaste, then left a jug of water on the bedside table.

Next, he called on Boswell, who in his delirium was conversing animatedly with someone no one else could see at the foot of his bed. Johnson touched his shoulder, and Boswell jerked round. 'Ah... it is you,' he said with a sigh of relief, his eyes slowly focusing on his friend.

'Rest now,' said Johnson, and he took a cold cloth and placed it tenderly on his friend's fevered brow.

The laird's ten daughters were suffering from varying stages of the malady, allowing Johnson to make some preliminary observations. The victim first suffered a prolonged fever, he noted, followed by visions. These visions varied in intensity, but at their most intense were powerful enough to induce the sufferer to harm themselves or others. The visions were accompanied by burning sensations in the limbs, followed closely by delirium, insensibility, in some cases even death.

Johnson retired to his room with a candle, a jar of salted cabbage, and a chest full of the laird's medical books. He unpacked the books and opened them out on his desk, then lighting a candle, sat himself down and began to read.

Chapter 5

*O*utside, the wind blew furiously, or rather sucked; for what is wind but a howling of air rushing in to inhabit a void? It moaned down the lum with a thousand voices, it rattled the doors in their frames, it shook the trees, and lifted slates clean off the roof. The murmuring among the servants was that the *Bean Sidhe* was abroad: a wild and tempestuous spirit that appeared whenever death was near.

Unable to sleep, the laird moved from room to room, his face a ghostly pale in the candlelight. With impotent fury he could have torn the hair from his head and beat his chest. He wanted to run outside and tear the shirt from his breast, to rip the soil from the ground and bury himself in it. Little Maireadh was breathing shallowly. Her mother, already weak from the ravages of illness, wept over her ailing body. Heart-rending screams issued from the girls' rooms, so that the servants were obliged to strap them to their beds. Meanwhile the devil stalked the corridors of Raasay House. Servants saw a black and silent shadow they called *Black Donald*, flitting from room to room, stealing through the corridors, vanishing around corners and peering in windows, smearing his malignant pestilence from person to person regardless of age, rank or sex. Even the laird had seen this apparition, and Johnson himself had been disturbed by its presence on more than one occasion.

Johnson flipped pages furiously by candlelight, but to his despair he was unable to find anything that might shed light on the curse of Raasay House. As he pored over his books, he glanced up briefly and caught a glimpse of his own tired reflection peering back at him. The candle flame guttered out, and his image was replaced by the face from the night before. It grinned mockingly from the other side of the window, its leering lips drawn back to reveal two rows of razor-sharp teeth.

'Get ye gone, Black Donald,' snarled Johnson through gritted teeth. 'I see you not!'

And just like that the vision disappeared, so that Johnson could not be sure if he had seen anything at all. With the weight of the world resting on his shoulders, he leaned forward until his forehead touched the reading desk, then despite everything...

...found himself walking through fields of rye, letting the fine ears run through his fingers. He came upon the women with their sickles raising their voices up to heaven, and the sound that they made was dirge-like and terrible. The sky overhead was grey and overcast. The men whose job it was to bundle up the sheaves of corn had constructed a huge man of straw some fifty feet high on the edge of the village. The women put down their sickles and followed the men. Johnson stopped one of the women to ask her something, pointing up at the strange construction with his stick.

'It is Saint Anthony,' she replied, her eyes shining with evangelical zeal. 'The Patron Saint of Lost Things.'

From out of the cottages poured a steady stream of sick men and women, young and old alike, carrying geese, lambs, goats and poultry under their arms. A ladder was placed against the straw effigy, and one by one they ascended. Cell-like cages had been built into the torso of the straw man. Once the last of the sick had crawled into a cell-space and closed the latch, Jeremiah Campbell appeared with a flaming torch in his hand. Cackling with demonic glee he lit the kindling at the effigy's feet. Johnson let out a cry of horror and ran towards the flames. A strong pair of hands held him back. As the flames leaped higher, the villagers surrounding the pyre joined hands. Their singing was frenzied, pagan in its licentiousness, accompanied by a cacophony of screams, squeals and grunts from the burning effigy.

'Do not waste your pity,' cried Campbell above the noise. 'It is Saint Anthony's fire! The village must be purged!'

He was dressed in the scarlet robes of an archbishop, but the face pointing out beneath the tall archbishop's mitre was the leering face of a fox!

Johnson awoke in a pool of sweat. With a pounding heart he flung a coat over his nightgown, then took up a candle and made his way to the library. Half an hour later he emerged with a renewed sense of purpose to assemble the servants in the kitchen.

'Mrs MacPherson,' he said to the most senior of the servants, a sturdy cook whose husband had only recently been consigned to his sick bed. 'What did you have to eat this morning?'

'I?' said the woman. 'Only a bowl of cabbage broth.'

'And to drink?'

'Just water.'

'And your husband?'

'He had the same as me.'

'Did he not have anything with his soup?'

'A little bread, I think.'

'And you? Did you have any bread?'

'No. It gives me terrible indigestion.'

'What did your husband have to drink last night?'

'A wee dram with his supper,' she admitted.

'And did you yourself drink any alcohol?'

'Heavens no!'

Doctor Johnson moved from servant to servant asking the same questions until he was satisfied, though something still bothered him. *None of the poison passed my lips*, he thought. *And yet...*

'Mrs MacPherson,' he said finally. 'Lock up the larder. Nothing is to be touched, unless it be the salted cabbage, which is an excellent source of nutrition.'

'Very good. Anything else, sir?'

'Pour the bedridden a good hot bath while you change their

bed linen, and give them a little of Mrs Beaton's powdered root mixed with water to drink. It is a natural emetic. It may also help ease their pain, and induce sleep.'

'If you say so, sir. Anything else?'

'I want you to pray, Mrs MacPherson,' he said over his shoulder as he put on his hat. 'Pray as if your very soul depended on it.' And with those words of advice he was gone, leaving the worthy woman more baffled than ever before.

Doctor Johnson had one last thing to do before he could be sure. Towards the rear of the house was a gated enclosure, within which a henhouse had been crudely assembled. The flattened earth surrounding the little wooden hut was strewn with blood and feathers. Johnson walked around the perimeter of the enclosure until he found what he was looking for, taking note of a gap between the fence and the ground, a small pile of displaced earth, and two little paths of pawprints.

He let himself into the enclosure and, as he stooped to examine some grain kernels scattered amongst the carnage, the last piece of the puzzle fell neatly into place.

Chapter 6

On the third morning the storm passed over, leaving tattered fragments of cloud strewn across the sky like corpses on a battlefield. Crows congregated on the edges of waterlogged fields, while the faint sound of thunder reverberated across the sea like distant cannon fire.

On the strip of waste ground beyond the village where Johnson had his vision, more bodies lay piled in a heap. The very elderly, mostly, but also children too weak to withstand the ravages of the disease. Nearby, a wooden stake had been driven into the ground, with a pyre of straw and driftwood shored against it. The minister looked to the hill beyond the village then consulted his pocket watch. He watched the sun climb like a benediction from behind the flat peak of *Dun Caan*. A good day for a witch-burning. Those villagers well enough to stand gathered sheepishly round the pyre. There was no sense of occasion. A sombre mood held sway over the previously hysterical crowd, as if they finally acknowledged the gravity of what they were about to do. The minister gave the signal and they brought forth the old woman, still in her nightgown, walking unsteadily on legs weak from praying. When she saw the pyre she began to tremble. Her eyes rolled in horror, but she did not struggle as they dragged her onto the pyre and tied her to the stake.

'Jeanette Beaton, have you any last words?' cried the minister.

The old woman looked sorrowfully at the faces in the crowd. These were the faces of her kinsmen and kinswomen; people she had grown with, fought with, consoled in their grief or shared in their joy; old ones she had healed; children she had delivered, protected, loved... Now she saw only fear and hostility on those same faces. It was the mindless face of the mob, united in hatred and ignorance. She caught the eye of one young crofter, who blushingly looked away.

'I delivered your wife's bairns, Iain Breac,' she murmured, finding her voice at last.

'And you, Calum Ruadh,' she inquired of another, who went to speak, then immediately closed his mouth again. 'Did I not cure your gout?

'And how is your rheumatism, Roderick MacLeod?' she asked a third. 'Are you sure your hands are strong enough to light that pyre?'

The man to whom she addressed this last remark began to tremble, and he nearly dropped the flaming torch from his hand.

'Ha!' she cried. 'Cowards! If my husband were alive, he would put the lot of you to the sword, and think no more on it! That is the kind of man he was. But I see no men here. Only a bunch of grandmothers afraid of their own shadow.'

'Enough, Jezebel!' cried the Reverend Campbell then, snatching the torch from the frightened man's grasp, he turned towards the pyre and lit the kindling himself. After a few moments the branches, still wet from the storm, belched a thick smoke which carried on a gust of wind, causing the onlookers to hack and cough. The minister tried again, and this time the flames took hold. The villagers stood rooted to the spot with horror and fascination, unable to tear their eyes from the dreadful spectacle.

The madman was now in his element. He opened his Bible and began spouting hellfire and damnation as the fire roared and crackled, sending burning embers over the heads of the crowd.

As the flames grew higher, the Widow Beaton's feet began to blister, and her vision shimmered with the rising heat. She looked hopelessly towards the hill beyond the village. She thought of her husband, and of her only son, Adam, who was in the grave before he could walk. Soon she would be joining them.

She hoped that it would be soon, that she would be spared the agony of the flames.

As the hem of her gown began to smoulder, she caught sight of two riders appearing over the brow of the hill, silhouetted in the rising sun. *It is he!* she thought exultantly. *They have come for me!* Then in a voice that could not be heard above the frenzied preaching of Jeremiah Campbell, Jeanette Beaton commended her soul to God.

*

At the sight of their Chief descending the hill in all his finery, the spell cast by Jeremiah Campbell was broken. The remembrance of old loyalties and oaths sworn in battle filled their hearts. Some of the older men removed their coats and ran towards the fire, beating down the flames. Two men grabbed a trough of water and doused the stricken woman's gown. By the time the riders had reached the edge of the village, the fire was extinguished.

The minister was beside himself with fury. 'You will explain yourselves,' he said through gritted teeth, his eyes rolling like a man possessed.

'I take full responsibility for the interruption of your Godly duties, Reverend Campbell,' said Doctor Johnson brightly, clambering down from his horse. Then turning to his mounted companion he said, 'If I may borrow your sword, sir.'

The laird drew his sword and passed it down to Johnson. The crowd moved forward, eager to know what the fat Englishman was about to do next. With a theatrical flourish he found impossible to resist, Doctor Johnson examined the naked blade with one eye closed as if looking for flaws, then satisfied, swirled it to the left and right like a swordsman making a few preliminary parries. Next, he turned his attention to the saddlebags slung over his horse. With a quick and graceful movement he split the nearest bag open. The contents of the saddlebag poured forth like sand. Johnson held out his hand, letting the fine grain run between his fingers. Yellow grain flecked with black. He caught one of the black grains between a thumb and forefinger, and held it up for the crowd to see.

'Your grain is diseased!' he cried. 'There is no witchcraft here. Only a terrible affliction that causes fever and madness in its sufferers. It is this alone that makes your loved ones sick, causing them to see things that aren't really there.'

'He lies!' cried the minister.

'Then ask yourselves this,' Johnson replied. 'How many of you have eaten the bread, or taken the drink made from rye?'

The villagers looked at one another and shook their heads.

'And your loved ones who are sick? How many of them?'

The villagers' expressions turned from confusion to shock. Despite their superstitious dread of the accused, the stranger's logic was undeniable.

'You men,' cried the laird. 'Bring the Widow Beaton down from there. She has suffered enough for today, wouldn't you say?'

Having lost the appetite for murder, the men picked their way gingerly over the still smouldering pyre and unbound Mrs Beaton, then took her body and laid it on the ground. She did not stir. Her face had the waxy pallor of death. One of the women, fickle to the last, let out a keening wail. The laird acted quickly, kneeling before the old woman. He placed his mouth over hers, pinched her nose, and blew the fire of life back into her lungs. The old lady's body twitched, then with a gasp her eyes sprang open to receive the unlovely light of day.

Three Days Later

The men were in the dining room. Doctor Johnson stood with his back to the fire letting the flames warm his rear, while Boswell and the Laird of Raasay sat patiently before him. Boswell looked tired; his cheeks were pale and his eyes sunken, but the last vestiges of fever had passed, as if carried away with the storm. The laird remained motionless, gazing impassively at the flames as he waited for Johnson to begin.

'Your grain was infected with cockspur, a type of fungus which is deadly if consumed in large enough quantities,' said Johnson. 'Rye, being wind-pollinated, is much more prone to cockspur than self-pollinated grains such as wheat or barley; thus the bread, the oatcakes, the whisky and the ale, indeed everything produced from imported rye, becomes infected. Thank God it was discovered in time. One more day would have been fatal.'

'We have you to thank for that, Doctor Johnson,' said Boswell.

'I might have noticed it sooner,' grunted Johnson. 'Only a certain nocturnal visitor convinced me that I, too, was going mad.'

Boswell glanced up, the shadow of some painful memory darkening his expression. 'You saw it too? You saw... *Black Donald*?'

'It was something a little less dramatic than that. The laird mentioned there were no foxes on the island, which is why it took me so long to figure out. Last winter the water between Raasay and Skye froze over, making it solid enough for any small mammal to cross, becoming trapped when the ice thawed. Oh, I am afraid he made rather short work of your chickens, but if you head down towards the bay, I believe you will find a narrow cave among the rocks where fishermen store their oars, and there you will find our little friend.'

'But if the poultry were fed with infected grain,' the laird reasoned. 'Then surely the fox will be dead?'

'Cockspur has a distinctive smell, and your sensible hens ate only the healthy feed. I found black kernels littering the floor of the poultry yard, which pointed me in the right direction. Humans, like cattle, are not so discerning.'

'If that is so,' said Boswell. 'Then how did you come to make the connection in the first place?'

'It came to me in a dream, would you believe? My suspicions were confirmed after a visit to the library, where I discovered that the phenomenon is not without precedent. Numerous accounts of cockspur-induced madness have been recorded throughout the Middle Ages. The *Annales Xantenses*, for instance, report an outbreak in the Rhine Valley as early as 857. It may also have been responsible for the mass hysteria that led to the Salem Witch Trials of 1698. Certainly, there are more than a few similarities between these cases. The ancients called it Saint Anthony's Fire, due to the burning sensation the illness produces, and the fact that the monks of the Order of Saint Anthony were first to recognise and treat the disorder. Symptoms include fever, convulsions, hallucinations, burning sensations in the limbs, and eventually, if not treated properly, madness and death.'

The poor laird, suddenly overcome with emotion, buried his face in his hands. 'Then we are ruined,' he groaned. 'And it is all my fault.'

Johnson patted his back. 'Console yourself, man. You were only doing what you thought was best for your people. And besides, the idea was sound. The good news is you may continue to harvest rye. Only certain precautions must be taken. First of all, the seed must be ploughed at a depth of at least four inches in order to avoid infection.'

'My dear Doctor Johnson,' the laird groaned. 'That is all very well. But as you ought to know already, the soil here is only a few inches deep at best. And we have already reaped the last of the harvest.'

Johnson smiled enigmatically, a magician saving his best trick for last. 'Fortunately,' he said, 'there is another way.'

At a prearranged signal, one of the servants came in with a silver tray covered in a white linen napkin. Johnson whipped away the napkin to reveal a salt cellar, a fork, and a glass of water. He salted the water liberally, then reaching into his pocket, produced a handful of grain and tossed it into the glass. Boswell and the laird leaned forward, watching with keen interest as the only the healthy kernels sank to the bottom. 'As you can see,' said Johnson, 'all you need to do is submerge the grain in a barrel of brine. It is then simply a matter of removing the infected kernels from the surface.' He demonstrated this by picking out the cockspurs with the tines of his fork.

Boswell was ecstatic. 'Bravo Doctor! You have surpassed yourself!'

The laird himself stood up and embraced his guest in a rare access of emotion. 'We are all indebted to you!' he cried.

Just then Lady Raasay, her face flushed with joy, entered the room with little Maireadh in her arms. The girl climbed down like a monkey and flew joyfully into her daddy's arms. The laird lifted his beloved daughter and spun her around.

'Doctor Johnson,' said Lady Raasay, 'We don't know how to thank you. But if there is anything we can do for you, anything at all, you only have to name it...'

'Well there is one thing,' said Johnson, blushing like a schoolboy.

*

The following morning, it was time for Johnson and Boswell

to take their leave of Raasay House. Now that the storm had cleared, the laird selected a seaworthy craft with a reliable guide who would convey them safely to Skye, their next port of call.

The Laird and Lady Raasay provided their esteemed guests with several luxuries for their journey: a knitted scarf and a bottle of brandy for Mr Boswell, and for Doctor Johnson, a brass telescope, a full translation of the Gaelic songs he had requested, plus half a dozen jars of the laird's very own salted cabbage. Johnson picked up one of the jars to scrutinise the label. '*Brassica oleracea doctorjohnsoni*,' he murmured, clucking to himself like a contented hen.

'One more thing,' said Boswell, as they readied to leave. 'What of the Widow Beaton, and the Reverend Campbell?'

'The poor lady is doing as well as can be expected,' Johnson replied. 'The women of the village are tending to her wounds, though it is the unseen scars that take longest to heal, if indeed they heal at all. As for Campbell, he left on yesterday's boat for the mainland, where he will be tried in Edinburgh under the Witchcraft Act of 1735.'

'What will they do with him?'

'The maximum penalty for any person claiming another human being has magical powers or practices witchcraft is one year in prison.'

'I can't say I feel sorry for him,' replied Boswell, 'though perhaps a spell in the Tollbooth will serve to dampen his enthusiasm in future.'

Nodding sagely, Johnson turned to observe Raasay House, and the green hills beyond, and the pier at Inverarish as they receded into the distance, and he smiled to himself.

Raasay would survive the winter.

A Hebridean Odyssey

Part II - The Grey Men of Glamaig

Chapter 1

hat is that mysterious, conical hill up yonder,' said Johnson. 'Wreathed in sullen clouds like a veritable Olympus?'

'She is called Glamaig, the Red Cuillin herself,' said Calum their guide. 'Which means *Greedy Woman* in the English.'

'How did it come by such a curious name?' asked Johnson.

'Och, no one can remember anymore.'

Calum MacLeod had accompanied Johnson, Boswell and their manservant Joseph from Raasay, rowing them over to Skye, where they hoped to investigate some of the island's more colourful myths and legends before tea.

'I should very much like to see it up close,' said Johnson.

'I doubt that you will find anyone who would show you the way,' said Calum. 'Glamaig is home to the *Fear Liath Mor*, the Big Grey Man, though they say it is more phantom than man.'

'And you have seen this apparition?' asked Johnson.

'Not I, sir,' said Calum. 'But I know a man who has, and lived to tell the tale.'

'Then you must introduce us,' said Johnson. 'I would have an account of the experience for my journal.'

'That would be very easy, sir. He frequents the inn where you are lodging tonight.'

The four men rode west along the banks of Loch Sligachan, then turned south through the Sligachan Glen, following a winding river of the same name. They stopped to rest at a spot where the current was not so rapid, but ran cool and clear over smooth pebbles, sparkling like liquid magic. Johnson sat on the bank, pulling off his boots and easing his feet into the icy water.

'Tell me,' he said, turning to their guide. 'Is it fit for human consumption?'

'The Sligachan is said to grant eternal youth to those who drink from her,' explained Calum, stooping to fill his flask a little upstream from Johnson's submerged appendages. 'Mrs MacLeod swears by it, and takes a cup each night before she goes to bed.'

'And yet judging from those washerwomen,' remarked Johnson, indicating with his stick three aged crones washing their linen on the opposite bank, 'either they themselves have not partaken, or else your preposterous claim is naught but a fantastic invention.'

'Bravo, Doctor!' cried Boswell, glowing with admiration. 'Your powers of deduction are remarkable. I stand in awe of your method, by which you sift through the silt of superstition to find the gleaming nuggets of truth within.'

'I assure you, Mr Boswell, that it is merely the application of many years of rigorous scientific discipline, and as natural as breathing; once you have the knack, of course.'

The three crones glared sullenly at the men on the opposite bank, as Johnson doffed his hat.

After they had rested, the company mounted and continued on their way, following the course of the river as it meandered through the glen. Calum lagged behind Joseph and maintained a sullen silence throughout. Boswell and Johnson forged ahead, taking note of the strange geological formations, a unique feature of the island, that rose up around them.

The Isle of Skye was, and still is, a land coloured by tales of fairies, phantasms, fauns, Tom-tumblers, melch-dicks, kitty-witches, hobby-lanthorns, Dick-a-Tuesdays, elf-fires, knockers, old-shocks, ouphs, Tom-pokers, tutgots, tantarrabobs, tod-lowries, bogles, swarths, sprites, giants and other outlandish creatures, and as they watched the morning mist roll down from those curiously-formed peaks it was not difficult to see why.

Finally, they came to a rude dwelling in the village of Broadford which acted as an inn, a last stop for drovers before they ferried their cattle across to the mainland.

After a supper of mutton stew with hunks of fresh bread, Boswell and Johnson were introduced to Fergus MacIvor, the old crofter who claimed to have encountered the *Fear Liath Mhor* on the summit of Glamaig.

'It was terrible, sirs,' said MacIvor, once they had brought him a whisky to loosen his tongue. 'I was coming down from the summit with a barrow of peat for my hearth, when I heard a crunching noise on the gravel behind me. For every few steps I took I heard a crunch, and then another, as if something was coming after me, taking strides five times the length of my own.' MacIvor took another sip of whisky to calm his nerves and continued. 'When I looked back into the mist, I *saw* it. At least twelve feet tall he was, with legs as big as tree trunks, talons like scythes, and grey hair sprouting all over his stinking hide. But the worst of it was the face: the creature's head was shrouded in unearthly light, like a saint from a religious icon. But this was no celestial light, sirs. No, this was diabolical hell-fire! Well I dropped my barrow and ran down the side of the mountain as fast as my legs could carry me. Nothing would induce me to climb Glamaig again for as long as I live. It is eerie up there among the clouds, and there are things that walk the summit that have no right to be amongst the living.'

According to those who knew him, Fergus MacIvor was a reliable man. He was also a devout Christian who had never been known to lie, which made his account of the Grey Man of Glamaig all the more interesting.

'Well Boswell,' said Johnson, once Fergus had taken his leave. 'Now I want to climb that blasted mountain more than ever. What say we rise early and attempt it?'

Chapter 2

When Boswell came down for breakfast Johnson was already at table, leafing through his copy of Ebenezer McFait's *Essays and Observations*. Boswell wondered why his friend chose such a ponderous text for a travelling companion.

'Why sir,' replied Johnson, glancing up. 'If you are to have but one book with you upon a journey, let it be a book of science. When you have read through a book of entertainment, you know it, and it can do no more for you; but a book of science is inexhaustible.'

Boswell sat down beside his friend while the landlady brought them each a hearty breakfast of porridge oats. After they had cleaned their bowls the landlady appeared again with a bottle and set it down on the table. 'Perhaps ye'd like a touch of something stronger t'set ye up for the day ahead?'

Johnson grimaced at the bottle placed before him, and fixing his landlady with a look of mock severity said, 'I am surprised at you, Madam. Alcohol only inflames, confuses and irritates the mind. It is true, as a young man I drank to excess, and suffered as a consequence. But now, in the autumn of my life, I find that abstinence suits my temperament far better.'

'Well I don't know about that, sir. But many a Skye man takes his *morning* as we call it, then touches not a drop more. It sets him up for the rigours of the day.'

Johnson picked up the bottle and squinted at the label.

'It is called Drambuie,' said the landlady. 'The recipe was

given to my grandfather by Bonnie Prince Charlie himself.'

'Indeed?' said Johnson. 'Well perhaps we may have a taste, after all. What's sauce for the goose is sauce for the gander, eh Boswell?'

The landlady poured out a dram for each of her guests. The liquor was brandy-based, infused with cloves and other spices and sweetened with heather honey. Suitably fortified, the two men took leave of the inn with a kind word for their hostess, and made their way to the stables, where Joseph had the ponies made ready.

It was easy enough to find their way back to Glamaig without their guide, following the trail of landmarks Boswell had sketched the previous day. As they trudged across the Sligachan, Glamaig appeared before them, its vast flanks of scree forming a perfect cone of granite. The peak seemed much taller than it had the day before.

'Are you sure you still want to do this, Doctor?' said Boswell.

Johnson was a heavy man already in his sixties, but his youthful spirit rose to any occasion. 'To have come so far and admit defeat? I'd be laughed out of the Literary Club.'

They rode as close as they could to the base of the mountain and left the ponies with Joseph, promising to return before nightfall.

It was a steep ascent, but not so sheer that they would need the rope Joseph had provided. As the two men climbed higher, they entered a thick fog which enveloped them entirely. Unable to continue, they decided to sit it out and open the package Mrs Mackinnon the landlady had provided. Johnson unwrapped a pile of oatcakes and a round of crowdie, a cream cheese made with curdled milk and rennet. 'I could get used to this,' he said, slathering a large chunk of crowdie onto an oatcake with his knife. 'The good woman makes it herself, using a secret ingredient handed down from her grandmother. I rose early this morning to discover what she feeds her cows to give the cheese its distinctive flavour. Alas, like her Drambuie it is a secret she will take with her to the grave, more's the pity. I could have had Mrs Thrale whip me up a batch when we got back to London.'

Once the fog had thinned a little the two men continued on their way. It was a tedious, laborious ascent, and Johnson suffered the worst of it, panting heavily as he dug his staff into the coarse earth, stopping every few hundred yards to catch his breath.

When they finally reached the summit, it became evident that Glamaig was not the perfect cone it appeared to be from the ground, but was joined at the far side to a long ridge of mountains stretching south for miles.

The views were breathtaking. Using the map provided in their guide Boswell was able to identify some of the more prominent features. To the south, the long ridge of mountains called simply The Red Hills appeared like the back of some vast, slumbering dragon. Far to the north across the Sound lay the Isle of Raasay, with the distinctive flat-topped peak of Dun-Caan appearing like a tiny hat in the distance. To the west, across a grassy plain dappled with cloud-shadow, the ragged peaks of the Black Cuillin stood in stark isolation.

The two men sat side by side, their backs to a cairn, drowsy and breathless but glowing with exhilaration. Boswell took a hipflask from his pocket, unscrewed the lid and drank the last of the Laird of Raasay's brandy, grimacing with pleasure as the fiery fluid burned a path to his belly.

'My dear friend,' said Johnson, noticing the urgency with which Boswell drained the last few drops from his flask. 'Perhaps I have been too harsh on you these past few weeks. It has not escaped my notice how much you have suffered since Edinburgh. After all, one who drinks to excess drinks to forget, do they not? And though I may not say it often, you do mean a great deal to me. Might I share some of your burden?'

But Boswell was already fast asleep.

The fog had followed them up the mountainside, its formless tendrils enfolding them in a caress where they lay. So dense was this fog that Johnson could feel its moisture like a cold breath on his face. The very air he breathed was thick and soupy. After a while he started to feel sleepy too, and before long both men had fallen into a deep and dreamless slumber.

Boswell awoke with a start. The sun was inching its way towards the horizon, gilding the pink wisps of cloud that lingered over the Black Cuillin. To the east the sky had begun to darken. The evening star shone as remote and lonely as the summit of Glamaig herself.

Boswell shook his friend awake, and the two men clambered to their feet. They had slept too long. Joseph would be worried. If they didn't leave soon it would be fully dark before they reached base camp.

The summit was eerily quiet. The receding fog presented an impenetrable wall of mist further down the mountain, like a crown of snow-white hair around a bald pate.

Something was moving in the mist.

As the men strained their eyes to see two monstrous figures emerged. They stood on vast legs, these mountain giants, with elongated arms that hung loosely by their sides. Their heads were relatively small, each crowned by a fantastic nimbus of light comprised of concentric circles of glowing, vibrant colour.

Boswell glanced suspiciously at the empty flask still cradled in his hand.

'That is no hallucination brought on by the consumption of alcohol, though I wish it was,' said Johnson, without taking his eyes from the fog monsters, who were observing them with the same intense scrutiny.

'Then what are we to do?' hissed Boswell.

'There is only one thing *to* do in a situation like this, Boswell. RUN!'

Boswell didn't need to be told twice. The two men took to their heels and fled south along the ridge of the mountain, staggering blindly in their flight. The fog creatures kept up easily, taking huge strides on their monstrous legs, crunching the ground with each step of their huge feet. Curiously, they did not appear to be coming any closer, but chose to remain within the fog bank, as if this element alone gave them substance.

As the men increased their speed so too did their pursuers, until Johnson finally stopped, resting the palms of his hands on his knees and panting heavily. 'It's no use,' he gasped between breaths. 'Leave me, Boswell. I can't go on.'

'You must go on!' cried Boswell. 'I won't leave you here at the mercy of these ungodly creatures.'

Johnson risked a glance at the figures several hundred yards further down the slope. One of them appeared to be mimicking him, bending forward with his hands on his knees. After studying the creatures for a few seconds, Johnson's entire frame began to shake.

'Now, Doctor,' said Boswell. 'Do not weep! We must face our fates like gentlemen.'

But Johnson's face was creased with mirth, and his girth was convulsed not with tears, but with laughter. He straightened his back, and did something that took Boswell completely by surprise. He stuck a thumb in each ear and waggled his fingers at the giants, sticking out his tongue like a naughty schoolboy. To Boswell's amazement one of the creatures did the same. Johnson let out a wild cry of triumph, and snatching the hat from his head he waved it in the air, only for his actions to be mimicked again by one of the fog creatures.

'Ah, Boswell, fear will make fools of us all!' cried Johnson. 'Those creatures nearly unmanned me, and yet there is a simple enough explanation, had we the wit to look. Follow me if you dare!' Johnson strode forward, with a reluctant Boswell close behind. As they approached the mist the creatures seemed to evaporate into thin air. 'See, Boswell? They are only shadows after all!'

Boswell struggled to keep up with his friend. 'But shadows that stand vertically twelve feet tall, with glowing lights on their heads?'

'Aye, it is a singular phenomenon, I'll grant you, but let's get ourselves safely down the mountain first, and I'll explain later. Joseph must be frantic with worry.'

They were not out of the dark yet. It was a torturous descent, and the mountainside presented many hidden dangers, the threat of a landslide not the least of them. Halfway down, Johnson lost his friend in the mist and had to locate him by sound alone. After that, they found that Joseph's rope came in handy after all, and used it to tether themselves together.

Chapter 3

Joseph wept openly when he saw the two men staggering down the mountain and ran to embrace them, a gesture which they found both touching and vaguely uncomfortable. Happy to be reunited, the three travellers climbed onto their ponies and began the long trek back to the inn. Though Boswell had a thousand nagging questions, Johnson remained tight-lipped, preserving his thoughts until he was comfortably ensconced, and could hold forth in his own inimitable style.

When finally the three men were seated round the table with a supper of cold ham and a tot of Drambuie before them, Johnson was ready to begin.

'Ebenezer MacFait mentions the Grey Man in this book, under a chapter entitled *Some Phaenomena Observable in Foggy Weather.*' Johnson placed his well-thumbed copy on the table. 'But the phenomenon was previously recorded in 1735 by French scientist Pierre Bouguer, who witnessed it first-hand while exploring the Periuvial Andes. Put quite simply, when the sun is at a certain angle behind the subject, it casts a shadow vertically against a fog bank. It only occurs at dawn or dusk, when the angle of the sun is in a direct line with the slope of the mountain. The figure appears gigantic, because there is no frame of reference in the fog.'

'I see,' said Boswell. 'But how do you explain the corona of light which appeared around the creature's head?'

'I am glad you asked that,' said Johnson. 'Have you ever

observed a rainbow?'

'Of course I have.'

'Well it follows the same basic principle. Rings of coloured light appear when the sun's rays illuminate a cloud of water droplets, creating the eerie halo effect, often referred to as the *glory,* which so unnerved us on the mountain. To quote MacFait: *All shadows converge towards the anti-solar point, where the glory also shines.'*

'And yet I *heard* those creatures,' argued Boswell. 'Or at least, I heard their footsteps. The last I heard, shadows have no material substance with which to affect the world around them.'

'Quite right, Boswell, and I must confess, the phenomenon threw me at first. But you will have observed that the summit of Glamaig is littered with countless broken shards of rock?'

'Yes. But what of it, Doctor?'

'As fog thickens and thins,' explained Johnson, 'the temperature fluctuates, and rocks expand and contract, causing them to shatter. When this happens on a slope, the smaller pieces of rock will tumble. These actions are, in fact, entirely responsible for the scree of which Glamaig consists. Even on a calm day, rocks will shatter and slide down the mountainside, which may account for the sounds we perceived, in our heightened state of alarm, as footsteps.'

'Remarkable, Doctor. But how do you account for MacIvor's lurid description of the Grey Man's physical appearance, the fur and the claws, where we saw only formless shadows?'

Johnson forked the last piece of cold ham into his mouth and chewed thoughtfully. 'Who knows what the mind, alone in lonely places, can create out of nowhere,' he said, wiping his mouth with his napkin. 'Illusions and hallucinations may be brought on by isolation, or from sheer exhaustion alone; indeed, the wind itself may whisper strange things to a man, when alone on the high places of the Earth. All that was needed was the phenomenon of the Grey Man, remarkable enough in itself, for MacIvor to fill in the details with his own vivid imagination.

Shadows, it would seem, are as a blank canvas to the suggestible mind.'

'Well I must congratulate you, Doctor Johnson. Your logic is watertight,' said Boswell. 'Truly, your mind is a lantern, dispelling the gloom of ignorance wherever you go.'

'And yet,' said Johnson with feeling, 'there were moments up there, Boswell, when I felt a closeness to some ineffable presence, a mystery far greater than ourselves, which inspired in me the profoundest sense of reverence and awe.'

'Quite so, Doctor Johnson,' replied Boswell. 'It is not for nothing that Scotland is known as *God's own country.*'

'Well I wouldn't quite go that far,' said Johnson. Then turning to the landlady he said, 'Madam. Would you be so kind as to bring me some of your delicious crowdie? And heavens to goodness, don't scrimp on the oatcakes this time!'

A Hebridean Odyssey

Part III - The Bird-Men of St Kilda

Dunvegan Castle, Isle of Skye, 19th September 1773

e arrived at Dunvegan in the midst of a thunderstorm, and were greatly relieved to find the Laird and his family at home. After drying our wet clothes we were ushered into the main hall to a rapturous reception.

Such were the delights of Sir Norman MacLeod of MacLeod's table, that we were in danger of never leaving, until a chance opportunity arose, and with it that indomitable spirit that leads men onwards to folly or to glory, whichever the whims of fate decide.

Sir Norman's realm is substantial, encompassing the isles of Harris, Lewis, Skye and St Kilda, this last being the remotest of the Western Isles, situated some forty miles west of the most westerly outpost of the Outer Hebrides.

Over dinner, Sir Norman shared some noteworthy anecdotes

concerning the inhabitants of that remote island, who rarely venture beyond the confines of their sea-girt fortress unless strictly necessary.

The Laird himself the St Kildans consider a great Lord, and his family seat at Dunvegan an Imperial Court of inestimable grandeur. The exploits of former Lairds and Stewards they recount with all the enthusiasm of historians reflecting on the heroic deeds of Alexander the Great or some other semi-mythical figure.

Only last year, a St Kildan's maiden voyage to the Isle of Skye caused quite a stir, his peculiar behaviour even attracting attention from a local newspaper, who cheerfully reported his antics in a daily column, much to the delight of the local populace. This simple-hearted soul considered everyday items such as windows and looking-glasses the devil's trinkets, whereas the simple act of riding a horse he considered a tremendous source of wonder and novelty. When some friends took the visitor up a mountain to show him which islands belonged to the Laird, he lifted his eyes and hands to heaven and exclaimed in a tremulous voice: O mighty prince, who art master of such vast territories! giving his companions much cause for amusement.

The poor fellow even attempted to take a tree back with him to show his fellow St Kildans, that island being bereft of arboreal ornament, but was put off by the difficulties involved in getting the thing onto his little boat.

The ladies of our company laughed with delight over such naïveté, until Doctor Johnson reminded them of their Scripture, which tells us: "Unless ye be converted and become as little children, ye shall never enter the kingdom of heaven," (a message that today's generation, with all of its subtlety and cleverness, would be wise to remember). I found myself envying the St Kildans their purity of heart and childlike sense of wonder, untainted by the stain of ambition or pride.

According to our host, the last missionary to stay on St Kilda for any significant length of time died in 1745, and though he was much revered on the island, since his passing, rumour had it the natives had reverted to their former ways.

THE STONE OF DESTINY

A young minister in our company by the name of John Ferguson, recently returned from missionary work in Africa, expressed an interest in taking up residency there as soon as possible, in order to restore the Light of the Gospel to their hearts.

When Doctor Johnson mentioned that he was very desirous to see St Kilda for himself, Sir Norman kindly arranged for us to travel over with the minister on the first available boat.

From *The Casebook of Johnson and Boswell*

Chapter 1

*Y*ou'll have your work cut out for you, of course,' said Sir Norman. 'They are a hospitable folk to be sure, but resistant to change. The last attempt to civilise St Kilda ended in disaster, when a missionary named MacKenzie brought with him more than the Gospel. Influenza wiped out the entire elderly population in a matter of days. The islanders have been deeply suspicious of incomers ever since, and guard their privacy jealously.'

'There are some who say they still practice heathenish ceremonies out there,' said one lady from Harris, whose brother had recently married a St Kildan, 'and murder their old ones as a means of preserving food supplies.'

Sir Norman tutted and shook his head. 'I have heard this rumour too, but I do not believe it. These folk may have their difficulties, with little use for the gospel as we commonly understand it, but I am unwilling to believe they are like those Druidic pagans of old, to treat their elders with such barbarity.'

Johnson had been listening to this latest discussion with great interest. 'And yet the practice is not without precedent, Sir Norman. On the island of Sardinia for example, men over seventy were sacrificed by their sons to the titan Cronus. In Rome they used to throw their elder citizens from a bridge, and in Sweden they were thrown from a cliff. The Heruli, a Germanic tribe from the fifth century, would place their sick and elderly on a tall stack of wood and stab them to death before setting the pyre alight, whereas the Japanese carried anyone over sixty up a mountain or some other remote place and left them to die.'

'Then we must be grateful that we do not live in feudal Japan, Doctor,' said Sir Norman, paying sly homage to his guest, 'or we might have been denied some crown jewels of English literature.'

'Indeed,' agreed the minister. 'A grey head is a crown of glory, if it be found in the way of righteousness.'[8]

'Amen to that,' said Doctor Johnson.

---

8   Proverbs 16:31

The Atlantic Ocean, 20th September, 1773

We set sail this morning with a gentle breeze bearing us westwards. Doctor Johnson has been charged with the unenviable task of investigating rumours of senicide, and has been "deputised" by the Laird for the duration of our stay. Mr Ferguson particularly is full of high hopes for the expedition, and I myself am not unmoved at the prospect of viewing this last and furthest bastion of Caledonia, and to meet the inhabitants of whom I have heard so much.

From *The Casebook of Johnson and Boswell*

The waves pounded the little boat mercilessly, throwing surf into the air, buffeting the passengers dangerously from side to side. Doctor Johnson stood at the prow as the craft pitched and yawed, entirely in his element. 'Bracing, is it not, Mr Boswell?' he cried, then roared with laughter as Boswell clutched the side of the boat and launched his breakfast into the brine. Mr Ferguson, his face a ghastly pale, clutched his crucifix and muttered the Lord's Prayer, his voice lost amidst the pounding of the waves. Even Joseph seemed nervous, whilst the captain did his level best to navigate the fragile vessel through the tempest.

'Get down, man,' cried Boswell. 'You'll drown us all!'

He was not wrong. Such was the weight of the redoubtable Doctor that the boat was leaning dangerously in his favour, threatening to capsize at any moment.

'I believe he is right, Doctor Johnson,' said Mr Ferguson, in a vain attempt to disguise the faltering note of fear in his voice. 'Please calm yourself.'

Johnson had a fanatical look in his eye, as one who scorns death, but when he realised he was putting his friends at risk he did as he was told.

The brooding, slate grey sky matched the tumultuous sea, and with the air so full of spray Boswell could no longer tell which was up and which down. As he leaned over the side and vomited again, he wished a wave would sweep him overboard and put an end to his misery once and for all.

At long last the purple smudge of an island appeared in the middle distance, which seemed at one moment to sink beneath the prow, then swing into view high above them, as the boat pitched and yawed on the North Atlantic rollers.

'Brace yourselves, gentlemen,' cried the captain. A monstrous wave came out of nowhere, gaining momentum until it towered above them, blocking out what little light was left. Boswell wondered if his prayers had been answered, instantly regretting putting the lives of his friends at risk.

Time stood still in the shadow of that immensity, and at last Boswell understood what it means to have your life flash before your eyes.

The wall of water came crashing down, but the boat did not capsize. Boswell clasped his hands together and, on his knees, thanked the Lord for ignoring his first selfish prayer.

The wave had thrown them dangerously close to the rocks, where the vision of a hulking black shape emerged through the pouring rain. Perched on the edge of a natural jetty, the big seabird spread his oil black, cherub's wings and preened himself with a beak shaped like a cobbler's anvil, calmly indifferent to the breakers that crashed around his webbed feet.

The captain looked fearful. 'It is one of Simon's familiars,' he cried. 'Employed to set a storm against the man who has come to supplant him.'

Doctor Johnson smiled at the notion. 'Who is this Simon,' he said, 'that can control the weather and the fowl of the earth?'

'His name is Simon MacCodrum of North Uist, though they

call him Simon the Magus here.'

As they neared the harbour a group of locals ran onto the jetty to greet the new arrivals, chattering excitedly among themselves. The women nudged one another like children, shyly hiding their faces with their shawls, while the men steadied the boat with wooden poles to prevent it from being smashed against the rocks, then threw ropes onto the deck. The visitors' portmanteaus were passed up to the men and duly carried on their shoulders to the village, where lodgings were hastily prepared.

'Tell me,' said Johnson as he disembarked. 'Is there an inn where we can we eat? I haven't had a bite since breakfast.'

'It is forbidden to eat on Fridays, sir,' said the boldest of the islanders. 'But breakfast will be provided on the morn.'

'On whose authority?' Johnson demanded.

'On the authority of Simon the Magus,' replied the man.

'I am beginning to take an aversion to this Simon,' said Johnson. 'Please take me to him.'

The islanders looked from one to the other, until the first to speak said quietly, 'Excuse me, sir, but one does not choose to see the Magus. The Magus chooses to see you.'

'Very well,' said Johnson. 'I am too tired to argue. Take us to our lodgings, please. Maybe I'll be in better humour by the morning.'

The village consisted of a single row of cottages halfway up a slope, overlooked by a grassy ridge of some prominence, which followed the semi-circular shape of the bay. Behind the curved strip of cottages the crumbled ruins of older settlements were organised in similar semi-concentric patterns, like strata of rock or the rings of a tree, so that the whole bay gave the impression of a vast, ruined amphitheatre looking out to sea.

Mrs Collins, a stout woman with a broad, weather-beaten face, high cheekbones, deep set eyes and arms like hams picked up the rest of the luggage and showed the guests to their lodgings, a low-built house fashioned in the same style as its neighbours, having a thatched roof weighted down with rocks and plainly furnished inside with a table, a few chairs and simple beds of straw.

Mr Ferguson asked the woman about the curious edict which prevented the villagers from dining on a Friday.

'Simon takes care of all our needs, both spiritual and temporal,' said Mrs Collins matter-of-factly.

'And where was this Simon ordained?' asked Mr Ferguson. 'The Scriptures say nothing about fasting on a Friday.'

'He?' cried Mrs Collins, 'Ordained? The Magus receives his orders directly from St Columba, with whom he converses regularly.'

John Ferguson was astonished, but refrained from questioning the woman further, as from her countenance it could be seen she would brook no argument.

The men bedded down on their mattresses of straw, which were dry at least, if not particularly comfortable. All slept soundly except for Boswell, who was disturbed by Johnson's snoring. Every so often the older man would splutter some imprecation about *whiggish imbeciles* or *canting apostates*, and in the throes of one particularly vivid dream he cried, 'Nay, Madame, the King of Prussia does not play billiards on a Tuesday!' by which point Boswell had had enough, and pulled on his breeches to take the night air.

The moon hung low in the bay, its silvery edges softened by diaphanous wisps of cloud, reflecting its broken image on the wine-dark water. The air was warm and balmy, the horseshoe bay protected by two great hills, *Oiseval* to the north-east and *Ruaival* to the south-west. Boswell was just about to step back in when his attention was diverted by a torch-bearing procession on the beach, coming from the direction of the harbour. In the moonlight they appeared almost as ghosts, wearing only white gowns, each girl no older than seventeen, treading lightly across the shingle on slender feet. Boswell wrestled with an urge to walk down the slope to join them. He watched the dancing lights cross the beach, then disappear in snake-like formation up

the side of the hill at the far end of the bay where a stream fed
into the ocean.

*

True to the villager's word, the next morning Johnson, Boswell,
Joseph and Reverend Ferguson arose with the first light of dawn
to find the table overflowing with the bounty of the island.
Bread, butter, cheese, eggs and some kind of roasted fowl called
guga, which was an acquired taste due to its excessive oily
richness. After they had eaten their fill the party of four went
out to explore the island.

The storm had passed over in the night, revealing a clear blue
sky with only a few scattered clouds overhead. They made their
way up the side of the hill, approaching the high ridge from the
west, following the path of the strange procession Boswell had
watched the night before.

From the highest point the entirety of the island was visible.
Apart from their horseshoe bay to the south-east, the island was
naturally fenced with one continuous high face of rock. The
unexplored side of the island sloped down towards a smaller
bay on the north-west, inaccessible by sea, with here and there a
ruined crofthouse or solitary sheep scattered along the way.

The surrounding expanse of ocean stretched unbroken in
all directions; except for the uninhabited sister-islands of Soay
and Boreray, which were little more than turf-capped rocks, the
island on which they stood, Hirta, being the largest island of the
St Kilda triangle, was completely isolated.

As the men took in this melancholy prospect, up popped a
head from behind a rock a little further along the high ridge.

'Ahoy there!' cried the head's owner, emerging from his hiding
place. He was a fat, red-faced little gentleman in a threadbare
frockcoat, his breeches yellow from excessive kneeling.
'Delighted to see you! It is not often we receive visitors to our
desolate outpost.' The stranger came trotting towards them

and introduced himself as Sir Charles Braithwaite, a visiting naturalist. He was amazed to find among his new acquaintances the world-famous Doctor Johnson and his companion Boswell.

'It is a privilege, sirs, a huge honour!' he cried, shaking their hands with genuine enthusiasm. The eccentric little man explained he was making a study of the various flora and fauna of the island, then as if to prove his credentials, he produced a pocketbook filled with sketches. 'See here?' he said, pointing to a perky-tailed little bird represented with some skill. '*Troglodytes troglodytes hirtensis*, the St Kilda wren, a subspecies of the Eurasian wren, and this one—'

'What about this one?' interrupted Johnson, pointing to a black seabird with a ridged, horn-like beak, a kind of prehistoric penguin in charcoal.

'Ah,' said Braithwaite, 'that is *Pinguinus impennis*, the Great Auk.'

'That is the bird we saw as we sailed into the harbour, is it not, Boswell?' said Johnson.

'Yes,' said Boswell. 'It does bear a striking resemblance.'

'Then you were most fortunate,' said Sir Charles Braithwaite. 'The islanders consider the Great Auk a rare delicacy, and have hunted them down to a single living pair. Simon has forbidden anyone from harming them on pain of death. We have that to thank him for, at least.'

'And there's that confounded name again,' said Johnson. 'Tell me, Sir Charles, who is this Simon, that has power of life or death over the islanders?'

'There is very little to tell,' said Sir Charles with a shrug of indifference. 'I keep myself to myself for the most part, and try not to get involved in local affairs. Simon MacCodrum, the one they call the Magus, has some queer ideas. He's a holy man. Belongs to an obscure priestly order called the Culdee, they say. Claims to receive messages from Saint Columba, no less! The islanders would lay down their lives for him, if it came to it, and he rules over them like a little God. No, I steer clear of politics and religion altogether, for the two are entwined, are they not? The birds are my only friends, Doctor Johnson. The birds, and my solitude.'

'If what you are saying is true,' Ferguson exclaimed, 'then this Simon is no more than a common charlatan, and I consider it my sacred duty to remove these poor misguided islanders from his influence.'

'Then I wish you good luck, sir,' said the naturalist with perfect sincerity. 'But now you must excuse me. The locals have very kindly agreed to row me over to Soay this morning to observe some puffin colonies. Have you ever seen a puffin, Doctor Johnson?'

'No sir, I can't say that I have.'

'*Fratercula arctica,* named for his little black hood, which reminds one of a monk's cowl. Totally monogamous, you know, like the swan. If only we humans were as loyal! That reminds me—are you familiar with an old folk tale called The Children of Lir? No? A wicked stepmother, jealous of the love her husband the king bears for his children, transforms them into swans, and is banished when she refuses to reverse the spell. Alas, the poor children are fated to live out the rest of their lives as swans. All that remains of their old selves is their beautiful singing voices, which folk come from miles around to hear.

'For five hundred years the Children of Lir migrate from lake to lake with the passing of the seasons, until finally they find their way to the ocean. The winter winds blow cold, and the elder sister shelters her two younger siblings under her protective wing. Then one day they hear the distant ringing of a bell—one of the first Christian bells in all of Ireland—and the swans follow the sound, knowing that the end of their curse is near. Saint Patrick comes to lay his hands on the Children of Lir, transforming them back into their human forms. Alas! They are now very old, and soon die of their infirmities: but not before Saint Patrick has baptised them. It is a very poignant tale, except that when Simon the Magus tells it he substitutes

Saint Patrick for Saint Columba and swans for black seabirds, such as cormorants or auks. It's why the islanders won't kill them anymore. They see them as the Children of Lir.'

'It certainly is a poetical tale,' said Johnson.

'This island is rich with such lore. I'm something of a folklorist, you see. I have been collecting stories from the islanders in the hope of one day compiling a book.'

'A capital idea!' proclaimed Johnson. 'I would enjoy reading some of the transcripts.'

'If you are interested,' said Sir Charles, 'then please do come for lunch when I get back. There's my house down there, on the eastern side of the island between those two hills. It's the only house with glass windows, you can't miss it.'

The men watched Sir Charles Braithwaite trot down the slope towards the harbour, hopping from point to point like one of those little puffins he loved so much. He seemed like an anachronism—a curious oddity whose personality contrasted sharply with the dour, weather-beaten faces and sullen expressions of the locals.

Hirta, St Kilda, 22nd September, 1773

The isle of Hirta, a rolling expanse of turf whose highest point towers some 1,411 feet above sea level, braves the cold North Atlantic with only her two little sisters Soay and Boreray for company. I fancy a giant has carved her from the mainland, towed her into the middle of the ocean and left her there, only for another passing giant to come along and press his thumbs down on opposite ends to create the south-eastern bay and north-western bay respectively.

Those hardy souls brave enough or stupid enough to make a life for themselves here have sacrificed luxuries the rest of the nation take for granted. Milk and meat are not to be relied on. The sheep of St Kilda are small and provide little of either, and what few crops grow depend on the vagaries of the weather. Fish, surprisingly for a community who make a living from the sea, are also hard come by, owing to heavy seas and unpredictable weather.

The St Kildans' primary source of sustenance is the seabird. Fulmars mainly—gull-like birds who nest comfortably along the cliff-ledges—but anything the natives can ensnare or entrap in their nets will do, and like primitive cultures the world over, that which they hunt they also revere, if the little clay idols placed in their window are anything to judge by.

Defying strong winds and crashing waves, the bird-man of St Kilda dangles precipitously from the cliff edge. His fellows support him from above, grasping both ends of a rope, the middle of which is looped around the bird-man's waist. In his hand is a stick with a noose attached, which he uses to snatch young fulmars from their holes.

The bird-man works barefoot. His prehensile toes grip the

narrow ledge as he scurries about the cliff face like a spider. He must be fearless. The fulmar, when frightened or threatened, ejects an astringent oil from its beak, and any man thus surprised is liable to lose his grip and fall eighty feet to the razor-sharp rocks below.

From *The Casebook of Johnson and Boswell*

Chapter 2

*J*ohnson and Boswell stood as close to the cliff edge as they dared, leaning over to watch the men at work. Afterwards, one of the bird-men shyly approached the visitors and introduced himself as MacPhee. He had quick, agile fingers and his eyes sparkled with a natural intelligence. He brought out some of his catch to show Johnson. These, he explained, were the very last of the colony: birds too old or weak to make the flight south for the winter.

In spring the young men would leap from the cliffs and swim to nearby Soay to gather the first eggs of the year. It was a dangerous business, MacPhee explained, but the first man back would be crowned King-for-the-Day, having proven his virility and worth to his kinsfolk.

Johnson asked MacPhee what he would do with the birds he caught.

'No part of her is wasted,' said the bird-man. 'The meat is stored in cleats to sustain us during the cold winter months, and the feathers are used as stuffing for our pillows. The oil from their bellies we use for medicine and lamp fuel and from the whole skin we can fashion a shoe which lasts for several weeks.'

MacPhee had a good grasp of English and was, unlike the majority of the islanders, talkative and friendly, having been born on Lewis and schooled in Inverness. He led the visitors a little further along the high coastal cliff to show them how they preserved the meat. The cleits themselves were little houses of loosely stacked stone with turf roofs, chest-high and shaped like beehives, as if a fairy village had sprung wholesale from the ground. MacPhee explained that the stones were stacked loosely to allow the cold sea winds to pass through, chilling and preserving the meat within. Johnson poked his head through the entrance to one of the cleits. The smell of rotting flesh was so overpowering that he took a step back. MacPhee shook his head sadly, explaining that it was an imperfect science, and the meat often spoiled from damp weather.

A derelict shepherd's bothy, not much bigger than a cleit itself, contained signs of human habitation, though whoever had braved a life there had long since departed. Boswell poked his head inside. A name had been scratched on the inner wall of the lintel stone, with a series of little scratches or tallies where someone had marked the passage of time. It was a lonely place, with the cold wind whistling through the holes in the wall, and a damp earth floor with scatterings of straw a poor substitute for a bed.

Boswell read the name aloud. *Rachel Chiesley.*

'I wonder who that was,' said Ferguson.

'I think I know,' said Johnson, removing his hat and lowering his head. 'This was the home of Lady Grange.'

'Of course,' said Boswell.

'Who was Lady Grange?' asked Ferguson.

'It happened before your time, Mr Ferguson,' said Johnson. 'It is a singularly sad and tragic tale. Lord Grange was a lawyer and Jacobite sympathiser. He was also fiercely opposed to the witchcraft act of 1734, which may tell you something of his character. His wife Rachel was a spirited woman, to put it mildly. She was prone to wild fits of violent jealousy, and not averse to causing public scenes, which caused her husband no end of embarrassment. Suspecting him of having an affair (which he probably was), Lady Grange took the liberty of raking through her husband's personal effects, where she found something altogether more damning than any love letter—evidence suggesting that her husband was part of a Jacobite conspiracy to overthrow the monarchy.

'From that point on, the unfortunate woman's behaviour became increasingly erratic. She threatened to take the letter to the authorities, foolish woman, claiming it was evidence of treason. She followed her husband through the streets of Edinburgh and waited for him outside taverns and gentlemen's clubs, crying out the most scandalous accusations and threatening to expose him. Clearly something had to be done about Lady Grange, who was fast becoming a liability. There was more than Lord Grange's reputation at stake. The letter implicated some very high ranking persons, not least of them his friend Simon Fraser, Lord Lovat, whom you may recall as the "Old Fox of the Forty-Five". On Lovat's orders, and with the consent of her husband, Lady Grange was abducted from her home on the night of January 22nd, 1732. She was taken to a number of secret locations around the western isles, before being deposited here on St Kilda in 1734, where she remained in isolation for the next six years. Finally, Lady Grange was removed in the night, and imprisoned in several other secret locations, blown this way and that like a leaf on the wind. No one knows exactly where she was taken after she left here, though it was rumoured she died and was buried on the Isle of Skye in 1745.'

'Begging your pardon, sir, but you are right on every detail apart from one,' said MacPhee. 'The good Lady never left St Kilda, but was murdered here on the very night you claim she was taken.'

'Nonsense, man,' snorted Johnson. 'What proof do you have?'

'The proof of my own eyes, sir. I was a lad of fifteen at the time. She fascinated me, you see, and I suppose I thought myself a little in love. Every night I could see her from my window as she walked the beach in nothing but her nightgown, crying at the moon and tearing her hair. She was always drunk, and seemed like such a tragic figure, like a beautiful butterfly trapped in a glass, or a white moth knocking itself blindly against an oil lamp. Then one night, six men came in their longboat. The bay was quiet and the water still as they sailed into harbour. They called to her that it was time for her to go home to her husband, that he was asking for her. She ran into the surf weeping for joy and clung to their legs, still weeping and laughing. Then to my horror, one of the men grabbed her by the hair and held her head under the water. She thrashed around for a while, then stopped moving. I was filled with rage and remorse. But what could I do? I was a fifteen-year-old boy at the time, and there were six of them. If they knew what I had seen them do, they would have killed me too. It was a terrible, sinful thing, and to this day I am unable to remove it from my memory.'

Doctor Johnson looked gravely at MacPhee. 'And you have told no one of this?'

'No one, sir,' replied MacPhee. 'You are the first.'

'It is a sorry tale,' said Doctor Johnson, slowly shaking his head. 'She never stopped loving her husband, and to betray her so cruelly seems wicked beyond belief.'

The men walked back down the hillside in respectful silence, leaving MacPhee to his cleits. As they neared the village, they passed a group of young girls leading their flocks back up into the hills. Some of their faces Boswell recognised from the night before. He decided to ask Mrs Collins about it when next he saw her.

The opportunity arose that evening, when Mrs Collins dropped by with some home comforts for her guests.

The men were all sitting round the table playing cards as Mrs Collins bustled around the living space, placing the wildflowers she had brought by the window and straightening out their beds.

'I saw something the other night,' said Boswell, casually raising the subject with the landlady. 'A candlelit procession walking along the beach before disappearing into the hills.'

Mrs Collins seemed to stiffen as she fluffed up the fulmar-down pillows. She answered her tenant without turning. 'They were going to the home of the Magus, to receive instruction in prayer.'

'What are they praying for?'

Mrs Collins stopped what she was doing and turned to face the men. 'To be with child, of course. Each girl receives a special prayer from the Magus which must be spoken by the light of the full moon, in order to receive the divine seed.'

'What blasphemous nonsense is this?' blurted Johnson.

I think it more likely that this Simon the Magus is deflowering the maidens himself,' said Boswell. 'There certainly seems to be an abundance of red-headed, green-eyed children running around the place.'

'You should not mock the Magus,' snapped Mrs Collins. 'If you knew Simon as we do, you would not speak so disparagingly of him.'

'But what has this Simon done for you,' said Johnson, 'that you hold him in such reverence?'

'Take a look around you, Doctor. Five years ago, before He came, a great pestilence was on this land. The people were starving, or dying from the smallpox. The fish floated belly up on the loch, a murrain took away our sheep and cattle, and our women were barren. All that has changed, now. The sheep bleat on the pasture, the fish multiply in the sea, and our womenfolk are fertile, all thanks to Him.'

'Impossible!' cried Johnson.

'No, not impossible! But you will see for yourself, Doctor Johnson. You have arrived at a very fortuitous time on this island; a time of transition, when the sun leaves the constellation of Virgo, goddess of the harvest, and crosses into the constellation of Libra, representing the balance of the seasons. After a night of revelry, during which time we feast and enjoy the bounty of the island, we go to the sacred place to prepare for our ascension. The equinox represents the end of our summer, a time of change, when the year falls into decline. It is only fitting, therefore, that the elders, during the last rites of our festivities, make ready for their ascension. I, too, am privileged, Doctor. For soon I will ascend to heaven in the arms of *Colmcille*!'

The men were all staring at Mrs Collins, who was standing in the middle of the floor, her face radiant and shining. Ferguson was incensed. 'You mean you actually have a *feast* on the sabbath?'

'And why not? Tomorrow marks the Autumn Equinox, when day is as long as night, and the last harvest is gathered in for the coming winter. What better time to enjoy the fruits of our labour?'

'Mrs Collins,' protested Ferguson. 'How can you reconcile such pagan ritual with the teachings of our Lord?'

'*Tut tut*, Mr Ferguson. We are God fearing folk, just as you are, but you have your ways and we have ours. Perhaps you will never understand. But you are welcome to join us all the same.'

'Madam. The only celebration in which I will be indulging,' said the minister, 'is the word of the Lord, through the reading of his works and quiet contemplation.'

'Suit yourself then,' said Mrs Collins with a shrug, and after dusting the mantelpiece and placing on it a small figurine from her pocket, she left the men to their thoughts.

'A true fanatic,' Boswell remarked once Mrs Collins had closed the door behind her, 'if ever there was one.'

'If what the woman is saying is true, then I fear the rumours of senicide are not entirely baseless,' said Johnson, examining the idol on the mantelpiece with a grimace of distaste.

'But she is mad, surely,' said Ferguson.

Johnson's reply was sobering. 'And yet how many people over the age of seventy have you seen on the island?'

*

Boswell arose before the dawn and made his way down to the beach for an early morning walk. His spirits were at a low ebb. With not a drop of alcohol to be found on the island, he was beginning to suffer the effects of withdrawal, and had gone out for some fresh air to clear his head and put some vigour back into his atrophied limbs. Starting at the harbour, he crossed the half mile stretch of shingle to the rocky southern arm of the bay, where he passed an agreeable hour clambering among rockpools in search of crabs, shells and other trinkets washed up from the deep, a pastime which evoked a warm rush of nostalgia.

As he was engaged in this agreeable diversion a thick mist rolled in from the sea. Boswell fancied he was exploring the surface of the moon, with the familiar sight of the harbour and village lost in a shroud of grey, the only sound the bobbing waves as they lapped against the rocks around his feet, making a curious *gulp gulp* sound.

So absorbed was Boswell that he hardly noticed the tide come in, filling the hollows, forming islands and new continents from the rocky outcrop. Fearing he would be stranded, Boswell hopped awkwardly from boulder to boulder and finally back onto the shingle.

As he headed towards the harbour the ghastly stench of rotting fish filled his nostrils, and he was seized by an overwhelming urge to look round. A hunched black figure stood in the place where Boswell had been standing only moments before. Its shape reminded him of the great auk they had seen from the boat. At first glance it could almost have been an old sea groyne or wood piling, half rotted away and covered over with seaweed. Then it started to move. Its legs seemed proportionally shorter than its body, causing it to waddle as it walked. Rather than producing a comical effect, the lurching movement overwhelmed Boswell with a paralysing terror.

He turned back towards the pier and forced himself to move. The *scrunch scrunch* of his feet on the shingle was accompanied by a curious *dragging* sound coming from behind. After several yards he turned again. The creature was closer this time, halfway between Boswell and its original position. All the while the rancid smell of rotting fish grew stronger. As the creature drew closer Boswell could see it was too tall for a great auk, and much nearer the size of a man, its shuffling gait causing it to sway hypnotically from side to side. For a moment, Boswell had the absurd impression that he was being followed by two dwarves, one upon the other's shoulders, doing an impression of a tall man, a black coat with empty sleeves thrown over them to maintain the illusion. It was a trick he saw once performed in a London theatre. But on this isolated, sullen stretch of beach, there was nothing funny about the absurdity that stalked him. It seemed an otherworldly entity, resembling simultaneously a great black bird and a cloaked person. Its head, too, was irregular, being joined to the shoulders with no discernible neck, and Boswell thought he could see a grotesque nose projecting from the middle of its face. Though the thing was as black and insubstantial as shadow, it carried with it an aura of disease and corruption.

It was moving quickly now, its tattered cloak flapping in the wind, trying to catch Boswell before he reached the stairs to the harbour. Boswell tore his eyes from the approaching grotesque and made for the pier as fast as his legs would carry him. He could hear the thing's flapping feet dragging along the shingle just behind him as he reached the stairs. Boswell felt only terror, convinced that if the creature caught him something terrible would happen. Finally his feet found the first step and he scurried up the stairs, nearly slipping on the seaweed. He expected any moment for a black, webbed claw or razor-sharp beak to snatch at his ankle. When he reached the pier, Boswell finally gained the courage to look down.

He could only see the depression of his own footprints in the shingle. The thing was gone, with no trace of it having existed.

Chapter 3

There was no sight sadder in all the world, to Mr Ferguson, than that of an abandoned church. It represented something altogether more sinister than the heathen villages he saw in Africa. Those people were as unsophisticated as babes in the eyes of the Lord, ready for their eyes to be opened by the Light of the Gospel. A neglected church, on the other hand, signified that a people had already closed their eyes to the Lord. They had seen the Light and rejected it, clawing their way back to darkness like crabs scuttling under a rock.

Mr Ferguson approached the ruin of St Margaret's Chapel, a forlorn-looking structure that lay hidden in a grassy hollow behind the harbour, surrounded by rows of uncared-for gravestones. He pushed open a rotted door that crumbled and flaked in his hands and stepped inside. A flock of pigeons fluttered up through a hole in the roof. Mr Ferguson looked sadly at the pews caked in bird droppings, and wondered if God, too, abandoned his neglected churches. And if He did, what things unseen by His eye scuttled in to seek shelter from the elements?

A shard of light came in through the hole in the roof and rested on a dreadful figure propped against the pulpit. It was a grotesque thing. A woven man of straw caked in bird droppings, onto which a layer of feathers had come to rest and become stuck. Ferguson stepped up to the pulpit and carried it from the church, grimacing with distaste.

He brought the mannequin to the middle of the dirt road, where a handful of curious villagers gathered round to see what he would do next. The minister emerged from his lodgings moments later with a flint and set the thing alight. His face shone yellow in the reflected glow of the flames. He looked up at the sharp, pinched faces of the villagers, and for a moment was reminded of mean, spiteful children.

*

The sea voyage had weakened Johnson's constitution and he felt the familiar irritations of a cold coming on, so had prescribed himself a comfortable seat by the fire with his book of translations. He had barely settled down, however, when he was disturbed by a chapping on the door.

Mrs Collins bustled in with a basket which she placed on the table. 'I heard ye were poorly, so I brought you some of my fruit loaf. Would you like me to cut you a slice?'

'Madam,' said Johnson, closing over his book and trying hard to disguise his irritation. 'It was right magnanimous of you, but I have already enjoyed an ample breakfast. Thank you.'

'Och I'm sure a wee slice or two won't hurt. I have the sugar and the dried fruit brought in special twice a year.'

'Well, maybe just a sliver then, Mrs Collins,' said Johnson, realising that resistance was futile.

'That's what I like to hear, Doctor. My Roderick used to love my fruit loaf, and I do miss having somebody to bake it for.'

Mrs Collins lit the stove and busied herself making a pot of tea. 'How about you, Mr Johnson. Is there a Mrs Johnson waiting at home to warm your bed?'

'There was once, Madam, though she died a long time ago.'

'And you have no thoughts of marrying again?' Mrs Collins, a natural busybody, couldn't help but notice Doctor Johnson's dishevelled appearance: the unbuttoned shirt-collar and sleeves, the dirty brown housecoat and battered slippers under the table.

Johnson laughed. 'Why, never, Madam. I am a creature of habit, and far too old and set in my ways to marry now.'

'Nonsense,' she said, picking up a napkin and brushing the crumbs from Johnson's shoulder, which managed to put him even further out of sorts. 'A handsome man like you? You need a good woman to take care of you.'

With a Herculean effort, Johnson changed the subject from his own marital status. 'And when did Mr Collins pass, if I may ask?'

'Och, five years past now. But he watches down on me, as I am sure Mrs Johnson looks down on you.'

'Which is all the more reason why a second match might be disagreeable to all concerned.'

'Mr Johnson,' said the landlady with patient condescension. 'We St Kildans do not believe in death. My Roderick chose the time of his passing, and has ascended to a state of grace, to prepare a space for me by his side in paradise when I too am called.'

'I applaud your purity of faith, Mrs Collins.'

Mrs Collins heaved a sigh, and rolled her eyes heavenwards in an expression of rapturous contentment. 'It is Simon who has restored our faith. He has called me back to the source, and I must heed the call. Very soon we will make our way to the north end of the island, where we will begin our festivities. At the height of the revelries Simon himself will appear among us in the form of Proteus, God of the Ocean. I and others who are ready will cast ourselves from the cliff edge onto the rocks below. Like husks being separated from the wheat with a winnowing fan, our gross bodies will be stripped away, allowing our spirits to be liberated. But are you all right, Doctor Johnson? You look terribly pale.'

Johnson's head reeled as if he had been struck a blow from a heavy object. 'Mrs Collins, I'm sorry but if you will excuse me, I still feel tired from all the strain of the voyage, and must rest awhile.'

'Yes of course, Doctor. Let me take your dishes, and I will leave you to sleep.'

*

Boswell returned at noon to find Johnson in a sombre, reflective mood. The Doctor had dressed himself more sloppily than usual. His shirt was buttoned in the wrong holes and his hose had holes in them. The Enkil Stone was on the table before him, which told Boswell his friend had a particularly vexing problem to grapple with. 'Ah, Boswell,' he said without looking up. 'I trust you have had a fruitful morning?'

'Nothing too interesting. Just a walk down by the sea.'

Johnson looked curiously at his friend for a moment. 'As for me,' he said finally, 'I received some new information concerning our good friend Simon, and none of it good.' Johnson went on to explain exactly what Mrs Collins had told him.

'And what do you make of it all?' said Boswell.

'I am afraid to draw too many conclusions, Boswell, but I fear that if we do not act soon, Mrs Collins and others of her generation are about to become the latest victims of Simon MacCodrum's peculiar brand of Christianity.'

Chapter 4

*O*nly four men attended afternoon service that day: Johnson, Boswell, Joseph, and MacPhee, who had taken a liking to his new friends and wished to make a show of loyalty.

Mr Ferguson had cleared the little church as best he could in the time he had given to him, scrubbing the bird droppings from the pews and patching up the hole in the roof.

The sermon itself was a sober and measured diatribe against sin, with Mr Ferguson impressing upon the small congregation the benefits of quiet contemplation, restraint and moderation. It was just the sort of sermon they needed to hear, devoid of grandiosity and spiritual posturing, but full of good sense and pious sentiment.

As the men made their way back to the village, preparations for the feast were already underway. The young lads were filleting fish, the women plucking fowl in their doorways or baking bread on crude stoves. Children ran from house to house wearing masks, shrieking with excitement, while the older men looked on happily, smoking their pipes and talking to one another, studiously avoiding the gaze of the newcomers.

Everyone stopped to watch Mrs Collins emerge from her house dressed in nothing but a white gown and a crown of wildflowers. She made her way down towards the shore, then proceeded to wade barefoot into the sea. When she was waist deep she stopped to raise her hands above her head and cried aloud in a clear, ringing voice. '*Seonaidh*, I give thee this cup of ale, hoping that thou wilt be so good as to send us plenty of seaware for enriching our ground during the coming year.'

One of the fishermen on the harbour raised an axe and split open a barrel of ale they had been saving for just such an occasion, which he kicked down the slope into the water. The crowd cheered as it bounced into the sea, seeping dark ale and froth everywhere.

'What is a *Shoney*?' Boswell whispered to MacPhee, watching jealously as all that fine ale seeped into the ocean.

'*Seonaidh* is a God of the Sea, chieftain of the Blue Men of Minch. He lives amidst great splendour in an underwater cavern. If we appease him he will send seaweed to our shores, but if we anger him he will send storms to shipwreck our boats. On Mabon, we give a libation to *Seonaidh*, that we might obtain a good bounty of seaweed for the coming year. The seaweed makes fertiliser to grow more grain, and more grain means more ale.'

'So what happens now?'

'They will take the rest of the ale, the bread and the meat over the hill to the horn, where they will feast and make merry until dawn, in order for *Seonaidh* to grant a good harvest.'

'And you will be joining them?'

MacPhee took off his hat and placed it to his heart. 'I am too old to be rutting on the hill like a stag, Mr Boswell. And besides, it would be a disgrace to the honour of my late wife.'

Pipers gathered on the dirt path to lead the procession, and as they passed each house revellers emerged, some with solan geese under their arms or baskets laden with eggs and cheese to join the procession.

Mr Ferguson had seen enough. He climbed upon a rock between the harbour and village and cried out from his improvised pulpit. The villagers studiously avoided his gaze as they went about their business. Johnson and Boswell watched the proceedings with mounting unease. The minister thrust out his arms and addressed the villagers in a booming voice. '*My hand will be against the prophets who see false visions and utter lying divinations. They will not belong to the council of my people or*

*be listed in the records of Israel, nor will they enter the land of Israel.
Then you will know that I am the Sovereign LORD!*

The men shifted uncomfortably; some of them paused, while
the women instinctively crossed themselves. But no one turned.
Some children laughed, and were quickly chastised by their
elders and hurried along. One boy picked up a clod of earth
and hurled it at the minister. It glanced against his face, but the
minister heeded it not. Some of the villagers looked aghast. The
boy's mother clipped his ear, then muttered an apology as the
crowd moved on, marching up the hillside to the song of the
pipes.

*

Once the last of the revellers had disappeared over the brow of
the hill an eerie silence descended on the village. The sun, now
over the yardarm, began its protracted descent, flooding the
bay with golden light, casting long shadows across the village.
Despite the beauty of the bay there was a definite chill in the air.
The group had unanimously decided to leave first thing in the
morning, having exhausted their welcome and nearly everything
else.

With their store of peat for the fire depleted, Mr Ferguson
offered to gather driftwood from the beach, hoping also to
gather his thoughts, which were sadly disordered. He headed
out with his haversack tucked under his arm.

The harbour was deserted now. Boats rocked calmly in the
bay, gently bobbing on the water. Lobster creels and fishing
nets lay unattended. As he walked towards the bay the minister
contemplated the sound of the tide as it rushed in over the
shingle, and the long sigh of its protracted withdrawal. Here
was the rhythm of the universe. Expand and contract. Inhale
and exhale. Advance and retreat. He watched a pale gold moon
rise above Oiseval. In the early evening light it seemed a pale
imitation of its nocturnal self, and he marvelled how something

so distant could influence the ebb and flow of the ocean, and at the same time something so intimate as the cycle of a woman. It was a thing of great mystery and wonder to him.

A thick fog bank rolled in slowly over the shoulder of *Ruaival*, shrouding everything in a funereal dullness. As he looked across the bay Ferguson caught sight of a pale shape flapping against the slate grey sea, like a bedsheet being whipped to and fro in the wind.

There was no wind.

It was a woman in her nightgown. But the movement was erratic, unnatural somehow. She was dancing on air, whirling and twirling as if being tugged and yanked and whipped around by some unseen force. Peals of laughter filled the air, but there was a frantic note of desperation to the sound, like that of someone trying to appease her tormentor. It sounded more like crying than laughter. Ferguson knew there was nothing Christian about the scene played out before his eyes, yet he longed to reach out, to let her know someone was there, that somebody cared. As he drew closer the figure stopped dancing and turned to see him for the first time. The apparition spoke sweetly, coyly, like a little girl, her hair blown hither and thither on the wind. *'Have you come to take me home?'* she breathed, then seeing some unseen horror over Ferguson's shoulder, the expression turned from one of playfulness to that of abject terror. Her mouth contorted in a silent scream. The figure turned and fled towards Ruaival, the grassy knoll at the far end of the bay. Ferguson cried out, and before he knew what he was doing he was giving chase. He followed the ghostly figure up the flank of the hill, climbing higher and higher until they were far above the sea. The wind had picked up now and was whipping at Ferguson's hair and clothes as he followed. When she was some ten yards from the edge of the cliff she stopped and turned to face her pursuer. Her face was deathly pale, her lips crimson red. She held out her long white arms and smiled.

Ferguson thought of the ebb and flow of the ocean, and how

it must be like the giving and receiving of love, an act he had never experienced before, perhaps never would. He felt a shiver of anticipation run down his spine, like the sea pulling back across the shingle.

'Dance with me,' said the pale apparition. Mr Ferguson took another step forward, and fell headlong into the cold embrace of the sea.

*

Doctor Johnson was in his armchair reading a maritime report from 1765, while over at the window Boswell and Joseph smoked their pipes. 'I am beginning to worry about Mr Ferguson,' said Boswell, pulling aside the heavy curtain made from a ship's sail and peering down towards the bay. 'He's been gone almost an hour now.'

'Perhaps we might take a walk to see if we can find him,' said Johnson, putting aside his maritime report, which was mainly dull but yielded some interesting tidbits, and provided welcome respite from the painstaking work of his translations. 'I could use the fresh air.'

The three men put on their warm winter coats and wandered down towards the bay. They followed the distinctive tread of the minister's hobnail boots round the bay to Ruaival, coming to a stop at the base of the hill.

'He must have climbed up here,' said Boswell. 'But why? Where was he going?'

'Let's split up and look for him while there is still light,' suggested Johnson. 'Boswell, you search the village. Joseph, you climb to the top of that hill, where you will be able to see over to the other side of the island. Here, take the telescope given to me by the Laird of Raasay. I will pay a visit to Sir Charles Braithwaite, who may have heard something on his travels.'

*

Joseph climbed high above the fog bank where visibility was clearer. He found a rock to shelter behind as he spied out the lay of the land. The pagan festivities had begun. Bonfires blazed all round the north-western bay on the uninhabited half of the island. Barrel after barrel of ale ran dry as the men slaked their thirst. Women danced naked around the flames, their sinuous bodies shimmering in the rising heat. Elsewhere, couples were pairing off, hardly caring who saw them, while the children ran free without a care, unattended, undisciplined, exposed to all that lewdness and licentiousness.

Joseph moved his telescope from face to face, trying to identify the leader. This Simon and his kind were nothing new to him. In his native Bohemia, every village had its own resident mystic, a local seer of visions and caster of spells, who might rise to a position of some prominence in the district, in some cases supplanting the authority of the church. These mystics cobbled together fragments of the Old Religion with Christianity to make it palatable, their charms and potions offering more instant gratification than mere prayers. Joseph was immune to their nonsense. He would laugh in this so-called Magus's face given half the chance.

He turned the telescope down towards a group of rocks, where Mrs Collins the landlady was being groomed for some ceremonial function. A young girl braided and put flowers in her hair, whilst another rubbed down her naked body with goose fat. The sight of her sagging breasts and heavy thighs exposed to the cold night air, with so many children running around, caused the blood to rush to Joseph's cheeks. The telescope moved swiftly on, coming to rest on a white-haired man who stood a little way off from the rest of the celebrants. He was standing on a high promontory of rock, his arms raised in a gesture of invocation towards the sea, crying out in a voice inaudible to Joseph from his lofty perch. Joseph was just deciding what to do next, when a hand clamped down on his shoulder.

Chapter 5

Ferguson awoke to darkness. He had no way of knowing how long he had been lying there. The pain in his ankle bit hard. He looked up towards a dim circle of light. He must have fallen down there when he was chasing the woman in white and passed out. When he tried to move a bolt of agony shot up his leg. He tried yelling, weakly at first, then more forcefully, until he was crying for help from the top of his lungs. He carried on this way until he was hoarse. No one came.

Ferguson stretched out his arms, feeling around the walls of his prison. There was a gap in the earth wall before him big enough to crawl through, if he could overcome his horror of enclosed spaces. He fell onto his hands and knees and tried moving forward, finding that if he put most of his weight on one knee he could drag himself through the horizontal passage without disturbing his broken ankle too badly. He managed to cover about five yards before he had to stop, then reached into his haversack to find some leftover oatcakes from breakfast. They were reduced almost to crumbs, but would give him the energy needed to carry on. He only wished he had stored some water as well.

When he felt ready, he gathered his strength and moved on. He seemed to be moving down a gentle gradient. A pale glow of light ahead kindled hope in his heart. He kept dragging himself forward until he could hear the distant surge of the ocean. A little further and he could smell the brine and feel the wind on his face. A few more inches and the moon swung into view.

Ferguson edged his way forward another few yards until he could poke his head outside. He almost lost his grip at what he saw.

Waves crashed against razor-sharp rocks some twenty feet below. He turned his head to look up at the grassy clifftop crowning a sheer face that stretched for miles in either direction. Overcome by a wave of vertigo the prisoner pulled his head back in and laid himself flat on the ground.

After he had regained some equilibrium, Ferguson propped himself against the wall of his cave to take stock of his situation. He considered his options. *I am trapped in a sea cave halfway down a sheer cliff,* he thought. *There is no way of climbing up. Firstly, my ankle has been badly sprained in the fall. Perhaps even broken. Secondly, the cliff face is completely vertical and I am not equipped for such a feat of agility. Nor can I go down. Even if I managed to throw myself clear of the rocks I cannot swim. No, there is only one course of action left to me. I must sit it out. Doctor Johnson and Mr Boswell will soon notice I am missing, and will surely organise a search party by the morning.* And with this glimmer of hope in his heart he passed out completely.

*

Joseph looked warily at the hand clamped onto his shoulder.

'So it's yourself,' said the hand's owner with a grin. 'And what brings Joseph out on a night such as this. Come to see the heathen in all his native glory?' To Joseph's great relief he recognised the voice. It belonged to MacPhee the bird-man.

'Mr Ferguson,' said Joseph. 'He go out. No come back.'

'I see,' said MacPhee, watching the golden ball of the sun inch its way towards the horizon. Campfires as numerous as stars in the sky were spread out across the north-west bay. He sat himself down beside the manservant. 'Well there's no point looking for him now. What good would ye be to any o' us if ye fell down a pothole in the dark and broke baith your legs? Nah, we'll sit tight until the morn, and I will help you look. In the meantime…' MacPhee produced a flask of whisky from his pocket, took his fill, and passed it to Joseph. 'Now, did I ever tell ye of the time I met the Faerie Queen, and lived for a spell wi' the little people under the hill?'

Joseph heaved a sigh and took a drink. It was going to be a long night.

*

Sir Charles' home was situated in a secluded spot, on a *col* or dip between the twin hills of Conachair and Oiseval, with views overlooking the village bay to the south, and north across a broad expanse of ocean to the sister isle of Boreray. The cottage itself seemed incongruous in such a barren setting, with its neatly-manicured lawn, glass windows and white picket fence.

Johnson rapped on the door. When there was no answer he tried the handle. The door was locked, which struck him as odd on an island where it was not the custom to be so distrustful. He peered in through a diamond-shaped pane of glass, shading his eyes to see if he could detect movement, and caught the reflection of Sir Charles Braithwaite coming up the garden path towards him. On reaching his visitor the naturalist offered his hand, which Johnson found cold and clammy to the touch.

'I am very glad to find you here, Doctor Johnson.'

'How was your trip, Sir Charles?'

'My trip?'

'Yes, you mentioned something about puffins on Soay.'

'Ah, yes. Most edifying.' Sir Charles fumbled in the pockets of his threadbare coat for keys. 'What brings you out here all alone, Doctor?'

'I'm afraid it's not a social visit. One of my company has gone missing. I rather hoped you might have bumped into him on your travels.'

Sir Charles paused, his key poised just inches from the door. 'Mr Boswell?'

'No, the Reverend Ferguson. He went out for a walk this afternoon and never returned. He didn't quite see eye-to-eye with some of the villagers, so I fear something bad may have happened to him.'

'Oh dear me! No, I can't say I've seen him, though I am sure there is a perfectly innocent explanation.' Sir Charles twisted the key around in the lock until finally it clicked open. 'We have only four square miles of land here on Hirta, so he can't have gone too far. But please, come in.'

Once inside Sir Charles lit the fire and heated a little samovar for tea. Johnson gazed with undisguised curiosity at the scientific paraphernalia strewn around the room, taking note of a magnifying glass, clamps, pins, modelling clay and jars of chemicals. His eyes moved to the newspaper clippings and scientific articles pinned to the wall, and a prominent wall-map of the Western Isles, where a single pin had been stuck midway between Iceland and Scotland.

'Rockall,' said Sir Charles, appearing at Johnson's side with a cup of tea.

'I beg your pardon?'

'Rockall. The name of the island. Well, it's more of a rock, really: a rock caked in guana and virtually unassailable from any boat. But it's a very important rock. It forms the topmost peak of an underwater plateau called Murias, a landmass that once existed above sea level. I plan to take an expedition there soon. They have colonies of seabirds that are quite tame, and a new species of sea snail that does not exist anywhere else on Earth.'

Johnson moved on, pausing to examine a display cabinet boasting a rare collection of butterflies. He picked up Sir Charles's magnifying glass and leaned in for a closer look. Each sample had been carefully pinned, labelled and mounted according to its size, colour and species.

'I see you have discovered another of my little hobbies,' said Sir Charles. 'What do you know about lepidoptera, Doctor?'

'I can tell the difference between a moth and a butterfly, but that's about it,' lied Johnson.

'There are four distinct stages of metamorphosis,' Sir Charles explained. 'Egg, caterpillar, pupa, and adult. The adult may only live a week or so, but in that short space of time, she graces the Earth with her beauty.' As Sir Charles became more animated, Doctor Johnson noticed for the first time several of his fingers were fused together, giving the hand a distinctly flipper-like appearance. 'Do you ever think about metamorphosis, Doctor Johnson? I don't mean simple change—I mean the ability to undergo radical transformation on a cellular level, to shed one's old skin, as it were, and emerge as something entirely new?'

'I have seen enough with my own eyes not to reject the idea out of hand, Sir Charles. But why do you ask?'

'The folklore of St. Kilda concerns itself almost exclusively with the theme of metamorphosis. That, and of course the sea, which is an ever-present motif. Take for instance the selkie, a seal-maiden who leaves her seal skin on the shore while she combs the beach for shells. A handsome young fisherman, bewitched by her beauty as she searches among the rockpools, finds her sealskin and hides it. Trapped in her human form, the seal-maiden has no choice but to marry the fisherman. In time she gives him three beautiful sons. But the seal-maiden never stops yearning for the ocean. Then one day, while the husband and sons are out fishing, the maiden discovers a casket that the fisherman keeps locked in his room, and on finding the key and opening it, recovers her stolen sealskin. The maiden puts it on and returns to the sea, leaving her husband and poor children behind, never to return.'

Johnson moved to the window as he listened, absentmindedly picking up a little idol which had been placed on the sill. 'Sir Charles,' he said, turning the clay figurine in his hand, 'who are the Fin-Folk?'

Sir Charles stiffened. 'Why do you ask?'

'Oh just something I overheard in the village the other day. A mother warned her child to be good or the *Finfolk* would get him. And I noticed the locals keep little clay dolls just like this on their windowsills, as if to ward off something evil.'

Sir Charles appeared at Johnson's shoulder, looking out towards distant Boreray. The reflection of his face, superimposed against the monstrous granite reef, appeared drawn and cadaverous in the flickering firelight, creating an eerie, disembodied effect. 'The Fin-Folk are a race of sorcerers and shapeshifters from *Finfolkaheem*, a city that lies so far beneath the waves that no light ever penetrates its sunken halls. They spend the cold winter months in *Finfolkaheem*, but in summer months they surface, taking up residence on Boreray. They come at night, rowing themselves over to Hirta in silence, searching the shores for a lone fisherman or a frolicking youth to abduct and take back with them. They are terrible.'

'You sound as if you half-believe these stories yourself, Sir Charles.'

Sir Charles gave a shudder as he moved from the window, as if afraid of being seen. He threw a slab of peat onto the fire and sat to watch it smoulder on the flames. 'And why not?' he said, motioning for his guest to join him. 'Living among these people as I do, you come to realise they are more than just stories. They are a way to help one come to terms with one's own condition.'

'And what condition would that be?' said Johnson, pulling up a chair beside his host.

'The St Kildans have a rather unique creation myth, which one could spend one's whole life studying, and still be no closer to penetrating its mystery. More tea?'

'Go on,' said Johnson, holding out his cup.

'The St Kildans believe they hail from Atlantis—a sub-continent of Atlantis called Murias, to be precise. The Murians were a gifted race of seafarers and pearl divers, ancient mariners whose hearts belonged to the ocean. When Atlantis was lost, the Murians chose to follow her beneath the waves, adapting to their new environments with ease. For ten thousand years the Murians lived in peace, farming the seabed, herding whales, raising teams of seahorses, and hunting shoals of fish with their faithful seals by their sides. But in time they grew tired of their undersea realm and wished to breathe the air once more. They longed to chase the deer on the hill and feel the sun on their faces. And so gradually nearby St Kilda was colonised. And yet within their hearts they still retained a kernel of themselves that belonged to the sea. Simon MacCodrum, the one they call the Magus, has taught the St Kildans of their birthright.' Sir Charles turned his head and looked searchingly into Doctor Johnson's eyes. 'He has shown them the meaning of transformation.'

'That is quite a tale.' Johnson looked again from the window to the map on the wall, and the whole truth of the matter became glaringly obvious. 'And this is the nonsense you feed these poor, ignorant islanders?'

A slow smile spread across the naturalist's face. 'All I have done is to show them where they come from—given them a little *push*, if you like.'

'Off the edge of a cliff, you mean.'

'If that is what is needed, then so be it.'

'I think it is time to dispense with the formalities wouldn't you say, Simon MacCodrum?'

Johnson's nemesis straightened in his chair, and seemed to grow before his guest's eyes. The obsequious, deferential expression left his face, replaced with something altogether more self-assured. When he spoke it was no longer in the clipped tones of an English schoolmaster, but with the lyrical burr of a Highland *dunnie-wassal*. 'So you have seen through my little masquerade, Doctor. I'm curious, what was it gave me away?'

'I heard tell of *MacCodrum of the Seals* when I was in Dunvegan,' said Johnson. 'A clan in North Uist who claim kinship with selkies. The name for seals in North Uist is *clann righ fo gheasan*, which means *children of a king under spells*, does it not? Rather like your Children of Lir, as it happens. The reality, however, is a little less poetical. Like others of your clan you suffer from a hereditary condition whereby the digits of the hand are fused together so the appendage resembles a fin or a flipper. Congenital anomalies such as these have, throughout history, given rise to folktales concerning mermaids, cyclopes, little-folk, ogres, chimeras, multiheaded monsters and so on. Your fairy tales are merely a way to come to terms with a rather commonplace and unexceptional hereditary malformation.'

Simon MacCodrum's lip curled in an involuntary sneer, though he instinctively slid his hands out of sight. 'I assure you, *Doctor* Johnson, not all phenomena may be explained away by the science you hold so dear. Indeed, you come at a very fortuitous time in our calendar. A time when you may experience first hand the limits of your paltry rationalism.'

'Mr MacCodrum. Let us not deceive ourselves here. What you are suggesting is nothing less than wholesale murder. You will return with me to the mainland at once to face justice.'

'I think not, Doctor Johnson. Indeed, in your current state of mind I doubt that you will be going anywhere soon.'

'What do you mean?' Alerted by the threat in his host's voice, Doctor Johnson staggered to his feet. He reached out a hand to steady himself, dropping his teacup to the floor. He looked at the contents he had spilled, his eyes focusing and unfocusing on the spreading shape it made on the tiles.

'But you are not well Doctor Johnson! Really, you must sit down.'

'You... You've poisoned me!'

'Poisoned you?' laughed Simon. 'No, Doctor. I have *liberated* you.'

'What was in that tea?'

'You have partaken of our holy sacrament, Doctor Johnson. A rare privilege, I might add. You have been given a concentrated dose of *Psilocybe semilanceata,* a hallucinogenic mushroom. Sit yourself down, man. Very soon you will begin to feel the effects, and you will never see things the same way again.'

Johnson slumped back onto his chair. He struggled to take stock of the situation. His thoughts seemed detached; not a part of himself. Despite the dangers of his situation a wave of euphoria came bubbling up unbidden from the depths of his being, washing over his senses, sweeping away all reason and judgement. His eyes darted feverishly around the room. The butterflies in the display cabinet appeared to twitch and stretch their wings, then all of a sudden broke free from their confinement to flutter around his head, shaking stardust into the air with every beat of their diaphanous wings. Johnson's eyes followed their movements and he laughed with delight. These were not butterflies at all but fish, shoals of fish with iridescent scales that shimmered and twinkled like silver coins in the refracted light. The colours of the room heaved and swarmed, swaying hypnotically with the oceanic rhythm of the universe. Johnson tried to stand. His movements were slow but he felt buoyant, suspended in the air, moving through some dense medium *(full fathom five thy father lies)* that somehow supported his body. He looked curiously at the stranger sitting across from him. This was not a mortal man at all but an ancient, barnacle-encrusted, sea-dwelling Triton *(them's pearls that were his eyes)* with cerulean skin and shimmering green hair, who controlled the ocean waves with one blast of his mighty conch.

He rubbed his eyes and looked again—it was Sir Charles Braithwaite, and yet not Sir Charles Braithwaite. Simon MacCodrum, and yet not Simon MacCodrum.

Doctor Johnson, it was safe to say, was not in his right mind.

*

Boswell hadn't had a drink these past three days. With a pounding head and dry mouth he made a cursory search of the deserted village, tapping on doors and peering through windows, looking for any sign of the missing clergyman. His heart wasn't in it. What he really hoped to find was a stray bottle of whisky or keg of ale that someone had left behind. He longed for just a taste of something strong. Finally coming to the conclusion that nothing was stowed away in any of the houses, he made a quick search of the roofless and derelict shells behind the village, then the ruins further up the hill, which had crumbled away until only the foundations remained. It seemed curious to Boswell that each successive generation should build their home a little closer to the ocean.

The sea-haar had now reached the village, a suffocating mist that brought with it the stench of dead fish and rotting seaweed. Boswell consulted his pocket watch. His friends had only been gone an hour, but it felt like a lifetime. Ever since his confinement in the vaults under Edinburgh's Old Town the thought of being alone filled Boswell with horror. He took a step back from the rolling mist, suddenly afraid. It seemed to be coming from every direction. The whiteness of the void was filled with a *chittering* noise like an approaching swarm of locusts. Suddenly a multitude of crabs came swarming in from the beach, a wave of hard shells scuttling over his feet like clockwork toys, disappearing into the surrounding hills as if in flight from something. Moments later Boswell was shrouded in a blanket of white, barely able to see his trembling hands in front of his face.

Four distinct shades not so much emerged as *emanated* from this mist. They were born of it, like a dense smoke being poured into a bottle. The long, thin aperture that Boswell had previously thought to be a proboscis or some sort of beak was a funnel through which these beings poured their essence, starting at some indeterminate point in the ether, then like molten metal being poured into a cast they slowly solidified, becoming monstrous shuffling things with nightmarish faces, black things with flippers or barnacle-encrusted pincers for arms, seaweed hair that reached the ground. Boswell searched around desperately for somewhere to hide. He flung open the first door he could find and backed inside, closing the door and shutting himself in pitch darkness.

They were jostling into position outside. Boswell peered through the gaps in the stone walls of the hut, watching as they surrounded his hiding place. They reminded him of the pillars of granite called sea stacks that flanked the island of Boreray, formed over time by wind and water. Hulking, prehistoric things with tombstone shoulders and grotesquely squat heads. The Watchers.

Boswell was not alone in his hiding place. Something was breathing beside him in the dark.

He didn't dare turn his head or move an inch, for he now realised he had blundered into the abode of Lady Grange. An icy, tingling closeness raised the hairs on the back of his neck. Had those things outside brought him here? Were they in league with the spirit shut in with him? No, the breathing was irregular, terrified, accompanied by a soft whimpering. It suddenly dawned on Boswell that the thing sharing his hiding place was just as terrified as he.

It didn't make him feel any better.

As the last rays of sun disappeared behind the brow of the hill, the air was pierced by a shrill and plaintive call the likes of which Boswell had never heard before in his life. It was a sound that belonged to the sea as surely as the foam and the wrack. It expressed a deep longing for the ocean, but it was also filled with a horror of the deep and an inexpressible sadness. The noise increased so that Boswell felt his eardrums would shatter, and raising his hands to block the sound he fell to the floor. Shut in with only the darkness and his invisible companion for company, he passed out completely.

*

John Ferguson was revived by the corrosive tang of brine in his nostrils. As he slowly came to, the full horror of his predicament came rushing back. He was trapped in a sea cave, with no means of egress, and no hope of being rescued. Outside, a passing bank of cloud plunged the cave in darkness. Ferguson cursed his own stupidity. With great difficulty, he turned his head and caught a glimpse of something white in the corner. Dragging himself by the elbows he crawled over to the spot, pulling slimy fronds of seaweed aside to examine his find. The bones were barely noticeable, hidden among a pile of driftwood and wedged into a shallow crevice against the wall. Ferguson could identify several varieties of seabird and the bleached bones of a cat, but the skull grinning up at him was unmistakably human. Strangely, he felt no terror or threat from vengeful spirits. It almost felt like company to him in the dim light, as the winds howled outside and the sea waves heaved and broke hard against the rocks below.

Ferguson wondered if this sad pile of bones had been the cave's former occupant, a hermit who had chosen a life of solitude over the heathen ways of the villagers.

As the cover of cloud broke, moonlight came flooding in, allowing Ferguson to examine more of his surroundings. The cave walls were daubed with some kind of primitive artwork. He took from his pocket the spectacles which were only slightly cracked from the fall and placed them on the end of his nose.

The technique was basic, primitive, childlike even, featuring a line of little stick figures, almost hieroglyphs, marching like lemmings off the edge of a clifftop. As they fell they sprouted wings; or was it fins? Elsewhere figures crawled out of the sea to give birth, transforming in reverse from sea-creature to human. Only when Ferguson moved back did the immensity and scope of the mural reveal itself. It was a story spanning millennia, a kind of prehistoric Bayeux Tapestry, depicting an ancient, amphibious race from a continent lost beneath the waves. From what he could decipher, this race gave birth on land, returning to the sea when they reached the age of maturity. Ferguson was reminded of penguins or sea turtles, who crawl onto the shore to lay their eggs in the sand.

At some point in their history war broke out between the Atlanteans (for that is surely who they were) and a race of similarly amphibious lifeforms. But these other lifeforms were grotesque, contorted, shuffling things, sorcerous shapeshifters who abducted mortal men and made them into beings like themselves. The Watchers.

Ferguson wondered if the bones at his feet belonged to the artist, a mad visionary who had chronicled the saga of these fantastic lifeforms before he died, daubing in a frenzy of activity those strange, amphibious beings, who had surely been here long before man ever set foot on the bay.

As Ferguson studied the riddles on the wall, he became so fascinated he failed to notice the passage of time. The water, which only a few hours before had been crashing against the rocks twenty feet below, was now on a level with the cave mouth, almost up to his ankles. In a sudden panic he sloshed over and stuck his head outside, noticing for the first time the high water mark on the cliff above. The cave itself, he only now realised, was festooned with seaweed. It hung from the ceiling in great garlands. So he wouldn't need to worry about dying of thirst after all. In only a few hours' time, the cave would be completely submerged.

Chapter 6

ohnson was no longer in Sir Charles' cottage. He had somehow found his way onto *Mullach Mor*, the high ridge that runs like a spine the length of the island from north to south, dividing the island in two distinct halves, each with its own bay and valley. He had no recollection of how he got there, but he vaguely remembered being pulled by a team of giant seahorses on a carriage made of seashells. By the time they reached the summit Johnson realised he was not the citizen of Atlantis he had previously supposed. The carpet of iridescent jewel anemones was only grass, the towering stacks of coral only cleits, the waters had receded, and he was Doctor Johnson once more, though the universe still blazed forth more vibrantly than ever before.

The morning sun, peeking over the horizon, cast its first beams across the Village Bay, while the pagan half of the island still belonged to shadow. Innumerable bonfires had been lit across the north-western bay that mirrored the myriad stars wheeling overhead. By Johnson's side was no Neptune or Poseidon with his three-pronged trident, but the master they called Simon the Magus, chieftain of St Kilda and spiritual leader of its people.

'What you mortals call time,' said the Magus, as if in answer to Johnson's thoughts, 'is merely nature's way of preventing everything from happening at once. The mortal brain, in its primitive, day-to-day level of consciousness filters experience until events and thoughts come plodding one after the other with a tedious inevitability. Only under the influence of the sacrament may we see reality as it truly is.'

Johnson fell trembling to his knees and ran his fingers through the grass. He had never really noticed grass before, and it was a tremendous source of novelty and wonder to him. Each blade, sufficient in and of itself, was perfection, replete with beauty and meaning. He stretched his fingers into the luxuriant foliage and grasped tightly. The Earth was spinning, hurtling through the cosmos, and he feared he would fall off if he did not hold tight. As he clung to the ground, he felt the souls of ancestors seeping up through the soil and into his fingertips, connecting him intimately to all life that had gone before. The grass held memories. He wept as civilisations rose and fell before his mind's eye. With a flash of realisation, he saw he had been present long before he was born into the (*sleeve? configuration? constellation?*) body known as Samuel Johnson. He had been a horseman of the great Mongol Empire sweeping across the plains of Asia; he had lived through the golden age of Islam; he was a beggar, a thief, a mathematician, a soldier in the Roman Empire, and a high priest of Mesopotamia. So many past lives receding into the distance in an infinite regression. Further and further into the past he hurtled. He was an ape in the jungles of Africa, then a rodent-like creature, then a giant amphibian crawling back into the sea. All the while Simon was talking, guiding Johnson through these stages, and his voice was indistinguishable from Johnson's own inner voice. He bore witness to the birth of the sun and the cooling of the Earth, and realised there was never a time when he was not.

And he saw a civilisation infinitely more advanced than our own, though whether they were born of the sea or descended from the heavens, Johnson had no way of knowing.

He blinked away his vision and looked down the slope towards an arm of the bay, a high promontory of rock named in maps the Cambir Peninsula but known locally as "the horn", in form like the shaft and head of an arrow, or more accurately a jutting phallus protruding half a mile out to sea. The revellers were leaving the embers of their bonfires and heading down *en masse* towards it, passing like a swarm of fireflies through an archway crafted from the jawbone of a whale. The candlelit procession formed two orderly lines along the length of the peninsula. Johnson watched in rapt attention as three figures dressed in white robes passed hand-in-hand between the lines like participants in some ritualistic dance. When they reached the end, they turned to face their kinsfolk and raised their linked hands. Johnson saw his landlady, Mrs Collins, holding hands with two of the island's elders. Mrs Collins looked up. When she caught sight of her master standing alongside Johnson her entire countenance lit up. She cried out ecstatically.

'Good Lord,' said Johnson. 'Surely she does not mean to jump.'

'From the sea we come, and to the sea we must return.' Simon spoke gently, kindly. 'Do not grieve to see Mrs Collins cast away her old skin. For now is the hour of her great transformation.'

'But this has gone on long enough,' cried Johnson, and turning his back on Simon MacCodrum he started down the hill using his stick for support.

To those spectators on the horn he appeared like Moses descending Mount Sinai, his face a picture of wrath to behold his people reduced to idolatry. The crowds looked uncertain as Johnson passed between them. 'Stop!' he cried. Mrs Collins looked curiously at the Old Testament figure coming towards her, then raised her eyes to the brow of the hill where her beloved Simon stood, his face smooth and impassive like a little God. Before Johnson could reach her, she spread out her arms. With the beatific smile still fixed to her face she fell backwards, followed closely by her two elderly companions. 'No!' cried Johnson, but it was too late. The three figures had disappeared over the edge of the abyss.

*

Ferguson scrambled knee-deep in water for a piece of driftwood large enough to use as a raft. Perhaps the tide might carry him from the cave, round the island to the bay. It was unlikely, but the thought kept him from losing hope. As he searched among the debris his eye caught a flash of gold in the water. He snatched something out of the water and held it up to the light. It was an old-fashioned poesy ring, the gold tarnished with age. The inscription inside the band read:

"Keepe faith till death, RC & JE"

Ferguson cast his mind back to MacPhee's story at the cleits, and the sad fate of Lady Grange.

Rachel Chiesley.

On a sudden inspiration he searched among the remains until he found the pelvic bone. It was broad and flared, while the rest of the bones were smooth and relatively small, indicating that this was the body of a female.

So MacPhee's claim that Lady Grange had been murdered there on Hirta and her body thrown to the sea was true after all. There before him was indisputable proof: this sad collection of bones, with a single gold band bearing both the victim's name and that of her assassin. For surely it was her own husband who had murdered her, even if it was not done by his own hand. The body of Lady Grange had been washed up here, trapped between rocks at low tide, and here it had remained for thirty years.

Ferguson wiped away a tear. How profoundly sad to be stolen away from the world like that, to be cruelly murdered and cast into the sea, unlamented and forgotten, then for the sea to wash the flesh from your bones and leave you stranded in some desolate hole. Despite his own predicament Ferguson closed his eyes and wept for the soul of Lady Grange. Had he been summoned by a ghost? Could it be that he had been brought to the edge of the abyss, only so that he could find these sad remains? Ferguson dislodged the bones one by one and placed them in his bag. As a man of God, it was his duty to give Rachel Chiesley the Christian burial her murderers had denied her. But in all probability he would not be leaving that prehistoric cave alive. His bones would be mixed with those of Lady Grange, to be the companion in death that both of them had been denied in life.

*

When Johnson reached the head of the peninsula where the three figures had been standing only moments before, he could barely bring himself to look. Mustering his courage, he leaned forward and peered over the edge. The bodies were pinned to the rocks some forty feet below, their white robes soaked in blood. Johnson's vision blurred with tears. He rubbed his eyes and looked again. There was something unnatural about the shape of the bodies. They appeared boneless, empty, like discarded gloves.

Beyond the rocks, the water rushed and whorled furiously in an ever-widening whirlpool, as if the ocean had opened its huge maw to swallow up the world.

Charybdis, the songs called her: daughter of Neptune, a great bladder of a sea-monster chained to the seabed, with flippers for limbs and a terrible, gargantuan thirst. Nothing could survive such a maelstrom. Then impossibly, miraculously, three sleek heads appeared just beyond the reach of the whirlpool. At first Johnson mistook them for seals. But there was something distinctly humanoid about the features, slightly smaller than human heads they were, hairless, earless, with huge, black, watery eyes, flattened noses and smooth, bluish skin. The three heads bobbed up and down in the surf for a few moments and they seemed to smile, then their crested backs arched and tails pounded the water, sending three glorious of arcs of glittering water into the air as the lifeforms disappeared under the waves.

Johnson stared hard at the empty sea, trying to fathom what he had just witnessed.

'Now you have seen us as we truly are,' said Simon, appearing at Johnson's side.

Johnson passed a hand over his brow. 'See? Yes, I… I suppose I must have.'

'And now do you understand why you were brought here?'

'Brought here?' Johnson looked genuinely perplexed. 'I came of my own volition, as a deputised emissary of Sir Norman MacLeod.'

'Tell me, Doctor,' said Simon, with all the restraint of a schoolmaster addressing an unruly child. 'Who is this Norman MacLeod, that he presumes to judge Simon MacCodrum?'

'As clan chief,' replied Johnson, 'he serves as your lawful representative. It is his duty to protect the rights of his tenants.'

'Have a care, sir,' said the Magus, turning on his accuser with a darkening brow. 'Do not meddle in affairs of which you have little understanding. My people are no more beholden to your laws than the fish in the sea, nor more answerable to your earthly jurisdiction than the birds of the air. No, sir. Go back to this Sir Norman, and tell him that we recognise no master but the ocean. And *she* will suffer no rival.'

Johnson looked, ashen-faced, at MacCodrum. He had never in his life been spoken to in that way. Then again, he had never seen his landlady transformed into a mermaid before. He turned towards the horizon with a pensive expression, then heaved a sigh of resignation. 'From the sea we come,' he murmured at last, remembering MacCodrum's words from earlier.

'And to the sea we must return,' replied Simon, and when he smiled it was like the sun peering out from behind a thundercloud. 'And now the festivities have come to an end, and we must return to our homes.' He gestured towards the dispersing crowd, the look of contentment on each of their faces plain to see. 'Today a seed has been planted, and tomorrow new life will spring forth.' Simon looked kindly at Johnson, who was still staring in wonder at the spot where the three wondrous lifeforms had materialised. 'Come,' said Simon, placing a friendly hand on Doctor Johnson's shoulder. 'I have something wonderful to show you.'

Ferguson couldn't feel his legs anymore. The water had risen from his chest to his chin. He had to tilt his head to reach the last pocket of air. Strangely, he wasn't afraid. *How beautiful life is*, he thought. *Even these last few breaths are precious. But when they are gone, what will I have lost? I have dedicated my life to God, and now He is calling me back to Him.* As he cast his mind over his past, Ferguson's heart became troubled. *Am I ready?* He wondered. *Is my heart pure enough?* He considered those he had "saved". Had it been enough? He had rescued children from poverty in Africa, sending them to England to be educated. He had founded an asylum, helping fallen women in Glasgow and Edinburgh. But what was it all for, in the final analysis? Was it not mere vanity? Could it be that he was trying to *buy* his way into heaven? What had brought him here to St Kilda, if not sheer hubris?

'Lord!' cried Ferguson into the shrinking air space, even as the water sloshed into his mouth and nostrils. 'Deliver me from the sinfulness of pride!' Then in a voice hoarse with emotion he cried, 'Behold, the dwelling place of God is with man. He will dwell with them, and they will be His people, and God Himself will be with them as their God. He will wipe away every tear from their eyes, and death shall be no more, neither shall there be mourning, nor crying, nor pain anymore, for the former things have passed away.' And with these words, the cold Atlantic Ocean sealed John Ferguson's lips entirely.

*

'Funny,' said MaPhee the bird-man, standing over the hole. 'I covered this over years ago. Someone's lifted the lid.'

'You think minister fall down here?' said Joseph.

'I think it likely. Here are his footprints.'

'Where hole go?'

'It leads to a cave. The main entrance is halfway down the

cliff-face. I never go in—folks say it's haunted. But if he is in there we should hurry, the tide's coming in. Very soon it will be filled with seawater.'

MacPhee retrieved a spare length of rope he kept in one of the cleits close by and looped it round his waist. 'There is no time to wait for help,' he said, handing the coils of rope to Joseph and kicking off his shoes. 'You're going to have to do this by yourself. Stand like this, with your heels wedged into the turf. Feed the rope through your hands as best you can. Don't let go! When I tug on the rope, and this is the important part, you have to pull me out.' The two men looked at each other. They both knew it was a perilous undertaking from which MacPhee would probably not return. 'I will not let a man die on my island without at least making an attempt,' MacPhee explained to Joseph's look of concern.

The bird-man stepped backwards over the edge with all the consummate ease of a veteran and began his descent, bouncing gently against the rock face as he made his way down. He had placed his life in this foreigner's large, calloused hands, and he prayed that Joseph wouldn't let him down. Or at least not too fast.

Ten minutes later Joseph felt the rope slacken. MacPhee had entered the cave. Joseph counted the seconds. By the time he reached sixty he started to worry. MacPhee was a strong swimmer. He had trained his lungs to endure long spells underwater. But everyone has their limit, and by this time of year the seawater was ice cold. When Joseph reached one hundred his brow broke into a sweat. No man could survive much longer than two minutes without oxygen. Still he kept counting. One hundred and fifty... one hundred and fifty-one... one hundred and fifty-two...

At last, he felt a faint tug on the ropes. Joseph tightened his grip and started to walk backwards. The weight of the two men combined was too much, even for a strong man like Joseph. He hadn't factored in how much heavier a body is when the clothes are saturated with water. He pulled for all he was worth, until his whole body strained with the effort; at last MacPhee broke the surface, dripping seawater and gasping for air, the rope looped around both himself and the slack body of John Ferguson. Joseph used every last reserve of strength. The two men were pulled clear of the water, but all Joseph could do was prevent them from going back under. The veins bulged like cords on his neck and his face turned purple with the strain but not an inch further could he raise them.

On the other side MacPhee tried to help by using his feet to gain purchase, but the wet rocks were too slippery.

Just then a group of six men were returning home from the festivities. They spied Joseph straining with the rope and ran to help. Taking up the strain they heaved, pulling the two men inch by inch up the cliff face.

Finally the rescued men were deposited back on dry land like a prize pair of flounders. MacPhee worked quickly. Drowning was a liability of his trade, and he knew just what to do. He laid the minister flat on his back, tilted his head, pinched his nose then blew air back into his lungs. Then he placed his hands on the minister's chest, one on top of the other, and pumped. The man vomited up a quart of seawater, coughing and spluttering back to life. His eyes slowly focused on his rescuers and he smiled. 'You are not St Peter,' he said. 'Where am I?'

'You are on St Kilda,' said one of the men.

The minister rolled his eyes to heaven and wept.

Chapter 7

ilhouetted against the dawn sky, the flightless auk spread his magnificent cherub's wings, letting the sun dry his oil-dark feathers. To passing fishermen he seemed wise, somehow. Old and wise. They tossed fish to him, ashamed to have hunted his kin in the past.

The village was slowly returning to life. The old women went back to mending their nets, the menfolk to their lobster creels. The boys returned to the hills to herd their sheep and the girls to their milking stools. Meanwhile, up on the high ridge of *Mulach Mor*, two old men sat side by side. They looked like old friends as they watched the horizon, and there they remained as the sun passed over the yardarm, though what they were watching for nobody could or would say.

Down in the churchyard Mr Ferguson the minister was digging a hole with a rotten piece of wood. Fortunately the soil was sandy and easy to excavate. His ankle had been carefully splinted, and provided it did not receive any major shocks it would heal well enough. But it sang with pain each time he put weight on it. When the minister had dug a hole deep enough, he took the earthly remains of Lady Grange from his haversack and placed them at the bottom of the hole, then filled it over. Next, he formed a cross from two pieces of wood and drove the marker into the soil.

Not far from the spot where Mr Ferguson the minister was praying over the grave of Lady Grange, Boswell opened his eyes. The sun shone through the gaps of his stone sanctuary, warming his bones. Whatever shade haunted this place it had gone now, leaving a sense of peace that Boswell hadn't felt in a long time. He stood, brushed himself off, and stepped out into the morning light.

*

The captain returned a day later than scheduled to collect his passengers. He took one look at the four men standing on the pier and smiled. 'So ye'll have met the Magus?' he said, as the men passed down their luggage.

'If you are referring to Simon MacCodrum of North Uist,' replied Johnson, boarding the small vessel. 'Then yes.'

The captain did not reply, but Johnson could tell from the gleam in his eye that he knew more than he cared to let on.

Once Boswell, Johnson and Joseph had settled in, the captain turned to help Mr Ferguson on board.

The minister took a step back from the edge of the pier. 'I have decided to stay,' he announced.

Johnson stood up on the wobbly craft. 'Good God, sir. After all we have been through, are you sure?'

'I have never yet deserted an outpost,' said the plucky missionary. 'And I am not about to start.'

With a shrug of his shoulders the captain started to row.

Johnson, for want of something better to do, fired off a salute as the boat pulled away. 'By God I admire your courage, sir. Is there anything we can send you from the mainland?'

'Paper and ink,' cried the minister, as the little boat left the harbour. 'And tobacco!'

The sea was gloriously calm. Perhaps, thought Boswell, *Seonaidh* was too busy getting drunk in his sea-cave to rouse the storm against them.

Doctor Johnson seemed more subdued than ever before, looking out to sea with a sombre, reflective mien. This was a marked improvement on the brash, argumentative Doctor

ANDREW NEIL MACLEOD

Johnson of old, Boswell noted, and he hated it. 'My dear friend, I can't help noticing how changed you seem these past few days. Would you care to share your burden?'

'Ah Boswell,' said Johnson, with a searching look at his friend. 'Where do I begin? It is true, I have had my head turned. The foundations I had always held as incontestable, those twin rocks of observation and judgement upon which I have built my entire system of reasoning, have all crumbled to nothing. I can no longer discriminate between truth and illusion. I feel like your Hume, no more than the sum total of my impressions at any given moment. And yet... and yet I have never felt more wholly *myself* until this moment. I have never felt more truly alive!'

Dunvegan Castle, September 26th, 1773

We returned to a magnificent welcome. Many had come to Dunvegan to hear the testimony of the great Doctor Johnson, who seemed for those who had gathered that evening like Captain Cook returning from some unexplored region of the Antipodes, rather than an Englishman just returned from a part of Britain populated by loyal subjects. However if the guests expected to hear colourful anecdotes concerning savage rites and barbaric practices they were to be sorely disappointed. Taciturn to a fault, my friend seemed weakened by our voyage, fragile to the point of frailty. Often I detected a slight tremor pass through his frame, and after the fantastic outburst provoked by Sir Norman's kind offer, I began to fear a return of the nervous malady that had plagued my friend since childhood.

From *The Casebook of Johnson and Boswell*

'So,' said Sir Norman. 'How fares our heathen subjects?'

The whole party hushed to hear what the good Doctor had to say on the subject of St Kilda.

'There is very little to tell, Sir Norman,' said Johnson quietly. 'They are a hard-working people, to be sure, honest as the day is long and God-fearing, but a little on the dull side, truth be told.'

'And what of the rumours of senicide?' said Sir Norman, provoking a ripple of polite laughter around the table. 'You saw no sacrifice to Neptune, or Poseidon, or some other god of the sea?'

'I'm sorry to disappoint, Sir Norman, but the simple fact is that life is hard enough for the St Kildan, and the life expectancy is much lower than it is in say, Surrey or Kent. It is only natural for the natives to succumb to illness or accident before they reach their dotage, and fortunate too, in a way, considering the lack of adequate resources or medical facilities on the island.'

'It is well,' said Sir Norman. 'Since the end of heritable jurisdiction, senicide and other such aberrations of nature are no longer private matters, but must be dealt with by the Crown. I'm afraid I could not long endure the negative publicity such a scandal would generate. You have saved me a lot of heartache, Doctor Johnson. If there is anything you want, just name it, and it is yours.'

'Oh God!' cried Johnson suddenly, passionately, surprising all with the ardour of his words. 'If only you had the power to bestow it! If only I had the strength to receive it!'

Epilogue

Nuair a thig Rocabarra ris, is dual gun tèid an Saoghal a sgrios

It was impossible to gauge just where the pillars started and where they ended. Even from the top of *Mulach Mor* they were immense. Cyclopean. Their foundations were hidden from sight, tucked away somewhere beyond the horizon, beyond the curvature of the Earth. The twin shafts filled the sky, thrusting upwards, disappearing into a cover of cloud. Despite their evident solidity the pillars were azure, almost translucent, as if made from the same ethereal substance as the sky, even as the moon at dawn or distant hills appear blue to the naked eye.

'Behold,' said Simon MacCodrum. 'The Pillars of Hercules.'

Johnson had seen many miraculous things on his travels, but nothing could have prepared him for this. Now he knew he had reached the very edge of the world. The edge of reason. 'My God,' he said quietly.

'You are privileged indeed, Doctor Johnson,' said the Magus. 'Only the chosen few may gaze upon the Pillars of Hercules, and even then only at a certain time of year: Mabon, the Autumn Equinox, when the continent of Murias once more emerges from the ocean bed to open her immense, subaquatic gates, and for a few magical hours she becomes visible to the naked eye. Can you see her, Doctor?'

Somewhere on the horizon, between the two pillars, a nimbus of gold set the surrounding whisps of cloud on fire. The more he looked, the more Doctor Johnson could see of the castellated walls, watchtowers and gilded domes of a magnificent, glittering city. 'I see it,' he said. 'I see it, and my heart yearns for it with a longing that is filled with such an inexpressible sadness that my heart breaks just to contemplate it.'

'And yet she is beautiful, is she not?'

'Yes,' sighed Doctor Johnson. 'She is beautiful.'

The two men kept their vigil wordlessly into the night.

THE CASEBOOK
OF SAMUEL JOHNSON, LL.D.
And JAMES BOSWELL, Esq.

THE STONE OF DESTINY - PART II

"Pulvis et umbra sumus" (We are but dust and
shadow...)
Horace

Dunvegan Castle, September 26ᵗʰ, 1773

fter the unfortunate episode at dinner the laird hastily summoned a doctor, who concluded that my friend was suffering from nervous exhaustion, but nothing that a few days rest wouldn't cure. Sir Norman insisted on looking after Doctor Johnson himself, and spared no expense in providing him with every little comfort that might help alleviate his esteemed guest's suffering.

Doctor Johnson insisted the antique book belonging to Professor Dunbar be restored to him, along with his own translations and writing materials. I must confess it was against my better judgement. Ever since he had opened that particular Pandora's Box my friend had been out of sorts, and after his experiences on St Kilda, I felt that any further research into the Tuatha de Danann and their history would only bring on a relapse of that nervous condition which had slowly infected his mind.

For three days and nights the Doctor worked in silence, only stopping for food, which was left by a maid on a silver tray at his bedroom door, and for his toilet bowl to be removed. Meanwhile I found plenty of diversion in sampling the delights of Sir Norman's well-stocked wine cellar, though I made a point of refraining from the "harder stuff", mainly to appease the naggings of my conscience, but also the stern reproofs of Doctor Johnson, whose excellent moral character continued to influence my decisions even in absentia. On the third day Doctor Johnson rose from his sickbed like Lazarus from his tomb, a man transformed; or rather, a man returned to his usual larger-than-life self. He roared with laughter and made jokes with everyone, even the stableboy and housemaids, and so endeared himself to all and sundry that his peculiar behaviour of the past three days was soon forgotten.

'So Doctor,' said I, the moment I had my friend to myself. 'Did you manage to unravel Adamnan's secrets?'

'Naturally,' said Doctor Johnson, his eyes gleaming with a strange intensity.

'Go on then,' said I.

'It was right under our noses all along, Boswell. The book itself is a rather straightforward—albeit fascinating—history of the Tuatha de Danann. But something about the message Dunbar left on the final pages irked me. "Follow in the footsteps of Dalriada's Kings", he said. It seemed altogether too vague, and yet at the same time strangely specific. Remember, Dunbar loved riddles, anagrams, codes and ciphers. He would never dream of leaving a secret message unless it had some kind of double meaning. I spent days trying to decipher it. Finally I assigned each word a number using a method employed by the ancient Egyptians, leaving me with 5,620,622.'

My friend paused in his narrative, urging me to admire his ingenuity. 'Go on then!' I cried.

'I almost drove myself mad trying to figure out which Biblical chapter and verse the numbers related to, but nothing made any sense. Then something occurred to me while leafing through that dog-eared maritime report on St Kilda. Perhaps Dunbar was revealing the location of the Stone of Destiny using traditional longitude and latitude. If so, 5620,622 might be rendered as 56 degrees and 20 minutes north, by 6 degrees and 22 minutes west.'

Trembling with excitement, I pulled down an atlas from Sir Norman's bookshelf and ran my finger down the meridian and along the parallel. 'It's on Iona!' I said at last.

'The north-eastern quadrant of Iona, to be precise,' said Johnson.

'But that would be like looking for a needle in a haystack!'

'Not necessarily. The island itself is only one and a half miles wide by three miles long. I believe our chances of finding the Stone are fair to middling, especially if we consider that Iona Abbey, where the Stone of Destiny was once enshrined, falls within this area. Of course I would have arrived at the truth eventually, even without

Dunbar's assistance. After all, Iona is the Stone of Destiny's spiritual home, and only after the threat of a Viking invasion was the stone relocated, during which time the library which housed the relic was allegedly burned to the ground. It is only right and fitting that it should be returned to its receptacle by the Stone's sworn protectors.'

'You mean this library still exists?'

'St Adamnan himself, as ninth abbot of Iona, helped to rescue the books, storing them in a secret location just moments before the Viking fleet landed on Iona.'

'And you think we'll find the Stone of Destiny inside this hidden library?'

'Either that,' said Johnson, 'or we will find the library inside the Stone of Destiny.'

'My dear Doctor you are speaking in riddles again.'

'I believe that one is a receptacle for the other. In fact I am willing to stake my reputation on it. After all, the Stone of Destiny, the Lia Fail, is said to contain a record of the entire history of the Tuatha de Danann. What could be a more fitting location for such a remarkable object than in a library? Indeed, what could be a more fitting location for a library than inside the Stone of Destiny?'

'Now I am hopelessly confused.'

'Ah Boswell, all shall be revealed in the fullness of time.'

The arrangements couldn't have been simpler. Sir Norman lent us one of his sailing boats, a brass sextant, provisions and a good map, and we had a very competent seaman in Calum MacLeod, our erstwhile guide.

We skirted the western coast of Mull, stopping enroute to explore Mackinnon's cave, which Johnson declared the most impressive natural phenomena he had witnessed to date. The cave is reputed to be home to a she-ogre and indeed, the interior space seems high enough to accommodate a whole family of Giants. Calum our guide told us of a piper who ventured in with his dog, hoping to outdo the fairies at musical ability (the piper that is, not the dog), only for the dog to come scampering out, trembling, hairless, and alone. But we have heard a similar tale too many times throughout Scotland to *take it very seriously. Nevertheless, we had only gone a hundred yards when our candles guttered out, and such a feeling of despair and sadness overwhelmed us that we quickly turned about and headed towards the daylight.*

It was a misty morning as we rowed into the bay of Iona and dragged our boat onto the shingle. When we were safely on dry land Johnson turned to me and we embraced one another cordially and with a tremendous sense of occasion. Here we stood, perhaps on the same bay on which Saint Columba himself alighted to establish his church, supplanting the old Druidic ways for the word of God.

From *The Casebook of Johnson and Boswell*

Chapter 1

The pilgrims clambered up onto a grassy bank and were immediately struck by a strong sense of being watched. Undaunted, Joseph and Calum entered a nearby copse of woods to find something for the pot, while Johnson and Boswell explored the abbey grounds. The sky was sullen and overcast as they approached the crumbling monastery. Even the patches of grass on the surrounding hills seemed muted and drained of colour, while the sullen wind howling through the ruins only accentuated the bleak impression of the place.

'I must say,' said Johnson. 'Even roofless and windowless, the monastery inspires in me feelings of reverence and awe bordering on dread. Here stood the first established monastery on the British Isles, where Christianity itself took root and flourished. And yet as I look upon the place I am filled with a deep sense of foreboding, and where I should find comfort, I find only unease.'

Boswell knew just what he was talking about.

As the two men approached the bell tower some loose masonry fell to the ground at their feet, narrowly missing their heads. They looked up in time to see a dark shape moving away from a medieval window above.

'Shall I have Joseph go up and drag the fellow, assuming it is a man, down for questioning?'

'No, Boswell. That would be unnecessary. After all, we are the guests here. Let us behave as if nothing untoward has happened, and see if our host introduces himself formally.'

An ancient causeway of cobbled stones called the Street of the

Dead ran all the way from the monks' landing place at Martyrs' Bay, past the monastery to St Oran's Cemetery, where the High Kings of Scotland from Kenneth MacAlpin to MacBeth were entombed. As Johnson and Boswell followed the medieval causeway down to the burial ground, they struggled to hide their disappointment. The monuments were little more than a scattering of gravestones lying flat on the ground, overgrown with weeds, the inscriptions mostly crumbled away to nothing.

'*Life's but a walking shadow,*' Johnson murmured, '*a poor player that struts and frets his hour upon the stage, and then is heard no more.*'

A sudden squall swept in from the sea, prompting the rusty Flemish bell in the belfry tower to creak on its hinges and ring dully in the pale afternoon. This was the bell of St Finian, Johnson explained, which legend has it only rang when a true king was coronated, or to announce the arrival of a royal funeral procession along the Street of the Dead. Boswell looked up and shuddered. 'Even the most hardened cynic might believe in ghosts after coming to this place.'

'I have spent half my life chasing ghosts,' mused Johnson. 'And yet perhaps I have been chasing myself all along. For what is a man, Boswell, if not a ghost?'

By way of reply Boswell turned his gaze seaward, where the gulls in their flight surrendered to the coming storm, buffeted this way and that on the rising tempest. '*Isle of sleep, where dreams are holy,*' he murmured. '*Sails to thee a King who sleepeth, With thy Saints we leave him sleeping.*'

'Those are fine words,' said Johnson. 'What is it from?'

'I don't know. It's a song my mother used to sing.'

'I always knew you had hidden depths, Jamie.' Johnson looked searchingly into Boswell's eyes for a moment. 'I am glad, after all we've been through, that you are here with me. I can think of no one else I'd rather share this moment with. And even if we do not find what we came looking for, it has been quite the adventure, has it not?'

Boswell, for fear of saying something that would ruin the moment, turned his collar up against the cold. 'The wind is picking up, Doctor. We'd best go and find shelter.'

While the storm gathered strength the men gathered armfuls of firewood and brought them to the only part of the old monastery that provided some protection, a courtyard surrounded by a cloistered walkway. Joseph and Calum had returned empty-handed, leaving the group with the prospect of a miserable night.

Johnson was toying with the brass telescope presented to him by the Laird of Raasay, when a clatter of stones out in the dark startled them all. Johnson looked up, only to find two shining eyes regarding him from beyond the circle of firelight. As his vision became attuned to the darkness, he could discern a hunched figure perched on the cloister wall, regarding them with animal cunning. 'Come, my friend,' said Johnson, squinting his eyes at the shadows. 'It is bitterly cold tonight, but the fire is warm. Come warm your bones—my friends and I mean you no harm.'

The creature tilted its head like a curious dog.

'Oh, you want this?' said Johnson, raising the telescope in both hands. 'Come! Come and take it. It's yours, if you want it.'

The creature leapt down from its perch and came loping towards the firelight. Boswell let out a gasp of surprise. It was more ape than man, semi-clad in rags with coarse hair covering its hunched back, a grotesquely extended jaw that gave the impression of a muzzle, and deep-set eyes glittering with inscrutable, simian intelligence. Tentatively the creature edged its way towards Johnson, reached out a paw and snatched the telescope from his outstretched hands.

'There you are my good fellow,' said Johnson. The creature retreated a few yards to examine its prize. First it sniffed, then raised the telescope to its eye the wrong way round to look at the men around the fire, gurgling with laughter at the effect. Johnson gestured with his hands for the creature to turn the telescope, and when it did so it dropped the device in alarm and hopped back to the sanctuary of the cloisters.

Johnson laughed. 'Come, my friend. There is nothing to fear here, though I am afraid we have no food to offer you.' The creature moved close to the fire again. Johnson patted his breast. 'My name is Johnson. JOHN-SON.'

'J-Junsun,' the creature mimicked gruffly.

'And this is Boswell. Boz-well.'

'Buz-wuz.'

'No. Boswell.'

'Boz....wull.'

'Yes, that's right. And you?' said Johnson, pointing at the creature. 'You are?'

The creature made a noise from somewhere deep in his throat that sounded like 'Thoth', and his eyes shone like flints in the firelight.

'Here,' said Johnson, reaching into his pocket for a dried biscuit. 'Though I am afraid we have no meat.' The creature snatched the biscuit and took a sniff, broke off a little piece, placed it on his tongue and tilted his head, before spitting it into the fire with a grimace of disgust.

'Eat,' said Thoth, pointing at his mouth and then his belly.

'I am afraid that is all we have,' said Johnson.

'You wait,' said Thoth. 'I bring.' In a flash he loped over the wall and disappeared.

'What an odd creature,' said Boswell. 'I wonder where he came from?'

'Goodness only knows,' said Johnson. 'Though he appears to have the rudiments of speech.'

'What was his name again?'

'Thoth,' said Johnson. 'I don't suppose the name has any significance for you?'

'Thoth! Was he not some sort of Egyptian deity?'

'He was,' said Johnson. 'Sometimes depicted as a man with the head of a baboon.'

'Well whoever named him got that part right.'

'They also had a sense of humour. Thoth is the Egyptian god of wisdom and learning, the deity who gifted man with the art of writing. He is the god of scribes, also depicted holding the scales of good and evil, whereby he measures the weight of a man's soul against a feather.'

'I wonder how he ended up here?'

'Who knows,' said Johnson. 'He most certainly is an oddity. Though in a strange way, he seems to belong to the place.'

Just at that moment Thoth reappeared from among the cloisters with a deer carcass slung across his shoulders. Calum and Joseph immediately set about butchering the carcass and roasting the parts on the fire, while Thoth contented himself with ripping out and eating the organs raw.

After the men had satiated themselves, Boswell turned to Johnson and, indicating their strange, ape-like companion, said, 'Do you think he has been baptised?'

Thoth's ears pricked up. 'Uhuh. Saint Oran baptise me. Take you to him.'

Johnson and Boswell exchanged glances. 'Surely,' whispered Boswell, 'being alone so long on the island has deranged his senses.'

'Let us humour him,' suggested Johnson.

Thoth scrambled over to the well in the middle of the courtyard, and gestured for the men to follow. Johnson and Boswell approached and peered down into its depths.

'Master down there,' said Thoth.

'Surely you don't mean us to climb down into that well?' cried Boswell.

'I go first,' said Thoth. 'You follow.' The creature hopped into the well, using a system of carefully placed handholds and footholds to clamber down into the darkness. Five minutes later a hoarse voice echoed up from the depths. 'You come. Is safe.'

Boswell looked at Johnson, whose shining eyes told him everything he needed to know. 'My God,' said Boswell. 'You trust this baboon?'

'I must confess,' said Johnson, 'curiosity has the better of me.'

Unable to decide who should go first, Johnson flipped a coin. Boswell called heads and lost. Joseph and Calum tied the rope around Boswell's waist and lowered him into the well. They fed the rope through their hands while Boswell used the handholds and footholds for support. Eventually the rope slackened. After a few agonising moments Boswell's cheerful voice rang out. 'It's quite safe!' he cried. 'The ground is about forty feet below.'

Joseph and Calum retrieved the rope and lowered Johnson the same way. When Johnson's feet found solid ground, he groped around blindly until he found his comrade, patting his face and feeling his nose until his identity was established. The two men stood in a few inches of water.

'Where is Thoth?' said Johnson.

'I don't know,' replied Boswell. 'He was here a few seconds ago. THOTH?'

High above the storm clouds broke and the moon shone down, revealing a horizontal tunnel branching off from the bottom of the well, some five feet in diameter, tall enough for a man to enter if he stooped.

Johnson took a compass from his pocket. The tunnel ran in a south-westerly direction towards Abbot's Hill, the elevated mound of grass overlooking the cemetery. 'Shall we?' he said.

'After you, Doctor.'

Johnson sloshed through twenty yards of tunnel before he realised the only footsteps he could hear were his own. He had lost Boswell somewhere back there in the dark. Turning was out of the question in that cramped passage. He pressed on, ignoring the rats that scurried around his feet, wishing he hadn't left the Enkil Stone behind on the boat. After nearly fifty yards the tunnel opened, quite unexpectedly, onto a spacious, circular chamber with a high-domed ceiling. Johnson estimated that he was somewhere underneath Abbot's Hill, which would account for the size and height of the chamber. He was reminded of the reading room of Oxford University, with a little bit of the British Museum thrown in for good measure.

The moon shone through a stained-glass dome overhead, illuminating walls stocked with a variety of musty, mildewed books. The main area was chock-full of crates and covered antiques, like a museum getting ready for an exhibition, or a stately home in the process of being closed for the summer. A tall reading desk stood at the far end of the chamber, and sitting at the desk, incredibly, a little old man in a monk's cassock. Upon his desk sat an impressively large and ancient-looking leather book, a book he was annotating with a very long quill he dipped fussily in his pot of ink. Johnson cleared his throat to speak, but the old man only raised a hand for silence while he finished what he was working on. Thoth came loping in sideways, pawing at the monk's feet. The old man reached down and gently patted the creature's head, before he finally put down his quill to acknowledge his guest.

'Welcome, friend. And you are...'

'Johnson. Doctor Samuel Johnson.'

'Ah. I see,' said the little monk, his eyes shining with pleasure. 'We have been expecting you.'

'You have? And who might you be exactly?' Johnson was still trying to find his bearings, and thought it might help if he adopted an equally officious manner.

'I am Oran.'

Johnson looked thunderstruck. 'You mean *Saint* Oran?'

'A simple Brother will do,' replied the holy man, blushing with modesty.

'Remarkable,' said Johnson, speaking mostly to himself. 'One of the twelve Culdee priests who accompanied Saint Columba from Ireland with the four sacred treasures of the Danann. Legend has it that a chapel could not stand on Iona until a living man consented to be buried alive beneath the foundations. And that man was you?'

'Guilty as charged,' replied the little librarian, beaming with pride. 'As you can see, I've made quite a comfortable nest for myself in the meantime. What do you think?'

Johnson looked around at the dust-covered antiques, the musty books, the curious little librarian and his simian pet, and his shoulders sagged. 'It all seems a bit of an anti-climax, if you must know the truth.'

'You mean it is not to your liking?'

'Please understand, I do not wish to be rude or ungrateful. I'm sure it's a fine place to live; it's just a little bit underwhelming, after all we have been through to get here.'

'That all depends on what you bring,' the librarian observed sagely, leaning towards Johnson with a conspiratorial wink. 'And what you seek.'

'And what about Professor Dunbar,' said Johnson, beginning to understand something. 'What did he find?'

The little librarian rocked with laughter. 'An elaborate fiction, I'm afraid. We manufactured those clues deliberately to lure you in. The real professor is enjoying a peaceful retirement somewhere on the Isle of Wight, and doesn't trouble himself with nasty things like quests. But *you*, Doctor Johnson. You are cut from a different cloth entirely. You see, we have been watching your progress for quite some time. The way you handled yourself in Edinburgh was impressive, and so we decided to test your mettle, so to speak. To see if you were worthy of the task we have set for you. Everything you have done since leaving Edinburgh, everywhere you have been, the trials you have faced and the people you have met, has been engineered by us, specifically to bring you to this point.'

'I see,' said Johnson. 'I was beginning to suspect as much. Well, here I am. What do you want from me?'

'Relax. Why not have a look around? Come on, let me give you the tour.' The librarian hopped down from his stool, and Johnson hadn't noticed how short he was before. In fact Saint Oran cut an entirely unprepossessing figure. 'Now this here,' said the little monk, pulling away a dust sheet, 'is the cauldron of the Dagda, which we brought over from Murias. It magically replenishes itself each time it is emptied. Very handy at weddings. And this one is the mythical spear of Lugh. We got that in Gorias, City of Fire. He who wields it can never be defeated in battle. Well that's what they say, anyway. And here is the Sword of Light from Finias... Ooh! It's still sharp! Ah, now this might interest you...' The librarian pulled away another dust sheet to reveal a magnificent, gilded harp. 'Dagda's Harp. Its music has the power to change the seasons, and to soothe the troubled hearts of warriors. The renowned warrior King Dagda himself would play this harp after battle, and its music would make men forget their wounds and their sadness over fallen comrades, and reflect only on the glory of battle.' The librarian plucked a single string, and the instrument rang out in that stuffy cavern, filling Johnson's heart with joy, sending waves of ecstasy tingling down his spine. Before the golden tone had even ceased to ring the librarian moved on, and shook out a glittering pelt. 'Now this I know you will like. The enchanted pig skin of Tuis, which has the power to cure the sick and wounded, and turn water into wine.'

Johnson was speechless. Here was this little man, showing him the sacred treasures of the Danann as if they were nothing more than tawdry wares, and he a common market trader.

'And the Stone of Destiny?' demanded Johnson.

'The stone of what?'

'The Coronation Stone. The *Lia Fail*. Jacob's Pillow, the sacred relic that is said to sing with joy whenever the true King sits upon it. The holy relic we set out to find in the first place.'

'Oh... that old thing! Are you sure there's nothing else I can interest you in? After all, you are standing in greatest library since Alexandria. As a matter of fact, this *is* the library of Alexandria. At least what we could salvage from the fire. Now let's see if we can't tempt you.' The little librarian dragged over a footstool and stepped up to examine some of the books on the shelves. 'We have Homer's lost work—a comedy, would you believe? We also have Shakespeare's *Cardenio*, and the lost books of the Bible (though they were never really lost, to be honest). We have *Inventio Fortunata,* written by a 14th century monk who travelled to the North Pole. We have *The Emerald Tablet of Thoth* by Hermes Trismegistus—a signed copy no less! We also have Ctesias's *Persica*, and Aristarchus's *Astronomical Treatise*, and Berossus's *Babyloniaca,* and Eratosthenes's *On The Measurement Of The Earth,* and Claudius's *Etruscan-Latin Dictionary,* and Origen's *Hexapla,* and—'

'Stop! *Stop!*' cried Johnson, clamping his hands to his ears, staggered by the sheer wealth of knowledge on display. These were works of art thought lost for ever, now brought tantalisingly close, like low-hanging fruit. Johnson's fingers twitched in anticipation.

'Feel free to take a look,' said Oran amiably. Johnson reached out towards Claudius's *Etruscan-Latin Dictionary* and immediately withdrew his fingers. 'It burns,' he cried, shaking his fingers and blowing on them.

'Of course it does. They are protected. Only the rightful custodian is granted access. We can't have any Tom, Dick or Harry getting their grubby little fingers on our books, can we now?'

Without any further ceremony, Oran wandered over to the middle of the room and flung aside another dustsheet from one of the covered antiques. 'I believe this is what you are looking for?'

Johnson was almost thrown back by the blast of energy that hit him. 'My God,' he said, almost falling to his knees. 'Can it be…?'

Chapter 2

*B*roadly speaking, the artifact that the librarian uncovered was shaped like a saddle, its blunted edges turned up like a sausage at the ends. But that is where any earthly similarities ended. The *Lia Fail* was black, as black as the void, a hole in the world through which all eternity might be glimpsed. Johnson could not tell whether he was looking at a solid object or peering through the fabric of reality into the abyss. Perhaps it was both at the same time. He was simultaneously drawn to it and repelled by it, like a magnet whose poles either attract or repel. His whole body began to tremble. For one fleeting moment of madness he was tempted to fall down in worship, before checking himself. 'I knew it!' he cried, trembling all over. 'I knew it! Dunbar was right! The Stone of Destiny was here all along, hidden by the Scots and moved from place to place to avoid detection!'

'Why not try it out for size?' said Oran, and he patted the saddle as if it were an ordinary chair.

'You would have me sit on the *Lia Fail*?' cried Johnson, aghast. 'The throne reserved for the King of All Elements, the *Rìgh nan Duil*?'

'Why not?' replied the librarian. 'By assuming stewardship of the Stone you will automatically become custodian of this library, and all of her treasures.'

'And I presume then that I would be taking your place?'

'Yes,' replied Oran, 'Should you accept this blessing, it would release me from my vows.'

'But come, friend, that is hardly an enticing proposition for me, is it now?'

'Oh, I don't know? To have the knowledge of the universe at your fingertips? To live forever?'

'Yes, but to be stuck in here? Never be able to leave the bounds of this chamber? That is the deal, is it not?'

'Well… yes,' said the librarian, looking awkwardly at his sandals. A fine sheen of sweat had broken out on his brow, despite his seeming air of indifference.

Johnson felt a need so all-consuming that it was like a burning fire within him. His throat was dry and his hands trembled by his sides. He looked around. It wasn't such a bad place to live, really. Those books! And the candles would presumably burn eternally, and then there would have to be some sort of den to sleep in. But how would he eat? And drink? Perhaps he wouldn't need to, if he was immortal. What earthly reason did he have to refuse? His wife was long gone, he had no children who depended on him, nor any emotional ties to speak of. What an illustrious crowning of his career it would be, as creator of the English dictionary, to end up the custodian of the greatest library in the history of the world! He would be mad to refuse such a bargain.

With a great effort of will, Johnson tore his eyes away from the Stone to address the little librarian. He seemed old and wizened by years beyond measure, and yet just for a moment, alarmingly, Johnson thought he was gazing directly into the pleading eyes of his old school chum John Dunbar.

*

While all this was going on, Boswell had blundered into altogether more commodious surroundings. It was not, it was safe to say, what he expected to find at the end of a dank, underground tunnel oozing with earthworms.

He found himself in a tented palace of silk under a canopy of red and gold velvet. Richly embroidered Persian carpets covered the floor space and large brocade cushions had been scattered around to lean upon, with brass lamps providing light, and a central table set for a lavish feast. A warm, aromatic breeze wafted in through a flap at the far end of the tent, through which he could hear the gentle bellowing of camels. Directly opposite, on the other side of this lavish spread, sat a dark-skinned man dressed in robes of silk, puffing on his houka. He was as plump as a baby, with gold rings on each of his fat stubby fingers. His flesh, smooth as a cherub's, shone with oiled fragrances. 'Come!' said the vision in silk, gesturing to the food on the table before them. 'Eat!' he said, and when he smiled, his eyes crinkled like a little Buddha.

Boswell sat down without any further preamble and broke a loaf of bread. 'Where is Doctor Johnson?' he inquired between mouthfuls of food. 'He will be hungry too.'

'Don't worry about him. He is well looked after.'

With a shrug, Boswell raised a goblet of wine to his lips and drained its contents. He set the goblet back on the table, and watched in astonishment as the vessel refilled itself. *Just like the stories I read as a child,* he thought.

As Boswell filled his mouth the Sultan clapped his hands twice, and a troop of dancing girls sprang into the room. A pulsing, seductive melody filled the air as the dancers performed for Boswell. Their ebony limbs swayed with lithe and supple grace. As he watched, Boswell's eyes glazed over. He seemed, to anyone watching, a million miles away.

'What is the matter, friend?' inquired the Sultan, his brow wrinkling with concern. 'You have indigestion? Come. Drink. Drink deep. In that cup is the cure for all pain. The cure for all sorrow.'

The music picked up pace, and the dance grew wilder. Veils of silk flew through the air as the dancers gyrated their bodies in time to the music.

Boswell raised the cup to his lips, and did as he was told.

It began as a tiny voice in his head.

Johnson could hear someone singing softly. There was no discernible melody or notes, but the song was tuneful, soothing—more humming than singing. As the sound increased in intensity, he realised that it was not a dream. The singing was real, and it was emanating from the Stone itself.

'Ahh,' said Oran. 'She is singing for you Doctor Johnson. Do you hear? It means that she likes you.'

'She?' said Johnson.

'Of course,' said Oran. 'The *Lia Fail* is a living entity, a relic from our home planet. A *chip off the old block*, you might say.'

Doctor Johnson took another step towards the black monolith and reached out towards it, hovering the palms of his hands just inches from the surface of the stone. He felt a powerful attraction, as close a feeling to love as one could conceive for an inanimate object.

'Go ahead,' said Oran. 'Touch her. She will not harm you.'

Johnson turned a questioning look on Oran.

'Trust me,' said Oran.

Johnson softly rested the palms of his hands against the smooth surface of the stone. It felt cold to the touch. Meanwhile, the singing in his head multiplied until it became a duet, then a quartet, and then a choir which rose and swelled above and beyond the confines of the Earth. It was the music of the spheres, filled with longing and ecstasy, touched with divine madness and a delirious joy. The circular room started to revolve in time with the music. Slowly at first, then gradually picking up speed. Faster and faster it turned, until Johnson felt he was at the hub of a spinning top. Light and shadow flashed furiously before his eyes in a whirring blur, and in an instant every page of every book in the library was exposed to the light, each letter made clearly visible, so that nothing was hidden, everything was revealed.

None of this is real, said a voice in Johnson's head, and with this simple, devastating realisation, the ground was swept away from under his feet. The library, the sacred treasures, the books with all their knowledge, even the little librarian, were flickering shadows projected onto a wall, like the magic lantern shows he loved as a child. The *Lia Fail* had dreamed them all into existence. Had it dreamed Johnson into existence too? And the world beyond those walls, was that also a dream? Overwhelmed with the intensity and meaning of the experience Johnson shut his eyes. To stop his head from reeling he focused on the stone, the only thing in the chamber that did not move, that had existence, an anchor in a sea of absolute chaos.

Its icy blackness was absolute, but he began to discern raised figures on its planes, hieroglyphs of power. The more he looked, the more he could see they were not symbols at all but stars, whirling galaxies and constellations of a strange yet familiar universe. The stone was expanding beyond the bounds of Johnson's vision, until he was completely enveloped in darkness, suspended in the breathless void.

Somewhere out there in the celestial maelstrom, a star was in the process of devouring itself. Debris from its destruction filled the void. Johnson watched as a chunk of black rock the size of St Paul's Cathedral came hurtling past his head. On reaching the Earth's atmosphere it was broken into a thousand fragments, each piece falling silently to earth.

In a panic Johnson tried to find his feet, and realised he was standing on a hill. The cosmos wheeled about his head. He gasped, and his lungs were filled not with the thinness of the void or the staleness of a vault, but clean night-air.

Johnson recognised his new location from Boswell's guidebook. It was the hillfort of Dunaad in the West, high seat of the Kings of Dalriada, a place he returned to every night in his dreams. But he knew instinctively that this was not a dream. Everything around him felt real. Solid. Near the summit of the old hillfort, he knew, was a footstep in the stone, a slight depression in the shape of a foot, and a basin of natural rock.

The Kings of Dalriada were coronated there by placing their foot in the hollow, and anointed with rainwater from the basin. It was a high throne overlooking Iona, from whence the entire Kingdom of Dalriada could be surveyed, from the west coast of Alba to the misty green vales of Erin.

Johnson felt afraid for the first time in as long as he could remember. The place seemed familiar and recognisable, yet his heart told him he was very far from home. He cried out for Boswell. All around the base of the hill, black shapes were gathering. Johnson watched in horror as they began crawling up the hill, groping their way towards him.

Follow in the footsteps of Dalriada's kings, he murmured.

He began to run, scrambling for the summit, falling over and picking himself up again. The shadow creatures were on him like spiders, clutching at his ankles, pursuing him relentlessly. When Johnson reached the summit, he looked on in horror as twelve black shapes came closing in, demons made of shadow, sucking and devouring the light from around them. Johnson put his foot in the place reserved for the Kings of Dalriada, then just as they were about to seize him he perched his rump upon a mossy throne and... *zaaaap!*

In an instant everything changed. Night became day. With a flash of lightning that illuminated the night sky the black shapes became beings of light: men and women, tall and indescribably beautiful, with blue green eyes, golden hair and a bluish tint to their opalescent skin. They were dressed in flowing robes of the finest silk, these beings, with a gentle kindness in their eyes that to Johnson was irresistibly appealing. Far beyond, all across the land, Johnson could see other hillforts, now no longer simple mounds of grass but towers of crystal. Beacons of light. Places of *seeing*. And he knew without knowing how or why that each of these places contained a fragment of the meteorite, like a giant fisherman's net cast across the land, a matrix of energy with the power to transform crude matter into light. Johnson had wandered into the realm of the Tuatha de Danann, existing in the same space as our own world, but beyond the range of our everyday senses. He looked down, only to realise that he was not sitting on a mossy rock at all, but a smooth block of obsidian.

The Shining Ones knelt to venerate him.

'No!' cried Johnson, 'You are making a mistake! I am no king—I am an ordinary man!' but the shining folk paid him no heed. They anointed his head with water from the basin. Saint Oran himself now stepped forward with the sword of light grasped in his hand. His whole body radiated the most indescribably beautiful light, and he was tall, taller than a man, and his face, lined with wisdom, was beautiful, like that of an angel. Saint Oran reached out with the sword and touched Johnson's shoulder. He was being knighted!

'I cannot do this! You have the wrong man! I am not the *Righ nan Dual*, but a mortal man! Boswell! Boswell!' Then, flinging himself to the ground, he covered his head with his hands.

When Samuel Johnson looked up again, Saint Oran and the shining ones were no more. He was overcome with a wave of despair. He was back in the vault under Abbot's Hill, but the walls had been stripped of books, and the treasures, even the Stone of Destiny, were all gone. It was a simple underground chamber, lit only by a few crude torches affixed to the earthen walls. There was nothing to suggest the existence of a library, or a librarian, or any of the fantastic artifacts Johnson had witnessed with his own eyes.

A groan signalled the presence of another beside him in the dark. 'What happened?' said Boswell, rubbing his head like a man awakening to a bad hangover. 'Where is the sultan with his hookah? And the soft cushions? And the scented candles? And the ladies all in silk?'

'Let me guess,' said Johnson. 'You were brought to a seat of power, and promised the world if only you took your rightful place upon it.'

"How did you know? It was exactly as you say. My host pulled away the tablecloth like some conjuror to reveal a solid block of stone carved into the shape of a throne. Come to think of it, it was rather like your descriptions of the Stone of Destiny.'

'But clearly you reneged on his generous offer, or you wouldn't be here to tell the tale. Come, what was it that changed your mind?'

Boswell's eyes filled with tears. 'I remembered my family, and... and I realised that I didn't want for anything. Not as long as I have them. And you of course, Doctor.'

'I am very proud of you, Boswell,' Johnson laughed. 'For had you taken that trickster up on his offer, you would never have seen your family again. Which is why I did not succumb to my own temptation, though I very nearly did. Who would be there to look out for you? It was a test, Boswell. A test of our faith if you like. But there is always a catch.'

'And the Stone of Destiny?' said Boswell.

Johnson smiled. 'I have seen enough treasures to last me a lifetime, Boswell. Give me a soft bed and a good book any day, and I'm richer than all the Sultans of Arabia. Besides,' he added. 'We have achieved what we came here to do. That is, to prove to ourselves once and for all that the Coronation Stone at Westminster is a fake, thus undermining the legitimacy of the current monarchy. Alas, it is a secret we must take with us to the grave. The security of the nation depends upon it. Come on,' he said, offering Boswell his hand and pulling him back to his feet. 'Let's get you back to your family. I believe we came in this way,' and he dragged poor Boswell through the narrow tunnel as if he were a wayward child.

Calum and Joseph were waiting back on level ground to pull both men to safety. Johnson and Boswell embraced their rescuers as if they had been away for decades, though according to the position of the moon they had only been gone a matter of minutes.

Boswell declined the dram of whisky Calum offered from his flask.

'Well Boswell,' said Johnson, dusting himself off. 'Perhaps

ANDREW NEIL MACLEOD

you mean to take your vow of sobriety seriously after all. I am very proud of you. If this was all we had achieved on our quest, it would have been worth it a thousand times over. I for one shall never again reach for knowledge beyond my grasp. I believe I shall be happier for it, too.'

As the men gathered their things the first blush of daylight illuminated the eastern sky, though the cloisters around them remained in shadow. A movement off to the left caught Johnson's attention. He turned to see a shape retreat into the shadows. 'THOTH!' he cried, but there came no answer from the surrounding arches. The curious creature had left something propped against a pillar. Joseph went to retrieve it. It was about five feet in length, wrapped in rags and tied with pieces of string. Johnson opened the rags, and the men all crowded round to gaze in wonder at a sword sheathed in a glorious leather scabbard. Johnson picked it up. The scabbard was embossed with the most intricate design, depicting the tall Danann ships arriving on Erin's misty shores. Everyone let out a gasp and took a step back. The steel sang as Johnson slid the blade from its scabbard. It was light and sharp, radiating a faint blue light. Its handle was inlaid with gold, silver and studded with precious gemstones. A blue Enkil Stone had been set in the pommel, so that Johnson could have balanced the whole thing on the tip of a finger.

As the company gathered round in wonder to admire the craftwork, the spiderweb of gold and silver on the handle shifted and changed. At first they saw the glittering Danann warriors in all their strength of arms, their enemies arrayed against them, then new figures emerged; witches and warlocks, werewolves and vampires, creatures to strike fear into the hearts of men, nightmarish creatures that Johnson himself had witnessed, and he realised that this sword was meant for none other than himself.

It was Calum who broke the spell. 'Aye,' he said. ''Tis a bonny bit o' steel, richt enough!'

'Unquestionably,' said Johnson, squinting an eye and looking

382

along the length of the blade for flaws that didn't exist. 'This is the Sword of Light, wielded by Lugh of the Silver Hand himself, the blade that destroyed the Fomorian Sea Giant Balor the Invincible, and banished the Sons of Belial to the lowest regions of hell.'

'Well, Doctor,' said Boswell. 'It would seem you were meant to have a treasure after all, whether you wanted or not!'

'Treasure?' said Johnson, sheathing the sword and passing it to Joseph for safekeeping. 'I think not, Boswell. This is just on loan. And once it has served its true purpose, it will be returned to where we found it.'

'Its true purpose?'

'By this hand and by this sword shall the serpent of the world be brought low,' Johnson intoned solemnly. 'So it has been ordained by the highest authority, the *Righ nan Duil*, King of all Elements, who has one foot in this earthly realm, the other in the realm of *faerie*. He is the King that is foretold, Boswell, who will regain his throne upon the Day of Judgement.'

'Doctor!' cried Boswell. 'That kind of talk is blasphemous! And here of all places!'

'Not if the One that is foretold is Christ Himself, Boswell.'

'These are all very weighty concerns, Doctor. And you believe this to be true?'

'Ah Boswell, I don't know! Everything has been topsy-turvy since we set off on this path. All I know is that it's time for us to go home, and for you to return to your family. For a while, at least.'

'My Dear Doctor Johnson,' said Boswell, linking arms with the older man and leading him towards the bay, where their little boat was waiting to carry them back to the mainland. 'That is the best offer I've had all day.'

Epilogue

Our journey back to Edinburgh was not entirely unpleasant, despite or perhaps because of the fact it was almost entirely devoid of incident. We visited the hillfort at Dunadd which had appeared to Doctor Johnson in his dreams, yet it proved to be an entirely unremarkable hill of grass, though the footprint in the rock was there just as the guidebook and Johnson had described. There was also a proliferation of mushrooms on that hill, being the same species the Doctor had ingested on St Kilda; though understandably he was reluctant to repeat the experiment.

We spent an uneventful night in the Saracen Head Inn at Glasgow, where we were pleased to receive letters from the Duke of Queensberry and Lord Chalmers, before making our way east the following morning. We just had time to see one more familiar face before embarking for Edinburgh.

From *The Casebook of Johnson and Boswell*

Johnson was giving Boswell a lesson in cosmology in Brodie's Famous Tea Rooms, using the condiments on the table to illustrate his example.

'There are four realms, or dimensions, that we know of,' he explained, shuffling the condiments around the chequered tablecloth like chess pieces. 'Let's say Heaven is this salt cellar, while this peppermill represents the lower-fourth dimension commonly referred to as Hell. Here is the realm of man, which shall be represented by this pot of mustard, and the realm of the Tuatha de Danann, which is represented by this delicious jar of honey. Both of these terrestrial realms, the mustard and the honey, exist together in parallel space-time realities, but there is a veil which separates them. In some places this veil may be thinner, such as on Iona, or on the hills of "seeing", each of which contains a fragment of the Stone of Destiny.'

'Hold on,' said Boswell. 'You mean there is more than one Stone of Destiny?'

'Yes,' Johnson confirmed. 'The Stone is extra-terrestrial in origin, shattered into a thousand pieces on entering the Earth's atmosphere. The Ancients declared the location of each fragment to be a sacred site, and raised earthworks, artificial mounds, temples and stone circles, or planted yew trees where they found them. The biggest piece, that which for seven hundred years was used to coronate the High Kings of Alba, is the heart of the meteorite. The Motherstone, if you will, carved into the form of a throne by Danann craftsmen. But each fragment contains tremendous power, and communicates with itself by means of cosmic vibrations, creating a vast web of energy across the entire northern hemisphere.

'Indeed, though they may be separated by geographical distance, they are as one, these sacred stones, and call out to one another across the vastness of space. I believe these fragments act as portals, Boswell. My vision of the hillfort of Dunadd is so vivid because I was really there. From my lofty vantage point I was afforded a glimpse of an entire network of energy lines running from one sacred site to the next, forming a vast pentagram across the entire North of Britain. Those who come into contact with these stones are afforded a glimpse into the world of the Tuatha De Danann, the "faerie realm". But to take possession of the Motherstone, the *Lia Fail* herself, is to hold dominion over both realms, straddling them like a Colossus. You see, the Stone of Destiny moves with alacrity between our world and the next, as readily as you or I may move from one room to another, which is why it was able to vanish before our very eyes in the scriptorium. The High Kings of Ireland and Scotland were more than just earthly monarchs, Boswell. They were masters both of this world and the twilight world of the Tuatha de Danann, the *fairie folk*, with whom they regularly conversed.'

'It would seem our fates are entwined with this elusive artifact,' observed Boswell. 'Whether we like it or not.'

'We find ourselves poised at the centre of a vast mystery, Boswell, which presents itself to us in the form of a riddle. The Stone of Destiny first seduces those who would take possession of her, by showing them their greatest and most secret desires. Only the pure of heart may face these temptations and triumph over them, earning the right to assume the mantle of power. I was afforded just a glimpse of this power when I reached out to touch the stone. It confirms to me a long and deeply held conviction: that only those who do not *wish* to rule, are precisely those qualified to do so.'

'So what happened in the Scriptorium was a test?'

'Everything we have done since we stepped out of your door has been a test, Boswell. Those Culdee horsemen who have been dogging our heels since Edinburgh are emissaries of light, guiding us and influencing us on our path to enlightenment. Even their name, Culdee, is a derivation of Keledei, the Order to which they belong. The Keledei sometimes appear to us diminished in stature, because their power on this earthly realm is diminished. Just as their demonic counterparts appear to us as monstrous.'

'You mean to say the Order of Keledei are angels?'

'I believe they are too mischievous and deceitful to be truly of that Order. No, we are in the presence of the old, Druidic Gods: mysterious forces beyond our control, always seeking to influence us and shape us in their own image. In the House of Thomas Weir, for example, our enemies tried to paralyse us by showing us our greatest fears. On Iona we were overcome by equally powerful desires. Fear and desire. Repulsion and attraction. We managed to conquer both, and I think have become better men because of it.'

'My dear friend,' said Boswell. 'These are all weighty concerns, and I don't profess to understand even half of what you have just said, though I do appreciate your lively demonstration. All I know is that I was very nearly breakfast for a pack of cannibalistic lepers, my daughter came close to being sacrificed in a satanic ritual, we narrowly escaped being torn apart by a pack of ravenous werewolves, we were almost burnt to a crisp, then drowned, and you came within a hair's breadth of having your brain replaced with an ape's, for goodness sake. Surely there is some meaning behind it all, besides some sort of cosmic "test"? I've got to believe it was all for *something*.'

'My dear Boswell,' Johnson replied, genuinely astonished. 'You mean you don't know?'

Just at that moment Mrs Brodie appeared to take their orders. 'And so did ye find what ye were looking for?' she asked, on recognising the three peculiar gentlemen who had come looking for a stonemason some two months before.

'Mrs Brodie,' said Johnson solemnly. 'We have been on a voyage to the very edge of the world and back, and have seen things to make your hair stand on end. We have been the guests of lords and dukes, enjoyed the hospitality of kings and sultans, and have tasted the nectar of the gods. But all of it pales into insignificance when I smell your delicious scones. Or indeed when I see your dear, sweet face again.'

And before the look of astonishment had even left Mrs Brodie's face, Johnson sprang to his feet and scooped her into his arms, waltzing the poor woman between the tables before setting her down again, breathless and confused, only to see her scamper back to the kitchen, muttering about madmen overtaking the town. But her face, flushed with pleasure, had shed at least ten years since breakfast, at least according to her scullery maid.

As for Johnson, he was still chuckling to himself as he placed a very generous tip under the napkin, and the three men stepped out into the morning sun, and whatever the day, full of such mystery and intrigue, might bring.

THE BOOK OF ELS

The Coming of the Milesians

he Tuatha De Danann were Lords of Erin, but the prophecy spoke of three invasions, the last of which would see this mighty race brought low.

There is little we know of the origins of the Milesian people, the last race to settle in Erin, but what we do know is that they came out of Egypt by way of Spain, and that their queen, called Scotia, was the daughter of a Pharaoh. The Milesians brought with them their craft and artistry in poetry and music as well as the arts of metallurgy and alchemy, and rivalled the Tuatha De Danann in powers of clairvoyance and prophecy. Some say they carried the blood of the Keledei's ancient enemy the Sons of Belial or *Drakon* in their veins, and were a slave people who had overcome their masters. Wherever the truth of the matter lies, the Milesians were more than a match for the Danann, and so a deal was struck between Scotia the Milesian Queen and newly-crowned Danann King Lugh of the Silver Hand, for better or for worse. It was agreed that each party would occupy exactly one half of the highly-prized "Emerald Isle".

Being the gentleman that he was, Lugh offered Scotia the

first choice. Being the wily daughter of a Pharaoh that she was, Scotia chose the visible half, effectively banishing the Tuatha De Danann to a land of perpetual twilight.

The Milesian People thrived, extending their realm to the east, where Queen Scotia established the Kingdom of Scotland in her name, and her priests took with them the Stone of Destiny from the hill at Tara and placed it on another hill and called that land Dalriada.

The fate of the Tuatha De Danann remains largely obscure.

Adamnan the Wanderer, Iona, 566 A.D.

Author's Note

I may have played fast and loose with certain historical facts, for which I hope I may be forgiven in the name of artistic license. My main offence was to take James Burnett, Lord Monboddo, a luminary of the Scottish Enlightenment, and turn him into a homicidal maniac. In fact the only similarities between my creation and the real Monboddo, beyond a cool name which sounds like a B-Movie mad scientist, is a shared interest in the development of apes, their capacity for speech, and an anticipation of Darwinian principles of evolution. Everything else is pure fantasy.

Speaking of which, it must be added that the orangutan, a critically endangered species, is a gentle creature far removed from the homicidal abductor of young women presented in this fiction, a misrepresentation for which I should be soundly flogged. I hope that by donating a portion of the profits from this book to the WWF Adopt an Orangutan scheme I can in some small way atone for this injustice.

As for the rest, I have shamelessly plundered from history that which I found shiny, fascinating, curious, mysterious, or just plain weird, and bent it to suit my own agenda. Curiously, some of the more outlandish parts are closer to fact than might be imagined, and vice versa.

In the final analysis, if any of the historical figures, events or locations alluded to in this novel sends the reader off to check Google or better still, to the library for verification, then I have achieved something worthwhile after all.

ANDREW NEIL MACLEOD

Did You Enjoy This Book?

*I*f so, you can make a HUGE difference

For any author, the single most important way we have of getting our books noticed is a really simple one—and one which you can help with.

Yes, you.

Us indie authors and publishers don't have the financial muscle of the big guys to take out full-page ads in the newspaper or put posters on the subway.

But we do have something much more powerful and effective than that, and it's something that those big publishers would kill to get their hands on.

A committed and loyal bunch of readers.

Honest reviews of our books help bring them to the attention of other readers.

If you've enjoyed this book I would be really grateful if you could spend just a couple of minutes leaving a review (it can be as short as you like) on this book's page on your favourite store and website.

About The Author

Andrew Neil MacLeod is a Scottish writer and musician with a deep and abiding love for British history and Celtic myth and culture. In the noughties, Andrew's band was signed to Warner Brothers, giving Keith Richards a run for his money while he toured the length and breadth of Britain with bands such as The Libertines.

Andrew has since taken up the pen as a means of artistic expression. For the last seven years he lived and worked in places as diverse as Malta, Abu Dhabi, Dubai and best of all, Le Marais, Paris, while he worked on his first two novels. Andrew has recently bought a holiday home on a remote Scottish island, which he will be renovating with his adored wife Amber and little Shi Tzu Alex. He looks forward to long walks on the beach, fish and chips by the pier, and cozy nights in before the log fire with a wee dram, while he works on his third novel. He also makes a great Cullen Skink.

About Burning Chair

Burning Chair is an independent publishing company based in the UK, but covering readers and authors around the globe. We are passionate about both writing and reading books and, at our core, we just want to get great books out to the world.

Our aim is to offer something exciting; something innovative; something that puts the author and their book first. From first class editing to cutting edge marketing and promotion, we provide the care and attention that makes sure every book fulfils its potential.

We are:
- Different
- Passionate
- Nimble and cutting edge
- Invested in our authors' success

If you're an author and would like to know more about our submissions requirements and receive our free guide to book publishing, visit:

www.burningchairpublishing.com

If you're a reader and are interested in hearing more about our books, being the first to hear about our new releases or great offers, or becoming a beta reader for us, again please visit:

www.burningchairpublishing.com

More From Burning Chair Publishing

*Y*our next favourite new read is waiting for you…!

The Fall of the House of Thomas Weir, by Andrew Neil Macleod

Edinburgh, 1773. A storm is coming. A storm that will shake the Age of Reason to its very foundations. Before Holmes & Watson, before Abraham van Helsing, there was Doctor Johnson & James Boswell: scourge of the hidden, supernatural world of the 18th century.

The Curse of Becton Manor, by Patricia Ayling

Rumour has it that Becton Manor is haunted. But that's all local gossip. Or is it? The Curse of Becton Manor is a gripping tale of betrayal through the ages, and how the ghosts of English past still haunt all the way to the present day.

Shadow of the Knife, by Richard Ayre

A genius criminologist haunted by his past. A brilliant detective with everything stacked against him. A mysterious murderer that can't be stopped. It's been two years since Jack the Ripper stalked the streets of London. Two years in which the East End slowly returned to normality. And then the killings start again.

THE STONE OF DESTINY

A Life Eternal, by Richard Ayre

What if you knew you could never die? How different would your life be? How different would *you* be? A cursed journey through a century of incredible change, seen through the eyes of a man immune to death, while he searches endlessly for the answers to what makes him so unique.

The Retribution, by Mike Wardle

A wronged man. A hidden treasure. A secret that could change the world. Wilbur Smith and Clive Cussler meet Bernard Cornwell in this story about the price of freedom, the cost of revenge, and the siren song of power and privilege.

Love Is Dead(ly), by Gene Kendall

Brad Burns has a big problem. Not his crippling credit card debt. Not his ex-wife, and current business partner, who still blames him for the messy break-up of their marriage. Not his lovable but spiky personality, which keeps him alive, but along. No, Brad's big issue is that he sees dead people. And those dead people have started to fight back.

Haven Wakes, by Fi Phillips

What if you discovered there was another, magical world alongside ours but just out of reach? What would you do if a being there wanted you dead, but you didn't know why? And how would you save their world – and ours – if all was threatened by evil? An exciting and enthralling journey through new worlds, both futuristic and magical.

The Infernal Aether series, by Peter Oxley
The Infernal Aether, by Peter Oxley (Infernal Aether, Book One)

London, 1865. A world being torn apart by supernatural terrors. A drunken adventurer who just wants a quiet life. A genius whose inventions tend to make bad situations worse.

When an exiled demon uses the power of the Aether to create Hell on Earth, Augustus Potts and his friends must face their darkest fears to save everything – and everyone they hold dear.

A Christmas Aether, by Peter Oxley (Infernal Aether, Book Two)

The adventure continues… With the end of the terror of the Infernal Aether, surely humanity is safe at last?

The Demon Inside, by Peter Oxley (Infernal Aether, Book Three)

London, 1868. Augustus Potts is in trouble. The runic sword which gives him his supernatural powers is slowly turning him into the one thing he fears and despises the most: a demon. He's not the only one: N'yotsu, one-time saviour of mankind, realises that the only way he can survive is to turn back into the evil demon Andras. When their closest friends and allies start to disappear, they find themselves in a race against time to save their souls – and the whole world.

Beyond the Aether, by Peter Oxley (Infernal Aether, Book Four)

The summer of 1869. When the famed demon hunter Kate Thatcher is kidnapped by the enemy, Augustus Potts and his friends must risk everything – including the safety of the entire planet – to rescue her before she is lost forever.

Burning Bridges, by Matthew Ross

The Isle of Sheppey. The discovery of a wounded, unconscious man left for dead sets in motion a series of events where mistakes once thought buried in the past are forced to the surface. With lethal results.

Push Back, by James Marx

They framed him. Tried to kill him. They were his fellow

police officers. But this time he will get revenge. This time he will Push Back. If you love action-packed thrillers in the vein of Jack Reacher and Jason Bourne, then you'll love Push Back.

Blue Bird, by Trish Finnegan

It is the blisteringly hot summer of 1976, and WPC Samantha Barrie is Wyre Hall police station's newest recruit. When young girls start to go missing, Sam finds herself at the centre of an investigation which goes far deeper than anyone expects.

Killer in the Crowd, by P N Johnson

Live music is in her blood, but as the death threats arrive, she fears there's a killer in the crowd. Described by Steve Harley (Cockney Rebel) as "utterly compelling... mystery in the music world".

Point of Contact, by Richard Ayre

A series of horrifying, unexplainable deaths. A race against time to stop an all-powerful madman. And the only person who can stop it all is battling his own demons.

The Other Side of Trust, by Neil Robinson

When the world is turned upside down, who can you trust? British Secret Intelligence Service agent Sebastian Friend is tasked by "C" to seek out who is responsible for a string of murders of prominent Iranian emigrees – but, as with everything in the shadowy world of espionage, all is not as it seems.

Spy Game, by John Fullerton (Brodick Cold War Series, Book One)

February, 1981. The Cold War is in full swing. Richard Brodick decides to follow in his father's footsteps and seeks an exciting role in what used to be called the Great Game, only to find that it turns out to be less of an adventure, and more brutal betrayal.

Spy Dragon, by John Fullerton (Brodick Cold War Series, Book Two)

Brodick is back. Despatched to Beirut at the height of the civil war, Richard Brodick quickly becomes embroiled with a mysterious Chinese operative known only as Fang. Finding himself in a new and dangerous game of double and triple agents, can he trust anyone: even himself?

Near Death, by Richard Wall

Is it possible to commit murder from beyond the grave? Sing Sing Prison, 1962. Joseph Hickey is executed for a series of gruesome murders. But what should be the end of the nightmare is only the beginning.

The Tom Novak series, by Neil Lancaster

Going Dark, by Neil Lancaster (Tom Novak Book One)

"Other thriller writers do research. Lancaster lived it. And now he is ready to tell you about it. His hero, Tom Novak, is a soft-spoken hard man who makes Jason Bourne look like a vegan Pilates teacher. If you like your thrills fast, gritty and authentic as all hell, then Going Dark should be top of your reading list." – Tony Parsons, Sunday Times bestselling author.

Going Rogue, by Neil Lancaster (Tom Novak Book Two)

Tom Novak is back. When a spate of deadly terrorist attacks hit the streets of London, Tom finds himself thrust into the middle of a fight for the survival of all he holds dear. When faced with the ultimate choice, which way will Tom go?

Going Back, by Neil Lancaster (Tom Novak Book Three)

Answering a call from an old friend, Tom Novak finds himself back in the one place he doesn't want to be, the home of his childhood nightmares: Sarajevo. Forced into a race against time to stop a terrifying new weapon, can Tom fight against the odds once more to save not just those he loves, but the world as we know it?

10:59, by N R Baker

A deadly virus. A world on the brink of destruction. An impossible decision. If you held the lives of those around you in your hands, who would you save? 10:59 is the most important book you'll read all year. An apocalyptic thriller with a difference, it will have you questioning everything – and everyone – you thought you knew.

Beyond, by Georgia Springate

Alex Duncan is just an ordinary 14-year old boy. His main worries are homework, girls, the school bully… and his sister Jenna, who has ovarian cancer, stage B. As his parents retreat into themselves, Alex is desperate to find a way to help, a way to make things better. To understand exactly why this is happening to his sister and, more importantly, what lies beyond this life.

The Wedding Speech Manual: The Complete Guide to Preparing, Writing and Performing Your Wedding Speech, by Peter Oxley

Your complete, practical, step-by-step guide to writing and performing a personalised wedding speech which will be enjoyed ' and cherished by your loved ones, friends and family.

www.burningchairpublishing.com

ANDREW NEIL MACLEOD